INTO THE ABYSS

INTO THE ABYSS

A NOVEL BY
DAVID MARSH

SEA CHEST
BOOKS

INTO THE ABYSS

Design by Jim Stopp

Library of Congress Cataloging-in-Publication Data

Marsh, David

INTO THE ABYSS / David Marsh

Published by Sea Chest Books

ISBN 0-9742909-0-4

First Edition

To Michelle

INTO THE ABYSS

Prologue

1972

IT'S DARK DOWN HERE—PITCH—and very, very cold. A minor earth jolt causes some turbidity, breaching an eerie stillness, but soon all is quiet again. This is the way it is year after year, decade after decade, century after century: always black, silent, icy, and virtually void of visible life.

Yet, swooping down into the stillness of this midnight cosmos, the *fast one* honed her sights on the realm she had known since birth. A marvel of evolution, science and speed, and flying faster than a peregrine falcon—thought by humans to be the swiftest animal on the planet—she generated a piercing glow, like a luminous torpedo, as she raced away from the clamor of the raging storm above and the mysterious surface.

Slicing through the *dysphotic zone*, or twilight zone, her body underwent a molecular transformation. Oxygen and new pressure-resistant proteins began feeding her muscles, and her lungs compressed into a state of dormancy, making her impervious to the effects of the increasing atmospheric pressure. Closing her eyes, she fell into the rhythm of the undersea.

Another creature, something tiny with colorful bioluminescent dots on a gelatinous body, bounced into her nose. It was a *hydroid*—a typical *benthic zone* dweller—perhaps hoping to secure a ride.

Sensing the approaching seabed, the *fast one* swished her tail fluke and *retroflexed*—arching her body to radically reduce velocity. Then she came to a gentle rest next to a shimmering *thermal vent*—a cone-like chimney, where it was suddenly much warmer.

The *fast one* loved this place. The naturally formed chimney was a spring of heat and minerals soaring up from the core of the earth, one of the few places of the abyss where life was in abundance—life thriving off the internal energy of the planet as opposed to the sun, a process called *chemosynthesis*.

As the *fast one's* luminosity softened, a *coelenterate*—luminous jellyfish—zipped by her huge eyes, making her blink. Scores of these lively critters darted in and out of nooks and cracks, pulsing and twinkling. The *fast one* rubbed against the chimney, the warm water embracing her smooth bioluminescent form. She massaged herself in the mineral-rich sediment, gleaning mellow vibrations, soothing and tranquil, affirming that all was well. She was safe. Life was still good, even though…well, she didn't want to think about that. Life was fun. Life was—

She snapped to attention, an alarm bell sounding off in her mind.

Something was approaching….

POSSESSING A FIFTY-FOOT WINGSPAN, the vicious *death ray*—member of the shark family—swam quickly, following the path where his echolocation sensors had located something large and fleshy. Then he saw her…and froze. Confusion and fear rifled through the giant predator's body. His appetite suddenly unimportant, he began to backtrack, minimizing the motion of his wings, lest he be seen. He'd never been this close before but he knew…he knew instinctively: She was definitely not one to engage.

As it so happens, even great whites, even super-giant squids four times her size were smart enough to stay clear of the *fast one.*

The *fast one* knew the large predator was fleeing, but her concern was directed elsewhere. Her sensors had located something much more ominous, something way up above.

A machine….

And it was descending.

The *fast one's* chemosynthetic organs pulsed. Her scaly skin once again radiated an ethereal luminosity, no less than a chunk of the sun, and then, in a burst of catapult-force, displaying an awesome power way beyond the capacity of her build, she flew.

PART ONE

FIRST CONTACT

-1-

Deadman's Bluff

(Present Day)

"THERE'S COLD CUTS AND POTATO salad. Make sure you clean up after yourselves…and don't leave the house! I expect you to act responsibly, as if I was here. And be sure to fluff up the cushions before you go upstairs."

Grandmother Phillips was leaving for an early evening of bingo, which basically meant one thing to fourteen-year-old Ashlyn and his sister, Autumn, younger by two years: They could escape! They could dip their feet into the ocean and stroll along the beach, if only for an hour or two—something they hadn't been able to accomplish in three weeks, since arriving at Grandma's country cottage which was nestled way off the beaten track of life, or more specifically, on a boring cul-de-sac on the fringes of Oregon's Columbia forest, two miles from the Pacific ocean.

The shadows were already long when Ashlyn and Autumn set off for the beach, the air warm not toasty, with lacy cotton ball clouds floating high above. Weaving through a gauntlet of pine trees, they could make out the notorious Deadman's Bluff. It stood tall, like a massive rusty-red citadel, scored and chiseled by eons of crashing waves.

But today the ocean slept.

Their grandmother had warned them about the bluff, but then again she warned them about everything and everyone. She'd rambled on about storms, shipwrecks, sharks, and winds that could pluck a grown man up from the ground. She even spun a wild one about a serpent lurking in those deep blue waters. Why if you didn't know better, the bluff was the most dangerous place on earth—one big stewpot of disaster. But Ashlyn did know better. This edict was yet another of his grandmother's suffocating rules. "Do you think Grandma really believes in sea serpents?" Autumn asked as the swish of the tide grew louder.

"Yeah, like she believes in allowances...and chickens with three heads."

"Discovery Channel says there's—"

"Eels! Moray eels like in Hawaii," Ashlyn interrupted.

Autumn looked a little nervous. In her mind, she could still hear her grandmother's words about washed-up body parts and unusual bite marks.

"So don't go in the water." Ashlyn slowed as they started to cross the bluff's ridge-top from where, supposedly, many had plummeted to their deaths. No doubt those poor idiots stood on the edge when it was blustery. But Ashlyn had already decided to play it safe; if there was even a hint of the weather changing, one swift moving cloud, they'd be out of there faster than a hound on a hare.

Cautiously peering over the cliff's edge, Ashlyn's eyes met a meadow of sapphire silk pierced by two gnarly sea stacks casting shadows on a narrow strip of red sand. The drop was probably one-hundred-feet. Just off to his right, he noticed a dusty trail, obviously the way down. "Yup sleeping like a baby. I'll just get my feet wet. If you think it might be too dangerous...seriously, you might wanna wait up here."

"Here?" There was a rustle as something in the beach grass moved, probably only a rabbit, Autumn figured; she still shuddered. "I don't think so."

The trail was steep and narrow, at times simply vanishing, leaving them precariously balanced over a row of razor-sharp rocks. "Don't look down," Ashlyn shouted with authority. "We're doing good."

Maybe he was reckless, he recognized that in himself, but at some level he just didn't care anymore. Less than a month ago his life was on track—he'd had dreams, goals, things were good. Then his mother died unexpectedly from a massive brain hemorrhage. And his world turned upside down—from laughter to tears in a day.

Without money, without caring relatives, he and Autumn were up-rooted from their Barstow, California home and placed into a state-run facility. It was there, waiting to be raffled off into some foster home, that Ashlyn first saw his estranged grandmother. She was only sixty, but in her wheelchair, dressed from head to toe in black, she looked like a withered old witch. Even then he had wondered: Were they being rescued...or captured?

Ashlyn carefully navigated himself over a ragged boulder and jumped down onto soft sand. They had reached the deserted beach.

Autumn pulled off her Reeboks and ran into a foamy backwash while Ashlyn stood still, inhaling the salty air, digging his toes into the warm red sand. Yes, he was alive...in spite of his grandma's rules and her stifling way of life. "Hey, look at that, over there." He padded through the surf toward an object protruding from the sand. It appeared to be a small boat, mostly buried. He tried pulling it...wouldn't budge. Excitedly, they began digging. Autumn found some *geoduck* shells to use as sand scoops, and they continued digging. So engrossed, they hardly noticed the time...or the clouds conjoining over the headland.

At last, an eleven-foot-long rowboat slid out of the hole, de-crepit but in one solid piece.

Ashlyn couldn't believe his luck. It was as if his mother was trying to heal his bruised spirit. Yes, he would definitely turn this decrepit rowboat into a sailboat and sail day after—

Grandma! She would never allow it. He could see her turning blue in the face, gasping for air as she did so often, and Lucy, her housekeeper, rushing off to find the oxygen tank. Not to minimize her asthma or any of her ailments, but Grandma sure knew how to pile on the guilt. Her wounded eyes would say, you did this to me.

Ashlyn quickly decided that no one, not even his grandma, could tell him how to grieve. She didn't know the pain in his heart. The boat was his, and that's all there was to it.

"What time is it?" Autumn suddenly blurted. "It's getting cloudy!"

The sun had vanished inside a web of white and gray clouds. The tide was beginning to come in.

Ashlyn checked his watch. *Dammit!* It would be dark in less than an hour.

Feeling a sudden chill in the air, Autumn reached for her sweat-shirt. "We better go."

Leave the boat? Her words were like hemlock. Ashlyn scoured the beach. "Is that a cave? I bet it's a cave!"

Autumn wasn't following her brother's gaze along the base of the escarpment; she was more focused on a swirling cloud. It made her think about spindrift—howling moisture-filled winds whipping around at fifty, sixty, even ninety miles an hour—according to her grandmother.

Ashlyn grabbed the boat's stern and started to pull. "I'm not ditching this! We're putting it in that cave!"

"We can come back tomorrow."

"Tide will take it and that will be that!"

"Better it than us!" Autumn held her ground, hands defiantly on her hips.

As Ashlyn glared back, a sudden gust rifled through his sandy blond hair, making him flinch. He saw the alarming look of uncertainty in his sister's eyes. And he'd be remiss to say that he didn't feel slightly unsettled. But the forecast said less than a ten percent chance of a storm. Ten percent. He glanced up at the sky. Okay, there were more clouds. But they didn't look like high-piling storm clouds. The boat was doomed unless— "Okay, you go back. I'll catch up with you," he suggested desperately.

Autumn sagged. She wasn't leaving without him. He was stubborn all right. Stubborn like an ox. She grabbed one side of the boat. "Pull, you idiot!"

Ashlyn was correct in that he'd spotted a cave, although the distance to it was deceiving. A half-mile and fifteen minutes later, they dragged the rowboat up to the cave's arching outer-wall. The entrance, accessed from around the curved wall, was already standing in the tide. For a brief moment, the sun on the horizon broke through the clouds.

"Tide's in, too late." Autumn cried breathlessly.

"Stay here! I'll round the wall and see if I can wedge it against something. This is great!" He shouted, fishing out of his pocket a key-chain light. "Storage for less!" He and was about to move on when a punchy gust almost threw him to the ground.

Autumn spat out sand grits, somewhat melodramatically. "See! Like that!" She snapped two fingers.

"We're wasting time!" Ashlyn tried to move on but his sister held onto his tee, shaking her head no. Her piercing blue eyes reflected a sparkle from the sun's final rays as they brushed over her face.

By appearance, no one pegged them as siblings. She was lean, tall for her age, with silky chestnut locks cascading to a slim waist, and pretty, blessed with high cheekbones and full lips.

She sighed, realizing it was pointless. "Alright…we go together."

So together they traversed the wall to the cave's entrance. Ashlyn flicked on his pocket penlight, and abruptly halted, trying to camouflage his surprise. The entire cave floor was covered by water. "Normal. Yup. I expected this."

"Of course you did," she remarked sarcastically.

Ashlyn scoped the walls. There were nooks, crannies, shelves, a sloping platform, which he figured would suffice as a ramp for the boat. But how deep was it over there? He moved in another few steps, water now lapping about his shins, and stopped.

"What?" Autumn whispered.

Ashlyn felt as if someone, or something, was watching him. *Shut up*, he ordered himself silently. *Be calm…okay…okay, I'm calm.* But he wasn't feeling even remotely calm. Perhaps it was his grandma's admonitions buzzing in his mind. *Sea serpent…huh, bull. Surely bull.*

"Either do it or we're out of here." Autumn's voice echoed around the cave, eerily.

Ashlyn pushed the boat ahead of him. It glided forward, quickly afloat. The water was green, murky, probably rising. He figured it would only take a few minutes to wedge the boat, add another ten or so to reach the rickety path to the ridge-top. How high would the tide be by then? And it was one thing standing at the entrance, but wading all the way into the pitch-black—

Autumn interrupted his thoughts. "What are we waiting for? Total submersion?"

Ashlyn trained the penlight back on the boat, now bobbing along ten feet ahead. "We're here, troops," he said. "Let's do it!"

They waded several paces, water still only lapping at their shins, when Autumn simply said "ouch" and suddenly she was no longer standing next to him, but going under like a rock. And as she completely disappeared, Ashlyn found himself diving head first into the cold salty water after her.

It was just a sinkhole but it certainly shocked Autumn. As her feet landed on the rocky bottom, she propelled herself back to the surface, treading water, gasping, coughing brine.

Ashlyn shot up right after her.

"Sinkhole," he yelled. "Stupid sinkhole." He tried to laugh off the mishap as he helped his sister find footing on the sandy floor back in shallow water. She was shivering, rivulets running down her puckered face.

The beam from his waterlogged penlight fell on the rowboat drifting back toward them. It had now been afloat several minutes.

No water inside it.

For the last hour, he'd been planning the boat's restoration—to fix the leaks, sand it, paint it, erect a mast, a sail....

It didn't have leaks, and Autumn was shivering. "Get in."

"What?" she blurted incredulously.

Already with two hands around her waist, he was lifting her up. "I'll ferry you."

Autumn didn't struggle, didn't object. Too dazed to think, she sat down on the bench seat and folded her arms tightly around herself. Her teeth began to chatter.

Looking around, Ashlyn saw that there wasn't really anywhere to secure the boat. Tomorrow he'd come back with rope and—

He shrieked as *something* below the water bit him.

Autumn watched aghast as her brother thrashed his arms down into the black water, his face posed in agony. Then he plummeted below the surface in a froth of violent bubbles. The sole thought that bored into her mind was shark. She screamed...but then there he was, back on the surface, his arms flailing, his eyes wide open in shock.

"What is it?" She screamed.

Ashlyn's terrified voice echoed from wall to wall. "It's got me! It's got me!"

Down he went again, only this time as his buttocks hit the sandy floor, the frightened crustacean he'd stepped on unlocked its pincers. Ashlyn rocketed back up, groping for his right foot, expecting to find at least one toe missing. They were all there, sitting squarely on his foot, only one bleeding.

Breathless, cold, and desperate to escape from this crab territory, he did something that didn't make much sense: He threw himself over the rim into the boat, clipping Autumn's sunburned back, before crashing down on the centerboard, hard on his back.

Grimacing as she held her sunburn, Autumn took a shivering look about her. "Smart! So now what…we staying the night?"

Ashlyn was almost content to lie there in repose. "Sure. Give me a second."

Just then a freak wave slid into the cave with an unexaggerated *BOOF*. The rowboat sort of bobbed up and skipped forward, gently, and then it smacked into the rear wall. Ashlyn bolted upright. Now he recognized the imminent danger. They were moving backwards, being sucked toward the entrance in a retreating countercurrent! "Get off the boat! Get off the boat!" he yelled! "Jump!"

As Ashlyn leaped off the boat, he could have sworn Autumn was right behind him. He could have sworn— "Autumn! Autumn where are you?" His voice reverberated through the cave, a chorus in alarm. Then he heard her cries—coming from outside the cave.

Autumn hadn't jumped.

What a boorish thought! Wading as fast as his legs would allow, Ashlyn charged through the entrance, where his panicked voice was devoured by a malicious gust. "Jump, Autumn! Dammit, jump!"

Autumn would have jumped if she hadn't lost her balance. But now outside the cave, she realized she would have to choose her moment carefully. The ocean was no longer calm, she could feel the power of the current roiling and churning beneath her feet. She was a good swimmer but she wasn't foolish. She had to stay with the boat—until a wave pushed her back to shore. Ashlyn was being reckless. "Go back! Current's too strong!" She shouted.

Ashlyn saw that the sky was quickly turning charcoal. "No jump now!" he screamed, while trying to run toward her, until his feet no longer touched sand. "Jump!" He cried in desperation, swallowing a mouth of saltwater. Now he could feel how strong the current was, its unruliness undermining his strokes, tugging at him, pulling him back. The old man of the sea was saying *no you can't swim to your sister!*

Screaming sheets of rain began to uncoil from the heavens. A flash of lightning scorched the blackened sky, and in that shocking nanosecond, Ashlyn glimpsed around him roving canyons in confusion, rising, falling, colliding.

The storms at Deadman's Bluff, known to start with the snap of a finger, had done just that.

Autumn was forty feet away, a silhouette engulfed in a fog of seething sea-spray, shouting something, which to Ashlyn seemed like a crazy, silent mime. He observed her pulling something up out of the water. It looked like...a palm frond. She tried to reach him with it. Not nearly close enough.

"I'm coming, Autumn. I'm coming!" Oh how he now regretted ever visiting this dreadful beach. Ignoring the burning in his triceps, the searing in his thighs, he held his breath and dived, figuring he could swim better against the current underwater.

He surfaced ten feet from the palm frond, gasping, snarling away his fiery body pains. He threw his arms into another extension, one more sweep forward. But this time his motion was feeble. The frond was getting further away again, fifteen yards, maybe more.

As his limbs went from jelly to numb, and his stomach heaved with a wave of nausea, he allowed his eyes to close, his body to slacken. He simply needed a moment's breather, a short rest. Time to regroup.

Ashlyn never saw the seething sixteen-foot white wall. But it broadsided him with the force of ten sledgehammers!

Down he went, breathless.

Down.

Saltwater blasted up his nostrils, scorching the back of his throat before entering his lungs. His ears rang like church bells. His eyes stung with brine.

Down he went in multiple somersaults.

Down in a tempestuous, unoxygenated vacuum.

He felt his chest simultaneously exploding and imploding from the lack of oxygen. He prayed for mercy, but the venomous ocean, showing none, tossed him aside as inconsequentially as a sliver of loose seaweed. He was desperate to breathe. Bursting to inhale. Maybe he would find an air bubble, a morsel of life's sustenance. All he had to do was open his mouth for one little bubble, one minuscule tidbit of air. One little—

Autumn continued to shout his name over and over, despite being unable to hear herself over the howling wind. Thirty seconds had passed since she last saw him. Even her mother's death hadn't created such emptiness. She had witnessed her brother's death. Now she too would die alone and—

—Ashlyn?

"Ashlyn!" She screamed, her heart pounding with the vigor of the mighty waves whisking her out to sea. Ashlyn had defied death. But how much more could he endure? She attempted to wrestle the palm frond to him. But it was suddenly gone from her grasp, snatched by the intolerant sea.

As lightning blanched the sky, Autumn noticed that *the killer pillars*—the twin sea stacks at Deadman's Bluff—were now but specks slowly disappearing into the distance. How would they ever get back? Even if they had oars, even a sail, getting back to the bluff would be—

—No, Ashlyn would find a way! Ashlyn, her genius brother, would have a plan, as he always did. All she had to do was pull him aboard.

Ashlyn was close now, swimming as hard as his failing strength would allow. Autumn slid down on her stomach, stretching out an arm, hoping that he wouldn't pull her overboard. She barely flinched as howling spindrift cut into her sunburned flesh. Yet in spite of her pain, she risked all, leaning out as far as she dared, her feet locking around the centerboard keeping herself anchored, not allowing the capricious boat to oust her. She was the fearless matador battling the wicked ocean bull. For a few seconds she lost sight of him.

Then he leapt up forcefully, and grabbed the rim. "Back up!" He yelled, a swirling wind whipping the words back into his face.

"What? I can't hear you!"

"Back up! You'll capsize!"

As another fiery talon ripped open the blackness, Autumn saw the alarmed look in her brother's eyes.

"Lean the other way! Stay low!" he shouted, coughing up bile and water, although not nearly enough to alleviate the nausea he was feeling. He demonstrated with signs, pushing back with an open palm.

She nodded and said something, although it didn't reach Ashlyn's ears.

Ashlyn waited for the perfect wave, and when he felt himself riding up, he yelled, "Now!" Then he hoisted a leg aboard, precariously tilting the boat. Autumn leaned forward and grabbed one of his arms, pulling with all her might.

The boat began to keel.

"No!" Ashlyn screamed.

Abruptly, Autumn fell backwards, the sudden weight shift dropping the boat back down. Like a snapping rubber band, Ashlyn lunged aboard, deftly latching onto his sister's legs. An eye-blink later, she'd have been overboard. In its execution, the maneuver was almost simple, if not according to his plan.

They held on to each other tightly...momentarily safe.

No...not safe at all!

There was water inside the boat...a whole lot of water. "Bail! Bail!" he cried!

Unable to navigate, they shot up heaving hills, surfed down their backsides, all the while bailing...bailing with their hands...bailing furiously. And as Ashlyn watched the coastline receding into the distance, he began to seriously think about death, that perhaps he was about to die. Until this moment, he'd been too busy fighting for his survival to think about death. Not that he was surrendering. No, he'd never surrender. He would bail and bail as fast as he humanly could, but the thought of death had parked itself in his mind, and he was calm and angry simultaneously—angry because of his inexcusable stubbornness; he hadn't listened to Autumn or his grandma, and now Autumn's untimely death would be on his shoulders. As for being calm, in a twisted way of thinking, the idea of death didn't scare him at all. Perhaps, his mother's spirit was guiding him. Or maybe it was his father helping him find strength and inner peace, even though Ashlyn never really knew his father. Twelve years ago, a few days before Autumn entered the world, his father had drowned somewhere close to where they were right now. Was it destiny or irony that the sea would take him and Autumn the same way? Would they at last meet their father?

And as these thoughts cascaded through Ashlyn's mind, the boat started turning in a circle, and he heard himself shouting: "Whirlpool!"

Autumn screamed as the wind, like a thousand squealing pigs, tore into her eardrums. Ashlyn pushed her flat on the floor. He held her tightly. And with their noses barely above water, he prayed for a miracle. He prayed hard, at the same time wondering if their bodies would ever be found. Then he closed his eyes and cried, "I'm with you, sis," and gasped his last breath, resigned to succumb to the curving black wall now enveloping them.

IF THE TWISTING CLOUDS ABOVE possessed eyes, the rowboat on the ocean's surface would have appeared as little more than a molecule. But from that same high-up vantage point, those lofty eyes would also have seen a spangle of illumination deep underwater—a glowing light that was rifling toward the surface.

AS THE ROWBOAT SPUN AROUND, faster and faster, Ashlyn once again withheld the urge to puke. With his eyes tightly shut, he waited for death, hoping that it would be swift and painless.

He remained unaware that a golden glowing light, just two thirds of a mile away, was speeding toward him like a luminous underwater rocket.

Coming....

Pulsing brightly....

Five hundred yards away....

One hundred yards....

The glow flew under the rowboat...and suddenly they were no longer spinning but racing forward—screaming forward, as if a jet engine had somehow magically become attached to the boat.

Ashlyn's eyes snapped open.

They'd survived the whirlpool, but what kind of cruel trick was this? They were riding a tidal wave into the cliffs at Deadman's Bluff.

The *killer pillars* loomed up....

Fifty yards....

Twenty....

Impact imminent....

Autumn instinctively shielded her face while Ashlyn squeezed his eyes shut in passive surrender.

For sure this was *Death.*

Perhaps it was a moment later, or maybe an eternity, that Ashlyn found himself rocking side-to-side, obviously being lullabied in the afterlife, when a harsh voice snapped, "Ashlyn! Ashlyn! Move!" Then he realized, it was Autumn's voice. "Get out!"

"We're dead," he mumbled in a daze, allowing his eyes to flutter open. He saw Autumn standing on the beach, holding the boat. But he stayed put, swaying with the swell of the surf, too confused, too exhausted, too unwilling to move.

Lightning scissored the sky.

He thought, strange having storms in the afterlife, and he blinked. His eyes felt horribly sore. He could taste bile in the back of his throat. He was shivering. How could he be dead? "We're alive?" He almost began to laugh. "We're alive!"

"Get out! Now!" Autumn shouted again.

Ashlyn placed one leg ashore…and froze.

Something was there. *Something* moving—

Gone.

Whatever it—

"No, there! What the heck?" He squeezed his eyes, hoping to rekindle his senses. "What's that?" He yelled, pointing.

Autumn looked, but whatever Ashlyn had seen, or thought he'd seen, it had vanished, except for a dim glow, which she shrugged off with indifference…and anyway, even that was now gone. For all she knew, it was a flitting lantern fish, the reflection of the moon. Who cares? Any moment now another wave could carry them back out. "Hurry, you idiot! Move your lazy ass! Now!"

-2-

Beneath The Waves

THE SONAR MAN SITTING AT station three aboard the F-frigate *USS Whitehorn* rubbed and then squeezed his tired eyes, but when he looked back at the *Heads Up Display* it was still there. "That's weird," he mumbled, turning to his supervisor. "Sir, either a glitch here...or something...weird. SIA negative."

His supervisor, Ensign Edwards, leaned over the sonar man's shoulder to study the *contact* on three. Edwards frowned as he noted the *contact's* anomalous speed and the absence of a flashing bar at the bottom of the screen, which would have indicated the substance identification—a flashing red bar for compound matter, such as a submarine; flashing green bar for organic matter, such as a whale. But in this case, the SIA—Substance Identification Analysis—was inconclusive. Ensign Edwards rubbed his chin thoughtfully. From a commonsense viewpoint, there wasn't a submarine or fish in the world that moved with this kind of speed, which surely meant the *contact* was a technical malfunction. On the other hand, it didn't look like a glitch. Edwards picked up the phone. "Bridge. Sonar. We have an unidentified high-speed contact on three, bearing zero-four-zero." On the ship's bridge, Captain James Swift watched the sonar on a large wall screen. Though his mouth was sealed, his top and bottom molars grated noisily. He'd witnessed this kind of aberration many times before—anomalous pattern of movement, speeds up to one-hundred-and-sixty knots, failed SIA, which at minimum was supposed to render a basic identification.

Abruptly, the contact vanished, at fifteen-hundred-fathoms, close to the seabed.

Captain Swift, a veteran of two engagements in the Persian Gulf, stroked an earlobe. This was the twenty-fifth such encounter in eight years, but the third in three weeks. The name for this anomaly—a sore subject in some circles—was the *Seabed Phantom*.

Five years ago, under the guise of maneuvers, the navy had conducted an extensive underwater hunt for the *phantom*. Thousands of man-hours, millions of taxpayers' dollars were pumped into the top secret *"Operation Kelp Weed."* Yet the *phantom* remained a conundrum.

Later, a senate probe into the misappropriation of navy funds had exposed the nonsensical endeavor. The press had had a field day....

NAVY SPENDS MILLIONS CHASING WHALE SHADOWS

Early retirements had followed.

The ship's XO—second in command—was the first to speak, as he turned to the captain and raised his eyebrows. "Glitch?"

The captain nodded in affirmative.

"Shall we continue on the present course, Captain?"

"Yes. Write your report as observed."

To his crew, Captain Swift appeared typically nonchalant. But if truth were told, his heart was pounding with an excitement he ordinarily only felt in battle.

This was the third sighting in three weeks.

It was back.

-3-

The Hand

AUTUMN CONTINUED TO SHIVER UNDER her blanket, both from shock and cold. Ashlyn wasn't much warmer in his bed. His eyes were red raw from salt and fatigue. By now he wanted to close them, fall asleep and forget the whole thing.

But that wasn't possible.

What had saved them? There was no doubt in his mind—and Autumn agreed—it was a miracle. But exactly what? This is where they differed.

Was it a freaky wave or something else?

Autumn rolled over on her pillow. Their whispered conversation was going around in circles, going nowhere. Autumn hadn't seen anything under the boat except for a dim glow, and by now Ashlyn wasn't so sure that he'd seen anything either. He raised his head off his pillow. "But what if I did see it?"

Autumn mumbled something, drowsily, before slipping off to slumberland. "What if I did see it?" He sighed and perhaps drifted off because he thought he was back there again.

A hand.

It appeared to be a hand holding onto the boat. Autumn had suggested that it was seaweed or some other vegetation somehow disguised by the milky sea foam. Ashlyn's dilemma was that it looked so absolutely real. Surely, he shouldn't dismiss it. Maybe it was a lifeless hand, not holding onto the boat but floating under it, a corpse washing ashore?

The constant replaying of the terrifying ordeal—especially the image of the mystery hand—haunted Ashlyn all night. How could they have escaped the whirlpool? What sort of tidal wave acts as a ferry? And the glow, the pulsing glow? Even Autumn saw the glow.

It must have been morning because Ashlyn found himself being nudged awake by his grandma. Somehow he upped himself and stumbled down to the breakfast table. Lucy, the housekeeper, was at the stove, cooking. Ordinarily this would have been of interest to Ashlyn because he liked to eat, and Lucy made delicious meals, including gourmet egg breakfasts. But food was the furthest thing from Ashlyn's mind. Lucy and Autumn were chatting but he couldn't grasp any of the conversation. Maybe he was still dreaming. He closed his eyes and listened to the sizzle of bacon.

As Grandma's confidante, gossip-keeper and nurse, all rolled into one, Lucy ran the bed-and-breakfast, when there were guests. Short and plump, with dimpled cheeks, and blessed with the warmest of smiles, she turned to Ashlyn and asked, "Poached, Béarnaise, over easy, scrambled?" The spatula was in her right hand hovering over four raw eggs.

Ashlyn's eyes were still closed, and Autumn, eating a bowl of oatmeal, nudged his feet as Grandma wheeled herself in.

"How do you want your eggs?" Grandma interjected in her heavy Scottish twang.

"Yeah," Ashlyn replied groggily.

Autumn covered for him. "Go ahead, Lucy, mangle them."

"Mangled eggs, coming up."

Grandma poured herself coffee. "Storm keep you up last night, Ashlyn?"

Two slices of whole-wheat toast popped out of the toaster, startling him. "Huh?" He looked up, not comprehending his whereabouts for a few seconds. His focus went beyond Grandma to the kitchen window. A gray day. Still raining.

Lucy spread a thick layer of butter on the toast. "It's supposed to clear up by mid-morning. I was thinking, perhaps we could run over to Don Davis, pick up those two bicycles. It'd be nice to get a little exercise. If it's all right with you, Mary? My treat."

For a moment, it looked like Grandma was going to overrule. She shook her head as she thought about bicycles…and drivers under the influence. "Just what do you think you'll find about town? A beach, aye. But not like it used to be. Bums, drunks and not much more! The world is changing, and I can't say it's for the better." Pointing a finger at Ashlyn, she snapped, "You better keep to the bike path! And don't let your sister out of your sight."

Ashlyn swallowed hard. Don't let your sister out of your sight. No kidding. She was letting them go.

Lucy smiled. The kids needed to start living again. "Are you eating, Mary?"

Grandma tabled her coffee. "Béarnaise would be nice, thank you, dear."

ASHLYN SAT ON THE EDGE of his bed, examining his injured toe—two inflamed puncture marks, slightly yellow at the edges. Pretty lucky, considering the crab attack was the exclusive injury of the evening. He cast a look outside. The rain was light but it was blustery. Autumn was out there feeding her pet rabbit a blueberry muffin. The rabbit Bigsey was now sentenced to a life outdoors. Back in Barstow, the fluffy little guy had been allowed the run of the house, and he'd slept in Autumn's bedroom. But this was Oregon, a new life, and Grandma was allergic to pets. In fact, Grandma suffered from severe asthmatic reactions to perfumes, noise, stress, and life.

Ashlyn carefully put his sock back on. The hand image crossed his mind. He rubbed his forehead, attempting to ease a thrumming pain. He didn't want to think about the hand. Think of something else.

The boat.

Yes, the boat. He wondered if it had sunk or smashed into a sea stack. What a shame. The boat had been a spark of hope. Something he really wanted. What else was there?

The hand.

It wasn't a hand…forget it.

Slipping into his shoes, Ashlyn grabbed his windbreaker and headed downstairs. He found Autumn and rabbit Bigsey outside the tool shed, the bunny's new shelter, which Bigsey didn't care for—too dark, too much rust, too much junk. Autumn was trying to place her Walkman headphones on the rabbit's ears so that he too could enjoy her *Dead Can Dance* CD. As Ashlyn approached, Bigsey bounced off into the bushes.

"Well that's a turnaround, Grandma letting us have bikes. I guess we must have done something right. Hey, what's the matter?" she asked, stringing the headphones around her neck. Her question was in response to Ashlyn's sullen face.

"Nothing's wrong," Ashlyn retorted defensively.

Autumn figured he was brooding over having to share the bedroom, not being able to set up his computer and subwoofer. With only four B&B rooms, Grandma couldn't afford to give up two rooms—just in case real guests knocked on the front door.

"Let's walk." He said, leading the way into the cul-de-sac, away from the ears in the house. The rain had now digressed into a fine mist.

Autumn pulled down her rain hood. "What's up?"

"Last night...I've been giving a lot of thought about last night...."

"We've got to give this place a chance, that's all," Autumn interrupted. She wasn't interested in talking about last night. "We'll make friends and...it'll be fun, like old times."

Truth was Ashlyn didn't make friends easily. She was the only friend he really had in the whole world. He stopped by a neglected timber fence overgrown with blossoming ivy. Sitting on one of the beams, he began massaging a spot above his left eyebrow, trying to banish the headache. "You sleep?"

"Some." Autumn leaned against the post next to him.

"It wasn't natural. I can't just dismiss it," he said.

Autumn nodded understandingly. "Yeah...well, last night's behind us. Be thankful we made it out of there. And let's not be so stupid again."

Absentmindedly picking red berries and tossing them, Ashlyn suddenly looked up. "Autumn, what if—" His faced was creased with consternation.

"What if what?"

"What if—" He stopped short, knowing she'd never believe him. No one would believe him. "You're right...it's behind us." He mustered a smile, a somewhat tenuous one. Autumn saw through the facade but didn't press the issue. It was a new day, they were about to get bikes, and anything was possible.

The weather didn't clear up that day. It remained overcast, raining on and off. It even got chilly enough to light a fire.

Early evening, Grandma went off to her bedroom because smoke sometimes brought on an asthma attack, while Autumn played Scrabble with Lucy, and Ashlyn sat in an armchair, a book on his lap that he didn't have the inclination to read. Staring aimlessly at the fire, glued by the somnolent ballet of flickering flame, he felt a horrible depression sweeping over him, affecting every thought in his mind. If gloom was a virus, then gloom was speedily devouring him, destroying his laughter and hope and sunshine. He didn't know why it was happening. But with each whisper of flickering flame in the fireplace, he sank further and further into a pit of depression.

Tears trickled down Ashlyn's cheeks as he slept that night. When morning came, as he lay in bed, feeling burdened and grief-stricken, he observed through the lace curtains a jetliner strafing a contrail. It was way up there, a tiny speck silently drawing a landscape out of a cloudless blue sky. The day reminded him of one of those that his mother had loved. Watching that contrail, Ashlyn began thinking—he'd been damn lucky to survive the whirlpool. Luck had sided with him. Why hadn't such fortune graced his mom? He was the one who'd found her after returning from a movie, crumpled on the floor at the foot of her bed. She'd been fastening her sandals when a blood vessel ruptured in her brain. The doctor had assured him that she'd gone quickly and hadn't suffered, and though Ashlyn was grateful for small mercies, and though he had grieved and cried, at a subconscious level he obviously felt guilty for not being there.

So guilt was the root of his gloominess.

He sat upright and took in a long meditative breath.

Outside, a cawing crow flew off the pear tree, and glided under the jet's contrail before disappearing into the sun's glare.

Was this a sign, the bird messenger disappearing into the light? Was his mom responding to his grief, helping him lift away his guilt?

He wiped his eyes. "I love you, Mom. I love you so much."

Abruptly, Ashlyn felt compelled to ask himself a very simple question: "Would you rather be dead?"

No, came his answer just as quickly.

He slid out of bed and padded to the bathroom. "Okay, Ashlyn, pull yourself together! Get on with your life."

The hand.

"No. Not interested."

The hand.

"Seaweed. Driftwood. There's nothing weird about that." He started humming, trying to steer his mind off the subject.

The hand.

"Not interested!"

Almost angrily, Ashlyn threw water over his face. He made himself think about the new bike and the new school he'd soon be attending, all the while brushing his teeth furiously. Yet the image of the hand kept looping through his mind—the strange hand under the boat. What did guilt have to do with that hand? His calming revelation was suddenly full of holes. "No, I am not losing control. There's a logical... leave me be!"

AFTER BREAKFAST, WHILE AUTUMN PLAYED with Bigsey, Ashlyn sat on the pavement in the front of the house. Lucy advised Autumn to simply give him space. So he sat alone, his face buried in his hands, sucking back tears—tears tasting of salt. Abruptly, he sat up, licking his lips.

Salt....

Salt like he'd tasted that night in the ocean...salt in his nose, in his throat, in his stomach—

No, he told himself. Once is dumb, twice is worse than dumb.

But although dumb, illogical, absolutely ridiculous, the idea seemed to make perfect sense. Closure, he argued. Nobody would miss him. He'd just be off on a long walk.

Checking his watch, he stood up, and before he knew it, he was heading back to the very remote, very dangerous—

Deadman's Bluff.

IT WASN'T A HOT DAY. It was actually cool, with a gentle breeze rustling the leaves in the trees, but Ashlyn felt hot, as if the atmosphere was void of air, a broiling day in a windless vacuum. His injured toe throbbed, his heart hammered, and there was every reason for him to hastily retreat.

But he couldn't.

Gingerly approaching the cliff's edge, almost daring not to look down but at the same time feeling compelled, he searched. His eyes followed the contours of the beach, probing every mound, every rock pool. He scoured, scanned, scoped.

But there was no washed-up body, no signs of the boat, no debris. Nothing but an ocean resembling moving cloaks of royal blue velvet even calmer and bluer than when he'd first arrived in Oregon.

For a brief moment, he felt a sense of relief. Perhaps now he could get back to being good old, normal—

Someone spoke— *"Ash—lyn."*

It was a quiet voice that came as a whispery wind from directly behind him.

Ashlyn spun around. "Who's here?"

No one.

Ashlyn was aware of a sudden stillness.

There was no wind, no seagulls, no movement anywhere. The sky was blue, the ocean bluer, yet something as black and wicked and heinous as a monster in a sweat-drenched nightmare had now cloaked itself upon his shoulders.

He found a breath somewhere inside a gasp…and his trembling legs were suddenly backtracking. And then he turned and ran as fast as he could.

When Autumn found him in the bedroom, he was sitting on his bed, shaking like a baby. His eyes were bloodshot. "Where've you been? I went looking. What's the matter? I'll go get Lucy." She turned for the door.

"No!"

She stopped in her tracks.

"I'm alright," he assured her in a calm voice.

Autumn sat on her bed, opposite. "Man, you look…awful."

Ashlyn tried to control his shaking. "Thanks for the compliment. I guess I shouldn't have swallowed Grandma's pill chest."

"You took pills?"

"No…just the chest. Nothing to worry about…really nothing."

"Want some aspirin?"

"No, no. I was just thinking about home and stuff. Not such a man after all, huh?"

Autumn's pupils drifted aside reflexively, the way they did when she didn't quite believe something. "Lucy will get us the bikes, whenever we're ready."

"Ten minutes. I gotta go to the john."

She nodded, grabbed a sweater, and trotted downstairs.

Ashlyn stared at his reflection in the bathroom mirror. His face was gray, his eyes sore and red. He inspected his hands, holding them up in front of the mirror, slowly checking his palms, his knuckles. "I'm okay. I'm okay."

Deep down, he knew otherwise.

On the drive to the cycle store, Ashlyn attempted to stay within the loop of Lucy and Autumn's conversation. Withdrawn behavior was suspect, and he didn't want sympathy. But the anxiety attack had left him feeling weak and he was still experiencing an overwhelming sadness. He felt himself sinking into a blue bubble where he could observe life's show as a spectator without connecting. When Lucy spun off a joke and Autumn began laughing, he couldn't even force a grin. His eyes felt moist, his tear ducts ready to erupt.

He turned to the window, surreptitiously wiping away a tear. Staring at the blue ocean, he tried to focus on something positive.

Sailing.

Yes, sailing. Maybe, somehow, he could still get a small boat and—

He winced as a pain—a brutal pain—shot through his abdomen. He grabbed his stomach, trying to suck in a breath...but couldn't. His face began to turn blue.

Seeing him grab the back of his seat in shock, Lucy slammed on the brakes, skidding the car to a stop. Then she threw herself across the seat to administer mouth-to-mouth.

Ashlyn halted her with his palm. "It's...I'm okay...I'm okay." Color was seeping back into his cheeks.

"Ashlyn, good lord, don't scare me. Has this ever happened before?"

"Car sickness. I mean not like that...I'm okay. Really. Really I am."

Lucy wasn't about to take chances. She immediately drove to Wayside Manor Hospital, where Ashlyn reluctantly agreed to be examined. When he surfaced from behind the ER cubicle, he was rolling his eyes, as if to say I told you so. Nothing wrong.

Doctor Logan smiled warmly at Autumn, stuffed his stethoscope into his white coat, and walked a few paces with Lucy for a private chat. "Normal temperature, blood pressure's good, healthy heartbeat. Apparently crying earlier, that's why the red eyes, and that might have contributed to his shortness of breath. He also might have some intestinal gas...but more than likely, this is a physical reaction to an emotional problem. Given his recent circumstances, not that unusual. If it persists—"

Lucy shook her head. "No, I think he's going to be fine."

"Yeah, I think so, too."

Ashlyn's spirits appeared slightly elevated on the drive home, although he felt foolish for causing the ruckus.

"Ruckus?" Lucy grinned. "What ruckus? The doctor's a dish. I owe you."

However, the incident put the kibosh on the cycle adventure for that day. Lucy said a day's rest would do Ashlyn good. They'd pick up the cycles tomorrow.

FOR THE THIRD CONSECUTIVE NIGHT, sleep was a demon for Ashlyn. He mumbled, tossed, groaned, cried, even screamed. Unbeknownst to him, his grandma was so distressed she spent half the night on her respirator.

When Autumn stepped out of her morning shower, he was sitting on the edge of his bed. He'd been there for an hour, not moving, not responding to any of her earlier conversation. But he stole her breath away by asking, "Hi, feel better?" as if she'd been the one in the gloom tank.

She sputtered, "Me? That's a good one. Where've you been?"

Ashlyn folded his arms. "Thinking. I've been doing nothing but thinking…trying to make sense of this…trying to put it into some kind of perspective." He got up and walked over to the window. "I know it's not exactly logical but…I've come to some conclusions."

Autumn unwrapped the towel from her head and threw it into the hamper. "Oh, sounds kinda serious."

He turned back to her. "You agree it was a miracle?"

So he was back to that night again.

She slowly nodded but all of a sudden she was dreading the conversation. Where would this lead? Grandma and Lucy were already concerned, and had discussed the idea of therapy; not that there was an abundance of cash for sessions, but they were going to monitor Ashlyn. If his condition deteriorated—

"By a wave?" he said, interrupting her thoughts.

She nodded again.

"It pushed us, what, two miles, three?"

"Hard to know. What, you still think it was a hand?" She asked, finding it hard to suppress a sigh of anguish.

Ashlyn almost smiled, and for a moment she was relieved. "I don't think." He answered as he gazed at her steadily. "I know...I know what I saw."

Autumn's heart ached for her brother, and she wanted nothing more than to snap him back to reality with hard-edged reasoning, but she was careful with her response. After several moments, she said, "Well, if you really saw it, what do you want to do about it?"

Ashlyn played with his fingers, awkwardly. "I don't know. Part of me wants to, you know, like investigate...really get to the bottom of this. But the rest of me wants to run, to run a hundred miles." He laughed halfheartedly.

Again Autumn was reflective before responding. "Well I guess if there really was a body, we're going to have to tell someone. Like, the sheriff, no?" She chuckled. "Boy, I can see Grandma's face. We'll probably be grounded a year."

Ashlyn took a deep breath. "Not a corpse, Autumn. What I saw was definitely not a corpse. It was...very alive."

"But—" Autumn stopped. "What are you saying?"

"I know you, I know what you're going to think, and I'm prepared for your reaction...I've thought about this a whole lot, and it's going to sound like, really crazy...like your brother's lost it...but what if the hand I saw wasn't human?"

Autumn puckered her brow. She opened her mouth but held onto her words, not really knowing what to say. If this were Ashlyn of old, good old normal Ashlyn not suffering from grief and psychosomatic ailments, she'd know he was pulling her leg, and she'd jump on him and punch him. But she was convinced that the traumatic incident that night had triggered a severe form of depression in him. She was only twelve, bright yes, but she didn't know how to respond. Was it best to play along, or should she try to snap him back to reality? "Not human?" she said, her voice cracking.

-4-

Tax Man

TAX AUDITOR JACK HENRY WAS a hard working civil servant. Good at his job, great at detail, but with the personality of a carrot, said his fellow workers behind his back. Jack was never tardy, had few or no friends and as far as anyone knew, was single. Aside from his work, fishing seemed to be his only other love. Often during lunch or after work Jack would hang out at the *Jolly Roger,* a joint frequented primarily by seamen, although Jack's interest in navy types was extremely vapid. Not simply fishing, he was hoping to gather tidbits of information that would prove his age-old theory: That the *Seabed Phantom* wasn't an unusual whale or dolphin, nor an anomalous ocean current, but something much more unique…and definitely very tangible.

Tuesday afternoon Jack returned from lunch extremely excited. He'd overheard two merchant marines chatting about a new hydroelectric venture to be spearheaded by retired admiral Andrew Lightstone, a name he knew only too well. So the good admiral had resurfaced. You can't keep a good man down, he mused. Jack had a hunch that this hydroelectric venture was camouflage for a new hunt. No, he had more than a hunch—of course it was camouflage. The admiral had searched for the creature several times before. In fact, it was the admiral who'd coined the phrase *The Seabed Phantom,* rekindling interest in the old Oregonian sea legend.

Jack threw his jacket onto the clothes hook and sat at his desk, thinking about how the admiral and he shared the same passion…or was it obsession? The difference between them was simply that the admiral had the financial means to catch it, but—and this was Jack's trump card—he didn't know where to search. Jack barely contained a spluttered laugh, which drew a dirty look from a suit to his right. Jack returned the glare, as he absentmindedly toyed with two piles of neatly arrayed manila folders on his desk—his afternoon workload. He was really too excited and too nervous to work. Soon he'd never need to work again. He'd have the last laugh on the miserable bunch in the room. He'd buy himself a Ferrari, a bright yellow one, and butlers and servants would be at his beck and call, and everything he wanted would be placed at his feet—all of it paid out of the catch of a lifetime.

Jack knew the admiral was destined to fail, as he had on every other occasion, unless he employed him, and paid for his maps, paid dearly.

Something made Jack shudder. What if he'd misjudged his own importance, or the maps' importance? What if the admiral, a notorious strongman, threw him out, or even worse, double-crossed him? Jack primed himself. Got to hang tough. Stand up for myself. I can do this! One hundred percent of squat is squat, and without me, he's got squat!

Jack figured he was worth twenty percent. But he'd ask for thirty…no thirty-five…no, fifty percent! What the heck! He deserved fifty percent for his ten years of diligence. Fifty percent of a capture that would be worth millions: royalties from theme parks, merchandising, spectacular shows, movies. Yes, one hundred percent of nothing is nothing! Fifty percent!

Pushing aside the manila folders, Jack did something he hadn't done since school days. He doused his freckled forehead with bottled drinking water, poured the rest over his shirt, and flagged down his superior. With sagging shoulders, handkerchief dabbing his nose, he feigned the flu.

On his drive home, Jack rehearsed his call to Admiral Andy Lightstone. "You wanna bag the phantom…how do A-zone ingression maps grab ya? Yessir, A-zone ingressions. Wham bam diddly dam. Stick that in your pipe and smoke it, Admiral Lightstone! Maps! A-zone maps!"

There was no direct line to the admiral. Leaving both voice and email, Jack was cautious, careful not to divulge much, just enough to kindle an interest. He said he would call at eight forty-five the next morning, and he left his name: Tax Man.

RETIRED ADMIRAL ANDREW LIGHTSTONE HADN'T heard the term A-zone ingressions for more than a decade. Not surprisingly, the telephone message piqued his interest, providing reason enough for him to arrive at his office earlier than usual that next morning.

Waiting for the call, Andy lit up a Davidoff cigar and sipped on a cafe latte, while leafing haphazardly through a pile of applications for his latest oceanic enterprise. For several weeks the real agenda of his venture had been a topic of conversation in local seamen's jaunts. There'd even been a blurb on the Internet. Most of the calls and emails were from crackpots and sensationalists, the occasional oddball scientist.

Lightstone leaned back into a plush leather swivel chair. He checked his gold Rolex. 8:40. Maybe this Tax Man really had something. Maps not seen in years. Maps thought to have been lost or destroyed.

The admiral's eyes roamed over the piles of news clippings and police and navy records stacked up on the floor, hundreds of files, some dating back fifty years. Miraculous sea rescues, attacks by a sea serpent, prehistoric monster, demon from the deep. Most legitimate witnesses had only seen it on sonar; few had anything to contribute.

Was it possible that this so called Tax Man's contribution might be more meaningful than all the other piles on the floor combined?

The admiral allowed the pungent smoke from the Davidoff to curl around his gums.

The phone rang at 8:45, right on cue.

Lightstone listened intently as the caller—who was amusingly nervous—surrendered a couple of little known suboceanic facts—but not of mind-blowing value. The caller then said he wanted to meet rather than chat on the phone.

Andy flicked cigar ash. "I'm a busy man. Just give me a justifiable reason why I should take time out of my very hectic schedule."

"Why take the time? M-m-maps and money, that's w-why; you got nothing to lose, the world to gain. I w-won't…I won't do this over the phone."

"Come on, sir. Indulge me. What are these A-zone ingressions? And what do they have to do with my hydroelectric project? Why don't you fax or email me a map or two?"

"Oh yeah sure. I'm gonna email ya. Don't play cute with me, Admiral. We both know what they are. You know w-what I got is…what I got is legitimate. We need to come to an arrangement."

Andy blew a long stream of cigar smoke. "Arrangement? Like what do you have in mind?"

"I told you, not on the phone. I don't like the phone. Look…if you don't want my information, I'll go elsewhere."

Never seem too eager. Andy lived by that truism. He gulped the coffee dregs from his mug. "Mister Tax Man, with all due respect, I don't know you from Adam. You might be friggin' Prince Charmin', or you might be the devil himself. You got something, tell me. Otherwise, you have a real nice day—"

"Wait—" Tax Man quickly dropped another bait carrot. "I have the Mayhem chronicles from Proteus." He then fell silent, obviously regretting himself.

Andy's pulse raced, but he remained calm and ice-like, despite his sudden rush of excitement. "Mayhem chronicles?" He replied nonchalantly. "Proteus? Proteus? Now where've I heard that name?"

Andy remembered very well. *Proteus* was the name of a submersible that had been deployed in an extensive sea hunt for the *phantom*. The submersible and her logs, known as the *Mayhem chronicles*, were lost at sea, at least presumed lost. Outside of an inner circle, little was known about *Proteus,* and *Mayhem* was not public knowledge.

Tax Man tried to compose himself. Stuttering horribly, he informed Andy that what he had to offer was going to cost. *No kidding,* Andy mused inwardly. *Why else would the schmuck be calling?* Though Andy found himself being lured into this Tax Man's net, he continued to hold an air of indifference. His coolness could save him big bucks later.

"I'm not saying nothing else…not on the phone," added the nervous voice.

"Yes, well I reckon maybe you're right," Andy agreed. "Okay…tomorrow night. Nineteen hundred hours."

Tax Man said that early next week was the soonest for him; he needed time to bag a certain key.

"Key?" Andy inquired.

"Why, the key to the phantom," replied Tax Man, in a well re-hearsed line.

The place and time was set, and Tax Man hung up.

Andy sat in his chair twiddling his cigar, pondering: Was the guy for real, stuttering, phoneophobia, maps and all?

-5-

Tones

IT WASN'T A NIGHTMARE THAT woke Ashlyn in the middle of the night; he couldn't even remember any of his dreams. He lay there listening for several minutes to a noise—hissing or running water. He figured the toilet was stuck, but he didn't want to get up. Now the sound was really beginning to bug him, and anyway his pajama shirt was soaked with sweat. Lazily, he allowed his feet to reach the floor, and somewhat wobbly found his bearings. He quickly unbuttoned his pajama shirt and threw it on the floor. In the dark, he groped for the bathroom, opened the door quietly so as not to disturb Autumn, and closed it quietly before flicking on the light. Squinting in the glare, he immediately saw that the toilet wasn't running. There were no running taps in the sink or bath, no leaking pipes. But the hissing continued, as loud as before. Clasping his hands over his ears, he realized—

It was him!

The annoying sound was in his head!

Ashlyn stared at his pasty-faced image in the mirror. He swallowed, swallowed again. He squeezed his ears, tapped them, cleaned them with a Q-tip, tilted his head, gargled with water…and held his breath.

Nothing made the hissing stop.

Autumn already thought he was nuts. She hadn't exactly said so in words but the expression on her face had been worth a thousand. What would she think of running water in his ears? Maybe she was right. Maybe the last few weeks had been an emotional overload.

Abruptly, the tone of the sound shifted, turning to a higher pitch for a few seconds, then lower…higher and then lower again, a pattern that repeated itself several times.

Then the sound stopped altogether.

And there was silence, an unearthly silence, save Ashlyn's heartbeat, now racing—quite normal given the circumstances.

Ashlyn realized that he was shivering. In a peculiar way, he found comfort in the normalcy of feeling cold. He grabbed a dirty tee from the hamper and returned to bed. With his eyes open, he lay back, wondering, thinking—all he'd wanted was a sailboat, a blue and white sailboat to build a dream on, not a living nightmare.

LOUD GURGLING NOISES MADE ASHLYN snap open his eyes. It was light outside. His stomach gurgled again. A very natural sound, his brain agreed. He was famished. As he brushed his teeth, he went over the events of the night. Though he couldn't explain the bizarre water noises, the notion of them no longer seemed particularly alarming. He wondered why he'd been so nervous in the first place. He noticed that he was feeling almost cheerful. For the first time in three days, his shoulders felt light and unburdened. He couldn't wait to get down to the breakfast table.

Lucy served up eggs Béarnaise, grilled tomatoes, muffins, toast, jelly, and he ate like a linebacker. The table was alive with chatter. It was good to be his old self again.

Lucy kept her promise; after clearing away the dishes she drove them to the bicycle shop. Ashlyn also kept his promise. With his new 16-speed touring bicycle under his rump, he stuck to the bike trail, as they headed toward Wayside-on-Sea, eight miles north.

At last, summer.

Once an old mining and forestry town, now a tourist haven, picturesque Wayside appeared virtually as it did in the days of the old Wild West. However, most of the buildings were re-creations built after the 1931 Columbia River fire ignited the wizened gorse in the hills above Wayside, sending a wall of fire helter-skelter into the town. The rebuilt Wayside was just twenty-five percent original.

As usual, the summer madness had caused the population to swell. The lodges, hotels and motels were overbooked, and the quaint cobblestoned streets were jammed with crowds, strolling, souvenir hunting, riding bicycles, and eating rock candy and cranberry ice cream—cranberries being the indigenous flavor of the coast.

Ashlyn and Autumn headed down the very chaotic Main Street, onto Taylor Avenue, to the ocean. They padlocked the bicycles at the bike rack, unloaded their towels and packed lunches, and joined the throng on the noisy beach.

The water was crystalline, calm. They swam, played Frisbee with Tom, a loner from California, and ate lunch.

After devouring her sandwich, Autumn ran back into the surf while Ashlyn sat on the towel, watching her, watching the gentle rollers and breakers swishing ashore. Somebody behind him was laughing—a robust lady in an oversized swimsuit. Nearby, two kids were playing beach volleyball. Everything seemed run-of-the-mill, in place. Everyone was having fun.

BOOM! BOOM! BOOM!

Ashlyn's heart pounded like a fiercely stuck drum! His skin goose pimpled.

HISSSSSS!

Coming from where?

Whirling into the eyes of the plump lady who was still laughing, he saw that there weren't any showers near her.

HISSSSSS!

It wasn't the surf. He looked up and down the beach. No showers anywhere. His heart sank. He clasped his ears, barely holding back the urge to scream for help.

Autumn was jumping rollers, waving at him. He didn't move—couldn't move. He just sat there listening to that hissing coming from somewhere in his mind.

He managed to zone out the crowd, the ocean, making these elements vanish into oblivion as if they didn't even exist. Perhaps he did this on purpose, perhaps surrendering himself to some unseen force.

The hissing changed pitch, as it had on the earlier occasion. A lower tone of hissing, going even lower yet, and then higher, and then much higher.

What did this mean?

His anxiety began to lessen as he found himself studying the different tones as though this were some kind of strange music coming from inside of him.

Then as swiftly as it had begun, the sound stopped.

Although alone, Ashlyn sat on the beach with a feeling that he wasn't alone. He decided to guard that thought. It was easy to get carried away, to believe the tones and the non-human hand were somehow connected.

There had to be a sensible explanation. Medical disorder? He didn't relish that idea, and instantly dismissed the notion. Perhaps it was an innocuous buildup of earwax. Both ears simultaneously, and in musical tones? No, that didn't really make sense.

A large shadow loomed over him, and his heart skipped a few beats as droplets of icy water landed on his shoulders.

"You're not swimming anymore?" Autumn said, shaking her hair.

"What?" He abruptly jumped to his feet. "You bet I'm swimming. Race you!"

There was no reason to confide in Autumn, he decided. Charging off into the surf, he was already trying to convince himself that nothing else would happen,

And for almost two hours, nothing else did happen.

But as he rode along the bike path braiding the sandstone cliffs, he could have sworn Autumn called him. He could have sworn she said, "Come here now." But when he drew his cycle level with hers, and asked her "What's up?" she claimed she hadn't said a word.

Ten minutes later it happened again. But over the wind and clinking wheel spokes, he couldn't grasp her babbling. Again, he slowed down and drew level with her. "If you want to talk, keep up with me! I don't have ears in my back!"

Autumn snapped back, "What's your problem? I didn't say anything."

Ashlyn thought this was odd but nevertheless shrugged it off.

The next time it wasn't quite so easy to shrug off.

He was in the shower at home, when a voice called:

"Ash-lyn…. Ash-lyn come…."

"Won't be long," he answered, believing Autumn was urging him to hurry up.

"Aware, Ash-lyn."

Ashlyn hurriedly turned off the taps, reflexively shielding his privates.

"Who's there?"

There was silence....

Silence that did not soothe Ashlyn's sudden anxiety. The voice had been beside him, breathing in his ear.

"Hello?"

Standing still, shivering in that silence, prickly goose bumps covered his arms.

Could he have imagined it?

Ghost? Poltergeist?

Vehemently shaking his head, he quickly turned on the taps, blasting his face in a stream of hot water. He didn't want to think, to think about anything. Closing his eyes, he allowed the hot water to massage the back of his neck and his shoulders, somehow hoping it would scrub away his woes, cleanse him through and through so that he could emerge a new man.

He stayed in that shower until the water ran cold.

IT WAS SEVERAL HOURS LATER, shortly after Grandma and Lucy had retired to their rooms, and while Autumn was outside at the garden shed, putting Bigsey to bed, that Ashlyn sat on the sofa in the living room, with his sketch pad on his knee, drafting a small ketch—a simple, inexpensive boat not so beyond the reality of his means.

"*Ahh-shsss...shsss....*" The sibilant whispers were loud in his ears this time.

Ashlyn stiffened, his eyes quickly surveying the room. There was no one there. The TV was off.

"*Ahhhsh...plssss...psssss...psssss...shsssss...air...ga...fo...ssss... Ashlyn... sssss... awa...air...sssss—*"

Ashlyn clasped his hands over his ears.

"*Ahhhsh...plssss...psssss—*"

As he staggered to his feet, his pad dropped to the floor. He turned toward the hall but didn't know where to run. Where could he hide? He froze in mid-step, realizing—

The whispers had stopped!

Too afraid to remove his hands from his ears, he stumbled back into the living room.

"Ashlyn?"

"Nooo!"

He found himself staring into his sister's eyes.

"What's the matter with your ears? What are you doing?"

Ashlyn continued to stare at his sister as if she were a stranger. Then with bittersweet joy, he began to laugh; he yowled in crumbling hysterics, while somehow managing to hold back tears that so wanted to gush.

"Are you okay?"

Lamely, he claimed to have heard a burglar.

Autumn slowly nodded. Given his behavior over the last few days, she decided not to press the issue.

ASHLYN DREADED SLEEP THAT NIGHT. He thought of listening to music on Autumn's headphones until morning, but he'd already acted crazy enough for one night. For Autumn's sake, he assumed a fake smile as he climbed into the sack, quickly finding the spongy spot on his pillow that he hoped would offer a sound sleep.

I'm not crazy, he reassured himself, *a little stressed, that's all.* Then his mind drifted to two of the whispered words:

AIR and *ASHLYN*

But maybe air was a broken part of Ashlyn, in which case it was just one word:

AIRSHLYN

What difference did it make? *Forget it,* he told himself sternly. *Count sheep...one sheep, two, three, four, five....*

Fortunately, he did sleep soundly that night. He wasn't perspiration-soaked when he awoke, and he couldn't remember his dreams, whether they were good or bad.

After breakfast, Lucy directed him to the dining room to polish the silver. As Grandma had said, "Bed-and-breakfast guests have to make due return." In other words, they must pay for their stay. Ashlyn was actually grateful. As long as he remained busy, perhaps his mind wouldn't wander.

After covering the mahogany table with newspaper, Lucy brought down the silver tea service and the wine goblets, and then sat at the head of the table to get them started.

Autumn was in an inquisitive mood and soon had Lucy spilling her life story.

Lucy had lived with Grandma for fifteen years, even before Grandpa died. After divorcing her abusive husband, she decided that her bruised psyche would heal better on the coast. Planning to be away a few weeks only, she'd rented a day-rate room from Grandma. But the days whipped off the calendar. When Grandpa died several months later, Lucy helped with the funeral arrangements. Then when Grandma got sick, not only did Lucy take care of the ailing woman, she found herself running the bed-and-breakfast. Somewhere along the way, she had traded rent for a half-share in the house.

"Fifteen years? You must have known our father," Autumn inquired.

"Met him a few times...handsome...big blue sad eyes. They looked right through you, they did. Yeah, good looking family."

"What was he like? Was he, like, always telling jokes?" Autumn asked. "Mom said he could make an undertaker laugh."

Lucy tabled the silver polish with a look of surprise. "Oh, I guess that must have been before, you know...his troubles with that ocean study. Shame...all that money on sea equipment."

"Ocean study? You mean environment study? He was an environmental activist," Autumn quickly corrected her.

Lucy looked up, her mouth ajar. Had she just put her big foot in it? How was she to know the kids didn't know the truth...that Jerry had lost his marbles and blown the family fortune, tens of millions? Trying to recover, she said, "Yes of course he was...he stood up for a lot of good causes, he sure did."

That part was true...in the earlier days.

"What sea equipment?" Ashlyn queried, pushing away the silver goblet he'd been polishing.

Reaching for the polish, Lucy felt decidedly uncomfortable. If their mother hadn't spoken about their father, she had no business telling the kids either. "Oh just stuff, he was a bit of a spendthrift, you know."

Ashlyn knew their father had been wealthy, old money, but unpaid back taxes had resulted in the seizure of the entire family estate. At death, he'd left his family penniless, the result of which was that they had lived their whole lives never more than one month away from eviction. So what was all this about an ocean study and money on sea equipment? "Doesn't sound like flippers and a wet suit," he remarked.

Now feeling awful, Lucy was at a loss for words. She rubbed the silver teapot with extra verve, almost as if she hadn't heard him.

Ashlyn dropped his polishing cloth. Okay, even if his father was a wild man with the cash—maybe he was a lot of other things they didn't know about—but his wife had loved him until the day she died, and probably only wanted to remember the good times. "Lucy!" He said a tad loud, getting her attention. "Am I missing something? I think we've got a right to know. He was our father!"

Grandma's somewhat bitter voice startled him. "You want to know?" Grandma parked her wheelchair in the doorway. "What? That he lost his mind and burned the family fortune? That he was a stubborn idiot; that no one could talk to him, not even your poor mother." Grandma gasped for air, a wheezing sound coming from her lungs. "He tore her poor heart out."

"You mean he blew the fortune on...sea equipment?" Ashlyn asked.

"Blew it?" Grandma exclaimed, her face trembling.

Lucy put down the teapot. "Careful, Mary. You don't have to put yourself through this."

"No I don't...but they're right." Gathering her thoughts, Grandma continued, "If he knew something...had some kind of training...what a fool, what an absolute, idiotic fool. What was it, that sea place he built, Lucy?"

Lucy frowned. "I think they just called it sea lab."

Grandma wheezed again. "Sea lab. No, Ashlyn, your father didn't blow it. Blow it is an error of judgment, a mistake, a little recklessness. He didn't blow it. He burned it! Burned it as if he'd built a ruddy bonfire! Every penny, even his stupid submarine—his sarcophagus—rotting on the bottom of the ocean! Gone!

"They took the house, the furniture, the cars, even the little knickknacks! Left your mom with nothing but the clothes on her back! Well, now you know. Your father, the big shot oceanographer, whatever he was...your father's legacy was a nightmare of debt!" Lowering her eyes, Grandma reversed herself out of the doorway, wheezing as she went.

"Mary, are you alright?" Lucy called out after her.

Grandma didn't reply.

Autumn's stunned eyes found Ashlyn's before he turned to Lucy. "He died in a submarine?"

Lucy nodded. "A fire. He radioed for help...too late."

It answered a long-standing question. Why Mom had always evaded any conversation about their father's grave.

Ashlyn's gaze hardened on Lucy. Now he wanted answers; he wanted to know everything. "A sea lab? Like for marine scientists? But the family business was banking. Why did he build a sea lab?"

Lucy picked up a silver goblet as if trying to hide behind it, stuttering that she didn't really know that much. "It's really been none of my business, Ashlyn. I really don't know."

Ashlyn could see that Lucy was uncomfortable, so he decided to drop the subject, for now.

But as Ashlyn and Autumn sat in the backyard talking about their father, one question seemed to defy all logic: Why didn't their mom ever mention any of this? Submarines and sea labs, oceanography—it was glamorous, exciting stuff.

Autumn brushed a fly out of her face. "Yeah, go tell that to Grandma."

Toying with a blade of grass, Ashlyn slowly nodded. He could understand Grandma's reservations. But why was Lucy being so cagey? What part of the story was she concealing? "Submarines don't sink every day," he said at length, dropping the blade of grass. "And when they do, it's news, big news, in the papers. I wonder if the library—"

"Yeah. Good idea," Autumn nodded in agreement.

THE DESKMAN AT THE WAYSIDE Public Library referred Ashlyn to Jim, the senior librarian, who was due back shortly. Meanwhile, Ashlyn decided to try his luck in the reference section.

Autumn went browsing. She was only out of Ashlyn's sight for a few minutes when she noticed a man on the balcony staring at her. He was tall, disheveled, bearded, with knotted white hair sprawling on the shoulders of a black leather suit way too warm for a summer day. As he shamelessly honed his sight on her, Autumn felt the blood draining out of her face.

Ashlyn was returning to the information desk when the same tall man came charging down the staircase, and flew past him like a giant bat in his baggy leather suit. He then almost collided with a man carrying a stack of books.

"Mr. Clark, your books. I've got your books! Don't you want your books?" cried the startled man with the books.

He was either about to miss a plane, or he was stone deaf, but Mr. Clark kept going, storming through the revolving doors, out into the brightness of the street.

"What's his hurry?" Ashlyn asked the man with the books, who turned out to be the senior librarian, Jim.

"He's an odd one. From his petrified look, I reckon he saw Casper," Jim replied, dumping the books on the desk as he placed himself behind the counter. "What can I do for you?"

Before Ashlyn could answer, Autumn grabbed him by the sleeve. "Did you see that? Holy crap! He scared me to death!"

"The weirdo?"

Autumn shuddered. "The way he stared at me…those piercing eyes."

Jim interjected, "Denton Clark, yeah, bit of an odd ball, but he wouldn't hurt a fly. You must have reminded him of someone."

Ashlyn looked concerned so Jim tried to explain. "He's a sponsor for our library, gives computers and stuff for the kids…spends most of his time alone, pretty much a recluse. He's an artist and pretty good too. Odd, yeah, but harmless enough." Jim held a broad smile.

Ashlyn gathered his thoughts. "Are you Jim?"

"All day and every day. Something else I can help you with?"

"Uh…yes. I'm researching a submarine accident. It sank around here, about twelve years ago."

Jim scratched his scalp under a mop of thick red hair, bringing down a snow of dandruff. "Submarine that sank? Submarine? Nah nothing around here Wait a minute…there was that mini…the submersible. What's-his-face? Don't tell me, on the tip of my tongue—"

"Jerry Miller?" Ashlyn prompted.

"Darn, I knew it. Yeah. Jerry Miller. Nutcase. Went on all them Seabed Phantom hunts. Obsessed. Yeah, that sank. Your best bet's the Western World, the newspaper. We don't carry issues that far back, but you can call the paper…in Portland."

Ashlyn's mind was spinning—his father a nutcase? *Seabed Phantom?*

Autumn asked Jim a question. "Seabed Phantom? What's that?"

"The Seabed Phantom? Well, that all depends on who you ask. Some around here say it's a huge light-emanating monster…prehistoric, more than a hundred feet long; moves faster than anything else on the planet! With a hunger for human flesh." Jim raised his eyebrows theatrically.

"It's real?" Autumn asked in shock.

"Sound real to you?" Jim grinned, before continuing not quite so melodramatically. "Yeah, well, once in a while someone catches it on video. You know, same old, same old, blurry crap. But there is the navy connection. They got hammered a few years ago trying to catch it. Well, that's it. Our very own Loch Ness monster, right here in Oregon." Jim looked down at his computer and began typing. Then he looked up again. "Come to think of it, that's his baili- wick—Denton Clark. Lookit." He shuffled Denton Clark's books, all relating to the ocean. "I reckon he knows more about the ocean than a fish stick."

Ashlyn swallowed hard. "If I wanted to ask him—"

Jim interrupted. "The Old Mill House…straight up the highway, up on the cliff. Look for the windmill. You can't miss it."

AS HE DEPARTED FROM THE library, Ashlyn's mind swirled. The *Seabed Phantom*—a light-emanating creature, a legend that others spoke of and wrote about. The hand under the rowboat had been a glowing, luminous hand. Could it have been the *Seabed Phantom?* His thoughts drifted to his father, in a submersible searching for the creature, blowing the family fortune searching for it. Was he really a nutcase or had something happened to his father like what was now happening to him? Did his father also hear musical tones and experi- ence overwhelming feelings of dread?

"Wow! What do you make of that?" Autumn said, interrupting his thoughts.

"Strange," was all Ashlyn replied. But he was already planning his next move. They needed to find out everything there was about this *Seabed Phantom.* And maybe Denton Clark was just the ticket.

But he'd leave Autumn behind…just in case.

-6-

Lightstone

HIS DARK BLUE SUIT WAS tailor-made, with a price tag of over two thousand dollars. The blue and burgundy silk handkerchief in his breast pocket perfectly matched his tie. His Lexus was new and the leather still smelled fresh. Andy Lightstone liked the smell of a new car. He checked his appearance in the rear view mirror. His sideburns were graying, but his hair was still dark and thick, though not closely cropped as it used to be. Funny how life turns out, he mused, as he momentarily thought about some of his old navy brothers—still living by the code.

So much had happened over the last few years. Maybe, if he'd walked the stately path typical of high-ranking naval officers in retirement, he'd look at himself differently in the mirror.

But there was no stately path, no politicking or lecturing for this four-star veteran. Andy was the navy's scapegoat broadsided by the *'Phantom'* fallout. Wounded but not fallen, he'd made new friends, found new supporters, and using southern charm and razor-edged acumen, he'd secured backing for endeavors such as hydroelectricity, mineral extraction and illegal mass production fishing. He didn't care a hoot where the financing came from as long as it flooded in, and it came in duffel bags, from mobsters, to be washed in the ocean so to speak. Andy Lightstone was a master exploiter of the ocean, and it was lining his pockets!

At fifty-three, and still dashing, he thought, this was his third *phantom* hunt, the largest since the navy's *Operation Kelp Weed*. Officially, the new project was tagged 'research-and-development' for his seabed mining operation. And in fact there was a hint of truth to that, for much of his team would be working on enhancing Extremely Low Frequency communications in a subocean environment. With ships, scientists, weapons, at his disposal, this was a multi-million dollar operation.

The admiral chuckled to himself. This time, he'd do it—he'd pluck from the ocean the greatest sea discovery in all recorded history. Success was going to taste ever so sweet. This wasn't just about vindication, proving the navy wrong—although revenge was a fine motivator for a military man—this was about marketing.

This was about money!

Cruising up the coast in his beige Lexus, Andy spoke ship-to-shore to his good friend and partner, Captain James Swift, who was about to retire from the navy. The two men exchanged information.

James Swift spoke about the recent *Phantom* sighting, which the admiral agreed was excellent news. *It* seemed to be daring them on.

Andy then talked about the mysterious Tax Man and his purported *Mayhem chronicles*—detailed maps of A-zone ingressions.

A-zone was nomenclature for abyssal zone—ocean depths in excess of thirteen thousand feet—and ingressions, in suboceanic terms, defined openings or tunnels beyond the seabed. The theory was that the entity emerged and returned to enclosures on the A-zone seafloor, and that there existed a network of subterranean passageways, or even an ocean below the ocean. But almost all the gathered information on A-zone ingressions sunk to the bottom of the ocean twelve years ago, after an oceanographer's submersible accident.

Andy was excited. If the maps still existed, then these ingressions could possibly take them right to the creature's lair.

James said he'd dock at Port Oxford in four days. He agreed to join Andy at Sam's Seafood Grill for the meeting with Tax Man and afterwards a renowned animal specialist.

The plan was coming together.

Clicking off the phone, Andy pumped up the volume of his beloved CD—*Phantom of the Opera*—still his favorite after all these years. Then, for the hell of it, he gunned the accelerator, just to see if his Lexus LS 430 really had some guts.

He pulled wide as he roared past a kid on a bike, and kept on flying.

-7-

Denton Clark

ASHLYN WAS ON HIS WAY to the Old Mill House, another three miles up the highway, when a blast of engine heat from a beige Lexus almost knocked him off his bike. He slammed on the brakes, steadying himself, before waving his fist at the driver—like it made a difference. The speeding Lexus roared off into the distance.

Until this moment, it had been an uneventful day without whispers or any anomalous occurrences. But the coastal hills were steep, and the going was slow.

The shadows were already long when Ashlyn, sweaty and fatigued, turned into a dirt road flanked by chain link. Behind the fence lay blankets of yellow four-foot-tall gorse lapping the base of a weather-trashed windmill, its blades frozen in time. Another half-mile around a curve, the road dead-ended at a gothic iron gate.

NO TRESPASSERS
DOGS PATROL

Ashlyn rested the bike on the kickstand. There was an intercom next to the mailbox, another posted sign:

PRESS AT YOUR OWN RISK

Ashlyn noted that it was a pretty spooky place, yet he felt only marginally apprehensive. He pressed the buzzer without knowing if it was operational, for it was silent. He was about to press again when—

"What?" snapped a surly voice out of the intercom.

"Uh hello."

"What do you want?"

"Hello…uh, Mr. Clark?"

"Who wants to know?" demanded the voice.

"My name is Ashlyn Miller. I'd like to talk to you."

Silence.

"Hello? Hello, are you there?"

"Can you read? Can you read English?" The voice demanded.

Ashlyn was momentarily thrown. "Can I read? Yes, I can read."

"What does the sign say? What makes you think you can come snooping around here?"

"I just…I only want to…to ask you some questions."

"Questions? No trespassers, that's what it says. I don't do interviews."

"Please—"

"Go away before I send out the dogs."

A snarling dog sound resonated out of the intercom.

"Please, I must talk to you. It's about the ocean and um—" Ashlyn cleared his throat. "The seabed phantom."

More silence before Clark responded. "Seabed phantom? What about it?"

Ashlyn nervously kicked a pebble. "Do you think…do you think such a thing exists?"

"No," Clark answered immediately. "If that's it, have a nice day."

"Please, wait—" Ashlyn cleared his throat. "Have you ever heard of any strange, like uh, weird rescues, I mean, at sea, you know, like, miracles and stuff?"

There was a dead space. "Miracles and stuff? No." There was finality in the voice.

"I see," Ashlyn replied, his voice sinking. "Sorry to bother you," he sighed, turning to leave.

"I'll tell you what, cycle up to the green door…the green side-door. I'll give you five minutes. Understand?"

"Yes. Thank you."

"Stand by."

Ashlyn looked for the security camera. He couldn't see one, but the man obviously had one because he knew of the bike.

The gate swung open.

Ashlyn parked next to a tree on the rambling lawn. The L-shaped, two story abode called the Old White House wasn't exactly white; it was a dirty yellow with a run-down appearance and a red tile roof. A hundred and fifty feet below lay the spectacular Pacific Ocean.

The green door was at the base of eight concrete steps. Ashlyn heard an electronic beeping sound as he approached, then a click as the door sprung ajar. There was no one there to greet him.

"Hello," he called out tentatively. "Mr. Clark?"

Nothing.

Entering the house, Ashlyn's leather soles made annoying squeaks on the wooden floorboards. He found himself in a large, heavily cluttered room with a soaring ceiling, junky furniture, strewn books, papers, empty cocktail glasses and a sweeping view window. The smell reminded him of Benny's fish restaurant: dank, musty, a hint of stale alcohol.

The door automatically closed behind him.

Still no sign of Clark.

Off to the side, he came across a large fish aquarium. He tapped the glass, spooking several occupants. He then moved around to the other side of the tank, and froze....

He was face to face with a mermaid—a twelve-foot-long pros-thetic in an open tank, her tail dangling on the floor. Nearby, another mermaid was propped against a stand, another lay against a book-case, and an unfinished merman rested on a worktable. Ashlyn now saw mermaid paintings on the walls, easels, others lying around.

His thoughts churned—*the hand*—not just any hand. Large, scaly, with webbed fingers. How many times over the last few days had he thought about mermaids as an explanation? Only it was too infantile, too ridiculous. It was still too infantile, still ridiculous, yet here he was in the middle of a maze of mermaids, with no doors anywhere except the green one he'd entered, and no Mr. Clark—just a big ugly fish staring at him through the glass, staring at him and moving swiftly toward him.

Ashlyn took an uneasy step back, when a voice startled him. "Harmless rainbow wrasses, magnified." It was Clark, standing barely three feet away, a long coil of his unkempt hair dangling down the side of his face. He was wearing a red silk robe, holding a bottle of whisky in one hand, a half-filled cocktail glass in the other, mostly ice, which he constantly swirled. He appeared to be forty-five, maybe younger, but haggard.

Ashlyn looked beyond his odd host, trying to see the concealed door or space he'd entered through. But there was nothing to see.

"Labroids dimidiatus," Clark added with a marginal slur.

Ashlyn nodded. "Uh-huh…neat aquarium."

"I know." With one swig, Clark polished off the brown liquid and quickly poured himself another. "Drink?"

"No. No thank you, sir."

"Good. So, what's on your mind?" He began swirling the ice again.

"Amazing…really amazing…all these mermaids."

"Do you sculpt?" Clark stooped down and placed the bottle on the floor, but almost immediately changed his mind and picked it up again.

"Er, I sketch, with charcoals. I can paint kind of okay, but I don't really have the patience."

"Keep it up."

"These are…amazing. Why do you—?"

"Nah, no questions. Remember, I don't do interviews. You talk, I listen." Clark glanced at his watch, almost spilling his whisky. He then led the way to a wooden desk, leaned against it and propped his foot up on a tattered ottoman, swirling his ice without taking his eyes off Ashlyn. They were the bluest of eyes, like blue marble balls and they seemed never to blink. Ordinarily this would have been un-nerving but there was something benign about this stranger, perhaps even melancholic.

Ashlyn began, "I'm interested in…er, weird, uh…unexplainable sea rescues." He looked back at the full-sized mermaid. "Like uh, a rescue by her."

"A mermaid?"

"Well, yeah, or…or something like it."

Clark's gaze returned to his ice as he slowly swirled the cubes. "A rescue by a real mermaid? Now that's interesting," he said face-tiously.

"But not impossible?" Ashlyn rejoined, wincing at his own na-iveté.

Clark's eyes suddenly looked fierce as they probed into Ashlyn's soul. "Don't you think that's something a crazy would say...or a little kid?" He raised his eyebrows.

Surely Ashlyn could have expected a more passionate response, considering all the mermaids. Searching for a comeback, he said, "The seabed phantom, what d'you know or think about it?"

"I don't know anything; I already told you." Clark's jaw hardened into a sneer. "Is that it?"

"No," Ashlyn sighed. "Look, what if something weird happened—" he stopped in mid-sentence. On the cycle to the house, he'd made the decision to gather information and say little. He definitely didn't plan to spill his guts to this eccentric stranger. But Denton Clark was a stonewall. There seemed to be no other way to draw him into a real conversation. And now, more than ever, Ashlyn wanted answers from this man of the mermaids. "Do you know Deadman's Bluff?"

Clark grunted that he did, took another swig of whisky.

Ashlyn continued, "Me and my sister, we were there; we know we shouldn't have been, but we were. And something happened."

As Clark nodded, his eyes momentarily lost focus.

Better hurry, Ashlyn figured, before he passes out.

The story of the night of the whirlpool spanned twenty minutes, considerably longer than the five-minute allotment. Clark appeared interested, nodding understandingly and refilling his glass at least three times before Ashlyn approached his conclusion. "The face was translucent—" He took a long look at Clark's largest mermaid prosthetic. "It was translucent, not really like her."

Clark nodded understandingly.

"Although I only saw it for a second, the hand...that hand was definitely webbed...and luminous." He paused, studying Clark's reaction—or lack of one. "Do you know something? Is this why you sculpt mermaids?"

Clark's lips turned slightly upward, almost a smile, and he cleared his throat. "Damn lucky to be alive. You and your sister are damn lucky. But come now, you really don't think a mermaid saved your...had anything to do with your...hey, be a hoot, wouldn't it?" He winked at Ashlyn, then stood up and cricked his neck.

"But...all this...what saved us then?"

Clark shrugged. "Currents, waves—simple forces of nature." Trying to usher Ashlyn to the green door, he said, "Do yourself a favor; get your mom to run you up to the dunes; it's great fun up there: sand bikes, river boat rides—"

"What sort of creature saved us? What's the seabed phantom?"

"Snap out of it, boy! Forget it! Now goodbye."

Ashlyn didn't move. "Forget it? Why? Because I'm on the right track and you don't want—?"

"Forget it because…what, you want people to think you're crazy? Forget it because it's hogwash. Forget it because it's nothing! Your sister's right, you imagined it."

"What about the hand, the bright light? She saw the light, too."

Clark shrugged. "Things aren't always as they appear. You thought you saw something, and maybe you even did, but it's not what you think. Face up to it, you were scared, disoriented, exhausted. What do you expect?"

"The moon's reflection?" Ashlyn retorted facetiously.

"I didn't say that. Could be a bunch of things. Pelagia noctiluca—it's a purple jellyfish, like luminous balls at night. They drift ashore in storms. Or orange cup coral—has a fluorescent pigment, emits a bright hue. Nothing abnormal about it, nothing mythical. Take my advice; stay away from Deadman's Bluff. It's a treacherous place! Now I mean it, goodbye."

Ashlyn still didn't budge. "But what about you? Look at these! Why do you do this?"

Clark sighed with frustration. "I'm a folklore romanticist, an escapist, that's all."

"You never saw one of these…creatures?"

"No, I see them all the time. That's why I paint them."

"What about the seabed phantom? Why was the navy searching for it?"

"I said time's up."

"Why was the navy searching for it? And my father, he had a submersible, and he was searching for it too. Is that all hogwash?"

"I have no idea what you're talking about," Clark nervously replied. But it was obvious by now that he'd really had more than enough of Ashlyn. Placing his palm on the base of Ashlyn's back, he forcefully pushed him toward the door.

Now Ashlyn felt really stupid. Could he have imagined the hand, the arm, the shape of a face, the eye? Was it really orange cup corral? But he remained stubborn. "You're hiding something."

"This interview is over. Whether you leave politely on your feet or without dignity on your ass is up to you."

Ashlyn decided, politely. He apologized for being pushy but it was too late—he was shoved outside, and Denton Clark closed the old green door firmly behind him.

Ashlyn dusted himself off. That was well done, he told himself.

DENTON POURED HIMSELF THE REMAINDER of the whisky, swigging half before reaching the bay window. His shoulders stooped low, as if the weight of the world had settled upon them. Staring at the orange orb setting on the horizon, he angrily tugged at a clump of his matted hair, until the pain evidenced itself in the form of moisture in his eyes. Perhaps it was a display of self-loathing, or maybe a masochistic idiosyncrasy. Either way, emotion vented, he turned around and pressed a remote control switch in his robe pocket, causing a concealed door between two bookcases to silently slide open.

And stumbling forward between the bookcases, Denton Clark disappeared into some other room of the mysterious house.

ASHLYN WAS TRULY GRATEFUL THAT no one other than Clark had watched him making a jackass out of himself. Fortunately, the man was a recluse and a drunk who would probably forget everything before he'd have the chance to share gossip.

Cycling back to the main road, Ashlyn made a decision: He was through with the *Seabed Phantom*, through with checking out weirdoes and digging up accounts from the past. Surely there were better things one could do during summer vacation.

I've got to start living again. I'm alive…I'm alive and I'm lucky. That's all there is to it. Let my summer vacation begin.

He took a deep breath to expunge all his demons.

And the rushing water tones began.

-8-

Air Ware

NIGHT HAD FALLEN WITH WINDY gusts howling and screeching through the doorjambs. Dinner was on the stovetop getting cold. No one had eaten; Grandma because she wasn't feeling well, Autumn and Lucy because they were too anxious—Ashlyn still wasn't home. He'd told them he was going to buy art supplies, that he'd only be gone an hour. That was four hours ago. They tried not to dwell on it. But something must have happened to him.

Autumn decided to check the street one last time before Lucy called the police. Autumn had done this at least a half dozen times already.

Opening the door, a biting wind assailed her, almost knocking her off her feet, and triggering in her an awful thought—that Ashlyn had been swept off his bike under a car. But as she moved quickly along the garden path to the gate, she was shocked—and extremely glad—to see him pulling his bike up onto the curb, his face chilled but smiling innocently.

Ashlyn's excuse was a flat tire. Autumn didn't believe him for a moment, and from Grandma's frown, she probably didn't either. Lucy palmed her hands together in praise. Ashlyn was frozen to the bone and starving—what else was she to do but put the meatloaf back into the oven? They could scold him later.

After dinner, when Lucy went up to bed, Ashlyn and Autumn sat in the living room, sipping hot cocoa, quietly chatting about Denton Clark. Autumn was disappointed that Ashlyn hadn't teamed up with her, even though there was merit to his logic—just in case Denton Clark was some kind of pervert.

Autumn blew on her hot cocoa before taking a sip. "Well, at least he seems to have knocked some sense into you." She figured that Ashlyn now accepted Denton Clark's explanation of orange cup coral as the mysterious ocean glow. "So we can forget about that night." Peering over the rim of the cocoa mug, she looked directly into Ashlyn's eyes. "We can...can't we?"

"You bet," Ashlyn agreed, and as they chatted, he appeared to be genuinely sincere and optimistic about the future. Of course, he didn't mention anything about his hypnotic episode after leaving Denton Clark's house—that for an hour he'd been sitting in a ditch by the highway listening to strange low-volume whispers and white noises; that he'd been in a cold sweat, too dizzy to cycle, and that even now his mind was buzzing. What would she think of that? Not that he had any intention of telling her.

It was getting late. Autumn went upstairs to take a shower. There was a three-hour multicolored cedar log burning in the fireplace, about an hour left on it. Ashlyn threw a cushion on the floor and sat down close enough to feel the heat on his face. He wondered if life would ever return to normal, like it was only a month ago, life without sibilant whispers and white noises, without the *Seabed Phantom*. His old life—Barstow, Mom, was now a world away, some other incarnation. What were the answers? He rubbed his forehead. At least his angst had subsided; surrender inducing a kind of odd composure. Even if the whispers were to start again at that instant, he'd give it his all to listen. In fact, he wished for them so that he could decipher their meaning. Up until now, he'd only been able to discern three words. He jotted them on his sketchpad.

AIR
WARE
ASHLYN

He rearranged them:

WEAR - AIR - ASHLYN
ASHLYN WEAR - AIRWARE

"Airware, like swimwear but with air?" He paused as something dawned on him. Could there have been a 'B' that he hadn't discerned?

B WARE...ASHLYN

Deciding not to linger on that, he tore the paper from the pad and threw it into the fire. "I don't think so! You don't scare me. You got something to say? Say it in plain English."

Ashlyn stayed by the fire, watching the dance of the flames, warming himself through, while waiting for answers. He waited... and waited. Perhaps half an hour went by or even an hour. A chunk of the log dropped off the grate, flaring up on the hearth. The log got smaller.

Still, no answers.

The glowing crimson embers under the grate began to turn gray. And with the fire almost extinguished, Ashlyn felt a chill in the air. The room became quite dark, and for a spell, without the crackle of flame, he felt the stillness of solitude.

But only for a moment.

"Aren't you going to bed?"

Ashlyn turned to see Lucy standing in the doorway, holding a steaming nightcap. "Yes. Yes, I am," he assured her.

-9-

The Call

"ASH—LYN...."

The voice beckoned in a soothing tone, *"ASH—LYN...COME...."* It was as if the voice was the ocean itself. In the dream, Ashlyn was at sea, not aboard a boat but in the water, rising up and down tall waves...up and down on a swaying carpet of navy blue... and he was beginning to feel nauseous.

The voice summoned again, *"ASH—LYN...."*

Ashlyn scoured the area, hoping to see a bright glow but all he saw was thick indigo-blue rollers surrounding him. Up and down he went, up and down in a monotonous rhythm.

He was feeling sicker by the minute.

A flash rifled out of the sky.

As he looked up, he saw a stream of luminous tentacles. "Monsters!" He cried in his sleep. He begged himself to snap out of the dream, but his eyelids, like deadweights, refused to open.

The tentacles shrieked as they stabbed down at the ocean, striking in rapid succession, churning the waves, making the waves heave and roll with an even greater intensity.

Ashlyn knew that if he stayed in that heaving swell he'd puke at any moment. He had to escape...and quickly! He threw himself into a dive...down into the undersea where the swaying quickly ceased and the horrendous noises faded into oblivion.

He found himself sinking into a silent world.

Down…down…down.

A tiny light blinked below…then another light, a bigger brighter, dazzling light, getting brighter yet.

What is that? he wondered, finding it hard to discern much detail through the intense glare. There were bubbles down there, thousands of blinding bubbles and…

Tones.

Yes, the tones were from down there.

Bubbles….

Light….

Tones….

Ashlyn tried to reach the light, to be with those tones. Yet the light remained unapproachable, at some distance beyond his gauge.

He suddenly realized that he was holding his breath because his lungs were aching. Thinking that he might be able to inhale some underwater oxygen, he took a breath. To his alarm, he sucked in a horrible thick tar scorching the back of his throat. His lungs were bursting with the hot liquid. He would drown unless—

Beset with panic, he began kicking…crazily kicking as hard and fast as he could, kicking for the surface…

"NO…ASHLYN, COME—"

Ashlyn was kicking his way to the surface when he awoke. The covers were off him, and he was coughing and desperately sucking in the air when Autumn, stirred by his nightmare, turned on her bedside light. "Are you all right?"

"What?"

"Should I get Lucy?"

Ashlyn pulled his wet hair away from his face. It had been a bad dream.

Dream?

No, not a dream…something more…something much more. At length, he replied, "What are you doing up?"

"Monsters, huh?" she said.

"I dunno…something."

"You wanna talk?" She switched off the light and snuggled back under her covers.

Ashlyn didn't respond right away, partly because he was planning his next move, and partly because if he told her the truth, she'd either try to justify the dream—justification according to Autumn—or she'd want to know what *they* would do about it. And now that he had a plan, he definitely couldn't bring her along. It was far too dangerous. Everybody said so. Lucy, Grandma, even Denton Clark; they'd all warned him about Deadman's Bluff.

"No," he said. "Forget it. Go back to sleep."

"Yeah, what sleep?" she replied sarcastically.

But Ashlyn wasn't listening. He was off in his own arcane world.

Yes, I have to go back, he told himself. *Tomorrow...tomorrow morning.*

He waited for his intellect to argue.

It didn't.

He was simultaneously scared and exhilarated. There was the possibility that he was being bewitched, that some unfriendly foe from the sea, a prehistoric sea serpent more than a hundred feet long with a hunger for humans, was now in control of his mind. But Ashlyn reasoned: This was his fate. Fate was destiny and destiny held no choices. Monster, mermaid, whatever it was, he would go because he had to go. Perhaps, like his father, he would perish at sea.

Then again, he'd already be dead if not for the intervention of this something under the water, this something that moved like lightning, that was luminous, that had at least one hand, and that was now telepathically sending him strange messages.

-10-

Creature

ASHLYN AWOKE TO THE SOUND of water—real water—fierce rain beating against the roof. And it was persistent. At noon it stopped briefly but the thunderheads regrouped for an even greater mid-afternoon onslaught. As the day wore on, he realized that his plan might have to be postponed.

Pressing his nose against the den's cold windowpane, he watched the front lawn, now resembling a duck pond, and as he thought about Deadman's Bluff, feelings of doubt and fear began to consume him. It was easy to reason the dream as a symbolic rendering of his mother's death coupled with his own near-death in the ocean, easy to dismiss his plan as a wild goose chase that could easily seal his fate. And by eight o'clock that night, when the rain finally stopped, he'd come to a final, intelligent conclusion: He'd have to be certifiably out of his mind to go anywhere near Deadman's Bluff, especially at night. And he wasn't out of his mind. With that diehard resolution, he took a very welcome sigh of relief, and settled back on the sofa to watch TV. At nine-thirty, he went off to bed, delighted to be off the hook.

Sleep came quickly, but it was brief.

He found himself consciously awake and tossing restlessly. He tried not to think. His heart raced.

Get up!

No!

Get up! Get up now! Get dressed!
No! I'm not going!
Yes you are!

He tried to remember the lyrics to an old Beatle's song his mother had adored—*Sergeant Pepper's*—anything to redirect his thoughts. But the lyrics trailed off into space, and his eyes popped open as if by alchemy. He stared at the window. Black outside. No rain.

No! I'm not going!

But he couldn't shut his eyes—they seemed to be on autopilot. He noticed Autumn's breathing was deep, her mouth open in delightful slumber.

"Lucky you," he whispered as he quietly slipped out of his bed. Creeping around the room in the dark, he gathered his clothes, his new flashlight and an old pocket penknife.

He was acting crazy; he knew that. But it didn't stop him. He stepped onto the narrow window ledge. The drain was gurgling from the rain run-off, and the after-storm air was cool, with a musty aroma. Flicking on his new flashlight, he composed himself as best he could. He took a deep breath, then another, and slid down the drainpipe.

He landed with an obnoxious squelch as his feet sunk into the muddy topsoil, surely loud enough to wake the whole street. He quickly stabbed off his flashlight, his legs shaking, his heart hammering almost as loud as the foot squelch. Standing there in total darkness, eyes on the house, he expected Lucy's or his grandma's bedroom lights to breech the darkness any moment. In a way, he almost wished they would, and then he'd have to dash back inside and forget this madness.

A gentle breeze rustled the trees sending down a flurry of raindrops, but all remained quiet. He took another few strides across the lawn, each step accompanied by loud squelches. He stopped. Waited. Nothing. He hurried away from the house and flicked on his flashlight.

That first time he'd walked to Deadman's Bluff, it was bright, sunny, Autumn had been by his side, and he'd felt adventurous. Now it was night, chilly, his stomach was knotted, every wind rustle spooked him, and part of him, perhaps most, wished to be snuggled up in bed. He mused, "Mom, I'm experiencing life. I'm really doing it." He thought about the feelings of dread he'd experienced the last time at the bluff. Had he imagined those? He walked slowly, desperately wanting to stop, to turn back. But something urged him forward. He had no plan. And his mind was a jumble of repetitive thoughts: Mermaid? Some kind of cetacean? Benign? Evil? He might never see Autumn again.

Turn back! Turn back now!

Chicken!

Fool!

He decided on a compromise. He would only scope out the ridgetop.

That's safe. Probably imagining this whole thing, anyway. Check ridge-top, split. Not chicken. Prudent.

He began to hear the swish of the surf...then the more thunderous pounding of the *killer pillar* sea stacks. Close. But so black he couldn't tell how close. He walked even slower. His flashlight found gorse flowers, then sagebrush, juniper—

The ridge-top.

On the far left, a distant headlight rounded the bay.

Okay, time to head back.

But he kept moving forward, as if his legs had a will of their own.

At the cliff's edge, he bent his knees into a sort of anchor position, ready to brace himself against any sudden wind burst. He aimed his flashlight down to the beach.

Something was moving...

Just a wave. He was breathing with irregular breaths, his throat dry, hands moist, trembling. "Now what?" He was hoping that he'd find himself saying "Home, James" but instead a ludicrous thought popped into his mind. And he knew where he had to go.

The cave.

A terrible idea...but he didn't even hesitate.

Probing with his flashlight for the old pathway, he tried to justify his decision. He didn't feel like he was in a trance because he was able to reason. His mind was active. Then again, how does a bewitched mind react? Bewitched? Was he already under a spell, subliminally following orders? He moved forward, gripping the flashlight tightly, prepared to use it as a weapon...just in case. In his other hand was the midget penknife. He'd jab both into the enemy's face, one after the other, while simultaneously kicking. What good would that do against a sea serpent?

"I'm crazy," he mumbled to himself, as he began his descent.

Down on the beach, he stood still, probing both directions with the flashlight. The sand was pristine, not one footstep. He stomach felt tight like a rung-out towel.

Don't be frightened.

"Easier said than done," he casually said aloud. "Talking to myself now. I see." He started to walk. Another thought occurred to him, perhaps the scariest of the evening—that maybe he was experiencing a nervous breakdown, or worse, insanity. It made sense, his manic behavior, the obsession, tones, voices. Soon he'd be in an institution, drugged. Lobotomized!

"I'm panicking...yes, you bet I'm panicking! Nervous breakdown? No. Why not? Dad was crazy. Why not me? Hereditary. Dad, now me!" Ashlyn shook his head. "Calm yourself, Ashlyn. I order you to be calm! You're not nuts! You're just...paranoid!"

He took several deep, relaxing breaths.

"Okay. I'm calm. I feel all right. I feel fine. Paranoia. Think about the crazy. You're right. If I were really crazy, I wouldn't think I was crazy."

It's what his mom had said about crazies: "The crazy ones never think they're crazy; they think they're normal. But the normal ones who think themselves crazy are either paranoid or artists."

Better paranoid than chicken.

He noticed that his stomach no longer felt tight. He was also walking faster, almost running.

AS HE APPROACHED THE CAVE, the tide's height was about the same as the last time. Rolling up his jeans, Ashlyn stuffed his Reeboks into his windbreaker and without hesitation waded around the cave's curved wall. He stopped at the entrance, flashlight shining in, and froze.

What he saw was impossible.

Unbelievable.

Fantastic.

Bobbing up and down was a royal blue lacquer boat with a small erectable mast. Not just any boat—the lost rowboat fashioned exactly the way he'd intended to retrofit it. Every detail was there—his rudder design, tiller, blue and white sails, even the buoyancy tanks. How could this be? He'd never mentioned the design to anyone, not even to Autumn. He waded forward furiously, and for an instant he forgot about the sinkhole, forgot about the entire world until—

THE HOLE! WATCH OUT! THE HOLE!

Ashlyn stopped inches from a plunging. "Thanks." he said re-flexively, no longer worrying about being crazy. He thought about this. Who was he talking to?

"Hello?" he called out tentatively. "Hello…are you here?"

Water slurped around the cave walls, the tide swished, but there was no response from his mind or anywhere else. "I think you're reading my thoughts. Who are you?"

Ashlyn waited for an answer.

None came.

"I'm here." Ashlyn's loud voice echoed back and forth between the cave walls.

Then there was a weird noise. It sounded like…wings flapping. "Oh hoh!"

Ashlyn ducked as a swarm of bats, squealing nightmarishly, swooped down from the far end of the cave. As they rushed by, Ashlyn realized that his chin was touching water, his entire body submerged. He eased himself out of the drink. "Shucks! I'm a regular Indiana Jones." His clothes clung to him, heavy and already feeling icy cold.

The boat drifted close by.

"What does this remind me of?" He was in a jovial mood, considering.

Grabbing one of the shiny new oars, he used it to levy himself aboard, and as he sat on the centerboard, his teeth began to chatter. He unzipped the windbreaker, took it off, wrung it out. It was nylon and he knew it would dry quickly. He removed his flannel shirt and tee and put back on the windbreaker. Now feeling marginally warmer, he removed his jeans and underwear, wringing those out too. When he put them back on, they still hung heavy on his legs, perhaps as cold as before. He was about to say, "Now what?" But he already knew the answer; at least he thought he did. It came to him as a very strong feeling or compulsion.

He picked up the oars, and began to paddle out of the cave.

Ashlyn hadn't sailed solo in two years, but he remembered an old sailor's credo: *Feel the wind…know it.*

He felt the wind blowing port side. Satisfied, he extended the mast, locked it down, clamped the shrouds, hoisted the jib, cleated it,

ducked under the boom and hoisted the mainsail, which fluttered and
clanged. "I know, I know, headlong." He tillered to port, allowing a
gentle breeze to fill the small sail. The obnoxious clanging quickly
stopped.

Ashlyn didn't know where he was heading, but even if he did,
given the utter blackness of the night, navigation was pointless.
"Okay, I'm trusting you." He relaxed his grip on the tiller, truly prepared to trust the unknown.

The swell was modest, the wind not as cold as his wet clothes.

BOOF!

The sound of exploding water made him abruptly stiffen—it
was waves crashing against the *killer pillars*—the twin sea stacks!

BOOF!

Hard to tell where those two massive rocky formations were
lurking…maybe to his left, no right, no left—

BOOF!

Behind him? Yes, thank God, behind, definitely behind. Ashlyn
breathed a sigh of relief. Too close for comfort!

Once again he relaxed his grip on the tiller. "Hello? Hello, can
you hear me? I'm here! Doing what you want. This is what you
want, right?"

The only sounds that returned to Ashlyn were the sea elements
and the swish of the hull slicing water. "That's nice. Keep me in the
dark. Yeah, I'm always risking my ass in tiny boats, heading out to
sea in the middle of the night! I do this sort of thing all the time. Hey,
you, it's pitch black! What do you have to say about that?"

Ashlyn's mind remained silent.

"Thanks, thanks, pal! Hey, did anyone ever mention, you give
scintillating conversation? Huh…I guess not."

He sailed on.

Sea bound.

Twenty minutes went by. Still nothing. As the coastal lights
began fading into obscurity, Ashlyn decided that he was far enough
out. Unwilling to risk the loss of his only navigable light, he sighed
as he tillered hard to port.

As the boat swung about, something blinked way off in the distance. At first, he thought it was an amber light from a boat. It was
moving quickly—too quick for a boat. As it neared him, the luminosity began to pulse, intensifying for a moment or two, then dimming, intensifying again, dimming.

Ashlyn's stomach knots took on a new severity. At a distance of perhaps two football fields, *it* seemed to cut its speed and its radiant glow softened into a milky cloud of light, with a hint of color.

It began to circle him, some unknown distance beneath the surface. Though Ashlyn had yet to take his eyes of it, he was unable to discern its size or shape. "Uh...hello."

It continued circling, silently.

"Hello. Can you hear me?" Now Ashlyn thought he could hear a quiet voice in his mind. "What? Did you say something?"

"Sssshsss... istshsss...tenshsss...shsssss—"

"I can hear you but I don't understand."

"Sssss...shssss...lisssh wisshin."

"Lish wishing?"

"Asssh...snnn isshssss you...shsss lisssen wisss shissss lisssen withssssshis—"

The voice sounded like a weak signal on the UHF radio band—a voice buried in heavy static. Though he struggled to make sense of it, Ashlyn could only clearly fathom two words: *Ash*—a part of his own name—and *listen.*

But he was listening, wasn't he?

Abruptly, the voice ceased.

Ashlyn watched as the glow stopped circling. He was squinting, trying to glimpse it—at least figure its dimension—when it startled him with a rocket-like spurt. Luminance surging, it shot right under the boat and zoomed out the other side, where it moved into another lazy thirty-yard orbit. Counterclockwise.

"Hello. I heard you...I think."

Long pause, then: *"Lissssten wissshten...Asshlynn, lisssten wissthen."*

Ashlyn repeated aloud, "Listen wisthen? You mean 'listen within?' I am listening. Wait...whoaaa...what's that? What's happening?"

Ashlyn gasped as currents of warmish tingles began falling down the back of his head and neck, as if the sun or a heat lamp was aimed at his neck. "What are you doing? What is that heat?"

"Ash-lyn." The voice in his head was pristine. *"Do you hear me? Ashlyn?"*

Ashlyn gulped. Almost too shocked to respond, at last he said, "Yes, yes, I can hear you...whoever you are..."

"Friend."

"Friend…great." Ashlyn couldn't help but think, better friend than enemy.

Now silent again, the glow circled the boat. *"You are Human?"*

The retort brought a smile to Ashlyn's lips. "Human, yes. I'm definitely human. I hear you well now, loud and clear. What's that heat I'm feeling? Not that it's bad. Actually, it feels good. It's nippy out here." Ashlyn placed his face just a few inches above the water, trying to get a better look.

The glow continued orbiting, slowly, silently.

Perhaps thirty seconds passed before it spoke again, *"Non-earth human?"*

Ashlyn frowned, contemplating the odd question. "Non-earth? No, I'm from here. Earth human. What are you?"

His underwater companion stopped moving. Ashlyn still couldn't discern its shape or dimension, except that it appeared to be larger than the boat. There was another long pause.

"Are others of your kind aware?"

"Aware? Aware of what? Aware of you?"

"Hmmmm." The voice in Ashlyn's mind seemed disappointed, and the glow now resumed circling in the opposite direction.

"Hmmm? A good hmmm or a bad hmmm?"

"Ash-lyn…you are aware?"

"To be honest, I'm not really sure what you mean."

The glow drifted directly under the boat.

Peering over the edge, Ashlyn once again lowered his face to the water. But all he could see was a mass of diffused light. "Can you be more specific?"

Silence.

With a sudden burst, *it* surged out beyond the starboard side. This time Ashlyn definitely glimpsed color—spangles of dazzling blue, green and red.

His underwater friend began a new slow orbit.

"It is not yet time."

"Time? Time for what? I'm here now."

No response.

It was now fusing into varying degrees of luminance: brighter, brighter yet, dim, very dim, similar to the pattern of the tones.

"Do you hear me? I don't understand."

"It is not yet time."

As the glow began to distance itself, the invisible heat lamp that had been keeping Ashlyn comfortably warm abruptly switched off. "Please, don't leave! It is time...it is! I'm aware. I'm very aware!"

The glow was probably two hundred yards from the boat when Ashlyn heard a long sigh.

"I feel you, Ash-lyn. You are good energy. In time!"

Moving very fast now, like a fiery torpedo, the entity took but a few moments to become a mere amber dot in the distance.

Balancing himself, Ashlyn stood up. "Please, I want to know you. I'm a friend too. We can discuss this like intelligent... please—"

It was gone!

Ashlyn's heart sank. His newfound friend had left him all alone, and night was once again as black as sealed eyelids.

How would he ever find the bluff?

A mile from the boat, the glow made a sharp U-turn, dispersing a school of giant kelp fish. The bioluminescent intelligence then throttled down, its bloom resurging into a dazzling brilliance.

When Ashlyn saw it, he knew what to expect and moved like lightning in readiness. He immediately dropped the sail, and secured himself on the floor.

THUMP—

The tiny craft lunged forward, no less than roller-coaster acceleration. Ashlyn held on as fierce wind and spray howled around him, chilling him to the bone.

It was perhaps not much more than a minute later that the boat's invisible brakes slammed on, and his flashlight beam skimmed over a slab of rock—the *killer pillar* at Deadman's Bluff. And then he was gliding through the entrance of the cave, streams of light—mostly his underwater friend's—bombarding the cave walls.

About five feet shy of the end wall, the light began to diminish. Ashlyn whirled, but before he could place one foot out of the boat, *it* was already outside the cave.

He watched *its* pulsing luminosity rapidly vanishing into the darkness. "Please...please wait!" His voice echoed loudly. "Will I see...or speak to you? I didn't even thank you for the boat."

Silence.

"I didn't thank you for saving my life."

Ashlyn sighed. Friend—*it* claimed to be his friend, a word that now conjured a warm fuzzy feeling in Ashlyn's heart. Back in Barstow, he could count his friends on one finger—if his neighbor Brandon qualified as a friend.

Pulling the boat partially up out of the water and wedging it against a shelf, Ashlyn wondered where his new friend was heading. How could a creature so large and so dazzlingly luminous and intelligent keep itself a secret from Man? In time, *it* had said. In time, what? In time *it* would— Ashlyn held his thought. "It's a *he*— a masculine intelligence, not an *it*." This seemed to be a reasonable deduction based upon...*intuition*. Okay, so in time *he* would reveal himself? Would he? Or was this the beginning and simultaneous end of a magnificent relationship that never was?

With his mind awash in thought, Ashlyn picked up the flashlight, noticing in the dying beam something shiny on the boat's floor. Thinking it to be a glimmer from a metal cleat, he almost ignored it, and was about to wade out of the cave when he had the urge to check.

As Ashlyn reached into the boat, instead of finding a secured metal ring, he scooped up something quite stunning—a shimmering oval-shaped pendant studded with gems: white gems, indigo blue, pink and violet.

-11-

The Castilian Cross

HE WAS COLD. HIS FLASHLIGHT was on fumes. There were no head-lights on the coast road. No moon. No stars. Not even a firefly to temper the blackness. Ashlyn hugged the bluff's sandy face, letting it guide him to the path up to the ridge-top. Holding the pendant tightly in his palm, his token of friendship, and perhaps of great monetary value, his mind grappled with something of even greater value: the word aware.

Are you aware? Are others of your kind aware?

What did *aware* mean to his luminous friend and why was it so important? Ashlyn shook his head as he tried to fathom its mean-ing — aware of what or who?

There was a hint of light at the ridge-top, or maybe his eyes had adjusted to the dark. Either way, he was grateful, and he began to trot.

THE HOUSE WAS QUIET AND dark, as it had been when he'd left it a few hours earlier. He felt giddy with relief. There were no search parties looking for him. He quickly scaled the drainpipe.

Back up stairs, he wasted no time trying to wake Autumn. But she was severely slumbered. Short of slapping her silly, he figured she'd remain that way all night.

He sat on his bed, examining the gleaming pendant, wondering about its origin. The diameter was three inches. The base appeared to be made out of bronze, or maybe gold. He would have to wait until morning to ask Autumn about that. She was good with gems and jewelry. There was a cross in the pendant's center embedded over a figure-eight lattice of gems. He guessed it was Spanish. Turning it over, he noticed a tiny inscription, and was just trying to read it when he felt a burning sensation in his abdomen.

He clutched his midriff, gritting his teeth to stifle a scream. The pain intensified. He buried his head between his knees, hoping to lessen the attack. No such luck. Doubled over, he staggered to his feet, his stomach now on fire. He needed water, desperately needed water to douse the burning. But as he took a step toward the bathroom, the floor tilted down and then rose back up, violently. Off-balance, his vision milky and defocused, he felt himself falling....

When Ashlyn opened his eyes, he found himself sprawled on the floor next to Autumn's bed. It was still dark outside. He realized he must have fainted. Sitting up, he felt the back of his head for a bump. But there wasn't one. No pain. No pain anywhere. His fall must have been broken by Autumn's mattress. Amazingly, she was still sleeping.

As he pondered on how long he'd been unconscious, the events of the night began refocusing in his mind—the boat, the creature, the pendant—

Where was the pendant? He was no longer holding it.

His angst was short-lived as he spotted it lying under Autumn's bed. Quickly retrieving it, he settled himself back on the floor, which seemed to be a safe haven—less distance to fall.

What was wrong with him?

A fiery stomach causing blackouts wasn't something he could brush off lightly. The doctor at the Wayside Memorial assumed that he was healthy, but the doctor hadn't performed any extensive tests, and he didn't know about his close encounter at sea.

Contamination had to be a possibility. In fact, a very likely possibility, Ashlyn conceded. Still, he felt passively calm. He'd already be dead if not for his newfound friend. In some ways, he was living on borrowed time. Fortunately Autumn wasn't suffering from any symptoms, at least none he knew of. Maybe he alone was susceptible or allergic to *him*. What a terrible twist of fate—to be on the brink of a friendship unlike any in the history of the world, only to have it thwarted by a biological incompatibility.

The gleam from the pendant caused a welcome shift in his

thoughts.

Booty.

Yes, perhaps booty retrieved from a sunken pirate ship. Ashlyn thought of the possibilities—after solving the mystery of *aware*, his friend could seek out the great shipwrecks of the world, and then pass the goodies onto him. What a team! What riches!

It is not yet time.

Would it ever be time?

Feeling chilly, he stripped off his damp clothes, and jumped into bed, donning his pajamas under the covers. He tucked the pendant safely under his pillow and pulled the comforter tightly around him. He was exhausted, but too highly strung for sleep. He thought back to the encounter.

I feel you, Ash-lyn. You are good energy. In time—

In time? What time? A month? A year? Ten years? What changes needed to occur to satisfy *him?* If he were *aware*, would that "right time" be now?

Aware?

Aware… good energy…simple enough words that obviously had higher meanings.

Consciously and perhaps, at times, unconsciously, Ashlyn re-played the conversation with his sea friend over and over like a video loop, until sometime during the middle of the night the tape stopped, and then it was dawn.

Smacking his parched lips, he sleepily opened his eyes. For a moment he forgot about last night, forgot about his dreams and eve-rything else except French toast, grilled pineapple and bacon. He could already smell the aroma. But as he lazily reached under the bed for his slippers—

"—Holy cow!" He threw his arm under his pillow. Sure enough, his palm slipped around the pendant, proving that it wasn't a dream. He was at Autumn's side in a flash, shaking her. "Autumn!"

She moaned groggily but both of her eyes remained sealed.

"You'll never guess where I was last night. Okay, okay, I admit it was dumb, it was crazy, but I was at Deadman's Bluff!"

"Later, I'm sleeping," Autumn muttered in a lazy mumble.

"Did you hear what I said? I was at Deadman's Bluff last night, again!"

"That's nice." Her eyes were still closed.

"You're not listening. The Seabed Phantom…he's real. I was with him. Open your eyes!"

Autumn burrowed her head deeper into the pillow. "That's great," she said without any cognition.

"Dammit, Autumn. Open your eyes. He's real! He's been reading my mind. He gave me a sailboat, exactly like I pictured in my mind—"

She was snoring.

Ashlyn shook her. "This is really important! You can sleep later."

"Leave me alone…in the morning."

"Did you hear what I said? Look at this!"

Autumn lazily opened her eyes, but closed them right away.

"Fine. Fine! You're out! I'm not taking you!"

She attempted to roll over but he grabbed her arm.

"What's your problem?" she snapped. "I don't care about your stupid dream."

As Ashlyn held the pendant in front of her eyes, moving it around teasingly, Autumn blinked, trying to focus on the vibrant green, red and indigo gems. "Where did you get that?" She sat up, reaching for the pendant.

"He gave it to me."

"Who?"

"I was there!"

"Where?"

One of Autumn's less attractive character traits was a habit of interrupting. But as Ashlyn briefed her on his night's adventure, she sat mesmerized, and didn't utter a word.

After finishing the account, Ashlyn placed the pendant in her palm—the most magnificent piece of jewelry she'd ever seen, yet her only response was one word, repeated several times: "Wow."

"Wow?" Ashlyn mimicked parrot fashion. "You don't believe me, do you? So I'm lying. I stole it 'cause I'm a total screw up."

"I didn't say that."

"You don't have to." Annoyed by her lack of response, Ashlyn folded his arms.

Autumn pretended not to notice him glowering as she buffed one of the gems. "These might be amethyst but—" she trailed a finger over a blue gem, "—if these are sapphires…holy wow!"

"And so? What am I? Liar? Crazy? Brave? What?"

"*It* gave this to you…at Deadman's Bluff?"

Autumn's eyes twitched nervously—at least to Ashlyn they appeared to.

Reaching for the pendant, Ashlyn scowled, "You weren't listening. *He…he* left it in the boat. *He* knew I'd find it."

"Okay…okay…okay…I believe you."

Ashlyn wrapped the pendant in tissue paper and placed it in his pocket. "No you don't. But you will."

BREAKFAST WAS A STRAINED AFFAIR. Despite the delicious servings, the teens ate slowly and in silence. Poor Lucy thought it was her food.

When Grandma wheeled herself in from the hallway, she was smiling, almost laughing, quite unlike her usual morning self. She poured herself a glass of fresh orange juice. "Good morning, good morning, good morning. Aye it is a good morning. Just toast, Lucy. Thank you, my dear. Well, I have some very interesting news. I just had a long chat with your Aunt Elizabeth."

Ashlyn frowned. Aunt Elizabeth? *Who the heck was she?*

"Aye, you never met her. But indeed you have an aunt in Scotland. A very lovely person I might add, and she loves kids. Got two grownups herself." Grandma's smile grew wide. "Well we were talking this and that and you know what, and suddenly, out of the blue, she had this wonderful idea. She suggested you go live with her for a wee while. Of course, I said, 'No ya couldn't.' But the more we got to talking…well, you've got your heritage there, and grand schools and youth clubs, and I was thinking…I bet you'd like it."

Ashlyn turned to his grandma, his face etched in semi-horror. "But we like it here, Grandma."

"We do…we like it a lot," Autumn agreed.

"In fact we love it," Ashlyn added.

"You'd love Inverness, too. You've got cousins you've never met…your age."

"No, Grandma, no." Ashlyn spoke adamantly.

Grandma looked slightly uncomfortable as she placed her empty orange juice glass softly on the table. "Well, it's just an idea."

The subject was dropped.

Just an idea—but Ashlyn could already feel the noose being tightened. This was more than just an idea.

SHORTLY AFTER BREAKFAST, UNDER A cloudless blue sky, Ashlyn and Autumn set off on their cycles for Deadman's Bluff. Autumn hadn't returned to the bluff since her close brush with death, and Ashlyn noticed her looking around nervously. He assumed she was reliving that night.

He was *wrong*.

Indeed, Autumn's heart was racing, but for another reason. Before leaving the house, she'd made the decision to believe Ashlyn. After all, if she didn't trust her brother, whom could she trust? But—and she gave a lot of thought to this—if the *Seabed Phantom* was real, then what exactly was it? According to the librarian, it was a sea serpent. Rifling through her pocket dictionary, she'd found two definitions of serpent. One was a noxious creature that creeps, hisses or stings. What stuck in Autumn's mind was how Ashlyn described its hissy sounds. If that wasn't bad enough, the second definition was just as alarming: Devil. But of course, she hoped that Ashlyn's creature was something entirely different from a sea serpent.

But even if *it*—whatever *it* was—was harmless, as Ashlyn claimed, it still left Autumn with a nagging feeling in the pit of her stomach. She was raised with traditional Christian beliefs, the Holy Bible plainly stating that God created Man to rule over the animal kingdom. Even recently her school class had discussed a related topic: Have animal rights activists gone too far? The class had decided that Man, the only species with rationalizing intelligence, had the right to dominate the animal kingdom because all other species were inferior. But if Ashlyn's creature could read Ashlyn's mind and give him a boat fashioned from his thoughts, then surely it was reasonable to assume that this creature was not inferior.

Something else had dawned on Autumn, making her even more uncomfortable. What if the creature had taken charge of Ashlyn's mind, like he once suspected? She tried loosening her shoulders. It's okay, she assured herself. Perhaps Ashlyn is only imagining it? Right—then where did the pendant come from?

"We're taking the bikes down to the beach," Ashlyn said, leading the way across the ridge-top.

"Why? No one comes up here, you said so."

"We need them with us."

"It's hard enough without a bike."

"You'll see."

So consumed in thought as she lugged her cycle down to the beach, Autumn hardly noticed her shortness of breath, or how difficult it was to wheel her cycle in the sand.

Finally, they were there at the cave entrance.

Ashlyn rounded the cave wall, breaking a long silent spell with a thespian open arm gesture: "Ta-dah!"

Truth be told, Ashlyn was relieved to see the boat. Someone could have easily taken it, but this was proof positive that no one, except crazy teenagers from California, ever ventured to Deadman's Bluff.

Autumn emitted an audible gasp as she laid eyes on the gleaming vessel. "Oh my gosh!"

Smiling proudly, Ashlyn marched into the cave, sidestepping the sinkhole, now plainly visible because of the low tide. "C'mon check it out," he beckoned.

Autumn followed slowly, her mind mired in a confused mix of logic, religion and superstition. The boat was beautiful—Ashlyn's boat, manufactured from thoughts in his mind.

But how was that possible?

Ashlyn ran a hand across the boat's polished surface. "Now that's what I call a paint job."

"How can it be? I mean, it's…impossible," she said.

Ashlyn stroked his chin pompously. "Impossible…impossible, do you mean something incapable of reality? Or something that's just darn difficult? Or maybe you mean really impossible, like…like this is an illusion, sleight of hand with light and mirrors?"

Looking askance at Ashlyn, Autumn rebuffed, "You know what I mean." Gingerly touching the hull, she found the paint to be smooth and silky. She couldn't help but feel that a creeping snake couldn't have made it. Intuitively, she felt that the boat was given to Ashlyn out of friendship, out of love. Her angst began to fade. "Did *he*, you know, tell you…*he* actually said, '*Hey, I'm giving this to you?*'"

"Well, not exactly those words; more a feeling. I know what you're getting at, and the answer is, think it through. You think someone else is reading my mind? Santa Claus, maybe?"

"But you do…you actually speak with *him*?"

Ashlyn nodded. "Just like you and me right now."

"Holy cow!"

Ashlyn untied the mooring rope and guided the boat toward the entrance. "We're going sailing. Get the cycles."

Still in a fog, Autumn followed Ashlyn back onto the sunny beach. "What they're teaching us…it's not true."

"What?"

"Genesis. It's wrong," Autumn replied.

"How so?"

"The Bible says we're supposed to be the only intelligent species. That's why we were given dominion over the world."

Ashlyn's expression abruptly hardened into a contemplative frown. "Doing a good job, aren't we."

"What?" She asked as if there was a connection.

"Nothing. Come on, my bike first."

Autumn hoisted Ashlyn's cycle over the bow. "Well what do you think? *He's* as intelligent as us?"

Ashlyn had asked himself that same question numerous times. Yet his answer came slowly. "Yes, *he's* intelligent. *He's* fast, mysterious…and unless we get a move on, the day's gonna be gone."

Ashlyn's plan was to sail the boat to the marina; he couldn't keep it at the cave for fear of tides and discovery. He hoped the ninety dollars in his pocket, his life's savings, would be enough to rent a short-term slip. They needed the cycles on board to get home from the marina.

Ashlyn sprinkled a handful of water over the bow. "I christen thee Sea Breeze."

"Cheese!" Autumn grimaced, trying to get comfortable with a bike wheel in her face. "Sea Breeze is a perfume, not a boat. Call it something like…Blue Mist."

Ashlyn pouted. "Blue is good. Sapphire…Sapphire Streak."

Autumn was shaking her head no.

"Sapphire Sun? Turquoise—"

"Turquoise Turtle," Autumn interjected in jest.

Ashlyn sprinkled another handful of water over the bow. "I Christen thee Indigo Night."

Autumn pulled a face of disgust.

"Empyrean! Indigo Empyrean!" Ashlyn pumped his fist in delight.

Autumn frowned as Ashlyn pushed off, jumping aboard moments ahead of the next wave. The mainsail quickly filled. "It means indigo heaven."

"Then call it Indigo Heaven." A gust of salty spray washed into Autumn's face. She grinned. It felt good.

Ashlyn tillered to port, and grinned as well…grinned big time. They were on the way…in his boat…named the way he liked it.

Not bad.

AS THEY SAILED TOWARD THE marina—a two-hour ride—they talked about theories and possibilities. Autumn suggested, "Maybe *aware* means are we, the human race, aware of *him*. Do we know he exists? And when you acted like, who the heck are you, *he* kinda got insulted."

"Sure. *He's* an insecure sea munchkin in need of a shrink." Ashlyn tillered into the wind.

"Yeah, well…who knows?"

Ignoring her retort, Ashlyn peered across the sea, his face reflective of his concentration, as if searching for a sign of his new friend, or a clue. He was compelled to know what *aware* meant. Further contact, true friendship depended on it. Sooner or later….

Autumn was studying the pendant, stroking the gems as if they were her pet rabbit Bigsey. "Are you going to keep it?" she inquired.

"No, I'm going to throw it overboard," Ashlyn replied deadpan.

"You know what I mean. We could sell it."

The ride got bumpy as a large motor yacht passed them. Sailing out of the yacht's wake, Ashlyn kept *Indigo Empyrean's* bow in line with the Wayside breakwater, now visible. "Sell it?" He shook his head. "Now why would I do that?"

Autumn handed him back the pendant. "Just a thought. It might make us rich."

While the boating traffic steadily increased, Autumn's eyes settled on a parasailist flying behind a speeding motorboat. Meanwhile Ashlyn fell silent for a few minutes. "How much do you think it's worth?" he asked at length.

"Allison Schuler's mom got a sapphire necklace, way smaller stones. Her dad paid five thousand."

"Five thousand, that all?" Ashlyn slackened the halyard, piloting the boat around the breakwater into the harbor channel. After passing a line of expensive yachts, he turned a corner into the main harbor, and dropped the sail, allowing the boat to drift in the current toward the dock. "No way…no way I'd sell it for five."

SMOKING A SMELLY PIPE, THE dock master checked his clipboard before slowly shaking his head. "Nah, no month to month rate." He moved off down the gangplank with Ashlyn in tow.

"Please, sir, there must be something."

"Like I say, day rate or happy sailing." The dock master chugged on his pipe as he stepped aboard his tiny weather-beaten harbor cruiser.

"Wait!"

The day-rate was twenty-five dollars, a big bite out of Ashlyn's pocket. But out of his pocket came his cash. Grimacing, he paid three days up front. It was partially refundable, prorated if vacated early. He was savvy enough to know it was a lousy deal but at that moment he didn't exactly have a bagful of options.

Fifteen minutes later, he was straddling his bicycle outside Boleshko's Jewelry.

The window sign read:

WE BUY OLD COINS AND JEWELRY

Loosening his palm holding the prized pendant, Ashlyn nodded at Autumn...and pressed the buzzer.

Air hissed through jeweler Petro Boleshko's hairy nostrils sounding like a leaky gas pipe, and all too often he snorted and grunted, attempting to dislodge wads of oppressive congestion. As he pressed his glass magnifying loupe against the pendant, Ashlyn eyed him closely, observing his every movement, looking for a sign—was he honest? Perhaps telltale was the crucifix on his tiepin. Of course, Ashlyn didn't know that it was a gift from the jeweler's pious son.

The jeweler turned the pendant over once, then pushed the loupe onto his creased forehead where it sat like a miner's light. He cleared his throat and in good English, but with a fairly thick Eastern European accent, asked where it came from.

Ashlyn wasn't a good liar. Nervously wiping his clammy palms on the back of his shorts, he replied that it was a family heirloom that he needed to sell because his mother had just passed away.

The jeweler coughed and clicked the back of his throat. "Understandable. How much?"

Ashlyn frowned. "How much?"

"Yes. What are you looking for?"

"Uh…what will you give me? I know it's valuable," Ashlyn replied. This was his second mistake. His first was entering the store.

The jeweler remained stoic, despite an inner rush of excitement. "How about a trade? A nice watch." He pointed to a fat diver's watch in the display case. "Or a necklace for the young lady?"

Autumn remained impassive. Ashlyn didn't need to verbalize his response.

"I see," remarked the jeweler. "If it's cash you want, the best I can do is a hundred."

"A hundred what?" Ashlyn asked in earnest.

"Dollars. We're in America."

Hardly believing his ears, Ashlyn extended his palm. "No thanks."

The jeweler held onto the pendant defiantly. "Not saying it's not worth more. But this is going to be a hard sell. Might have to sit on it, months, even years. See that gold clip, three years." He pointed to a gaudy money clip.

Ashlyn didn't give a hoot about the gold clip. His pendant was valuable; he knew that much. If the jeweler didn't want to pay for it—

"Okay, a hundred and fifty," the jeweler snorted,

"Forget it." Ashlyn replied instantly.

"Tell you what, leave it with me, I'll get it appraised. That's best. I'll broker it for you."

Ashlyn hesitated. He didn't know much about brokering but it sounded like a reasonable idea. If the pendant were appraised at least he'd know its true worth. "How does brokering work? How about security?"

"Security? Don't worry; it's safe with me. Never had a problem. I'll give you a receipt." The jeweler reached for his receipt book.

"Write down that you're responsible for…one hundred thousand."

The old jeweler laughed, then coughed, this time grabbing a handkerchief from his pocket and expelling something awful into it. "How old are you?"

"What's that got to do with this? Just give it back." Ashlyn unclenched his fist into an expectant palm.

"Suit yourself." The jeweler handed Ashlyn the pendant, swiftly interjecting, "No one's gonna give you a receipt like that. The jewels are worth…maybe not that much. Maybe next to nothing even."

"Then we're wasting your time. C'mon, Autumn!" The teens started for the exit.

"You want a receipt? Okay, I'll give you a receipt. Two thousand dollars."

In Ashlyn's mind, this was the jeweler's first mistake. "Two for something worth nothing?" Ashlyn twirled the pendant. "One hundred thousand...a receipt for one hundred thousand, fifteen hundred in cash right now, good faith...and we can do business."

The jeweler guffawed and it sounded awful. "Funny guy, funny guy."

Ashlyn reached for the door handle. "See ya."

The jeweler waved his arm beckoningly. "Okay, okay, you're tough. I'll tell you what, forget the cash, five thousand security receipt, it's a deal."

Ashlyn shook his head no.

The jeweler curled up his tongue, sucking his smoke-stained teeth in contemplation. For a moment, Ashlyn thought that he'd boxed himself into a corner, pushed too hard. But then the jeweler said, "Wait here," and abruptly disappeared into the back of the store.

BOGDAN BOLESHKO, THE JEWELER'S SON, heard his father's footsteps on the steep wooden steps. Quickly clipping the last wire of the homemade bomb he was assembling, Bogdan stuffed the device inside a red cookie tin and slipped it under the divan.

When his father entered the room, Bogdan's feet were already propped up on the coffee table, his hands cradling his neck, his focus on the portable TV.

The jeweler didn't say a word as he crossed the floor to the wall safe behind the old picture frame.

Bogdan observed him from the corner of his eye, anticipating the coming outburst.

"What the— Where's the money?" the jeweler exclaimed, whirling.

"Where do you think? Rent," answered the twenty-five-year-old nonchalantly without taking his eyes off the TV.

His father stepped toward him. "I don't need a mother or a bookkeeper. I need my money! I need it now."

Bogdan, who could pass for a cool California surfer rather than a preacher man—suntanned, faded jeans, cropped blonde hair, studded ear, goatee—didn't budge. He quietly answered. "Rent, pop."

"Yeah, rent. I got a live one downstairs that's gonna pay my rent for the rest my life…and yours."

"Yes I know."

The jeweler wasn't in the mood for games, so he went straight for his son's Achilles' heel. "For Christ's sake, I'm your father. Now give me my Goddamn money so I can make some Goddamn money!"

Bogdan detested the secular ways of the world, his father's irreverence included. Yet, he also loved his stupid father and couldn't bear to watch his decline, squandering everything, pouring every hard-earned cent into a world of booze, gambling and sordid flicks. Exerting as much control as he could muster, Bogdan shuffled the blasphemy aside, and said nothing at all. He simply kept his eyes on the tube.

"I've got a fortune downstairs! I want my Goddamn money! Do you hear me? I want my money!"

Now turning to face his father, Bogdan said, "You're being childish. It's for your own good."

"You mess with me, so help me, so help your damn god, I'll go to the cops. It's my money, dammit!"

Bogdan stroked his goatee thoughtfully. His father had threatened him before and done nothing. Besides, his conscience was clear, his actions right in the eyes of the Lord. He could even tolerate the blasphemy, given that it was a charade born from childish desperation. But a thought suddenly occurred to Bogdan. Maybe the Lord intended for his father to suffer. One can only shield another from harm's way to a degree. As they say: "You can lead a horse to water, but you cannot make him drink." If his father refused to heed the advice and the love, so be it!

Bogdan yanked the cash out of his pocket and threw it on the floor. "Go ahead! Go to the poker game! Drink it all away. See if I care!" Then he paled. This wasn't a way for a man of the cloth to act. "Pop, I'm sorry. You're right. It's your money." Sinking to his knees, Bogdan scooped up the cash. "Whatever you do with it."

"Straight up, son, there's a fortune downstairs. I swear. You'll see. This time, we'll get your church on the air. We will."

"Yeah, pop. Sure."

"C'mon down with me. I might need your help."

DURING THE TIME BOLESHKO WAS gone, the teens heard muffled voices, nothing distinctive, maybe an argument, then a brief silence followed by two sets of footsteps. Then the jeweler shuffled through the door with a younger man, probably a surfer, Ashlyn thought.

Running his fingers through his hair contemplatively, the jeweler held his gaze on Ashlyn. "Well...seems you kids got yourselves a deal."

Even though he felt like yelling with glee, Ashlyn curtailed his joy to a small, professional smile.

The agreement was hand-written on a plain piece of paper. Ashlyn filled out his address, not his telephone number, explaining, "My grandma's old and very fragile. I don't want anyone calling her. It's important! No calls! I'll call you."

"No problem," the jeweler replied, signing the document. For Boleshko this was another good sign. No telephone number. Probably bogus address too, which, in his book, meant stolen goods.

Boleshko turned to his son, and rambled off something in a foreign language—Czech, Polish, or whatever. Ashlyn only understood three words: "Pastrami on rye."

As the surfer strolled out the front door, presumably to get a sandwich, he winked at Autumn, but Ashlyn didn't notice because Boleshko was already counting fifteen hundred dollars into his palm.

The jeweler clicked the back of his throat. "You drive a hard bargain, young fella."

Wearing the best poker face he could muster, Ashlyn shrugged his shoulders, and shook the jeweler's hand. "Thank you. Nice doing business with you."

On that parting note, Ashlyn and Autumn, calmly stepped out onto the sun-baked sidewalk.

From across the crowded street, Bogdan the bomb-maker watched their facade evaporate; he watched them slapping each other high-fives and pumping their fists. For an instant, Ashlyn actually stared back at him. But Bogdan knew his disguise was solid. He was a tourist in black Speedo shorts, dark sunglasses, cranberry ice pop and beanie, lazily leaning up against a lamppost on his bicycle.

As the teens climbed on their cycles and set off toward Taylor Avenue, Bogdan the tourist dropped the ice pop and pushed off from the lamppost.

Bogdan the surfer, the tourist, the bomb-maker, was now Bogdan the tail.

SMARMY JEWELER PETRO BOLESHKO CLOSED up the shop and placed a closed sign in the window. His heart pounded as he thought about his new prized pendant. Honest kids don't peddle million dollar pieces. And boy, the pendant had to be worth at least a million. It was maritime, probably seventeenth century. The stones were diamonds—even the purple ones Autumn had mistaken for amethyst.

Boleshko placed the pendant atop the glass counter and snapped six digital photographs, all the while pondering on how to best profit from it. He knew many private collectors who didn't give a hoot if a piece was contraband, as long as it was unique and very valuable. To make such a deal, he first had to ascertain the pendant's exact origin. He needed photocopies of any and all pertaining documents—salvage rights, bills of sale, auctioneer's papers, government seals, curator appraisals, anything else that might prove its identity and ownership history. The curator at the maritime museum in Portland was out of the question, so was MARAD—the U.S. Department of Maritime Administration. These were the official channels where perhaps nasty questions would be volleyed.

A name sprung to his mind—the big Swede.

Boomer Larson.

BOOMER LARSON OWNED A STOREFRONT in Old Town where he peddled antique seafarers' collectibles, such as sextants, sundials, astrolabes, old wooden capstans, and the like. With a shoulder-stooping six-foot-six lean frame, Boomer was a treasure hunter, diver, relegated topside after a bout with caisson disease—the bends. Unlike many sufferers, Boomer had mostly regained the use of his knee joints, however the sparkle in the forty-six-year-old eyes, once his trademark, had faded along with his desire to recount any of his incredible deep-sea encounters—and he'd had plenty of those.

It was after store hours when Boomer closed up shop and pulled down a wooden ladder ascending to his mezzanine living quarters. Despite the day's handsome take, he wiped his tired face with a sigh.

The gargantuan Swede switched on the news, and swigged a shot of Stoli. He was just rolling an herb cigarette, a habit he'd developed after his third divorce, when his phone rang.

"Boomer Larson?" the voice on the other end inquired.

Boomer lit his smoke and inhaled. "This is he. Yah."

"Petro Boleshko...remember me?"

"Sure, yah." Boomer replied, still holding the smoke in his lungs.

The jeweler and Boomer had done business a couple of times before, peddling pieces of eight. Nothing spectacular.

"I've got an antique pendant. It's what I would call er...dramatic," said the jeweler.

Boomer exhaled. "Marine?"

"I believe so. It's a cross, studded with diamonds. The gems alone are in the half million range."

Boomer whistled. "Way out of my range, bro."

"Of course, but I was wondering, er...would you be interested in helping me identify it?"

"Identify it? That's not really my thing, Petro. Why don't you call MARAD? Department of Maritime Administration. Those guys harbor all the records."

"I know, but...there could be a nice commission here."

Boomer suspected that the piece was contraband, and he had mixed feelings about that. His little storefront would never make him rich but it was an honest, uncomplicated living, which suited him fine. But he refrained from shucking off Boleshko because a buddy of his, Carter Benwall from Los Angeles, was arriving later that evening, and would no doubt find this quite interesting.

Agreeing to meet for dinner, Boomer told the jeweler he'd bring a friend. "Yah, Carter's writing a book on sunken treasure. Between the two of us, we should figure it out."

ASHLYN AND AUTUMN ATE MUSHROOM hamburgers at Tony's on the pier, a lively joint with a sawdust-covered floor, where waiters in long white aprons danced on tables for tips amidst yelps and hollers.

Sipping a beer at the restaurant's sports bar, Bogdan watched Autumn rocking with the spirit, while Ashlyn appeared less involved, almost detached.

Indeed, Ashlyn's mood had taken a downward spiral. The thrill of a substantial windfall from the pendant now meant less and less. In fact, the earlier adrenaline rush after leaving Boleshko's had all but gone as his thoughts returned to *aware*. It dawned on him that the same *aware* mystery had probably precipitated the downfall of his father; that he too must have experienced a close encounter only to have *aware* elude him, leaving him confused and lost, searching, spending his entire family fortune, searching, being branded nuts, searching, and even going to his death with his eyes on the ocean floor, searching.

Was he on the same dead-end road as his father?

Ashlyn remained thoughtful and slightly nauseous on the cycle home, which made him anxious. He couldn't help but think that any minute now he'd feel another hot poker in the stomach.

Perhaps the mushrooms were too greasy.

Yes, he decided, it was the mushrooms.

He never thought of looking back over his shoulder, but even if he had, he probably wouldn't have realized that he was being followed. Bogdan the bomb-maker was a clever tail, staying a hundred yards back amidst a group of cyclists.

"Pop?" Bogdan spoke into his cell phone. He was at the cul-de-sac where the teens lived, having watched them enter a house at the end of the street. "I'm on Dunbar. The address they gave you, that's where they went."

The jeweler was taken aback with surprise. "What? They...they must have spotted you."

"No, no way." Bogdan took a sip from his water bottle. He was only marginally breathless. "I was too far back."

"Doesn't make sense. They're probably hiding in the back yard."

"No...they're upstairs, I saw them through the window. Now what?"

Boleshko fell quiet as he pondered. He usually read these situations well. He'd been so sure the address was phony—the crook's standard MO. But even if the address was correct, did that prove anything? No, he decided. The boy was obviously not too clever; he hadn't thought of covering his tracks. Boleshko remained confident that the pendant was stolen. Yes, he told himself, absolutely, and those thieving, sharp-talking punks weren't going to get another cent from him. "Alright, son. Hang around for another ten or fifteen minutes, just in case."

ASHLYN RETCHED. HE WAS STOOPED over the toilet bowl, his head swimming, his back covered in a dewy sweat. Autumn was beginning to feel ill-at-ease listening to his feeble explanation. She also had eaten the mushrooms, and there was nothing wrong with her. It was obviously something else.

Flushing the toilet, Ashlyn stood up, proclaiming himself to be as right as rain again. However, his deathly white face spoke another story.

Autumn shook her head. "Maybe I should get Lucy."

"What for? You'll make her nervous for nothing."

"I don't know. If you hadn't passed out in the car the other day—"

"I didn't pass out." Ashlyn dumped the towel in the hamper. "Mild sunstroke. No big deal."

She looked at him suspiciously.

"Really," he insisted.

IT WAS DARK WHEN BOGDAN returned to the jewelry store. His father was out, probably gambling, Bogdan thought. Upstairs in the loft, Bogdan retrieved the cookie tin from under the divan, and carefully placed it into a plastic bag.

He then cycled straight to the wharf, frequently looking over his shoulder to make sure no one was following.

Turning into Boat Yard Alley, Bogdan switched off the bike's dynamo light, but kept on cycling. Any pursuer would need a light to navigate the network of gangplanks and bridges now veiled in darkness, but Bogdan knew the terrain. Even in the pitch black, every narrow bridge and horseshoe gangplank in that yard was indelibly imprinted in his mind.

No one was following.

Bogdan rested his cycle next to an old Volkswagen at Pete's Fishery. He entered through an unlocked door, dead-bolting it before moving on. He then headed to the back of the store, weaving through a corridor of empty wooden tubs and crates. These had an incongruent purpose: They were the seats and his pulpit for his Sunday sermons.

This was Bogdan's church.

In the back room two men were waiting, Pete, his best friend, who also looked much like his brother, and a stranger of slight build, purposely holding himself in shadow. The stranger was from a different district of the organization, and after today Bogdan would never see him again.

Stepping forward, Bogdan handed the stranger the plastic bag containing the explosive device. "The lid sets the timer. Remove it slowly till you hear a click. Then replace it. You have five minutes."

The stranger nodded.

Bogdan took out a smoke. As his lighter flickered, the stranger stepped back further into shadow. Bogdan smiled. "Leaving a signature?"

Again the man nodded.

As it so happens, the signature was in his car, a four-foot stake that read: Sinners.

The rendezvous was over.

THE BIG SWEDE BOOMER LARSON and his buddy Carter Benwall met the jeweler at the King's Inn, a quaint village pub on the boardwalk. Carter, a forty-year-old with a baby face beaming behind John Lennon specs, wore a buzzing illuminated bowtie for laughs. He and Boomer drank Stoli straight up, the jeweler Heinekens.

Boleshko quickly got down to business, pulling from his breast pocket the digital prints of the pendant. The item itself was safely tucked away in his safe. Carter and Boomer exchanged deadpan glances.

"How did it find its way to you?" asked Carter.

Boleshko sniffed and made a clicking sound from the back of his throat. "A young man brought it to my shop, found it in his attic after his mother died. I'm brokering it."

"Rock-and-roll, the old attic find. All I found in ours was rat poo." It was Carter. He honked the buzzer on his flashing bowtie. "Whammy!"

Boomer acknowledged with a wooden smile. "Waiter, two more Stolis," he called out.

Carter leaned forward. "Where is the item?" he asked in a melodramatic whisper.

Boleshko downed his beer. "I have it."

"Yes. You have it. And you want me to identify it...so how about we drop the cloak and dagger stuff? I need to see it." Carter pursued.

"The photos are all you need. I assure you, it's authentic."

"Well that speaks of trust, doesn't it?" Carter retorted.

The jeweler remained passively indifferent.

"All right, let's say we identify it and you sell it. What's our cut?" Carter asked.

The jeweler cleared his throat. "If you can provide identification, complete identification, curator photocopies, MARAD documentation, five percent."

"Five. Hmmm. What's yours?"

"I told you. It's not mine. I'm just a broker."

"Really. What if it's hot?"

"Five percent for identification, that's all."

"Payable when?"

"One week after you deliver the correct information."

"How do we know you can move it?"

"Mr. Benwall, you are barking up the wrong tree. Identify it and you get paid. It's that simple. Nothing more, nothing less."

Carter removed his specs, cleaned them with his napkin. Carefully examining the photographs, he sighed and shook his head, appearing to be stumped for answers. "This is going to be tough. Five percent for a lot of work; I don't know."

Truth was, Carter almost had the identity pegged. The pendant bore three conjoined insignias: the crest of Prince Philip II of Spain, the crest of the Castilian knights, of which there were several orders; and the last crest, even though he didn't recognize it, was certainly the crest of a sea captain. Pendants studded with gems weren't awarded solely for bravery. This pendant had been awarded to a captain after returning to Spain bearing great riches from the Americas. The task of identifying the last crest—the key to the puzzle—was simply a matter of spinning through files on his notebook computer. Carter figured it would take him less than fifteen minutes.

Boleshko held firm on five percent, and the deal was cemented.

After four rounds of Stoli, the tab running on booze and food—shepherds pie followed by cranberry ice cream—the two experts unexpectedly stood up, Carter wobbling. "We'll let you know if it's edible, I mean saleable, I mean valuable. Whatever. Rock-and-roll." He honked his bowtie, and with Boomer on his heels departed, leaving Boleshko at the table to pay for the whole caboodle.

ASHLYN WAS CAUTIOUSLY EDGY ABOUT putting food in his stomach that night, even though Lucy had prepared one of his favorites—chicken casserole with potato flour dumplings followed by cinnamon and brown sugar baked apples. He ate sparingly, which brought on looks of concern, especially as his mood was somber and he'd hardly spoken a word. Not that Ashlyn cared to have a conversation at that moment. He was thinking about *him*. He couldn't stop thinking about *him*. Perhaps his desire to connect was an obsession, he recognized that in himself——addicted as if by an opiate.

But was there anything wrong with that?

Who, if they had the chance, would not want such a friendship, to interact with an equal from the sea, not a pet, a playful dolphin but one to share thoughts, ideas, experiences?

"If only I was aware," he muttered aloud without even realizing.

"Aware of what?" his grandmother asked as Lucy began clearing away the dishes.

Ashlyn looked at his grandmother sheepishly. "Huh?"

Autumn turned to Ashlyn, holding her breath while Grandma reiterated, "If only you were aware of what?"

Ashlyn blinked nervously. "Uh, nothing." He stood up from the table. "Do you need help with the dishes, Lucy?"

"Almost done," Lucy replied, tying an apron around her waist.

"Well, okay."

As Ashlyn headed off to the living room, Grandma turned to Autumn. "How's he doing?"

"Fine. Why?"

"He looks troubled," Grandma replied suspiciously. "Never mind."

"I THINK I'LL WATCH TV with you guys for a while," Lucy said sitting on the sofa next to Ashlyn. "Casserole too salty, huh?"

"No…it was delicious; I wasn't hungry, that's all."

Lucy slowly nodded.

Rubbing his stomach, Ashlyn added, "New philosophy…if I'm not hungry, won't eat…. Why, you think I need to?"

Lucy smiled. "I wish I was like that. So, what aren't you aware of?"

"What?"

"You've got us all guessing. Sounded kind of important; aware of what?"

Ashlyn felt the blood draining from his face.

"It's a poem," Autumn quickly interjected. "He wrote a poem."

"Oh that," Ashlyn added, running with Autumn's cover. "Yeah, forget that one."

Wrinkling her nose affectionately, Lucy's eyes widened. "You write poetry? That's marvelous. I used to, a long time ago. It's very therapeutic. So let's hear it."

Ashlyn shook his head. "I don't think so."

"Don't be shy."

Even though the television was on, Ashlyn sensed the room turning painfully quiet. Closing his eyes as if to escape the scrutiny, he surprised himself as a poem began to flow from him.

"Pinpoints of light spiraling under me....
Shadows I cannot understand....
Moving faster in that water than ever on the land.
There's a heat upon my back, a breath of fresh air in my soul.
And simple words we hear every day...that make no sense at all.
If I can solve this riddle so bizarre and without rhyme....
Then I'll have discovered the magic of why it is not yet time.
So simple in its concept, a journey impossible to compare,
I only know that I must do it....
Or forever wish I were aware."

Ashlyn opened his eyes, wondering how and from where that came. "There's more, but it's kinda incomplete," he said.

Lucy smiled warmly. "Very esoteric, over most people's heads. But I love esoteric poems. I didn't know you were so deep, Ashlyn. Oh my—"

Lucy's attention shifted to the television where Channel 7's *"On-the-Scene"* news team was showing the charred remnants of a local gay and lesbian bar that had been bombed. The female news reporter announced that there were only two minor injuries due to a swift evacuation following an anonymous phone tip. In the parking lot behind this bar, a billboard was found with the word *"Sinners"* painted on it in blood.

As the television coverage returned to the studio, the anchorman announced that this was the third gay bar bombing incident in Oregon in five months.

Lucy shook her head. "Why some can't tolerate others, I'll never understand. It's over my head, like your poem, Ashlyn."

Autumn nodded in agreement. Ashlyn didn't say a word, for his mind was elsewhere....

AT BOOMER'S SEAFARER'S STORE, the two treasure-hunting experts talked shipwrecks, smoked dope and drank vodka. Boomer's interest in profiting from stolen goods equaled a carnivore's interest in lettuce, so it was late before Carter fired up his Compaq notebook. Unlike Boomer, who was cash comfortable, Carter was financially challenged—better known as flat broke—and this pendant looked like it was going earn him some serious cash.

He flipped through a series of windows bearing details on salvage rights and Armada history, and hey presto!

Carter blinked.

He wiped his eyes, and checked again, and double-checked. And his shoulders began to sag.

This was disastrous. Calamitous. "Whammy, dude! It's a fake!"

Boomer casually leaned over Carter's shoulder and quickly saw his buddy's dilemma.

Boomer picked up one of the digital photographs. Sure enough the pendant appeared to be a piece of Castilian antiquity. The third and final crest belonged to one Captain Luis Hernandez De Cordoba, shipwrecked in 1605. But therein lay the problem. The shipwrecked vessel was still on the ocean floor, covered in seaweed. Undiscovered. A large smile gradually lodged itself on Boomer's face.

What an odd guy, Carter thought. Now that they weren't going to make a cent, Boomer was coming alive, eyes like sparkling spangles. "It's a fake, man! Putty! That's why old phlegm-throat didn't bring it to the pub. He must think we're idiots or something!"

Boomer shook his head. "That old jeweler will peddle hot, not fake." Boomer again compared the photograph with the image on the computer, trying to figure the catch.

Was it a replica made with real stones? Possible....

But another idea now forged into Boomer's mind. "What if the Cross didn't go down with his ship, yah?"

"Oh sure, De Cordoba gave it to someone before he sailed," Carter retorted cynically.

"Why not? His wife, his mistress, boyfriend?"

"Come on, bro. It was his ego externalized, clipped to his tunic by Prince Philip himself, right there, for the world to ogle."

Boomer was still grinning.

"He never took it off...even in bed. I know I'm right on this, Boomer."

"Yah. Makes sense. All of it. But I tell you, my friend, I'm sure, more than sure, it's not a fake." Boomer clasped his hands in a very animated fashion.

Carter was still puzzled. If it wasn't a fake, then— He whistled as the penny dropped. "Not claimed! Holy fried eels!"

That a treasure hunter had salvaged, or partially salvaged, the De Cordoba wreck without staking a claim, without becoming the legitimate salvor, was a crazy notion. But it wouldn't be the first time, although Carter had never heard about it with such a famous ship.

The monumental question was: Where was all the other treasure from De Cordoba's ship, the *Nuestra Senora De Begona?*

"Exactly my point!" Exclaimed Boomer.

The treasure-hunting friends began plotting. Boleshko had mentioned that the pendant belonged to a young man. They would have to question this young man. If stolen, they needed to find out from whom, where? If they did their homework correctly, traced back all the leads, then surely they would find themselves on a direct path to the *Nuestra Senora De Begona,* and riches beyond their wildest dreams.

Now that excited Boomer.

Carter pulled off his bowtie. "What about phlegm-throat? We tell him there's no claim, first thing that little weasel is going to do is run out and file one."

"Yah, well, I guess we'll have to do it first." Boomer replied with a roguish grin.

Boomer's desire wasn't to jockey the pendant, to benefit at someone else's expense. The salvor-in-possession claim would be for leverage purposes only, to get the attention of all third parties.

Once found and confronted, the person who unofficially owned the pendant would more than likely cooperate rather than face a long court battle and potentially lose the pendant on a salvaging technicality.

As for Boleshko, they didn't want to squeeze him either. They'd play it by ear. Hopefully, he'd be reasonable, and they'd all celebrate.

Stoli on the rocks…lots of Stoli.

Rock 'n' roll.

It was dawn by the time Boomer called his friend Toby Hollingsworth in the Florida Keys. Toby was enthralled by this discovery from the *Nuestra Senora De Begona,* and agreed to help his old chum with the salvage paperwork. He said he'd file papers right away.

For the next few hours the ex-treasure hunting mates played ping-pong facsimiles.

-12-

Time

ASHLYN SAT UP ON HIS elbows, his neck and back cold from perspiration, his ears ringing with a spacey wind.

Whsssssss-whisssssss-swhooosssss....

His eyes were open but he was only now coming awake. Or was he still sleeping?

Whsssss-shssshsss...feel-sissing-issss-you....

As these harsh, unintelligible whispers filled his mind, Ashlyn pinched his cheek to make sure he was awake. "Hello...hello is it you? What am I doing wrong? I can't understand you."

He took a deep breath, actually a sigh of frustration, which seemed to activate a kind of magic button because suddenly he felt warm rays streaming down his neck, the same kind of energy he'd felt on the boat.

After several moments, the whispers faded, and except for a single noisy cricket chirping outside, there was silence. And then....

"Ashlyn." Crystal clear.

Ashlyn gulped.

"You are good energy."

"Thank you. So are you." Ashlyn didn't give much thought to the meaning of his friend's words.

"We are drawn to each other. Are we not?"

"Yes...we are definitely...definitely drawn to each other."

"I wish to see you."

"You want…you want to meet?"

"Yes."

Ashlyn felt a tinge of panic, but answered with the feelings of his heart. "I would like that too."

"After the sun rises, take the boat."

"The boat? Where to?"

"Out."

"Yes, but where?"

"I'll find you. Now sleep."

"Wait…is it okay if I bring my sister?"

"Sister?"

"Autumn."

No response.

"Hello, are you there?"

"Yes. Bring Autumn."

"Great. North, south, straight out?"

No response.

"Hello?"

No response.

"Darn…you still didn't tell me anything. What you are? What's your name? I don't even know your name." Ashlyn sighed.

"Koa'ee'ee'ilee."

"Ko what?"

"Till the sun rises…sleep!"

"Sleep? Sure."

Silence.

Ashlyn pulled the cover up to his chin, his heart pounding, the prickly heat still tickling the back of his neck.

How could he sleep?

Only a few hours ago, in pursuit of the meaning of aware, he'd thought he'd never hear from *him* again. Now, about to come face to face, he was terrified.

Was he up to it? The delegate from Man to meet the intelligent…er, being from the undersea. "Pleased to meet you…but what are you?"

What about aware? And not yet time? No longer important?

Ashlyn's thoughts flitted from one to another: contamination, the meeting of a lifetime, danger, subjecting Autumn, every concern countered with rationale, capriciousness balanced by reasoning, until at some juncture in that melting pot of thought, he must have spiraled into a deep somnolent slumber because his next conscious realization was the early morning sun filtering through the blinds.

Autumn was already downstairs. He quickly joined her, but could only eye-signal her that something was afoot. He nonchalantly tore open a mini-packet of Cocoa Puffs, and was about to pour the contents into a bowl when there was a knock on the front door.

"Who could that be?" Lucy said, untying her apron. Ashlyn stood up, but Lucy was already on her way to the door. "No, eat your cereal. I'll get it."

Lucy opened the front door to Boleshko, standing there in a dark suit with black shoes, shiny enough to see reflections in them—his detective getup. With a snap of his wrist, he flicked open a leather wallet revealing a phony identification badge. It looked like a sheriff's star. He introduced himself. "Peter Boleshko, criminal investigator, Great Western Insurance. Good morning."

Lucy blinked, somewhat shocked. "Yes."

"I'm investigating some stolen jewelry, ma'am." This was an old ploy Boleshko had used many times before. "I'd like to speak to Ashlyn Miller, if he lives here."

By now Grandma was in the hall, demanding to be told if Ashlyn had done something wrong.

Boleshko was evasive, insisting on speaking directly with the boy. Grandma started wheezing while Boleshko worked hard to withhold his own respiratory malady.

"What are you doing here?" Ashlyn demanded as he approached the front door, Autumn right behind him.

"I'm investigating a jewelry theft." The jeweler said officiously, stretching his back to make himself look taller and meaner. In past situations, the scowl on his face had often prompted a confession or a pathetic excuse—I found it, I didn't know it was stolen, please take it back. Sometimes the person simply ran.

But that didn't happen here.

Ashlyn frowned. "A jewelry theft? What's that got to do with me? I told you I didn't want my grandma disturbed." Ashlyn walked forcefully toward the jeweler who took a nervous step back. "I'll handle this, Grandma."

"You know this man?" Grandma asked between hyperventilating gasps.

"I was doing some business with him. It's nothing—"

Grandma interrupted, "Business, what kind of business?"

Ashlyn found himself fumbling for an answer, which made Boleshko grin. There was friction. Good.

"I'll deal with it, alright, Grandma!" Ashlyn said after finding his larynx; and to the jeweler he snapped one word through snarled teeth: "Outside!" Ashlyn pushed past the jeweler and led the way down the garden path.

Boleshko thought to himself, kid's got balls.

He followed Ashlyn to the front gate, where Ashlyn about turned, his right hand fisted but on restraint. "I knew I shouldn't have dealt with you!"

"Save it, kid. This is serious," Boleshko barked back.

"You can have your money back! I want my pendant!"

This was a strange response from a thief, the jeweler thought. "Oh yeah?"

"Yes!"

The jeweler nodded thoughtfully. "Okay, show me the certificate of ownership, the registration."

Ashlyn frowned. "What?"

"Certificate of ownership. Curator document, salvage document, whatever proves it's yours. Show me that, I'll give it back to you."

"Ashlyn!" Lucy called from the doorway. "Ashlyn, what's going on?"

"Nothing. I'm coming."

"Well?" The jeweler clicked the back of his throat. "Maybe your grandmother can throw some light on this."

Ashlyn was momentarily caught off balance. Certificate of ownership? Curator document? All he could think of surfaced as a contrite, boyish whimper. "Why are you doing this? I have your receipt."

"Not good enough."

"What do you mean? It's what you gave me."

"Yes. But I don't peddle stolen property."

"It's not stolen."

"Then prove it. Lets go inside and get the papers."

Knowing that he was losing this battle, Ashlyn decided to go on the attack. Poking a finger into the jeweler's chest he snarled, "Look, you bird-brained maggot, any papers I have are my business! The security agreement is the only paper that counts! And it should be plenty good enough!"

"But it's not," said the flannelmouthed jeweler almost in song, pushing away Ashlyn's finger.

"Ashlyn! Come here right now!" Lucy called.

"You can deal with me...or the police, my next stop. Up to you," the jeweler retorted smugly, sensing the winning flag, not that he would dare call in the cops even if the boy agreed.

"Ashlyn!"

"It's not stolen. I swear it."

"I believe you. So, you find it? Lying on the beach?"

Ashlyn looked back as he heard his sister's footfalls. "Ashlyn, you better come."

"Okay, suit yourself. You'll be hearing from the police." The jeweler said with a raised voice so the ears in the doorway could hear.

Bullied, backed against the wall, Ashlyn found himself saying what the jeweler wanted: "Alright, alright I found it."

"No problem." The jeweler replied. "I'll make sure it gets back to its rightful owner. Oh, and do have a nice day." Straightening his tie, the jeweler turned around, so internally jubilant, he forgot all about his fifteen hundred dollars.

"What did he want?" Autumn inquired.

Ashlyn banged his clenched fist into the doorjamb, but his rage was so strong, he didn't even feel it.

GRANDMA SAT ASHLYN AND AUTUMN down in the lounge. The lecture that followed was without a raised voice, although at that moment Ashlyn could have easily screamed holy murder. The insurance man, whoever he was and whatever he wanted, was only one slice of a much larger problem, Grandma said. He was ostensibly the pea that tipped the scale. Parenting teenagers was the issue, the real problem. It was a major responsibility to keep them off drugs, alcohol, to nurture their studies, police their friends. And while her disabilities made it impossible for her, it wasn't fair to ask Lucy to fill those shoes.

Wiping her eyes, Grandma continued, "I'm fond of you, you know that, very fond of both of you, and Lucy adores you, too. During summer vacations you'll come and visit us."

"Visit? What do you mean? Where are we going?" Autumn asked.

Grandma's answer confirmed Ashlyn's fears: Inverness, Scotland, to live with Grandma's niece. "There are grand schools there, youth clubs." Grandma assured them. "Aye, you're going to love it."

Grandma had finished speaking but the teens sat in catatonic shock, as if speared by harpoons. When Ashlyn found his voice, it emerged almost as a whisper. "If we go, when?"

"It's not if, Ashlyn. I'm sorry. I know it's sudden—"

"When?"

"Monday!"

Monday. Four days.

THE DAY WASN'T GOING WELL. Ripped off by the jeweler, then tortured by Grandma's mean-spirited news, it was almost noon when Autumn and Ashlyn left the house, pedaling their bicycles furiously, fearing they'd blown the meeting of a lifetime.

"No way I'm going to school in Scotland," Autumn yelled, her face flushed blood-red, as she tried to keep up with Ashlyn. "I'll run away!"

Though he felt the same way, Ashlyn kept it to himself. At that moment, all he cared about was getting aboard *Indigo Empyrean* and meeting his friend somewhere out there in the blue yonder.

It took them thirty-five minutes to reach the marina. They chained the cycles at the fence, and hurried down the ramp to *Indigo,* where Ashlyn noticed something strange. The quiet, lazy harbor they'd moored at yesterday was now a tumultuous place with dense boat traffic on both sides of the channel. The harbor patrol was out in force and there was a distant symphony of sirens and horns.

Ashlyn cast off quickly, tacking in search of wind. Oh for a pair of speedy Crusader engines and no traffic. In lieu, he settled for a tortoise's pace along Marina Pass.

Rounding the breakwater, the sirens built to a crescendo, and the commotion unveiled itself as an excited crowd on the beach yelling at a line of white triangles speeding along the shoreline. It was a national regatta.

"How are we going to meet up in this?" Ashlyn griped, as he tillered straight out to sea, per his friend's instructions, only it was already past noon, not sunrise.

Autumn didn't say a word.

The conditions for sailing were good, a light breeze, hazy sunshine. As they headed southwest at an easy ten knots, a speedboat buzzed them, the scrawny youth at its helm in hysterics over his whitewashing maneuver.

They sailed on, away from the speedboat, steering away from all other craft, on and on.

It was one-thirty, then two-thirty.

No sign of *him*.

By now, the closest vessel was a speck in the distance. Ashlyn was nervous—perhaps not as goosey as the last time, nevertheless his stomach was tight.

By three-thirty, the clouds had burned off, and the regatta's excitement faded somewhere off to the east.

They were eight miles out, looking for a glimpse of underwater light.

But there was nothing.

Maybe it was best, because of Autumn, Ashlyn decided. It had been a stupid risk bringing her. Next time he'd go alone...if there would be a next time.

He was about to turn *Indigo* around when Autumn shouted: "I see something! There...there's a light!"

Ashlyn saw nothing. "No...it's just the sun's reflection."

Autumn yelped as the boat abruptly lunged forward.

There were no signs of a glowing light from under the boat, but without a doubt, it had to be *him!* They were zipping along faster than any amount of wind could propel them.

Ashlyn swallowed hard. Oh, why did he bring Autumn along?

"Where is he? I can't see anything. Are you chatting?"

"I'm concentrating!" Ashlyn gathered himself, but while the wind and spray rifled through his hair, not a word settled into his mind.

Indigo Empyrean was now positioned on a course back to shore. And the butterflies in Ashlyn's stomach were turning into nasty knots. "Hello...can you hear me?"

"Do not be nervous."

Ashlyn gulped. School exams made him nervous; airplane take-offs made him nervous—this was terrifying.

"I am a friend."

"Yes...I know."

"Ashlyn...feel."

"I am feeling."

In reality, he was thinking about the librarian's account of the prehistoric monster, a one-hundred-foot-long flesh-eating—

"I will not hurt you…I will not hurt you or your sister."

"I didn't mean to think that. It's just that I—"

"You are wondering what sort am I? To you, I am not sure what I am."

Not exactly the answer Ashlyn had hoped for.

Autumn nudged him. "We're really flying."

They were heading north at sixty knots—a huge speed for a tiny sailboat, but a casual gait for their underwater pilot.

Ashlyn nodded. "Yup, flying."

They still couldn't see him, couldn't even discern a speck or hint of his bioluminescence, but the entity below was now the undisputed master of their vessel, turning when he wanted to turn, accelerating and slowing regardless of their rudder position or wind in the sails.

A speedboat turned into their path, but their underwater pilot veered away with a head-snapping sprint, the sort of breakneck speed that would have shamed the international regatta racers.

Ashlyn's face was thoughtful yet tense. Autumn assumed that he was engrossed in a serious telepathic conversation. But at this moment all he felt was an internal silence.

"Ashlyn." The telepathic voice was soft, yet Ashlyn jumped. His verbalized "yes" drew a querying look from Autumn.

"Go within…feel. Breathe deep!"

Ashlyn sighed. It was simplistic to say 'feel' and 'go within' but what did that really mean? He took a few deep breaths and closed his eyes, not really expecting to feel anything.

But he did feel something, and quickly—a tingling sensation, like a warm energy running in all directions through his body. "Whoa, is that you? You're doing that?"

"No, it is you. Breathe…feel."

"Are you sure? It's heat."

"I am sure."

Ashlyn opened his eyes, half expecting to see his arms glowing from the heat. They looked normal, and Autumn was watching him expectantly. As his anxiety began to melt away, he addressed the entity, "I don't remember how to say your name."

"Koa'ee'eeee'ee'ileeee."

"Koa'eeily?"

"Koa'ee'eeee'ee'ileeee."

"How about I call you Ko for short?"

" And I call you Ash?"

Ashlyn chuckled. So, he had a sense of humor.

Autumn nudged his elbow. "What's happening? Where's he taking us?"

"Somewhere ashore I guess. I don't know."

"What does he look like? Is he like a merman? Is he big?" Autumn asked.

"He's not sure how to describe himself. I hope he ate lunch already."

Autumn's jaw dropped.

Ashlyn winked at her. "I'm kidding."

Autumn's attention shifted to some approaching white water. "Looks like rocks ahead."

Ashlyn also saw the line of jagged rocks. Getting closer...very close! They could now hear crashing waves. Surely their pilot would veer away.

Mini-clouds of spray shot up into the air, and into the boat. They were about to hit!

Autumn's eyes widened. "Ashlyn! What's he doing?"

Ashlyn reflexively grabbed the tiller. "Ko! The reef! Too close!" Ashlyn winced as they sailed through narrow gaps in the rocks—past jagged shapes as sharp as surgeons' scalpels—expecting the boat to be ripped up at any moment, yet....

"The reef. Beautiful?"

They flew along unscathed.

Ashlyn released the tiller. "Yes, beautiful."

With pinpoint precision, Ko moved along a perilous path that would certainly shred to pieces any vessel trying to follow them.

Through the arches of a chiseled sea stack, they curved around the headland, passing a large yellow house standing atop the cliff. "Denton Clark's house!" Ashlyn yelled, pointing it out to Autumn, when, with a sudden burst of acceleration, Ko barreled forward on a collision course with the face of the escarpment!

Autumn shrieked!

Ashlyn glimpsed the cave opening an instant before they roared into the enclosure, and then daylight abruptly vanished, replaced by complete darkness. Ashlyn felt the boat's brakes seemingly slamming on, and he steadied himself as the boat came to a choppy stop.

Water sloshed against the walls, gulls cawed outside, but in the pitch black of the cave, the voice in Ashlyn's mind turned silent. If

Ko was in the cave, he wasn't emitting even a hint of light.

Autumn squeezed Ashlyn's hand as she spotted something—a tubular glow under the boat. Then she squeezed his hand even harder!

Though still underwater, she saw that their underwater pilot was larger than the boat, bearing shimmers of red, green and blue, and he was beginning to pulse, his glow swelling into a gleaming incandescence illuminating the entire cave.

Ashlyn took a deep breath.

Time to meet his friend.

Barely causing a ripple, Ko swam to the boat's starboard side, then broke to the surface, soaring up eight feet above the water, smiling.

As Autumn gasped, Ashlyn froze, his mouth open in awe! He was looking at a real merm—

Well, sort of a merm— Well, no, not really—at least not based upon the accepted imagery in literature.

And Ko wasn't a *'he'*.

Leaning against a pillar-like rock, her tail steadily moving to and fro for balance while *her* color and luminescence periodically morphed—blue and emerald into violet, then indigo and amber, even salmon color like the folklore mermaid—her gaze was firmly upon Ashlyn. He could have never imagined her like this.

Ko's upper torso, endowed with small breasts, undeniably proved that she was female, and she had long upper limbs that ran to a pair of five-fingered hands, webbed where palm and fingers graced each other.

But here ended all mermaid similarities.

Sweeping out of her wide-barreled back was a translucent dorsal, tapestried with strands of pulsing iridescent color, that she sometimes dislocated into two dorsal fins, elevating and lowering them as gracefully as angels' wings. The upper part of the binary dorsal crested on her crown as a singular plume, about three inches wide, like a spectacular Mohawk hairdo, crowning a snoutish face.

And Ko was long. Although nothing like the one-hundred-foot monster, from the tip of her crown to her hefty tail, she probably measured about thirteen feet.

But to Ashlyn, Ko's most incredible feature was her eyes. They were well-separated, huge green and gold half-moons, smiling at him coyly.

Without brows or ears, she was equipped with gossamer-like gills on the sides of her face, and her elongated mouth bore two rows of minuscule teeth.

Ko wasn't pretty.

She was beautiful.

Her entire persona was a picture of love.

Ashlyn thought, a real mermaid, not a human-fish, but a luminous, rugged design built for the deep-sea.

"A mermaid? Explain this?" she inquired, caressing the back of her head, a nonchalant mannerism not unlike a human's.

Ashlyn grinned. "Oh, just a mythical name for a fish that looks half.... I mean you are a bit...well, not really. Put it this way, nobody—at least nobody who is considered sane—believes you exist! Like I said, you really don't look anything like a mermaid."

"Are you disappointed?" She moved her head to one side, a photographic pose if ever.

Ashlyn was about to pat Ko's head affectionately, but quickly retracted his hand, realizing his presumptuousness.

"What's happening?" Autumn asked. "He sure looks like a she."

"I know. Cause she is."

"Are you communicating?"

"Yes...I'll tell you later."

Ko splashed a small amount of water on her face. *"Mermaid, I like it."*

"What do you call you?" Ashlyn asked as he climbed out of the boat—Autumn following—onto a narrow shelf crusted with barnacles. There were several of these shelves in the cave.

Ko said a word sounding like *Ee'quee'huwuee'hana.* There were way too many high-pitched "E's" for Ashlyn to grasp it with any sort of accuracy. Ko agreed he should abbreviate the name to *E'qu'huana,* which sounded like the iguana lizard but with a "Q".

"Yes," she said enthusiastically, *"Iquana."* Again, she splashed water on herself, diligently.

Autumn nudged Ashlyn. "Is everything okay?"

Ashlyn quickly relayed the conversation thus far.

"Ashlyn...please tell Autumn I wish to borrow her hand."

"Borrow her hand?"

"She will feel something. Will she accept?"

"Like what?" Ashlyn asked, his suspicious human mind demanding an answer.

Running her webbed fingers over her plume, Ko turned expectantly to Autumn.

"Wait! What will she feel?"

"I do not know how to explain it...know I will never hurt you...or your sister." Closing her eyes and tilting her back her head loosely, Ko attempted to convey to Ashlyn a feeling.

Ashlyn also closed his eyes, hoping to gain an insight, and for several moments he wasn't sure if he felt anything, except perhaps shame for doubting this beautiful being.

Then suddenly something made him gasp. "Oh boy!" he said aloud, opening his eyes, turning to face his sister. "She wants you!"

"What?" Autumn grabbed his arm.

"Get ready!"

"What?"

"Don't be nervous. She's wants to...open you up a bit."

Autumn took a step back, her heart taking flight with a slight panic. "What do you mean?"

"What's the big deal...just a bit? You might feel something interesting."

Ko smiled, and a few droplets of water slid off her short but numerous teeth.

Autumn's eyes were wide open, nervous.

"Relax. You're going on a mind ride! Might be fun!"

Autumn released Ashlyn's arm, but she was still concerned. "What do I have to do?"

"First off, just say yes or no."

Autumn held her gaze on Ko. "What do you want me to do?"

Ko nodded her head, and a few moments later Ashlyn voiced Ko's reply. "She says relax. She won't hurt you."

Slipping off the rock, Ko glided around the boat, slowly approaching, a long arm reaching for the young human female.

Autumn was spellbound. She would never forget that first touch. Ko's hand was four times larger than hers, cold, scaly, oily, like a pulsing wet fish.

Ashlyn would never forget Autumn's hesitancy, the flicker of jealousy he felt when Ko started to pulse. He could actually see the energy moving in perceptible light waves, flowing into his sister.

Although gentle, the electric current so startled Autumn, she grabbed Ashlyn's hand.

And in that instant, Ashlyn felt pulsations swirling through his own body, bathing and relaxing him.

Then something extraordinary happened.

Ashlyn felt his spirit jumping out of his body, as if through an exit hole on the crown of his head. His inner being, not his body, was flying right out of the cave.

Language could not possibly describe the adrenalin rush, the euphoria Ashlyn felt. Like an eagle, he was soaring above the cliffs, feeling the elements moving through him, or perhaps it was the converse—he was the wind causing wings to fly and massive tree branches to bend and sway. But at that very moment, he also sensed himself being the soil under the tree roots, stony and sandy and moist, while simultaneously living as each seed and fruit born from that soil and every footfall that graced the land, every mammal, every bird.

With the blink of an eyelid he must have traveled hundreds or even thousands of miles because he found himself atop a snow-crested mountain, drifting as a misty cloud.

Then he was falling over the precipice, falling inside a glassy waterfall, only now he realized that he was the water.

With this powerful knowing, his heart beat vigorously. He was aware of Ko's heartbeat, of Autumn's, of the heartbeats of the tiny crabs scuttling all the way back at the cave. He could feel the pulse of the kingfisher flying above Deadman's Bluff and the kelp bass swimming offshore, all blending in time with the beat of his own heart.

He could even see himself, at that very same moment, swaying in a field of long grass, feeling a strong breeze upon his face, knowing that he was one blade, all the blades, and they were no more or less than strands of his own wind-tossed hair.

It all made sense.

There was only one life force, encompassing all, existing in all, being all, and it was immense and never-ending.

Ashlyn suddenly felt himself returning to his body.

The journey had ended.

He opened his eyes and saw Ko submerging herself. He shivered at the sudden coolness in the cave, the contrast from the preceding moments making him feel alone and empty.

Autumn also felt the same way.

Surfacing, Ko abruptly discharged a siphon of gas that shot to the roof. She then leaned up against the shelf.

Ashlyn knew she was gauging his reaction. After a silent spell, he heard her voice:

"Aware."

"Aware."

"Now you know."

Yes, now he knew the meaning of *aware*.

"The magic you felt is within you…always."

"I've heard it said that all life is a part of a larger whole, but I guess I never really figured it so. I mean we really are connected. If only we all knew."

Ko blinked, her eyes seemingly responding with an affirmative. Half pulling herself out of the water, she leaned against the shelf, while the teens sat, dangling their feet in the water.

As Ashlyn chatted with Ko, he learned that he was the only human with whom she had ever shared tones, with whom she truly *felt,* sensing and sharing emotions and thoughts. She had attempted to connect with other humans but, as far as she knew, none had heard her.

Ko studied how Ashlyn rested his elbow on his thigh, his hand supporting his chin. She wiped her mouth and mirrored his pose, relaying how she'd watched humans on ships and beaches, dancing, playing, but all too often killing with machines too foreign for her comprehension.

She dived again to recharge her breathing apparatus. She did this about every fifteen minutes.

Back up on the shelf, she asked: *"Why do humans make so many machines?"* She couldn't comprehend how and why humans gained so much pleasure from material possession. However, one type of machine brightened her eyes—if that was possible. *"Flying machines… I am awed by them, I admit. Perhaps I was a bird once."*

Ko then dropped down into the water, flapping her binary dorsal like a distressed turkey. Maybe she could fly underwater but her efforts above left something to be desired. Then she began to cackle—a real audible sound.

So, Ko was a clown, a klutzy clown, and they all shared a laugh.

Ko's color, which for some moments had been a luminous primrose, then turned slightly gray as she drifted back to the shelf. *"Teach me …teach me human."* Her eyes sparkled with childish anticipation.

How do you teach human? Human wasn't a language, but in a way, perhaps it was. Ashlyn leaned forward. "Human 101, getting someone's attention without the use of a machine." Placing pinky and forefinger to his lips, he sucked in a large breath and blew a deafening, wax-loosening wolf whistle.

Ko recoiled, but her eyes were rapt. Running a hand to her mouth, she puckered, blew, managing to produce nothing but a stream of raspy air. Undaunted by the teens' laughter, she tried again. Nothing. After making a pouting face of disappointment, she submerged herself…reemerging with her face distortedly ballooned.

"Oh, no!" Autumn screamed, anticipating the worst.

Ko bared her teeth and gave it her all—and a massive shriek of a whistle—ten-plus on the Richter scale—exploded from her mouth.

Autumn shrieked.

Ashlyn cringed.

They all covered their ears—even Ko who didn't have ears.

"More, more, more!" Ko was clicking and clacking but as Ashlyn's palm greeted hers for the congratulatory slap, he saw something in her eyes that sent a shudder down his spine. Her laugh became a grimace, and then she clutched her side and quickly dove out of sight.

Ashlyn watched, white-faced, not daring to believe what he now suspected.

On the floor of the cave, Ko curled herself into a fetal position, her luminescence dimming to that of a tired light bulb. She covered her mouth as a dark milky cloud, not seen above, oozed through her fingers. Yet somehow, barely conscious, she managed to draw from her *chemo-reserve.*

At that moment, up on the shelf, Autumn and Ashlyn observed Ko *luminescing*—becoming brighter and brighter, blindingly bright.

"What's wrong with her?" Autumn shouted as harsh white light filled the cave.

"I don't know." Ashlyn cried back.

Then Ko surfaced, her luminance quickly softening, her face materializing through the glare. Now pulsing a gentle violet light, she returned to her place against the shelf. She looked up at Ashlyn, smiling, as if nothing had happened.

Ashlyn knelt down. "You're sick."

Ko took Ashlyn's hand. Her color was turning indigo, like the boat. She looked spectacular again. *"It is the way it is."*

"The way what is? What do you mean?" Ashlyn wiped seawater out of his eyes.

"I like it, with you humans." She tried to assume a more comfortable position on the hard rock, as her tail gently swayed back and forth making ripples. *"Ashlyn, would you like to learn, to see and hear with your heart, to use all your senses?"*

"You're avoiding my question."

"Ashlyn, look!" Ko turned to *Indigo Empyrean,* where one of the oars began to shake and shimmy—as if by alchemy—then it jumped out of the boat as if it were alive and flew into Ko's open palm.

As Autumn gasped, Ashlyn's jaw dropped wide open. Ko laid the oar on the shelf while she waited for Ashlyn to respond. *"The other stick. Your turn!"*

Ashlyn's unpronounced thoughts were enough for Ko's comprehension.

"You can, Ashlyn. I will teach you...if you want."

Ashlyn was quiet.

Ko raised herself out of the water a bit more, until she was level with Ashlyn's shoulders. *"I will teach you, you will teach me. A fair exchange. Come with me, Ashlyn, and I will take you to a new world."*

"Come with you? I don't think that's possible."

"I will teach you a new magic. You will fly with me and soar like—"

"But I can't. I would love to see your world but I can't."

"The first human."

"I can't."

"You can. It is a choice."

Ashlyn swallowed. "No, Ko, It's not a choice. I can't come."

Ko lowered her eyes. *"You do not wish to be my friend?"*

"I do. But we can be friends here...in this cave."

"That for me is not a choice. I am hunted here."

"Hunted?"

"That is why it is not yet time...but for you, Ashlyn—"

"Who hunts you? Who knows you exist?"

"You can come in the machine."

Ashlyn furrowed his brow. "Machine? What machine?" He spoke this aloud, evoking a querying look from Autumn.

Ko closed her eyes, gently rolling her head from side to side as she sought for the name of the machine, probing into Ashlyn's mind for the answer. Ashlyn found himself imitating her, moving his own head around his shoulders.

"Submersible," she said suddenly.

"Submersible?"

"It comes out of the cliff."

"Submersibles don't come out of cliffs, Ko."

"Through an opening below the surface."

"You've seen this?"

"Yes."

"Wow. James Bond."

"James Bond?"

"Uh, nothing. Where did you see this submersible that comes out of the cliff?"

"A distance of no more than five hundred lengths from here. We passed by it; the human inside searches for me. He spends his life searching."

"We passed by it?" A thought occurred to Ashlyn. "The yellow house with the orangey-red roof…it comes from below that house?"

"Yes."

Ashlyn's face paled as he considered the uncanny coincidences: Denton Clark with a submersible, hunting Ko, staring at Autumn as if he'd seen a ghost. Did Autumn remind Denton of someone? Almost everyone thought Autumn was a carbon copy of their mother. Ashlyn's mind flashed back to the conversation in Clark's house: *Have your mom take you to the dunes.* He didn't say, *have your dad* or *parents take you*, he said *mom*. Was this a presumption, or a knowing?

It couldn't be, his father was dead. He died in a submersible—Grandma called it his coffin—and he left behind a world of debt. Left behind a world of—

Autumn noticed Ashlyn's altered countenance. "What's wrong?"

Ashlyn didn't know how to answer. The coincidence was overwhelming. Was it two men or one? Two lives intertwined with the seabed phantom—Ko—or one? Was his father still alive hiding under the identity of Denton Clark? Ashlyn wanted to scream, no! But his gut screamed, yes!

Having followed his thoughts, Ko looked deep into Ashlyn's

eyes. *"You think he's your father?"*

Ashlyn's mind made tally of the contradiction, the preposterously incomprehensible notion that Denton Clark was his father—the man who'd taught his mother to love the planet. What could he know about love? How could he act so differently from what he preached? To leave his wife, his family, just so he could escape a few debts. "No," he answered, "He's not my father. My father is dead."

Ko understood. She truly sympathized, but said nothing because nothing she could have said would have quelled Ashlyn's pain. Only time would do that. She slowly slipped back into the water and lethargically swam.

Ashlyn turned to Autumn, and with an attempt at masking his anger, gave her a quick summary, bypassing Denton Clark. "She wants us to go with her. She wants to show us places no one's ever seen."

Autumn's eyes sparkled. "Underwater? Radical! How do we breathe?"

"All we have to do is…borrow a submersible."

"Oh, is that all?" Autumn grinned.

Ko surfaced. Beyond her, through the cave's entrance, the ebbing sun began to show its amber face. *"I have much to share with you, Ashlyn. Get the machine. It will be good."* She nodded, seemingly quite satisfied with herself.

Ashlyn watched in wonderment as she morphed into a luminous turquoise. She was so childlike, so naive, and so clueless on human matters. She didn't understand the complexity of machines, and the human way of buying and owning property. How could he explain that he couldn't climb into someone else's submersible and simply take off?

But even if he did gain access to this submersible, how would he drive it? And of course to complicate matters, there was Denton Clark. Even the man's name now repulsed him.

Ko nodded, and then she smiled. *"Trust your desire…picture it… feel… see!"*

PART TWO

ABYSS

-13-

Hunters

AT THE HOUR THAT ASHLYN, Autumn and Ko departed from the coastal cave, Admiral Andy Lightstone and his partner Captain James Swift sat down at Sam's Cigar Lounge to interview an odd little man calling himself, for some oblique reason, Tax Man. With a dry mouth and shaking hands, Tax Man opened an attaché case and removed two photographs, which he placed neatly on the table. They were close shots of a man's face, top of the head clipped, neck clipped. The shot on the left was a lean face, dark hair, handsome. Andy instantly recognized the face—the man who'd coined the term A-zone ingressions. Sure enough, his name was scribed on the bottom of the photo, along with the date, thirteen years ago.

Tax Man cleared his throat. "Yes, I'm aware that you knew him; you were at the funeral."

There was no name on the other photo. It was a tired face, sagging under long, scraggly white hair with a salt-and-pepper beard. What linked both photos as a possible identity match were the bushy brows running over the bridges of the noses, drooping lids, and the eyes themselves—pools of deep blue, piercing, as if possessed.

The two navy men inspected the photos, carefully.

Tax Man took a sip of Perrier to soothe his nervous throat. "This, as you see, taken thirteen years ago, a year before his death." He placed an index finger on the top edge of the right photo. "This, six months ago."

Next, Tax Man pulled from his attaché a page with two finger-prints, one taken from an old passport fifteen years ago, the other lifted from a whisky glass, dated by a certified lab only four years ago. Both prints were identical.

Andy examined the documents. He snorted in mild surprise but his body language implied indifference. Tax Man then produced an-other document, a surveillance report describing the mystery man's deployment of oceanographic experiments, some as recently as three months ago. Finally, he produced three night-scope photographs of what appeared to be a dark shadowy object near a cliff, possibly a submersible.

Andy twirled his cigar in the ashtray. "Okay, according to this, Jerry Miller faked his death. B.F.D. He shook off a few debts. Why should I give a rat's ass?"

Tax Man absentmindedly curled the photo's edge. "Maps...the... the maps, A-zone maps—"

"Yeah, yeah. A-zone maps. Out of date, and a wild theory at best." Andy pushed aside the ashtray. The retired admiral knew how to crush an adversary.

Nervous, but not a total fool, Tax Man found some inner strength. "Guess we won't be doing business then." He picked the lemon wedge off his glass, ate its tart meat, even made a comically sour face, gathered his documents, and smiling, started for the exit door.

Out of earshot, Andy turned to James: "Miller might be an as-set. He's got the hardware, and the knowledge."

James nodded. "What about Tax Chump? He's excess baggage. Miller must have sea access. We check out beach front sales over the last twelve years, rap on a few doors—"

Andy didn't seem very convinced. "Why's he calling himself Tax Man?"

James twisted his lips, took a sip of brandy. "Maybe he is a tax man, an accountant."

Andy held his unlit cigar under his nose, savoring its aroma. "Or an IRS agent who doesn't blow the whistle on his man."

"Meaning he's shooting for a bit more than a civil servant's pat on the back."

"You better bring him back here."

When Tax Man returned, he was still shaking—a disposition that Andy swiftly realized didn't surrender him to the ranks of idiot.

Tax Man understood the value of the phantom, its revenue potential in movies, TV shows, cereal boxes, candy wrappers, toy tie-ins, fast food promos, et al. And all he wanted was a "reasonable percentage."

"Percentage?" Andy repeated. "You're a smart man. You must realize I have investors. First position, second position, third."

Tax Man raised his voice, slightly. "A hundred percent of nothing, that's what you have! I deserve it!" This was the moment Jack Henry had been waiting for, when he could demand his fifty percent.

But when Andy asked him what he had in mind, out of Jack's mouth came a wimpish, "Small…small percentage, just cut me in, and look, I'll even throw in all your tax planning."

Captain James Swift and Andy Lightstone couldn't help liking Tax Man. He was in sync with their objective. And three percent net for the Jerry Miller package wasn't outrageous at all. In fact it wasn't anything other than a deal.

They shook hands on it.

Shortly after Tax Man departed, Andy looked up as a muscular six-footer, with curly black hair, collarless shirt, and designer blue jeans approached the table. Ed Lazerath was a marine acquisition specialist who boasted himself the best in the biz, claiming to have bagged live and unharmed giant squids, man-eating great whites and massive seawater crocodiles.

Pretending to be impressed, Andy Lightstone smiled and nodded, despite knowing that the Madagascan authorities called Ed Lazerath an animal mercenary, a euphemism for 'poacher'.

Ed downed his beer before resuming. "A three-foot-long prehistoric fish, like the coelacanth found in the thirties, might raise some eyebrows, but it ain't worth the bucks. For that you need size. Take the fifty-foot prehistoric shark Megalodon, the undisputed heavyweight master of the ocean! Think that wouldn't pack 'em in? Hell, Jurassic Water Park! Bucks frickin' galore! Now this Gigas Hydromermadis, mermaid, right?" He raised his eyebrows. "I'd be glib, I mean, I'd be outright lying if I said I wasn't…you know, human face, animal body…" His cynical smile grew wide, but his audience remained stoic.

After a sticky pause, Ed's grin reformulated into a sycophantish nod. "Man, that'd be some sight wouldn't it? Er, yeah, from what you say, definitely seems to be something. Hell, I'll fish for it, whatever, whatever it is, I'll fish like a son-of-a—"

Andy re-lit his cigar. "You have a problem?" he asked with a stone-cold glower.

"No, no problem…no problem at all," Ed replied quickly. "If there was I'd tell y'all. Honesty is my motto."

Andy blew cigar smoke above his companions' heads and rinsed his gums with a mouthful of brandy. "I like that in a man. How much, how long will it take?"

"Cut to the chase man. Gotcha. Fifteen hundred a day, thirty thousand up front. You pay all costs, boats, traps, cameras, the works. I'll do my very best and I am the best, but there's no guarantee. If we catch it, I get ten percent off the top. As for what it's—" He took pause in mid-speech because Andy was shaking his head. When he continued it was with a slightly diminished verve. "—Uh, I guess I could…I could go with five percent off the top."

Andy placed his cigar in the ashtray, leaned forward, somewhat menacingly. "Five hundred a day, one day up front. When we bag it, so long as you do your part, so long as you…fall in…you do understand what fall in means?" Andy leaned forward so close that his scowled face appeared as a tight close up to Ed. "Left is left, right right, and o-four hundred is not o-four-ten. You do understand that?"

Andy waited for the man to nod, before continuing. "Five hundred a day, I supply the hardware. When we bag it, you get two hundred and fifty gees. Call it a bonus. No percent, no bargaining, no trouble. Yes or no." Andy leaned back into his chair, while holding a firm gaze on the marine specialist.

Realizing it was his cue, Ed blinked. "Er, yes, right…I could do…something like that," he mumbled.

Then there was a sticky silence broken by Andy. "Time frame?"

"Time frame, well, course I'll have a better idea when I see it on sonar. I see it on sonar, I'll be able to tell you what it had for breakfast, where it's going for dinner. I'll even tell you what it's thinking."

"What it's thinking?"

"Animal kingdom's all the same, thinking one of two things: How to eat you…or how to prevent you from eating it."

-14-

Back Home

THE SUN'S CROWN WAS ALREADY bleeding into the indigo horizon when Ko said good-bye two miles outside Wayside Harbor. They'd been together several hours and Ashlyn felt emotionally and physically drained from the sustained telepathic conversation. He had much to relay to Autumn, but decided to hold off on the dampener, Denton Clark, at least for a while.

He questioned himself: Could he be mistaken? Could it be pure coincidence? Father or not, this man was probably his only means of ever seeing Ko's world, of ever becoming fully aware. Still, the name sent shivers down his spine.

He looked up at the sail, now luffing, trimmed it in tight, let it out a tad, found the edge, and held it. A good tight sail on the edge would get them back to the harbor. He then realized that Autumn was chatting and asking him things, probably had been for some time.

From Autumn's perspective, Ko and the cave had been the experience of a lifetime. It was mind boggling that Ko was technically a fish yet she was a spiritual, God-aware, truly *aware* being. "Do you realize what this means?"

Although Ashlyn nodded, Autumn suspected that he hadn't considered the implication—the biblical notion that Man should be Ko's ruler. "What an obnoxious idea that would be, don't you think? Like one man being the ruler of another; how many wars were fought over that?"

Again Ashlyn nodded.

Autumn rubbed her shoulders. "Not that I would tell, not that anyone would believe us anyway! I wouldn't believe us! We've just made one of the most major discoveries in the whole world, in all of history, and guess what? They'd strap us up in straightjackets! We might as well have discovered a spaceship and gone to Mars. We're the first to make contact and no one, no one else in the whole world knows."

Ashlyn remained silent, still thinking about Denton Clark.

Waving her hands in front of his face, she said, "Hey! At least tell me something...like...like how did she make the boat? By magic?"

Ashlyn took a deep breath. "Magic? Yeah, in a way I guess it was magic." Doing his best to appear unruffled, he began with the account of the boat's creation, which Ko had assembled with the magic of sheer hard work. Understanding the human love of possessions, Ko had reasoned that the object would stir Ashlyn's heart and hopefully conjoin them in friendship.

After finding the rowboat, she'd set about transforming it into Ashlyn's vision, which she'd inadvertently tapped into. But boat building turned out to be enormously difficult. To patch the holes she'd used a mixture made from *seahucks*—a type of conical shell—shark egg yolk, squid ink, and oyster pearls, which she also used for paint. After grinding up the elements with her teeth, and blending them inside kelp bulbs, she fermented the mixture at a shimmering hydrothermal vent four thousand fathoms below the surface. Then she painted the boat above water in fifteen-minute intervals. The mast and sail came from a small sunken ketch, and she completed the assembly using glue made from fish bone and sugar-kelp. Broken coral shards, sharks' teeth and kelp were her only tools, and she'd stressed that no life form, not one living fish or plant had been harmed in the creation. It took her six days, and she'd never done anything like it in her life before.

Autumn caressed the boat's smooth finish in admiration of Ko's handiwork. Indeed, the boat stirred her heart, too; it conjoined them all in friendship. "Do you realize, Ashlyn, the magnitude? This is huge! This is so bigger than life! And you're like so...dead."

"Well I can't please everyone."

"What about the submersible?" Autumn asked, pulling on her sweater. It was getting chilly. "Surely, she doesn't think we can get a submersible, does she?"

Ashlyn steered the boat around the breakwater, angling them into the harbor. "Yup. Yup, she does."

"That's pretty far out. From where?"

"From…Denton Clark."

Autumn frowned as she tried to digest this. "Denton Clark? The creep with the…she actually said, Denton Clark's got a submersible?"

Ashlyn nodded slowly.

"But that's totally insane. Wait a minute—"

Autumn's mind raced. Denton Clark had a submersible. He sculpted mermaids. He had stared at her like he'd seen a ghost— "Ashlyn," she blurted, "All the—"

"Coincidences," Ashlyn interrupted, running his fingers through his hair.

AT DINNER, ASHLYN AND AUTUMN picked at their beef potpies. They hardly ate, hardly spoke. Skipping TV, they went straight upstairs. Autumn had remembered seeing a box of old photographs in Grandma's room. On a hunch she decided to sneak in and borrow it. Back in her own room, she found what she was hoping to find: photographs of their father.

Ashlyn picked out a honeymoon shot. His father's eyes were pale blue, penetrating, yet ironically kind—just like Denton Clark's eyes. Ashlyn sighed.

Sitting on her bed, Autumn studied the photograph. "A lot of people have similar eyes."

Ashlyn shook his head. Why else did Denton jump out of his skin at the library? Autumn was clearly a clone of her mom. The photograph was proof of that. The evidence was circumstantial. But what other facts did they need? *Father* stamped on Denton Clark's forehead?

"You know it's him, just as I do!" Ashlyn ambled over to the window. He stared outside, focused on nothing, just thinking. The idea of placing himself before Denton Clark and humbly asking or begging for his submersible churned his stomach.

Autumn looked up from another wedding photograph. "He was messed up…his mind wasn't rational."

"You got that right!"

"Think about it…Ko's world," she reminded Ashlyn, as if he

needed to be reminded.

"He's not going to give us a damn thing, and I, for one, am not going to give the bastard the satisfaction of spitting in my face…again."

"We have nothing to lose, everything to gain."

"What about dignity?" he snapped.

"You're a hypocrite, you know that. Only a few days ago you were hiding up here, talking to yourself and shaking like a baby. You think Grandma and Lucy hadn't talked about a shrink? What if Ko hadn't called you? What if we hadn't met her? Then what? How would you be now? Talking to yourself? Talking to who? Searching for who? For a mermaid, a sea serpent? Oh yeah that sounds real sane." Autumn caught her breath. "Maybe he's a liar and a deserter and a cheat, but look at us…are we so perfect? You tell me, big brother. You tell me, 'cause I don't know." Once again, she fixed her eyes on the old honeymoon photo.

Ashlyn sat down next to her. "You forgive him?"

Autumn thought about that for a good long moment. "Maybe I do and maybe I don't. Honestly, I don't know what I feel. I just want to go with Ko…go anywhere…as long as I can take Bigsey, as long as we can forget Inverness, I really don't care."

"You think I want something different?" Ashlyn lay down, staring up at the ceiling, his hands cradling the back of his neck. His mind flashed back to Ko's words: *Get the machine.* "Like in just take it?" he mumbled.

"What are you thinking?"

He massaged the back of his neck, "Nothing," he replied, smiling as his mind toyed with a really brainless idea—*yeah, duck Denton Clark's security and his stupid secret doors and snatch it right out from under his nose.* Chuckling aloud, he abruptly sat up. "Hey…what if we really could?"

"Really could what?"

"Sneak in…jack it."

"Oh yeah, like it's just like, 'here I am…all yours! Help yourself.'"

"Maybe it is."

"Even if we snuck in, it's not a car!"

"I bet I could figure it…just computers, software—"

"Yeah, well, forget it. You won't be able to sneak in. He's not an idiot."

Ashlyn wasn't listening, and Autumn suddenly knew from his expression that he was having another brain wave.

"Now what?" she demanded with a sigh.

"Why steal, when we can buy."

"A submersible?"

"If I ask Ko for more treasure."

Autumn rolled her eyes in weary disbelief. "I thought they cost millions—"

"But if we can sell—"

"But we can't—"

They both fell quiet.

Then something occurred to Autumn. "What if we're wrong?"

"Wrong about what?"

"What if he's not our father?"

-15-

Flashback

Tax Man Jack Henry and his new hunting partners arrived at Denton Clark's house earlier that afternoon. Denton now realized that in spite of all the IRS audits and the hounding and snooping, the tax auditor wasn't seeking an arrest. These people weren't after his blood. All they wanted was his brain, and everything he owned.

Andy Lightstone laid down what he referred to as the house rules. For full cooperation and complete access to all the equipment, Denton would receive a get-out-of-jail-free-card. Furthermore, he could remain in the house, which from now on would be considered team property.

As Andy spoke, he probed through the contents of several drawers, helping himself to two of Denton's Cuban cigars. "The word 'no' henceforth disappears from your vocabulary. Maps, theories, photos, everything you own is now the property of the team! Work with us, the sun will still shine. But if you become even the slightest problem, if you tax me, pardon the pun, my good friend here will tax you, or do whatever it is they do to tax frauds. Understand?"

Lamely and obediently, Denton agreed to everything.

Andy poured four glasses of Scotch. "The capture of the phantom, may it bring us joy."

Denton held up his glass like the others, yet his mind drifted off to another place, another time.

How did it all happen?

It seemed to be another incarnation when he was once Jerry Miller, the entrepreneur, philanthropist, daredevil advocate of environmental rights, dangerously riding an outboard tender across the bow of a speeding Japanese whaler. It was a lifetime past when he had lain down in a human chain before an indiscriminate bulldozer in the Selvas des Amazonas. In those days, he was wild, spunky, wealthy, the loving husband of Julie, doting father of Ashlyn, recently blessed with the news of a baby girl on the way.

Surely, only a selfish, loveless man could have conceived of such a wretched idea, ditching his old life and family, solely to escape financial difficulties.

But Jerry's entropy began on a night when logic, rationale, and sanity took a slow departure from his mind. His memory was foggy; there were gaps in his recall, but he remembered being thirty-two miles offshore aboard an unlit dinghy with Raul, his partner and best friend, on a stakeout of DALCO's oil platform, attempting to snap damaging infrared shots of illegally discharged drill mud—toxic fluid from drill bits—contrary to the company's claim that they properly disposed of the waste. An hour before dawn, after they had just bagged the evidence, a forty-foot motorboat flew out of the night, heading their way.

Jerry flipped on the boat's spotlight, and desperately pulled the starter, while Raul blasted the emergency air horn.

The motorboat charged on, its roar deafening!

Jerry knew it was too late…then nothing.

When a small wave smacked him in the face, Jerry opened his eyes, realizing he must have lost consciousness. The taste of blood, fuel and saltwater was in his mouth, in his stomach. Floating on his back, feeling light-headed and nauseated, he spotted the motorboat circling, its fog light sweeping. The driver was on the radio, claiming to have found one decapitated body, but nothing else. Jerry's heart ached for Raul.

For a brief moment, the boat's light blinded him. Maybe the driver saw him or maybe, conveniently, not.

The light moved away, searching elsewhere.

Soon after, he must have blacked out again. When he opened his eyes, a view of the coastline was whizzing toward him, fierce wind and sea spray was slashing into his face, and his arms and chest were wedged tightly against *something*. Straining to keep his eyes open, he attempted to roll onto his side, and for a moment he thought he was wedged inside an armpit, which didn't make any sense at all.

Then he took a closer look...and screamed.

He next remembered ambling along the coast road with the sun rising beyond the cliffs. According to the motorist who offered him a ride, he was delirious, talking about murder, Raul, and a luminous two-armed fish-thing.

"Hallucinatory shock," his doctor said later. The delirium was brushed off as expected given such an accident. After receiving thirty-three stitches on his scalp, neck and shoulder, Jerry was released from hospital. It was the same day.

The incident was ruled an accident, which surprised no one who had listened to the boat driver's frantic emergency call. The investigators concluded that Jerry's dinghy had been purposely running without lights until the last second. No one seriously questioned his survival or how he made the thirty-two-mile trip to the mainland.

In the weeks and months following the accident, depression consumed Jerry. He was plagued by whispers, rushing water sounds. He lost weight, became reclusive. And then he made the decision of his life—to find *it*.

Perhaps others with far less exalting quests would have found themselves in arm-restraining jackets en route to the cuckoo's nest. But in Jerry's case, his new jacket was a diving suit.

He spent a king's fortune on hardware including several submersibles, remote vehicles, even a manned seabed workstation. He hired a team of renowned scientists and divers, and he combed the abyssal depths of the Pacific Ocean—while the debts piled up. He combed the ingressions and canyons of the benthic zone—while the debts soared.

He combed, he combed, he combed.

Two years into his search for redemption, bankruptcy parked itself at his front door. A fortune spent, a fortune lost, Uncle Sam still had to be paid.

It was the end of the search...the final curtain.

Only the *Seabed Phantom* was still firmly embedded in his soul.

-16-

Dad

IT WAS THURSDAY, AN OVERCAST morning with a cold wind. Cycling up the coast highway, Ashlyn pulled his beanie over his ears. In just two days he was supposed to board a plane to Inverness, where it would surely be a lot colder yet.

With time slipping away, Autumn had finally convinced him that acquiring more of Ko's treasure would only lead to another Boleshko. So they were back to plan one.

Denton Clark.

Both now agreed it was possible that Denton Clark was exactly who he appeared to be: a reclusive eccentric with a submersible and a mermaid fixation.

Up ahead, Ashlyn could see the windmill, motionless in the field of yellow gorse. He turned to his sister. "This is it. Are we sure we want to do this?"

Autumn put on a burst of speed. "Be strong."

Turning off the coast highway, they cycled past a green Oldsmobile Cutlass Supreme parked on the side of the dirt road. Ashlyn thought the driver, a large man in a dark suit and sunglasses, looked like a traveling salesman taking a rest.

Approaching the large gothic gate, Autumn felt a rush of nervous excitement, but Ashlyn felt uncomfortable. He slid off his bike, tentatively approaching the intercom. He hesitated. This was a bad idea.

"Press it!" Autumn's voice came as a command, full of authority, rather unlike her.

Sighing, Ashlyn gritted his teeth, and pressed the buzzer.

No answer. Good. Denton wasn't home.

"Press again," Autumn demanded. And Ashlyn was about to oblige when—

"I'm not interested!" Clark's voice crackled out of the speaker box.

"I don't care!" Ashlyn's rejoin was loud and angry. "For once in your life, do something right!" *Where did that come from?*

Inside the master video control room, Denton viewed Autumn and Ashlyn on eight different monitors, his hand passing over the glass on monitor 2, over Autumn's face. My God, she looked so much like Julie.

For once in your life, do something right.

They knew.

Denton tugged his hair. Oh how he hated himself for his charade, for his gutless behavior. Twelve years ago he'd made the decision in a snap—to siphon the reserve accounts, hide the hardware, manufacture a new identity—without even thinking about the consequences. The stark coldness of his ploy only began to dawn on him after his staged death had been enacted. He'd wanted to contact Julie but suspected the feds were watching. He'd decided to wait for the right time. The right time, huh! The months flew. The years peeled away. And now, here he was, broken, defeated, and caught anyway.

Denton pressed the speaker toggle embedded in the control desk. "Go away, for your own good. Go! Never come back here!" He made himself sound angry, fighting back the true depths of his emotions.

"Dad?" Autumn said with a tender determination, "We have to talk to you."

As Denton watched Ashlyn grab his sister by the arm, he quickly boosted the audio. Over the speaker came Ashlyn's incensed whisper: "What are you doing? Only what we agreed!"

His emotions in turmoil, Denton ran his shaking hands through his matted hair, his mind as confused as his children's outside. Then he lashed out, pounding the side of his fist on a red oblong relay in the control desk—the gate control.

And the gate swung open.

My God, what am I doing? were the words in Denton's mind but what he verbalized was, "Ashlyn, use the same door as before."

The teens pushed open the green door leading into the cluttered mermaid room. Denton was there, sitting behind the desk, wearing the same red silk robe as before. He stood up, slightly hunched. His eyes looked sad, tired. Autumn stared at him, unsure of her feelings. She wanted to smile as if that might break the ice, but held back, speechless. Ashlyn opened his mouth but also found he was without voice.

Finally, Denton spoke in a soft, pedestrian manner. "How are you?"

"Good," said Ashlyn, an automatic, mindless response.

"Fine," Autumn acknowledged, staying in line with big brother.

"And your mother?"

In unison, the teens turned to each other. It was an admission. So he was their father.

"She's okay?" Denton asked.

"She passed away six and a half weeks ago, sir," Ashlyn replied.

Denton didn't move, but the pain was evident, at least to Ashlyn. It was the subtle drooping of his facial features. "I'm so sorry. She was still so—"

"Thirty-four. A brain hemorrhage."

Watching the man, knowing him to be in pain, Ashlyn's pent-up anger started to dissolve, like a suddenly unclogged drain. He felt only pity for Denton Clark.

Denton sat down at the desk, opened a drawer, and pulled out a fresh bottle of whisky. "Things are difficult for me. But I think I can arrange a trust fund—"

"We didn't come here for money," Ashlyn retorted abrasively.

"Ashlyn, Autumn, I don't expect forgiveness." Denton lowered his eyes, held them on the whisky bottle. "I know I don't have the right to be your father." He took a swig, a short one.

Ashlyn took a step forward, laying his hand flat on the desk. "You're presumptuous. We're not here because we want a father. We're here basically for one reason. We need to borrow a submersible. I understand you have one."

Considering the nature of the request, Denton's reaction was infinitesimal. He placed the bottle on the table, and looked up at Ashlyn, almost nonplused.

"I'm sure you know why," Ashlyn added.

Denton rubbed his face. "Didn't we have this conversation before? I told you there's nothing there."

"Cut the crap! You gonna lie to the end? It's a moonfish, right! And you never ditched your family! You ugly son of a—"

Ashlyn would have continued, but Autumn kicked his leg and mouthed, "Only what we agreed!"

What they agreed was to be cordial and polite, no matter what—vinegar doesn't beget honey. Ashlyn hesitated, then dropped his animated arms, took a deep breath and began again, somewhat cordially. "We need some help. I think we deserve that. We have an opportunity to go...we've been invited somewhere—" his eyes settled on the large mermaid prosthetic. "If you must know, we've been invited somewhere with her."

"What?"

"With *her*. Only she doesn't look like that, except her tail...a bit."

That one floored Denton. Eyes, mouth, body posture, all simultaneously came alive.

Ashlyn wiped his perspiration soaked palms on his pants. "That's why we need your submersible."

"It's true!" Autumn added. "We were in a cave with her. She promised to show us places no human's ever seen."

"You talk to her?" Denton said in astonishment.

"I do...telepathically. Autumn can't but—"

"—But she held my hand and we prayed." Autumn interjected, smiling proudly.

Denton shook his head, seemingly disappointed. Perhaps jealousy, Ashlyn thought. They'd accomplished something he'd failed at, something that had ruined his entire life.

"I know you've spent years searching for her," Ashlyn said trying to sound somewhat compassionate. "She knows that, too. But she's afraid of you. She opened her heart to you, but you hunt her. You never communicate with her, even when she sends you tones. But I do communicate with her."

"Enough! I don't want to hear this!" Denton said in a stern voice, rising from the desk.

As Ashlyn's shoulders sagged in defeat, Autumn stepped forward. "Please," she pleaded. "She wants to teach us to see and hear without eyes and ears."

"Do you understand? No more!" Denton said with raised voice.

Ashlyn looked at his father with contempt. He knew it would come to this. "So you won't help?"

"You don't understand. It's too dangerous. There are people—" Denton paused, trying to piece together his thoughts. Then he said what he thought was best. "I want you to leave, and I don't want you coming up here ever again. If you've got any sense, you'll stay away from this thing, whatever it is you think you're playing with. Now go! Go! Get outta here!"

"You know something," Ashlyn scowled back, "I'm glad you weren't around. Boy, we were lucky. Mom always had great things to say about you, but you're nothing! Nothing but an old drunken coward!" He turned to his sister. "C'mon. The air's bad in here!"

At the door, Autumn wiped her eyes, and turned around for a last word. "She's not a thing. She's a being. A kind, intelligent being."

The door automatically closed behind her.

-17-

Unmanned

IN OCEANOGRAPHY THE ABYSS MEANS 'the deep', that area of the ocean beyond the realm of indigo blue, where sunlight never penetrates. It is black, icy cold, at least thirteen thousand one hundred feet below the surface, where plant life cannot survive and atmospheric pressures are deadly to all but a few species—those that can survive on chemosynthetic energy—the internal energy of the earth, as opposed to the photosynthetic energy of the sun.

For humans it's an alien, inhospitable place.

But there is another abyss—the bottomless pit kind. And as Denton Clark watched his children leave, this is where he found himself. He should have never allowed them in. His weakness had put them in danger. He'd failed them again.

Failures in his life seemed to be like his drinking: chronic.

Andy Lightstone had given him an ultimatum: Cooperate or the man they called Tax Man would turn his file over to the IRS. Fortunately, Lightstone's mob hadn't yet moved into his house; that would take them another twenty-four hours. But they were watching and, for all Denton knew, listening. He'd spotted one man watching with high-powered glasses from the fly bridge of a *'79 Skipjack* anchored a quarter of a mile offshore; and another pair of eyes was parked at the turnoff to the highway. Ashlyn and Autumn must have passed him on the way up to the house. No doubt he would still be there in his green Oldsmobile when they cycled back down.

Denton fell down onto his worn sofa. "Think!" he ordered himself as he tried to force the effects of the alcohol into submission so that he could think. Even if he wanted to, how could he get his son the submersible while his new partners were watching?

As he leaned back into the worn cushion, he squeezed his eyes shut, and his head spun into a black vortex of ideas and memories.

He saw Ashlyn as a newborn, he saw his wife, the submersible, *the being,* and Andy's men...Andy's men spying on him...watching his every move.

What could he do?

Oh, how deeply he despised himself. What a coward. Ashlyn was right. If only there was a way. He angrily tugged at his hair.

WHILE DENTON'S ANGUISHED MIND SOUGHT for an answer, Ashlyn and Autumn cycled silently along the coast road, also in search of an answer. Ko had said Ashlyn should trust his desire, and picture it. Was a submersible supposed to magically appear? As farfetched as this sounded, Ashlyn was willing to try anything.

He pictured in his mind a small deep-sea submersible, but within a few moments his logical mind was saying:

Be realistic! Think of a plausible way.

Plausible? Realistic? How did Ko expect him to find a submersible? If it was so easy, why didn't she acquire one for him?

Trust your desire.... Picture it.... Feel.... See....

Again, Ashlyn tried to sustain the image of a submersible. In his mind he saw it turning around, heading straight toward him. But then his mind drifted to other thoughts—Denton Clark, Grandma, the scumbag jeweler.

Ashlyn pulled to the side of the road, looking disgusted with himself. "Let's face it. It's a pipe dream. We'll never get a submersible. We're going to Inverness."

The last thing Autumn wanted to hear. "I believe Ko. She wouldn't have told you unless it was so."

Ashlyn's face sagged in defeat. "She even said it's not yet time. She's right. It's not."

Autumn set her bike on its kickstand. "What's not yet time?"

"Time. This, us, now! I mean, she didn't exactly say, but it's obvious. Our association. Maybe humans aren't evolved enough."

Autumn shook her head, defiantly refusing to accept this. "I'm not going to Inverness."

Ashlyn bowed his head. "I'm sorry."

DENTON CLARK HADN'T MOVED FROM that same place on the sofa since Ashlyn and Autumn left his house, as his mind spun with discombobulated thought, wrestling for a way to give Ashlyn his submersible; and just when he was about to surrender to the lower gods or more aptly the demons of the bottle, an obvious, truly salient idea dawned on him. He recalled that Ashlyn claimed to be telepathically communicating with *it*.

Opening his eyes, he leaned forward, a wily grin forming on his face. The eyes spying offshore wouldn't suspect foul play as long as he remained visible. So moving to his patio in plain view of their skipjack, he placed his notebook computer on his lap, and began typing a set of programming instructions for his submersible. Several times he looked up, even waved to the goons. Who knows, maybe they thought he was writing his memoirs.

That his plan was risky and reckless and financially imbecilic meant little to Denton. His submersible *Proteus II* had cost him a whopping forty-four million dollars, and there was a strong probability that it would crash or end up somewhere on the seabed never to be found. But, as crazy as it sounded, if the *being* found the submersible and transported it to a cave, Ashlyn might just be able to figure out its operating logistics.

Yes, the plan was ridiculous and idiotic, and maybe just crazy enough to work.

Sixteen feet below the house a series of tracks, conveyers and elevators called *autobahn* kicked into gear. *Proteus II,* a twenty-eight-foot-long exploring submersible, started moving slowly toward the launch catapult.

A red light began flashing.

The underground sea door opened allowing a surge of seawater to thunder into the ninety-foot-long tunnel.

Proteus II's engine revved. A second red light turned amber. A buzzer sounded. And as the catapult's tightly wound coils snapped open, the submersible shot forward, thirty-five-thousand pounds of thrust gunning her down the flooded tunnel. It took all of three seconds for her to fly out into the Pacific Ocean, inertia forcing her through the pounding surf.

She was on her way.

Denton thought he glimpsed the splash, a flare of sunlight on metal, but already the conning tower was submerged. He almost laughed, his first joyous moment in a long time. He stopped short of fully relaxing. Knowing his house was undoubtedly wired, Andy Lightstone would soon be looking for Ashlyn and Autumn. Whether any of them found his submersible or not, his kids were on a dangerous path.

Deciding to form a contingent plan, Denton typed a new set of instructions on his notebook, and he recorded a voice message, which he instantly remoted to the memory chip of his satellite phone, hidden in a small compartment under the guest bedroom closet. If necessary, sometime later, he'd transmit the message to a local journalist.

The task accomplished, Denton reformatted the notebook's hard drive, erasing every last byte of data that had ever existed on the system. Taking a long, deep sigh, he closed the lid, leaned back and tried to think back to better times.

TWENTY MINUTES AFTER ITS EJECTION, all nine of *Proteus'* battery-powered motors disengaged, and the suddenly inanimate alloy beast slowly sank toward the midnight seafloor.

Another beast, a curious looking *cuttlefish,* relative of the squid, took one look and fled. Other less cautious breeds swam up to investigate.

The deeper the submersible sank, the hues around it darkened. Bioluminescent jellyfish were suddenly in abundance. An eight-foot-long *ribbonfish* stayed close until a mushrooming cloud of sediment billowed up, and with what sounded like a roar to the locals, *Proteus II* hit the seafloor, vanishing inside the sediment cloud. Nearby, a giant squid shot off an ink plume and jet-propelled the hell out of there, hightailed by a red and gold *hatchetfish.*

Proteus II slowly reappeared.

One by one, the denizens of the deep returned to investigate, some attempting to take a bite, others merely to use it as refuge from predation.

With its nose burrowed in the sediment, the uninhabited Kevlar capsule sat motionless, apparently dead, pursed into its final resting place, perhaps for all time.

"WE CAN'T WAIT TILL THE last minute! If Grandma suspects she'll never let us out of her sight. If we're going to do this, we do it now!" Ashlyn yelled above the roar of a high-revving Mazda. They were cycling to Wayside, talking about escape, becoming runaways, which seemed their only viable option. Ashlyn hoped that some time in the not-too-distant future, maybe only a few days, a week, or a month, he'd become the man Ko though he could. But in the mean-time—

"Tonight, after supper, we're on our own!"

His plan was to live aboard *Indigo Empyrean*, using a small tent as a cabin. His entire purse was fourteen hundred, enough for food and sundries for a few months. Meanwhile, if Ko obtained a bounty of treasure, they might still be able to acquire a submersible and whiz away to her world.

Yes, living aboard *Indigo Empyrean* and sailing south was his game plan, although something about it was missing. Checking his watch, he decided to pull off the highway, hoping to get some quick advice from a friend.

They stopped in a tranquil gully. While Ashlyn sat on the ground and placed himself in a meditative trance, Autumn waited patiently, sitting for a while watching the ocean, then tiptoeing around on the dry undergrowth so as not to disturb his telepathic conversation. Stooping to check out some unusual looking stones, she noticed him grimacing, holding his side in obvious agony.

As with the other occasions, the pain ripped through him, no less than a seared poker spearing his organs. Jerking with a spasm, he dug his fingers into the dirt. As his irises swam back into his eye sockets, he felt Autumn's hands behind his neck, helping him sit up.

He must have passed out.

"I'm okay," he said, waving her off, knowing he was sounding like a stuck recording. "I'm okay." *How many times had he said that recently?* He began breathing steadily. "Hey, I guess I was just cy-cling too hard…got a stitch, that's all."

"You fainted. You were unconscious for at least five seconds. I don't think that's something to shrug off."

"I didn't faint. I took a breather." Rising to his feet with relative ease, he changed the subject. "Anyway, Houston, we have a prob-lem. I didn't reach her."

"How do you know you're not sick?" Autumn asked, eyeing him suspiciously.

Brushing the dirt off his pants, he answered, "Quit it, I'm fine. I wasn't able to connect. Maybe I'm doing something wrong."

"You sat there an hour, nodding your head, making expressions. I thought you were yapping on about your whole life."

Ashlyn shrugged. "Did I say I was a whiz at this telepathy stuff?"

IT WAS MID-AFTERNOON WHEN Ashlyn steered *Indigo Empyrean* around the breakwater. He reasoned he'd have better luck connecting if they were out at sea, somewhere closer to Ko's realm.

It was decently breezy, the sky overcast. They close-haul sailed, leaning out the boat, utilizing the conditions to muster maximum speed.

Ko was out there....

But the clock was running.

-18-

A machine

JEWELER PETRO BOLESHKO WAS LOCKING up his store for the day when Boomer and Carter arrived with the salvage papers. As Boomer explained that he'd filed the papers to guarantee a better financial return for the pendant, the veins in Boleshko's neck bulged and foam and venom exploded from his mouth in a tirade bordering on the demonic. In essence, Boomer and Carter were liars, pigs, cheats, excrement, and vile things born from mothers of the red light district.

Snatching the salvage title documents out of Boomer's hand, Boleshko held them tightly to his bosom, as if possession would somehow change the title.

"Actually, we made those copies for you," Carter interjected, stepping back to avoid a wad of the jeweler's mouth foam.

Poor Boleshko's face had now turned an unnatural rubicund. "You're a thief! You're a dead man!" He kept the insults flying as Boomer calmly spoke about the pendant and the arena for a gigantic sale. Finally, Boleshko fell silent, save for his breathless wheezing.

Resting a hand against the display counter, Boomer repeated what he'd already said several times. "We're not cutting you out. You make out, we make out, ten, twenty times what you thought, even fifty. I've seen it before. Shipwreck hype!" Boomer could see the tabulations in the jeweler's eyes. "No offense, Petro, but I know how you work; yah, you'd have sold for gem value."

Boleshko scratched his scalp in confusion. It's true that he'd been hoping to sell the pendant underground for close to its gem value. He'd have settled for a hundred thousand. But this was insane. "Why should I trust you?"

"Put it this way, you don't even have to part with the pendant till auction day. And when you see the size of your take—"

Carter was nodding and grinning. "I swear, pops. We'll be rolling in it! Rolexes and Rolls Bentleys here we come!"

Boomer grinned, quite relieved that the jeweler had settled down. "The press thinks we've discovered the Nuestra Senora De Begona. Reporters will be all over us, so this is very important—we're not going to lie! We just say very little. *Where is the ship?* You'll be briefed later. *How much treasure?* We smile. Big smile. Hey, if we do this right, the jackpot. First things first, the youngster you got the pendant from—"

"—Out of the picture." Boleshko quickly interjected. "He found it, he admitted it."

"We still need to speak to him. We have to be absolutely sure no one can spoil our party."

OVER AN HOUR HAD PASSED since Ashlyn and Autumn set sail. It was cold and gray, and both wished they had warmer sweaters.

"Nothing?" Autumn asked, blowing warm air on her hands.

Ashlyn shook his head. No sign or word from Ko. Even though he'd already made the decision to run away, he desperately wanted Ko's advice—at least he needed her to endorse his plan.

Ko was nowhere—

Just then Ashlyn felt the sensation linking him with his new friend—the sash of tingling heat running down his neck and shoulders.

"I hear you, Ashlyn. Know my heart is touching yours...touching it always."

"Ko!"

"I am here."

As Ashlyn prattled on about Inverness, Denton Clark, the benefits of more treasure, he suddenly realized Ko was talking about a machine she had discovered.

"I said I found it...your machine, the submersible."

"You found a submersible. That's crazy. How? It has to belong to someone."

"You did it, Ashlyn. It is yours. You created your desire and you have your submersible. On the sea floor."

Although her words resounded clearly in his mind, Ashlyn sat silently stupefied.

"Ashlyn? Do you hear me?"

"On the sea floor? You found it lying on the sea floor?"

"Yes."

Ashlyn tried to think about this logically. A submersible on the sea floor might be full of water. Perhaps it was the fire-destroyed submersible that had belonged to his father. Did that matter? Given that Ko was able to transform a miserable little rowboat into *Indigo Empyrean,* she could probably do the same with a submersible.

"I do not believe it is destroyed...my senses tell me that it is good."

Ko then relayed her news. Shortly after locating the submersible, a foreign presence had tracked her. Projectiles were fired and two machines chased her. She had purposely silenced her mind to prevent those human hunters from reading her signals, although she sensed them still close by. Being in the open sea was now a big risk.

Ashlyn found himself thinking of Denton Clark, the obvious perpetrator. At that moment all he wanted was to pummel the man's face, but Ko suggested he dismiss such thoughts for they were destructive. *"You are now the master of this machine, the submersible. This is what counts...this and nothing else, for now."*

Ko promised to bring the submersible to Ashlyn at sundown.

Ko was right, Ashlyn conceded. She should escape from the area immediately. As for the inert submersible on the seabed, the story of its abandonment was perhaps irrelevant. Could he really be the master of this submersible? This is what mattered.

The plan had suddenly been kicked up a notch.

Escape.

Escape with a real submersible—whether his desire had created it or not—at sundown! Ashlyn checked his watch.

Two hours.

"Well?" Autumn's voice snapped him out of the reverie. "Are you going to keep it a secret or are we in this together?"

AFTER JUMPING OFF *INDIGO EMPYREAN* at the marina, the teens tore through the streets of Wayside gathering supplies. At Walden Books, Ashlyn purchased *Benthic Zone,* a chronicle of seabed explorations and submersibles. Whizzing up and down aisles at the supermarket, they grabbed flashlight batteries, candles, matches, a plastic bucket, two giant bottles of soda, four bottles of water, a carton of energy bars, a box of cereal, Kit Kats, a loaf of raisin bread, and a jar of peanut butter, which was about all they could carry.

Back aboard *Indigo* with the sundries, Ashlyn noticed a mere inkling of amber sun gleaming through a gap in the swirling clouds. He estimated forty-five minutes, maybe an hour to nightfall.

There wasn't enough time to return home and be back before dark. He thought about that for a moment. They might never see Lucy or Grandma again.

Perhaps it was best this way.

Autumn froze in her tracks. "Leave me behind! I'm not going without Bigsey!"

He'd forgotten all about Bigsey. Chewing on his bottom lip, he grumbled, "It'll be too dark! We won't see the breakwater!"

"I mean it! Leave me behind!"

Ashlyn grimaced. She was right. They couldn't leave poor Bigsey behind. Somehow they'd have to navigate the breakwater in the dark.

Like racers, they cycled home in less than twenty minutes. Through the front door, they acted normally, wearing happy, smiling, albeit flushed, faces. "What's for supper?" Ashlyn called out breathlessly. Whatever it was, Lucy's menu flew in one ear, out the other.

Upstairs, supposedly to wash their hands, they stuffed their backpacks to the brim, and tossed them through the window followed by the bed comforters. They wrote a quick note—*Dear Grandma and Lucy, we're sorry, but Inverness just doesn't cut the mustard*—

Once back downstairs, they saw Grandma watching TV, Lucy busy in the kitchen batter-frying red snapper. "Fifteen minutes," Lucy yelled.

"We're ready," Ashlyn replied.

Outside in the yard, Autumn ran to get Bigsey while Ashlyn rummaged for some bungee cords and an old plank of plywood to use as a luggage platform.

What a sight: Two cycles, side-by-side linked with a wooden plank running saddle-to-saddle supporting luggage, comforters and caged rabbit atop—a tandem for a bunny. There wasn't any space for a human bottom on this contraption, so they scooted.

They hadn't gone far when a battered white Cadillac passed them and screeched to a halt. Ashlyn immediately recognized the driver as the slimy jeweler. Two men were accompanying him.

"Hey! I want to talk to you!" Boleshko yelled through his window.

"Faster!" Looking over his shoulder, Ashlyn saw the Cadillac making a U-turn. "The grass!" he shouted to his sister.

Getting his drift, Autumn nodded, and they made an abrupt left turn, veering off Shelby Street onto a grass embankment, coasting down to the street below, which ran parallel.

Unable to follow, the Caddy stayed abreast on Shelby Street. Boleshko stuck his head out the window. "Kids, kids, what's the hurry? Look at that, blankets, luggage. Where are you going?"

Ignoring him, the teens kept on scooting, furiously.

"It's me. Your jeweler," shouted Boleshko.

By now the teens had picked up some speed as they reached the hill leading to the highway. The trio in the car—Boomer and Carter being the other two—held a quick conference. The kids were obviously fleeing. "See I told you! They stole it!" proclaimed Boleshko. "Forget these little cretins."

"Keep going. I need to know where they got it." Boomer insisted.

After hearing a loud tire screech, Ashlyn looked back and saw the Caddy charging down the hill. It came dangerously close, but swerved out wide as it accelerated by, rocking them with a blast of hot engine air, and churning a cloud of oily smoke into the early evening.

Then, in a maniacal maneuver, Boleshko attempted to slide into a flashy TV style roadblock. But Boleshko wasn't a flashy stunt driver. Tires shrieking, wheels locked, the Caddie skidded the breadth of the road, bouncing up on the bank with a painful crunch before nose-diving into a shallow ditch. As gravel smoke belched up around the car, three car doors simultaneously opened.

Ashlyn and Autumn held their ground ten yards back, shaken by the jeweler's erratic behavior.

"I'm making a citizen's arrest!" Boleshko scowled.

Ashlyn waved dust out of his face. "Who? Yourself for that stunning piece of driving! You almost killed us, you maniac!"

"Are you resisting?" Boleshko pointed his finger, like it was a gun. The other two men fanned out.

Ashlyn was confused, nervous. Autumn, too. Arrest for what?

They must have looked like trapped rats, because the tall sandy-haired man stepped forward making calm-down motions with his hands. He whispered something to Boleshko, and then introduced himself.

"I am Boomer Larson, my good friend Carter Benwall. You guys aren't under arrest. But we have to talk to you…about the pendant."

Ashlyn glared at Boleshko, then beyond the men. The sky was bruising. Perhaps twenty or twenty-five minutes of daylight remained.

"Where did you get it?" Boomer asked.

"What difference? I don't have it! He does! Come on, Autumn."

The teens scooted forward a step or two. But Boomer quickly blocked their path. "I'm sorry. This is very important. The pendant has an interesting history. You stole it, yah?"

"Me? I'm not a thief! He is!" Ashlyn glared at Boleshko. "It was a present."

"Okay…if that's your story, from who?" Boomer insisted.

"What difference? We've done nothing wrong, and we're in a hurry."

"I appreciate that. A little more information and you can be on your way. From who? Who gave it to you?"

Ashlyn decided that a quick lie was in order. "If you must know my mother."

Boomer pulled his hair into a ponytail. "Nice try. Tell me the truth. We won't press charges. You got it from who? Where?"

"I don't believe this! It is the truth! Look, we're late for something, and you have no right to detain us!"

Boomer shook his head. "Number one: that scooter is illegal; two: you're running away; three: you're making it difficult for yourselves; four: you don't have to. I could go on."

Ashlyn turned to Autumn. She shrugged. Ashlyn thought back to the documents Boleshko had demanded earlier—proof of ownership papers. He didn't have any documents except for Boleshko's dumb receipt. Maybe certain types of jewelry had to be registered. But Ashlyn couldn't fathom why. Surely, the pendant could be an old family heirloom. He stumbled for a slam-dunk lie, something they'd have to believe, something no one could disprove. And suddenly, he had it. "I am telling the truth. It's been in our family ever since my dad found it."

"Yah, your dad found it!" Boomer said with a cockeyed grin.

Ashlyn's grin was bigger. "Yes sir. He was a famous deep-sea hunter. He found it in a shipwreck."

Boomer raised an eyebrow. He was suddenly genuinely interested in this yarn. "Famous? Tell me his name?"

"Jerry Miller. I am Ashlyn Miller."

Boomer absorbed Ashlyn's words. He thought about them, then he nodded. This made sense. This made perfect sense. "You're Jerry's son." He smiled. "And you're his daughter? You weren't even born."

-19-

Argonaut

KWINKIDINKS—IS WHAT AUTUMN USED to call them as a toddler, and sometimes still did. And boy was this ever a *kwinkidink*—a coincidence. When Ashlyn was a baby only a few months old, Boomer would often hold him in his arms, while mother Julie scurried for a diaper or a meal, and doting father pored over a marine chart prepared by Boomer. Those were the days when Boomer worked as Jerry Miller's team captain. He was also the closest person to Jerry beside Julie. The old memories came sweeping back. So the pendant really did belong to Ashlyn and Autumn—Jerry's kids. And they were running away from their wickedly strict grandmother.

"One, two, three…heave!" came Boomer's command. All hands were pushing on the Caddie's bumper.

"It's going!" shouted Carter. As the Caddie rolled back onto the blacktop, Boleshko threw himself behind the steering wheel and hit the brakes.

They all piled in, bikes in the trunk, Bigsey onto the front seat next to Autumn and Boomer, Ashlyn and Carter into the back.

"Where to?" Boomer asked, having agreed to give the kids a ride.

"The marina," Ashlyn replied, without explaining.

The Caddie took off with a groan and a roar, sounding like the exhaust pipe had been sheared off. Ashlyn grimaced. He hoped the car would last the seven-mile trip to the marina.

During the ride, Boomer tried his hand at avuncular advice, strongly advising the teens against running away. When that counsel fell on deaf ears, he suggested an alternative—his place for the night. Ashlyn kindly declined that offer too. "Come on, guys, it's a pad, clean, warm. Do you have something better?"

Smiling, Ashlyn dangled his slip key. "We're staying on a boat."

The conversation switched back to the pendant. "What else did your father leave you?" Boomer asked.

Ashlyn shrugged. "Debts."

"You never thought to sell the pendant before?"

Again Ashlyn shrugged.

"And there are no other pieces, no other treasure?"

"We don't have any."

"I see. Do you know where he found it?"

"Sorry guys…I was a baby."

"You understand it's unauthorized salvage. Your father didn't always go about things the right way."

No kidding, Ashlyn thought.

Boomer assured them that they were the rightful owners, if not the deed holders, and he'd carry out the sale and make sure they were compensated. Boomer's eyes locked onto Boleshko's in the rear view mirror.

The old man wheezed. It was getting dark. Boleshko switched on the headlights, as he turned into Via Marina and pulled up at the public parking gate. Boomer rested a hand on the door handle. "Are you sure about this? I don't have a palace, but we could make do. I've got blankets, food, marshmallows in the microwave."

"We're fine. Really," Ashlyn insisted.

As Boomer helped the teens out of the car, he handed Ashlyn his cell phone. "Hold onto this for me, will you? Memory one's my home number."

Ashlyn thanked him, promising to call the next day. They shook hands on it. Boomer watched as they scooted away on their odd contraption, slowly disappearing into the early evening.

Arriving at the harbor gangplank, Ashlyn estimated ten minutes or less remaining twilight. By the time they loaded the gear, most of that time was eaten.

Ashlyn hoisted *Indigo's* sail….

THE WAYSIDE MARINA IS A natural cove fortified by a man-made breakwater bracing it from the pounding Pacific. Ostensibly, the breakwater is a bulky rock at the harbor's entrance with passage to and fro through two narrow channels on either side. It's a straightforward ride for vessels with spotlights and engines. But *Indigo Empyrean* didn't have spotlights, only two flashlights and two little sails. The breakwater was already cloaked under a veil of darkness. Perhaps, there was a faint outline of the rock.

Perhaps imagined.

But they heard the waves pounding, a booming *I'll-tear-you-to-shreds WHOM-BOOF* coming from the ocean side. Across the channel on the bay, the sound was swishy. Regular surf. Ashlyn used the varying sounds as a navigational method.

Swish-shooosh.

WHOM-BOOOOOF!

Ocean side was closer. Much louder.

"We're gonna hit it!" Autumn screamed. "Tiller that way!" She pointed right—starboard. She could never remember which side was which.

"Where's the wind?" Ashlyn yelled in frustration, tugging at the jib. "Keep the flashlight on it!"

"Tiller! Tiller!" She cried again.

"Where's the wind?" He couldn't see the breakwater, but he could feel the current pushing them toward the bay side. At least he thought he could.

"Turn, Ashlyn!"

"We're okay. Hold on!"

WHOM-BOOF!

"We're gonna hit!"

"Hold on!"

"We're gonna hit! I can see it!" she screamed!

She was right. They were close…and suddenly Ashlyn could see the sloping man-placed rock less than ten feet away. It was almost in his face.

Wind!

WHOM-BOOF!

A stinging, salty spray shot over the rock into his face. Bigsey squealed. The boat rose up, way up, caught in a soaring swell. Autumn screamed again. Ashlyn yanked the main halyard. The sails filled, and the rock disappeared. They were past it. Out of the harbor.

The swells were two to three feet. Wind moderate. Cold. They turned the flashlights off so the coast guard wouldn't see them. In that regard, they'd been lucky slipping out of the harbor.

Somewhere ahead, somewhere in the blackness, was their meeting place, the Kingston sandbar, a marine sanctuary where dolphins lived. Hidden. Without lights, just bells. Ko would be there, safe from the humans hunting her.

LIKE A BLADE OF DEATH, the hull sliced through the water at thirty knots, the wide girth of its wake like a foamy river, its engines droning loud underwater, unsettling to most life forms.

She was searching…hunting.

The ship's name was *Argonaut*. Twenty-eight hundred tons of black painted metal, two hundred and forty feet long, two decks, two masts, two towers. Officially, she was in the business of seabed farming, mineral exploitation, biology exploitation, and salvage. Unofficially, she was the largest of three extraction vessels chartered by Andy Lightstone. Still bearing cannon, remnants from the old days as a whaler, she was equipped with laser-guided technology, state-of-the-art sonar transducer array mounted on the keel, space-age control room midships, and an A-frame on the stern supporting a 16-ton 3-man submersible named *Gracy*.

Since Tuesday she'd been cruising that spot thirteen miles offshore. The captain wondered if his prize would show itself again this chilly August night. Eager eyes watched the sonar. The crow's nest lookouts observed the liquid realm through infrared nightscopes, their fingers on siren buzzers. The crew slept with their boots on. *Gracy's* launch team was on standby, in perpetual readiness.

Eleven P.M. Nothing sighted so far.

"COAST GUARD?" AUTUMN WHISPERED. THE bright dot they'd been watching for ten minutes had developed a drone. Ashlyn couldn't tell whether it was a pleasure cruiser or a larger vessel, but its solitary light had now turned into many. Maybe it was a thousand yards away, maybe only five hundred.

Autumn gripped Ashlyn's arm tightly. *Indigo Empyrean* was running in total darkness, a mere speck on this vast black ocean. To a crow's nest lookout, even if they were spotted, they'd look like a piece of driftwood. Autumn reached for her flashlight. But Ashlyn stopped her, calmly but firmly shaking his head. His hand was on the tiller; their sails were filled.

It wasn't the coast guard. It was a party yacht, music and laughter trailing from it as it passed them several hundred yards north.

Back to peacefulness. The creak of the mast, the gentle plop of water, a wispy breeze generating marginal sail-flap. "You okay?" Ashlyn asked.

"Why shouldn't I be?"

"Just asking," he said.

Autumn reached into Bigsey's cage, tickling the little fluffy guy behind his ears. The rabbit jumped on her arm, as if to say, "C'mon, girlie, bust me outta this prison." Autumn abruptly sat up. "Did you hear that?"

Ashlyn raised his eyebrows. "What?"

"Over there. A bell."

"I don't think so...it's a gull."

"I know the difference between a gull and a bell," she insisted.

There it was again, distant but definitely an echoey clang. Then another. She was right. Ashlyn flicked on his flashlight, tillered to port and...bingo.

The Kingston Sandbar—and it was teaming with wildlife.

They slackened the sail, gliding by clanging buoys into the marine sanctuary. Their crisscrossing flashlight beams moved over seabirds, dolphins, sea lions—a lot of sea lions, who seemed to be resting peacefully, hardly perturbed by the boat's intrusion. But there was no sign of Ko. No submersible waiting for them on the sand bars.

Not knowing how long they'd have to wait, Ashlyn dropped the anchor. They both donned an extra sweater and another pair of socks, before wrapping themselves up in their bed comforters. Dinner was peanut butter sandwiches on raisin bread washed down with Sprite, Kit Kats for desert. Bigsey ate cereal. The cold damp sea air was already settling on the topside of their comforters. Autumn kept her flashlight lit under her comforter, cozy and reassuring for Bigsey. She stroked the little guy through his cage. "There, there. Everything's fine."

"THIS LOOKS INTERESTING," *ARGONAUT'S* SONAR man said to the first mate as he tabled his coffee mug. The sonar man was monitoring three *contacts* on his scope, fifteen degrees west, bearing five degrees. The *contacts* were ascending, now at fifty fathoms. He estimated their speed at fifteen knots. "Hey, is that three…or four?"

Correction: four *contacts*; now at twenty knots; ID scan: organic. The sonar man figured their dimensions as ten or twelve feet long.

The first mate squinted in confusion. "No, that's not four, it's three."

The sonar man slowly nodded.

Correction: three *contacts*, after all. Now they were on the surface. No, diving again. The sonar man smiled: "Dolphins, going for a midnight swim." He canceled magnification mode and took a greedy gulp from his coffee mug.

"WHAT'S THAT?" AUTUMN WHISPERED, AN element of alarm in her voice as a large gray fin brushed by the boat. There was a splash, and she saw the fin again. *Oh no,* she thought, *shark.* Ashlyn grabbed his flashlight, and in the narrow beam, the shark shot up out of the water. He jumped back in shock.

Autumn shrieked.

"What's wrong?" Ko said, running a hand over her rainbow colored plume. *"It's me…and my friends."*

Ashlyn now saw several gray fins circling the boat, and then, as if the fins belonged to *one mind*, three bottle-nosed dolphins stood on their flukes and moon walked backwards, whistling, clicking, and flapping their flippers.

Poor Bigsey quailed and peed.

Ko explained that the cetaceans were her helpers for the evening. Ashlyn's eyes roamed beyond Ko and her so called *friends* to the sand bar. "Where's the submersible?"

Ko rested a hand on the boat's rim. *"Ashlyn…I was thinking the cave…your cave. I will bring it there instead."*

Ashlyn shook his head. "Deadman's Bluff…but it's dark."

Ko's eyes metered puzzlement over the irrefutable observation. Indeed it was dark and would remain that way until the sun rose. The cave at Deadman's Bluff was her choice because the seas there were rough; it was concealed by sea stacks, and more importantly, because the hunters in their ship were close to their current location. But sensing Ashlyn's anxiety, she suddenly knew she had to escort the humans to the cave before retrieving the machine, even though this meant a double journey for her and the dolphins, a double risk.

Just as Ko comprehended Ashlyn's feelings, Ashlyn found him-self sensing Ko's disquieted state, as if her disappointment was his. Ko was pushing her luck, spending hour upon hour in the open sea. What sort of friend would condone such a prolonged stay in the area? He shook his head. "Sometimes I'm more capable than I realize. Go! Get outta here! See you at the cave!" He raised his thumb.

Emulating him, Ko raised her thumb, and then with her cetacean escorts by her side, dove out of sight.

As Ashlyn hoisted the anchor, he noticed patches of fine mist descending out of the sky. On the starboard side, a sliver of low-lying fog crept along as if it were a living entity. Soon sections of the coast's fairy lights began to disappear.

ASIDE FROM BEING A PARAGON of speed and agility able to outma-neuver whizzing projectiles, Ko was immensely strong. She could easily displace ten times her own water weight. But her speed and strength only became fully manifest when she allowed her internal chemical energy to *bloom,* when her anatomy coruscated and pulsed with great intensity. But these processes also generated a detectable electrical field, a sort of signature calling card that would allow the men in the ocean machines to identify and track her.

So right now, Ko wasn't *blooming.* As such, she was reduced to a mere fraction of her might, which is why she had solicited the aid of the cetaceans.

This was a dangerous swim for the dolphins. The submersible *Proteus II* was lying on the seabed eleven hundred feet below the surface, as deep as the dolphins had ever dived before. At this depth their bodies looked painfully distorted from deep-sea pressure.

Resting a hand on the submersible's quarter, Ko discovered that the machine was even heavier than she'd imagined.

In fact, the submersible was anomalously heavy. Typically, when a submersible lost its operating power, the automatic ballast would make the craft buoyant, so that it would float to the surface, per its safety design. But Denton Clark had reprogrammed the auto-matic ballast, so that when the engines switched off compressed air reversed out of the ballast tank. Now, sitting on the seafloor, *Proteus II* was almost as heavy as its dry dock weight, about eighteen thou-sand pounds.

After running a tattered trawler's net over the submersible's nose, conning tower and skids, Ko placed three rope ends into the dolphins' mouths. As the dolphins pulled, Ko pushed from amid-ships, and with some excessive tail fluke thrusting, *Proteus II* lifted out of the sediment, groaning as it skipjacked across a rocky groove, sending numerous bioluminescent critters hurriedly into hiding places.

In bursts, the submersible traveled as fast as it ever had on its own muscle—but only in bursts. By Ko's standards, they were moving at a sea horse's pace. The dolphins needed breathing time-outs, and every eight to ten minutes they had to surface for some nice cool oxygen. Of course Ko—the only non-mammal—didn't need to breathe above water, but she went along anyway, always in forma-tion, always in the middle, emulating the dolphins' movements, only using tail and dorsal for propulsion, with her arms firmly tucked in. And she consciously refrained from *blooming*.

It was a stimulating game for the dolphins and they were happy to oblige. After all, their *Iquana* relative was a worthy companion who, to some considerable degree, knew how to communicate with them.

Ko, the fourth dolphin.

AT 03.10 THE SHRILL CRY of a klaxon siren pierced the quiet on *Ar-gonaut's* decks. Lights sprang on. Bunks emptied. Bodies surged onto the main deck. Captain Mason, still wiping sleep from his eyes, was briefed. It was the *three-four contacts* mystery, which sonar now admitted was five *contacts*, including something inorganic—a tubu-lar object, possibly a submersible.

Captain Mason ordered a new course matching the *contacts'* position, heading one-four-zero degrees.

Full throttle.

KO AND THE THREE SEA mammals had just dived back down to the submersible now resting on a weedy slope sixty-five fathoms below the surface. They were only three miles from Deadman's Bluff but Ko sensed trouble. She arched her back and swooped into an upright position, breaking formation with the cetaceans for the first time that night. Gliding some twenty feet above the submersible she concen-trated on the signals. As Ko sought for answers, she could feel the change in her internal biochemistry. It was automatic. Unstoppable. Whenever there was imminent danger, her energy glands reactively charged. Her companions, who had followed her up, were suddenly no longer swimming in the darkness, but in brilliant chemosynthetic incandescence, nearly as bright as the midday sun.

"SIGNAL! ELECTROCHEMICAL!" SHOUTED THE keen sonar operator into his microphone.

A few seconds later, another shrill klaxon rang across *Argonaut's* decks. Following the alert, the orders came over the public address in rapid-fire succession. "E-team to the launch platform immediately! Stand clear…A-frame is moving! One quarter ahead!"

Argonaut's decks were alive with frenetic activity, men shouting, running, manning spotlights, and gearing up *Gracy,* the ship's squat, yellow and white submersible.

"Lower her away!"

Supported by an A-frame, they swung *Gracy* out over the bow, while seventy feet below the submersible, on the ocean's surface, swirls of fog silently slithered and coalesced.

KO'S COMMUNICATION WITH THE DOLPHINS was curt, precise: *"Trouble comes! Trouble comes here! Wants to kill!"*

The dolphins were nervous. Ko sensed their panic, but couldn't understand why they swam around her instead of fleeing. And why was she picking up an inordinate degree of echolocation? With a gentle push on the elder dolphin's dorsal, Ko told her companions, *"Go! Go now!"*

But the cetacean trio immediately boxed Ko back into the formation. The game with the *fast one* wasn't really a game—the dolphins had known that all along. They were her shields, and they would remain at her side until the end.

Ko was mystified.

What were all the other signals? It seemed like hundreds of…dolphin signals?

AT THE KINGSTON SANDBAR, HOME of hundreds of marine animals, as the gray of dawn approached and smoky ribbons swirled off the ocean like steam from hot soup, the early morning peacefulness was shattered. Not by a blast from a poacher's shotgun, or the crunching of a boat running aground, but by an eruption of clicking, clacking and splashing—the clamor of three hundred bottlenose dolphins throwing themselves into the water. The cry had been heard—

Bottlenoses in trouble! Bottlenoses in trouble!

Ten, fifteen abreast, like soldiers in lines, the dolphins cannon-balled away from the sandbar, triggering a discordant chain reaction—sea lions roared, an army of waterfowl, honking and cawing, took to the skies, the bells on the buoys clanged wildly, and the triggers on their motion detectors set off warning sirens heard all the way on the mainland.

THE SUBMERSIBLE *GRACY* WAS LOWERED down through the foggy carpet into the Pacific, unmanned at this juncture for safety reasons. Her crew went down next, lowered on ropes. After sliding into claustrophobic positions inside *Gracy's* sphere, the surface technicians, donned in bright orange suits, spun the hatch closed. Through a bullhorn came more instructions. Wire mesh lines were released. And in a froth of black bubbles, engines at full throttle, *Gracy* took off after the catch of a lifetime.

KO FELT THAT HER ONLY option was to break formation, to use her speed. Although no denizen of the ocean could catch her, and none would normally want to, the human shooting devices were marvels of velocity, and they did want to catch her.

"Go!" She urged her loyal friends again. Then, with a thrust of her tail fluke, a sweep from both arms, she shot forward, stranding *Proteus II* and her helpers.

She was gone, but the dolphins could feel the power of her jet stream, the awesome current left in her wake.

Ko was in full *bloom*, a brilliant luminous speeding bullet. She went west, straight out, heading for deep water. Then she flew down, rocketing through the *thermocline*—the transitional temperature layer—into frigid water, down toward the seafloor. Her dorsal fin, tail fluke, arms, all producing maximum thrust, immaculate equipoise. The seabed zoomed up on her. She still hurtled down, till the last second...and turned. Seamlessly. No deceleration. A flip of her tail fluke and she was speeding horizontally a foot above the seafloor, giving spangles of light to this black cosmos. She went up and over the sharp edges of the ridge, down into the chasm, following its craggy contours, doing ninety, one hundred miles an hour. Then up out of it, across the rocky plain, into the kelp field, zigzagging over the hill and into the canyon, where she really flew. One hundred and thirty miles an hour.

They were tracking her—she could feel their sonar. Once before when this had happened, she felt some sort of light beam moments before being struck. She had almost dodged it, but a piece of the projectile nicked her. If she felt the light beam again, she would dive into the sediment, bury herself.

She turned again, sped up, crossed over another ridge, and down into the slope. Now feeling relaxed, she continued at her fastest speed, heading into very deep water. Her angst was gone. It wasn't a feeling—it was a lack of feeling. Their sensors had lost her.

ASHLYN CHASTISED HIMSELF FOR NOT bringing along a compass. This stupid oversight was now costing them dearly. For the best part of an hour, they had been cloaked in ominous gray swirls. The fog had blanked out all of the fairy lights on the coast, and they had no way of knowing where Deadman's Bluff was. For their wellbeing, Ashlyn decided to drop the anchor and wait.

He had just pulled his comforter back over his shoulders when a pain gnawed into his lower side, evoking from him a gurgling gasp, almost as if it was his last.

This time, the pain quickly subsided. But it left him feeling dizzy and nauseated. As he leaned over the boat's side, his head spinning, a cold sweat ran down his neck. He felt the strength draining out of his body. He tried to vomit, unsuccessfully. Lying down in a fetal position, not knowing what would happen next, he thought that he might even die.

He felt Autumn caressing his head. "Drink this, it's 7up."

"I need to sleep." He reached for her hand affectionately. "You too." He felt Autumn tucking the comforter in around him, and then he closed his eyes, hungry for rest.

Nothing in particular awoke Autumn, but as she wiped sleep from her eyes, she shrieked, snapping Ashlyn awake with a start. "What's wrong—?" He stopped in mid-sentence as his eyes settled on the massive bow of a ship looming out of the fog.

Ashlyn feverishly hoisted the anchor, yanked the mainsail halyard. Every few seconds the ship seemed to double its size. They could hear voices, commotion, maybe the sound of a winch. The ship slowly vanished, consumed by the fog, but Ashlyn knew it was still bearing down on them.

Indigo's sails were now hoisted…but where was the wind?

"What's that?" Autumn yelled, even more terror in her voice, as a low growl crept up from somewhere behind her. Within seconds the growl was a deafening roar.

"On the floor!" Ashlyn shouted. "Get down on the floor!"

Bursting through the fog, he saw it—a mass of diffused light flying right over their heads, its scream thunderous, its reptilian breath as forceful as a hurricane force wind. In that instant, *Indigo Empyrean* spun. Grabbing hold of the tiller, Ashlyn felt spindrift lashing into his face. He saw the mast looping circles, creaking torturously. He prayed that it would hold. Autumn screamed. Bigsey peed.

Then it was beyond them. *Indigo* stabilized. Now they could tell that the roar was nothing but a familiar rotary sound.

Briefly, the patchy cloud lifted, and they saw a coast guard *Sikorsky H-60 Jayhawk* helo hovering above the ship, which was anchored, not bearing down on them, after all. Nerves, or maybe the fog, had made them think that it was.

The helo's powerful searchlight probed the ship, named *Argonaut*, from bow to stern. Through a megaphone, the coast guard was saying something about broken rules, fines.

In actuality, the ship was two miles offshore, against regulations; it had invaded a dolphin playground, against regulations; the captain had launched an unauthorized undersea exploration inside marine-protected waters, a heavy fine. They were told to remain anchored. A coast guard vessel was en route. They would be boarded. Possibly impounded.

Yes, *Argonaut* was in big trouble.

AND SO WAS THE SUBMERSIBLE *Gracy* in big trouble. At a depth of eighteen-hundred feet, *Gracy's* crew had been ready to fire the laser-guided pellet, designed to subdue the target and to implant a homing device into its skin, crust, blubber, whatever the *thing* had.

But then *something* hit them broadside.

The submersible's skin shuddered. Nervous eyes inside the spherical cabin jumped to the closed circuit video screen. But all they saw was stardust and the sub's spotlights tapering into black infinity. Oceanologist/copilot Wade Coleman stuck his nose against the side viewport. He saw nothing. Really nothing. The spotlights shot fore and aft, not sideways.

THUD....

The lights in the cabin blinked as a metallic vibration scurried along the curved walls of the tiny sphere. Coleman kept his nose on the viewport, his rubbernecked face straining to see something.

Something large and gray streaked across the video monitor. Then there it was, dead ahead through the portal. The pilot veered right...into another charging bull!

Reversing full throttle, a fin brushed the front viewport. Copilot Coleman shouted, "Get outta here!"

THUMP! THUD!

The submersible creaked.

THUMP! THUMP!

The lights flickered. The sonar went haywire with *blips, spikes,* and then an aberrant vertical line. The weapon's man shrieked, "Surface! Surface!"

THUMP! CRACK!

The pilot stared at an empty, meaningless orange screen. "Array's gone!" The array was a group of underwater antennae providing the sub with sonar and global positioning capabilities. "We're running blind."

All hell now broke loose. Thump after thump, the submersible was hit from the fore, aft, above, below. There were fins everywhere...bottlenose faces everywhere.

The submersible tilted over, way over. "Surface! Climb! Climb!" Coleman yelled at the pilot.

"I'm trying." The pilot shouted back, ramming the joystick full throttle reverse. His eyes stared at the leak detector light, praying it would hold. At these depths, even a tiny leak could have the lethality of a laser beam slicing through meat, bone—or a human being.

The cetaceans were smart. Not merely clever performers for a freebie fish lunch, they knew the humans inside the machine were running scared. Their job was done. No need to inflict further terror.

It took *Gracy* fifteen agonizing minutes to reach the surface. And when her conning tower finally strutted out of the liquid realm, the crew was greeted by yet another surprise, an unexpected shaft of dazzling brilliance from the Jayhawk H-60's spotlight.

FORTUNATELY, THE COAST GUARD HADN'T spotted *Indigo Empyrean.* But daylight was around the corner, and just when Ashlyn was telling Autumn his concerns, they started to move faster....

Faster and faster and faster.

Ko.

-20-

Daylight

KENNETH FORBES, AUTHOR OF THE book *Benthic Zone* wrote: "...submersibles are petite, extremely compact, often spherically-shaped capsules."

In the cave at Deadman's Bluff this submersible didn't look at all petite. *Proteus II* was bulbous. Sitting mostly out of the water, white with a blue funnel tower, also called conning tower, rising five feet above her deck, the submersible was twenty-eight feet long including skids, eight wide, and weighed eighteen tons. Wading tentatively around the sub, Ashlyn felt overwhelmed. He was now supposed to be the master of it, a real-life practicing submariner. "Well, it looks good. Yeah...doesn't seem to be any...any major damage on the outside."

Autumn rolled her eyes. The expert's solid evaluation!

Ko, in deeper water at the back of the cave, was edgy, and made no effort to hide that fact—a moody side of her personality that Ashlyn had not seen until now.

With a boost up from Autumn, Ashlyn landed on the deck, which ran about a foot-and-a-half-wide around the conning tower. He looked for signs of damage, running his hands over the metal, but noticing nothing even remotely suspect. Carefully examining the hatch wheel, he could feel Ko's penetrating eyes upon him. "I know you think we should just jump in and boogie off, but you're going to have to bear with me. This isn't one, two, three." He retorted defensively. "Patience the doctor said."

Ko's translucent dorsal seemed to quiver when Ashlyn glanced at her. She gave him a subtle nod of encouragement, but Ashlyn could still feel her disappointment. Maybe she didn't understand the importance of preparation. "This is the first time I've ever seen one of these, and all I've got is this book! And this *thing* is stuck!" He whined, referring to the hatch wheel that wouldn't budge.

"You have all the knowledge you need. You must trust yourself...truly trust yourself. Feel it...and know it."

Ashlyn grunted as he struggled with the hatch wheel. "Sure, Ko." He couldn't help thinking that her pep talk was all well and good for her world, but in the human world, the submersible was a precision instrument. Yes, he'd bragged before that it was just computers and stuff, but now that it was here in front of him, big and bulbous, the real deal, he couldn't even spin the hatch wheel. And what about its safety? Yeah, its safety. Why did it sink in the first place? Had Ko stopped to think about that? And even if he couldn't find anything to suggest an abnormality, did that prove anything? Who was he to know? Perhaps, this submersible was a death trap, just plain unsafe!

"Then we'll make it safe," Ko responded.

"Exactly! How about starting with this stuck, er, wait, what's this?" He noticed a small metal lever on the underside of the hatch wheel. He was able to leverage it upward. Once again gripping the wheel, it now spun with relative ease. With a self-effacing grin, he turned to Autumn, "Well, how was I to know?"

Opening the hatch, he stared down into the belly of the sphere, as it was called in tech-talk. Dark. Smelled musty. He turned back to Autumn. "Flashlight."

She reached up and placed the light in his expectant palm.

"Book."

His young assistant handed him the *Benthic Zone* book. Ashlyn tucked it into his waistband. "Courage," he called out, hoping to borrow a dose from somewhere.

Autumn smiled. "You've got all you need." She was beginning to sound like Ko, the eternal optimist.

Ashlyn climbed through the small opening, then down ten metal rungs into the submersible's sphere. He expected to find at least some water on the floor, but his feet landed on coarse flooring, almost like rubber, bone dry. He took a quick stock of his surrounds, now understanding that the author of *Benthic Zone* was, after all, correct.

It was extremely compact.

It was like an airplane cockpit with switches and dials all around, three bucket seats—pilot, two crew—three aircraft-sized acrylic viewports—port, starboard and bottom. He assumed aft view was supplied by video. He decided he'd read up about that later.

There was no sign of any water damage.

Easing himself into the pilot's seat, he gripped the navigation joystick, which was rather fat and housed several toggles and sliding switches. "Fairly new, this baby I reckon."

"Baby?"

"Figure of speech, Ko."

"Figure of speech?"

"It's how we…forget it, no baby here. If I can just find the autopilot we'll be flying." He laughed. "Get it, autopilot, then I wouldn't need to figure…. Forget that too."

Some of the gadgetry seemed a bit familiar—speedometer, bathometer, sonar, radar. Then there was *Echo Sounder*, which seemed fairly obvious. Many switches and dials were repetitive: Battery meter one through nine; thrusters one through six; external lights, etc. There were analogue instruments and gauges and several digital screens.

Batteries first, he told himself, running a hand through his hair. He then proceeded to toggle all nine of the battery switches. If they caused a result, he didn't know it for there was nothing revealing to observe or hear. He flipped the *aux. power* switch, assuming aux stood for *auxiliary*.

Still nothing.

He pressed the faces on the digital windows to see if they were pressure sensitive, but they didn't appear to be. They remained black. Flipping switch after switch, dial after dial, he sighed with frustration over his inability to cause a reaction.

Perhaps he needed a key, he decided. But then where was the keyhole? He winced at the thought of being a failure in Ko's eyes. But he was stumped. The machine was one-hundred-percent dead.

He stuck his nose back into the book, hoping to find some wonderful words of advice, but he had a sudden urge to look up.

He blinked, focusing on a small black switch amongst the dozens of toggles and dials on the sphere's ceiling, a switch that didn't bear an identification label. He reached up, and flipped it.

BEEP!

The main screen began to glow with a greenish hue. "That's what I'm talking about!"

There was another beep, and on the screen there appeared an image of a whale's body with *Proteus II's* logo superimposed. Then the logo faded into a common digital icon: 06:12.

"Well done, Einstein." Ashlyn wiped his brow as he took another studious look at the hardware. Retrying the *aux. power* switch, the sphere's interior lights flickered on, bathing him in an orangey-red light while music filled the sphere—oldies rock. A blinking LED revealed the audio system on the floor next to the pilot's chair. He switched channels. Lousy reception. He hit the CD button—Enrique Iglesias. He turned the system off.

Tapping a finger on the control surface, he pondered on a very important question: How long had it been submerged?

"Trust...you are the master of the machine."

"Right," he mumbled to himself. I am the master of—" He heard footsteps. "I'm coming in."

"Watch your step," he yelled back. He heard his sister muttering about the stale, stinky air.

Climbing down the ladder, Autumn whistled in awe. "Cool... way cool."

"Yes it is. Sit in that seat, and don't touch!"

"Aye-aye, sir," she replied mockingly, plunking herself down on one of hard plastic seats angled behind Ashlyn. "So, are you the master of it yet?"

"Yes, I am the sub master. Master Sub to you."

Autumn shook her head, barely stifling a facetious giggle.

Another digital window beeped, and its black face sprang to life with information.

BAT. SYS. A-OKAY

"Battery system. Great. Ninety percent." Ashlyn was about to engage one of the thrusters, when a buzzer startled him.

Loud repetitive bursts.

Autumn's eyes widened. "What's happening?" she cried.

Ashlyn's focus moved back to the digital clock icon as it dissolved into a red flashing warning sign:

TURN ON CARBON DIOXIDE SCRUBBER

Without even looking for it, he located the scrubber switch on the top row of switches, as if he'd flipped that switch a thousand times before. Perhaps he'd simply noticed it earlier.

The air fan began whirring, and the alarm ceased. "The air should get better now."

Autumn sat back in her chair. "Not bad. Was that in the book?"

Ashlyn shrugged. Maybe it was.

"Okay, now what?" she asked.

With his sister's eyes upon him, Ashlyn felt a sense of pride. He was, after all, the captain. Hoping to put on a show, he pushed one of the thruster controls forward, expecting to get at least some reaction or feedback, an engine sound, a computer message.

But nothing happened.

He engaged all the thrusters. Still nothing. He sighed. Where was the ignition for this thing?

"How much air do we have?" Autumn inquired.

"Shush, I'm concentrating."

"No, I have an idea. How much air do we have?"

Tapping the meter to make sure it wasn't stuck, Ashlyn answered, "Twenty-two hours. Why?"

"Twenty-two hours? That's a lot, isn't it? Why don't we just close the lid and let Ko take us?"

Ashlyn held up the book. "Won't work, air pressure. The engines have to be running to provide proper air pressure."

Ashlyn's statement was correct. While it was true that Ko could push them substantially faster than the engines, they'd never get there alive—wherever there was—without automatic pressure regulation. So closing the "lid" and hoping for the best wasn't the answer.

Putting his nose back into the book, Ashlyn skimmed pages, searching for information on ignition systems.

"Go within, Ashlyn. Go within...reach for the answers."

Ashlyn felt an element of desperation in Ko's voice, and he sensed her becoming even more restless. Admittedly, she'd had one hell of a night, and she was fatigued, but so was he. He closed the book, wondering if he could truly become the master of this vessel. Looking rather fraught, he absentmindedly—perhaps absentmindedly—tapped the digital clock, which abruptly beeped…and the time icon disappeared.

So *it was* pressure sensitive after all.

The window displayed a new message.

SYS. CHECK | YES | | NO |

OR MASTER POWER | YES | | |

At last, computer language Ashlyn understood. The on-board computer was volunteering to check out the submersible. Ashlyn pressed **YES** for Sys. Check, and the computer began reading and calibrating the different systems.

ARRAY SENSOR....... OKAY
ARRAY LIGHTS........ OKAY
BAROMETER........... OKAY
BATHOMETER .... OKAY

Outside the cave, the tide was ebbing, the sun boring its head through the fog. Ko swam back and forth lethargically as if bereft of energy, while aboard the submersible, Autumn rubbed her temples, trying to ease the pain of a headache. She hadn't spoken for a while, daring not to interrupt her brother who was now virtually seeing double out of bloodshot eyes. "Backup oxygen, two lithium hydroxide canisters, manual valves, four pressure compensators, alarm triggered…one atmosphere normal."

The screen's image returned to the master power prompt.

SYS. CHECK | YES | | NO |

OR MASTER POWER | YES | | |

Ashlyn wiped his eyes, trying to reason why the submersible was in perfect working order, primed with full oxygen and 98% battery capacity. Should he care how the submersible came to him? Surely, the only thing that mattered was that it was his to use. Captain Ashlyn Miller, the submersible's master.

I guess so, he told himself, pressing the screen's affirmative for master power. A new prompt flashed:

MASTER POWER IN FIFTEEN SECONDS

Another alarm buzzer sounded.

WARNING... THRUSTERS NOT SUBMERGED

MASTER POWER   YES   ☐

Ashlyn quickly vacated his seat to go topside, Autumn following with a barrage of questions.

What he saw up there did not hearten his spirits.

The tide was out! The submersible was sitting in less than four feet of water, a full five shy of the aft thrusters, and from the cave entrance to the surf there existed a bank of dry sand, six or seven feet wide.

Ashlyn sighed. "We're stuck here for a while. You okay, Ko?"

"Yes...okay," Ko answered.

But her tired glow epitomized their combined effervescence.

In hindsight, bringing the submersible into the cave had been a poor decision. With the dolphins long gone, *Proteus II* had become a prisoner of the cave.

As Ko submerged herself in the shallow water, Ashlyn sat on the deck, his shoulders stooped, his weary face looking older than his fourteen years. His mastery of the sub would have to be postponed.

Until the tide came back in.

-21-

Interrogation

THAT HIS HOUSE HAD BEEN bugged was no surprise to Denton Clark, yet it still churned his stomach. With his head buzzing from an obvious hangover, he sat on one of his dining room chairs surrounded by hostility—Andy Lightstone and six obedient goons.

Smoking a fat Dominican cigar, Andy paced the room. "Your kids were here, with important information, yet you didn't *think* you needed to inform us?"

Denton reached for the whisky bottle on the coffee table, placed there as an incentive. But with a lightning-quick stride, one of the goons tossed it to Andy.

Andy swirled the bottle and spat out a flake of tobacco. "I've got kids too. I'm not without compassion. I understand. If it was me, hell, you bet I'd have invited them in. But why didn't you inform us? Don't you think that's a breach of trust?"

Denton's eyes met Andy's, but he said nothing.

Andy moved in closer, to within a few feet of Denton's face, his lips pursed in frustration. "When did their association with the *being* begin?"

Denton frowned. He rubbed his aching forehead. "It's not an association...they're just kids."

"When?" Andy repeated.

"I... I don't think they said."

"Of course, they didn't." Andy took a puff of his fat cigar. "Tax evasion, falsifying your own death, what do you think? Ten to fifteen?" He turned to Tax Man.

"At least."

Denton swayed. "I'm an alcoholic. If I don't get a drink—"

Andy swirled the whisky around the bottle teasingly. "Talk to me, you can drink all you want. We'll even run out, get you a truck load." He tossed the bottle to Ed Lazerath, and made a fist, cracking several finger joints. "What did your kids tell you the other times they were up here? What kind of conversation?"

"Other times? Er, yeah, you know, nothing much. Small talk. I think they said, 'Er…so you're our dad.' I hadn't seen them in—" Denton silenced himself as Andy, shaking his head no, snapped two fingers.

One of his goons hit a button on the tape recorder. It played back, Denton saying: "Didn't we have this conversation before? I told you there's nothing down there." Ashlyn's angry voice followed: "Cut the crap! You gonna lie to the end?"

Andy signaled the goon, stop tape. Menacingly, Andy pulled up a chair and sat a foot out of Denton's face. "What did your kids tell you?"

Denton shook his head. "Nothing."

Andy drew his arm back and forcefully backhanded Denton's face, leaving behind a set of dark pink knuckle-prints. "The other conversation with your kids?"

"I…I told them I didn't want them to get hurt. I told them not to go there." Despite his swimming head, Denton realized his slip up.

Andy twirled his cigar ominously. "Go where?"

"The lighthouse," Denton replied without hesitation, a decent cover-up job.

"The lighthouse?"

"Uh-huh. That's where they thought they saw it…but it was orange cup coral."

"That's where they met…the being…the kind, intelligent being, at the lighthouse?"

Denton was silent. Andy signaled the goon, play tape. The tape continued: Ashlyn's voice, calmer: "…we've been invited somewhere…if you must know, we've been invited somewhere with her." Denton's voice, astounded: "What?" Ashlyn's voice: "Only she doesn't look like that, except her tail…a bit." Another pause. Ashlyn continuing: "That's why we need your submersible." Then Autumn's voice: "It's true! We were in a cave with her. She promised to show us places no human's ever seen."

Andy raised his hand. The goon stopped the tape. "Cave. Doesn't say anything about a lighthouse. So is it a cave and a light-house? Or just a cave?"

Denton appeared confused.

"What cave is it, Jerry?"

"I don't know."

"Sure you do."

"No, no. Don't think they said."

"And you'd tell me if they did?"

Denton lowered his eyes.

"Life's a bitch, isn't it, Jerry?"

-22-

The sphere

HUNGRY, NERVOUS, AND HEADACHY, Ashlyn sat on the sand at the cave entrance watching the tide, thinking about Lucy and Grandma. They must have been angry when he and Autumn didn't show up for dinner. But at some point during the evening their anger would have fused into worry, then Lucy would have searched their room and found the note, which he'd left in the bathroom, and they would have called the police. By now they must be worried sick. Causing them grief didn't sit well with Ashlyn. Being dishonest didn't sit well with Ashlyn. If only his grandmother had been more open to—

Autumn interrupted his thoughts by dropping her 7up bottle on the sand, "Stop worrying. I'm starving; let's order pizza."

He looked up at her, befuddled.

"Why not? Use Boomer's phone."

"A pizza?" Glancing up at the ridge-top, he began to weigh the risk. Yet, the more he thought about it, the more reasonable it seemed that Autumn had a point. The cops would be inclined to do little, if anything, especially when told about Inverness. He could already smell the melted cheese and pepperoni. It was a dangerous idea but....

Twenty minutes later, Ashlyn rendezvoused with the pizza deliveryman on the road above the bluff.

Piping hot, with extra cheese, it turned out to be a great idea. Ko even tried a slice, not much to her liking.

Afterward, they rested on the warm sand at the cave's entrance.

It was seventy degrees, slightly overcast. With his belly full, sleep was not difficult for Ashlyn. But he awoke with sand grits slapping him in his face. The air was humid. Clouds were swirling ominously across the sky, some turning into dark thunderheads.

As another strong gust swept across the beach, he jumped to his feet. "Autumn! Up! Up! We're in for some bad weather."

After loading the gear into the submersible, Ashlyn secured an extra rope onto *Indigo Empyrean.* He hoped she'd survive the storm. Venturing back to the beach to check if they'd forgotten anything, he spotted five moving dots way down the beach. He charged back into the cave.

"Maybe swimmers," Autumn said with a strained grunt, as she pushed on the submersible's side. They were all pushing—Ashlyn and Autumn from amidships, Ko at the stern where the water was seven or eight feet deep.

"In this weather?" Ashlyn shook his head. "It's a search party."

The submersible wouldn't budge.

CAPTAIN JAMES SWIFT AND HIS crew of four marched headlong into the erratic wind, their hands shielding their faces from seething sand pellets. An overhead gull screeched, no less than a warning. Feeling raindrops, the first brief spattering, the men looked to their leader. Turn back? But James concluded there was still time, and he motioned with a wave of his arm: forward.

KO'S WEBBED HANDS SLIPPED OFF the submersible's stern....
"Ashlyn!" She was *blooming*, giving off her brightest luminescence of the day. Ashlyn knew that her only option was to strand them. But instead of answering with words of encouragement, his eyes rested on *Indigo Empyrean.*

A plan.

CAPTAIN SWIFT AND HIS MEN were just turning into the cave's entrance when something big and blindingly bright flew at them. Like animals frozen in a truck's headlights, they stood breathless and stunned. In an eye-blink, *it* screamed by them, slicing air, kicking back a rush of kinetic wind that lingered on their faces. Whirling as one, they watched in awe as it charged across the waves—now they could tell that it was a bright blue sailboat without a mast, seemingly jet-propelled by a white glowing energy from under its hull. In a measure it was a speck, then gone.

And they were still speechless.

AUTUMN AND BIGSEY WERE ALONE aboard *Indigo Empyrean*, hiding underneath the sail that Ashlyn had quickly jury-rigged into a boat cover. Through a gap in the canvas, Autumn watched lightning flaring the blackened sky. She felt a nervous twang. Not for herself, for she had complete trust in Ko, who was whizzing her across the ocean. Her nerves were for Ashlyn.

ASHLYN DARED NOT BREATHE, DARED not move, dared not peek down to see what the men below him were doing. His cranny was tiny, an oblique cavity half-filled with stale, pungent seawater, its base covered with barnacles and algae as slippery as ice. But it was well-camouflaged eight feet above the cave floor. Ko had located the crevice using her sonar. She had lifted him up into it, and made sure he was deep enough inside to avoid being seen. There, in the poky hole, his head skewed to the right, his back hunched and knees half-submerged, he held onto a nub of slippery rock. For sure, if he let go he would water-bomb down. Adding to his discomfort, his right leg was beginning to cramp. He bit his lip to distract himself. He tried to concentrate on the banter of the men below. They were elated at finding the submersible. While one of them chatted away on a cell phone, another stumbled into the sinkhole. There was an immediate explosion of profanity and the cave rang with laughter.

Ashlyn's leg kept twinging. Again, he bit his lip, perhaps too hard. He tasted blood. Knowing the cramping would get worse unless he moved that leg, he settled on wiggling his toes, curling them back as far as he could. The pain seemed to lessen.

"Give me a hand," one of them said below.

Ashlyn heard the man being boosted up onto *Proteus II's* deck, the hatch opening, then hard-soled shoes on the metal rungs stepping down into the hull.

Moments later, the man's voice called out: "Clear...there's a pizza here...cold...ummm still good. Luggage, blankets, sundries, that's it."

Ashlyn heard him climbing back up the metal rungs, being helped down off the deck.

One of them said, "Tide's coming in."

Come on tide, Ashlyn thought. Come on storm! The onslaught

would be their eviction orders. The leg twinge jolted him, a stabbing pain below his knee. Suppressing a groan, he waited for the cramp to depart.

But it was stubborn. It stabbed! It gnawed! If he didn't shift position, move his leg just a—

I can do it, he convinced himself. Grimacing, he dared to reposition the leg just a—

It slipped.

It slammed out of the slippery crevice with the speed of a flying karate chop!

Ashlyn felt himself sliding, his unbalanced weight pulling him down. He dug his fingernails into the slimy nub, clawing at algae, scraping into something sandy underneath it, his lopsided weight still trying to drag him down into the drink.

But he hung on.

He knew he'd made lots of noise and his left leg was now a dangling pointer, begging those below to look up and say, "Oh look, a leg; I wonder what's at the other end?"

He could hear them talking again…talking about the tide, the submersible. Good. They hadn't heard him. As long as they didn't probe with their flashlights, he could maintain that weird position, his leg hanging there like some sort of weird, biological stalactite.

Ashlyn's jaw hardened as the conversation below turned shocking. They started talking about catching it.

The men weren't searching for two runaways. They were hunting Ko!

Ashlyn's blood chilled for a second time in as many seconds. One of them, obviously the leader, said, "Who's gonna stay?" It wasn't a popular question. The leader slapped one of them on the back. "You?"

"Tide's coming in…all the way," came the reply.

Another interjected, "Skipper, another hour, two, this cave's gonna be completely under."

"So what? Get in the submersible, kick back, wait."

"For what?" The man replied, "Rigor mortis?"

Lightning blanched the cave. In that nanosecond, Ashlyn was as visible and vulnerable as a target pigeon. Still, heads were pointed the other way.

They were moving to the cave's entrance where the water was still very shallow. Their voices became distant, but still discernable.

No one wanted to stay back. The skipper told them that a technician in a Zodiac dinghy was on the way with a homing device; after attaching the bug to the submersible, the volunteer would leave on the dinghy.

Ashlyn was furious. So this was their plan to capture Ko. Cautiously lowering his head, his hands clawing even tighter against the slippery nub, he saw that the water was beginning to cover the submersible's two lower aft thrusters.

A rolling thunderclap boomed, and for several seconds Ashlyn couldn't hear the men. When the thunder ebbed, he realized he had missed the turning point of their conversation—two men had agreed to wait for the technician and the Zodiac. Almost immediately, the others departed. The two remaining—bouncer types in suits and ties, one with a hooked nose, the other wearing an evil goatee—talked about the easy thousand bucks they'd just made.

Lightning scorched the sky.

Ashlyn counted…eight seconds…nine…come on thunder… eleven, twelve….

KABOOOM.

Letting go of the nub, he slipped out of his hiding place and straight-legged down into the water. His splash was muted in the thunderclap. When he surfaced, silently treading water, he was glad to hear them talking about baseball.

So far so good, Ashlyn. They didn't hear you.

He swam to *Proteus II's* aft. Lifting a foot onto the left lower thruster, he hauled himself out of the water, freezing in place as rivulets gushed out of his water-bloated clothes, splashing down obnoxiously loud. His heart was thumping almost as loud as the splashes.

More baseball chat.

Move, Ashlyn, right.

He was sliding on his belly up to the deck when a long burst of lightning floodlit the cave, stopping him dead in his tracks, horribly exposed.

"It's gonna be a dandy," remarked Evil Goatee.

"Nah," said Hooknose, "You're not from 'round here, are ya?"

Lying flat on the deck, Ashlyn dared not move, or breathe. Just then the rain started washing down in sheets. Knowing where their eyes would be, he rose to his feet, swung around to the far side of the conning tower, and leapfrogged straight into the hatch. He missed the first few steps, and landed hard on the fourth rung. His chest slammed forward, thudding against the metal. It hurt, and it was noisy.

Hooknose thought he heard something. There again, there were storm sounds, cave sounds, echoing sloshes. He probed his flashlight over the submersible, around the cave walls.

"Something?" asked Goatee.

"Nah."

They got back to baseball.

Ashlyn grabbed the hatch handle—heavy due to his lack of leverage in the funnel—yanked it, heaved it, pulled it up and over him, down shut.

CLANG!

It so happened to be in serendipitous sync with a gnarly thunderclap. He flicked on his flashlight, and hastily spun the wheel. He knew it wasn't truly locked and wouldn't be until it became pressure-locked. That wouldn't happen until he fired up the thrusters.

How did he know this? Was it knowledge from the book or were these facts flying out of the universe?

Master of the sub?

He wedged the flashlight into one of the hatch's wheel spokes. Jam-locked was better than nothing.

Standing motionless, he waited to hear the men scurrying after him. But all he heard was the chatter of his own teeth and the constant, quick-firing pings of water dripping down into the sphere. The clamor of the storm, the waves, the men, were gone.

He climbed down the metal ladder into the sphere where it was dark but not black due to some collateral seepage from his wedged flashlight. After using both comforters to smother the front and side telltale viewports, he whipped off his wet clothes, pulled on a pair of long pants, a shirt, then another shirt and a sweater. He still shivered. Not from cold. He slipped into the pilot seat, activated master power.

MASTER POWER IN FIFTEEN SECONDS

He then mobilized the oxygen flow, turned on the scrubber, flipped switches for the external cameras and video monitor. His hands skipped over the camera light switches and the outside lights.

Mustn't turn on the outside lights—

He made a mental note!

The video monitor bloomed into an image. At first, nothing discernible, but as Ashlyn twisted the camera joystick—bingo! Hooknose and Evil Goatee were scrambling to higher ground.

Good. Stay away from my submersible.

Ashlyn went over his options. There was enough depth at the stern to fire up the thrusters, not enough to propel the submersible out of the cave. However, once the thrusters were engaged, the pressure-lock would activate, and Hooknose and Goatee wouldn't be able to spin the hatch. On the down side, firing up the thrusters would alert the men. He decided it was better to wait...until the first sign of danger. Yes, why alert the enemy early and give them time to block off the entrance, or shoot.

Shoot? They'd shoot, anyway. He felt panic rising in his bones. Wait a minute, the submersible is made out of Kevlar and titanium. Bullet proof.

Was that also from the book?

He couldn't recall, but he knew it was true.

But what if they shot at the thrusters? What if the thrusters didn't work? He hadn't been able to test them. The computer said they were functional, but he'd never fired them up because of insufficient water depth. Maybe they'd cough and splutter like an old car engine, or take forever to come up to speed—

Shut up, Ashlyn. Stay calm.

Right. Of course, they'd work. Probably instantly. They had to. Come on tide.

The digital clock blinked 18:01.

DENTON CLARK OVERHEARD HIS CAPTORS whispering how they'd found his submersible at Deadman's Bluff, and that his kids had managed to shake off the hunting party, but they were about to fall into a carefully laid trap.

Restraining the vomit that wanted to rise in his throat, Denton reminded himself that he wasn't helpless. Even though Andy Lightstone thought he'd stripped him of his right to choose and think, stripped away his equipment, computers, his maps and drawings—and even though Andy's goons were all over his house, following him to the bathroom, back to his study, disallowing him access to the yard, basement and balcony, denying him use of the phone, fax and computer— Denton was still able to talk, even though they often told him to shut up, and as long as he could talk, he had some control.

Denton's house was very large and contained many rooms. Andy's men thought they had checked them all. Of course they couldn't check the ones that didn't seem to exist, including one closet-sized secret space containing an array of voice-activated equipment that responded only to Denton's voice. The benefit of this was enormous. Denton could make a surreptitious phone call and dispatch a prerecorded message, like the one he'd recorded yesterday, without anyone knowing or suspecting.

Denton cleared his throat before speaking in a loud, precise voice. "I'd like to make a phone call."

One of the two goons watching him scowled. "Quiet you!"

"Phone connect to channel seven TV now, please." Denton asked.

"I said quiet!"

Denton shrugged his shoulders. "Go on, play!"

"What?" The goon snarled, as if he'd been told to go on and play. Putting down his paperback, the goon stood up and took a few menacing paces when Denton started muttering and complaining. The goon was six-three, three hundred pounds, but his buddy told him to relax. "He's in la la land."

Meanwhile, in the secret room, Denton's voice had already triggered an untraceable sat.link telephone call to channel seven's news reporter, Dan Shockbottom.

At that very moment the reporter was already listening to the edited recording.

Ten minutes later, Denton activated another phone call, this one to the US navy depot in Port Oxford.

-23-

Prank Call

WITH A MINI-AUDIOCASSETTE IN his hand, television newsman Dan Shockbottom departed from Video Edit #3 at Channel 7, and marched along the narrow corridor to his office.

Just pushing forty-five, with thick wavy brown hair, graying sideburns and a silky baritone voice, Shockbottom had an airy, striking face, almost too pretty for a man. While some thought he was blessed for having such physical attributes, Dan suspected that his looks actually impinged on his career—too pretty for the big scoop. Television journalism was always a tough gig, he knew that, but after being fired from D.C. and recently Los Angeles, he was back to square one, back to where he'd been born and raised, the land of the boondocks, where the chance of breaking a major story was about as remote as Easter Island.

Entering his office, Shockbottom dropped the audiocassette into his top drawer, and kicked back with his feet on the desk. He had to admit that this prank call, now one of a stash of recorded tapes in his drawer, was really bizarre.

The tape had begun: "Mister Shockbottom, you are listening to a recording, which I made purely in the case of the worst case scenario. The lives of two teenagers are at stake! This is an emergency! Repeat…emergency! This is not a prank call! The lives of Ashlyn and Autumn Miller, are in grave danger…."

Shockbottom had listened to the entire tape, several times. Still thinking about the tape, even though it was probably a prank, he figured it was worth a couple of quick calls. His agenda for that night was light, his only other assignment being weather duty—showing the folks on the coast what they already knew: That it was blustery and wet.

With elbows lethargically slumped on his desk, Shockbottom dialed the sheriff's office, and asked in a noticeably humdrum manner if there were any recent missing teens.

When Deputy Thomas P. Sunshine mentioned one file, the case of Ashlyn and Autumn Miller, Shockbottom quickly slid his legs off the desk. "Ashlyn and Autumn Miller?"

"Why?" Deputy Sheriff Thomas P. Sunshine asked. "Low priority case. Runaways. You got something says it's not?"

"Uh…no. Nothing…I'll let you know."

"Wait up, I need to know—"

Dan had already hung up. Maybe he had a scoop for the night after all.

DEPUTY SHERIFF THOMAS P. SUNSHINE'S nose twitched. It always twitched when he smelled trouble. Pulling out his handkerchief, the deputy pondered a course of action regarding the case of Ashlyn and Autumn Miller. He thought about radioing the sheriff, but he didn't really have anything substantial to report. But the itch in his nose was proof that something smelled foul.

It was just yesterday that the sheriff had placed the Millers' file into the low-priority cabinet for runaways. Come morning, it was back on the sheriff's desk for reexamination after some old folks claimed to have seen three men in a white Cadillac abducting the teens. Then, only twenty minutes ago, Sheriff Wiggins had received another panicked call from the kids' grandmother, although at first it didn't seem to be related to the file. She said three U.S. naval officers were demanding to search her house.

So, as the sheriff headed on out to calm down that situation, wouldn't you know it, in comes the call from the slippery, keeping-secrets-to-himself reporter.

Deputy Sheriff Thomas P. Sunshine sure felt that twitch in his nose. He wondered how the press was always one step ahead of everyone else. Maybe they committed all the crimes, just so they'd have something to report.

18:35….

At the cave entrance there was still no sign of the technician, no sign of the Zodiac, and Andy's men were under siege. Standing on the slippery rock pedestal, angry seawater tugging at their knees, hard slicing rain chilling them to the bone, the stench of fear had now taken hold of their senses. They thought about wading around the cave wall to the beach, but that would place them ten feet further out to sea. Even if they timed their sprint to elude those fierce swampers, they'd still be in five or six feet of water. If they stumbled, fell, if they didn't move like lightning, they could be sacked and gashed to shreds on the rocks. But even if they did move like lightning, the brutal undercurrent could still snare them, pull them down like rag dolls, down to the bottom on a one-way ride to hell.

The men decided that the beach wasn't an option.

The alternative was the submersible.

Kicking off their shoes, they stepped off the rock pedestal into chest-deep water.

Ashlyn watched them on his monitor. The moment they made their move, his nervous but competent hands went to work. He'd spent the afternoon reading, comparing, flipping switches, and for the last half hour he'd performed numerous dress rehearsals. More importantly, he had Ko's words of encouragement firmly embedded in his heart and mind.

"I am the master of this submersible. My knowledge comes from the universe. I am the master of this submersible...Oh boy!"

Working with cool but urgent efficiency, Ashlyn pressed the start-up command. There was no sound, but the master window displayed the affirmative message:

READY

His hands flew to the buoyancy disk—ballast control—a three-inch circular disk in the control surface. He turned the positioning arrow from seabed to surface. *More buoyancy.* That's right, he reassured himself.

"I am master of the submersible. I and this submersible are one."

There were three gears for power distribution, each controlled by sliding knobs in pegged tracks on the joystick, eight positions—one eighth power to full power. Without a second guess, Ashlyn slid the forward thruster up three pegs, aft and amidships one peg. Hovering mode.

There was a brief metallic clank, a slight shuddering of the boat. Again, without hesitation, Ashlyn gently tilted the joystick forward. Instantly, he heard the whir of turbines.

"Yes!" They worked!

FIRST TO REACH THE STERN, Evil Goatee was attempting to hoist himself up on the deck when he heard a clanking sound. He paused, looking about in bewilderment. Then he felt something pushing against his foot. *What the hell's that?* he moronically wondered.

Hooknose, a slower swimmer, was patiently waiting for Evil Goatee to board the submersible, but when he saw the turbines spinning, his face twisted in panic. He jostled for a foothold on the skids. He even tried to grab a piece of a thruster. "Move!" he yelled at his half-witted partner.

Only now, Goatee realized what was happening. In desperation, he tried to hoist a leg up on the deck....

ASHLYN WIPED HIS BROW. WITH the turbines engaged, he watched the control surface springing to life.

HATCH LOCKING NOW

Lights blinked, dials illuminated, digital windows flashed red numbers: temperature, barometric pressure, speed—zero. The master window displayed a new message:

SPHERE PRESSURE

ONE ATMOSPHERE...NORMAL

For a fleeting moment, Ashlyn hesitated, feeling the first signs of a panic attack.

"You are the master of this submersible."

Echo sounder.

Whether it was Ko or his own inner voice, the solution was abruptly in his mind. He immediately flipped on *Echo Sounder*, a navigational tool that diagrams graphical representations of the terrain. His next thought was—

"Camera...lights."

Turning on the aft camera and lights, the screen turned a light gray. Perhaps an amorphous form existed within the image…maybe rocks, sand, the cave floor. Ashlyn tilted the camera joystick up, way up…he saw the engine's jet stream, foamy green churning water, the underside view of the aft thrusters, bubbles…foam…legs.

Human legs, trying to get aboard…

Ashlyn anxiously increased throttle to the halfway mark.

EVEN THOUGH THE TURBINES WERE kicking back a fierce jet stream, Goatee tried to force his way through the pressure. Briefly, his face lit up. He felt that he was winning. Then— "Nooooo," he shrieked as his right leg flew backward, catapulted like a leaf in a raging rapid.

Without thinking, his partner tried to grab that flying leg. Given the circumstance, Hooknose would have grabbed at anything. But the speeding leg smacked him squarely in the face, sending him whizzing backward…backward like a sardine in a Jacuzzi jet…backward with his hooked nose flattened.

And Goatee still held on, desperately resisting eviction. What was he thinking? Even a half-wit would have let go. But Evil Goatee, stupid man, hung on, his face twisted, his body aching to be released. And as he fought to draw his legs onto the submersible's deck, the pitch of the turbines wound up an extra few notches.

Another sardine flew.

THE SUBMERSIBLE SHUDDERED, GROANED. THE aft rose two feet above the cave floor, then bounced back down, hard, bouncing Ashlyn off his seat, just as an alarm buzzer sounded. Now really panicking, he glanced at the message:

WARNING… NOT FULLY SUBMERGED

The alarm kept buzzing. The submersible skittered right and jolted against the cave wall, again throwing him. The aft lifted up. The alarm was relentless. Painful vibrations scurried under his feet. Something crunched and rattled.

Ashlyn's heart pounded. For a moment, his brain felt like mush. *Not deep enough. Not deep enough!*

He immediately reduced throttle, but had the smarts to keep feeding ballast. As the submersible settled back on the cave floor, the vibrations subsided.

Ashlyn's heart was still racing but the submersible was now

purring at a safe idle.

Yes, he wanted to escape from the cave at that very instant, knowledgeable master or not. But the water in the cave was still too shallow to fully float the submersible.

He was frustrated, anxious, worried to death about Autumn, knowing she was alone aboard *Indigo*, cold, afraid, unable to communicate with Ko, and night was falling fast.

A sudden dreadful thought made him gasp. *The men?*

He quickly searched with the camera but could only see dark, murky water. Thinking he must have killed them, he felt sick to his stomach. It wasn't his intention. He only wanted the men off his boat. He saw himself being hustled into a packed courtroom, an interminable fusillade of camera flashes—Ashlyn Miller, two counts of murder.

No, it was an accident.

Urgently, he pulled the comforters off the viewports and pushed his eyes against the glass.

A pair of legs swam by.

Thank God—at least one of them was alive. Ashlyn's hopes spiraled for the other.

Just then an aberrant face three times its normal size jumped at him, the eyes wide open, livid. It was Hooknose, magnified by the glass. Shaking his fist, trickles of blood swam out of his nostrils and a bubble left his mouth as he worded a curse.

Goatee's legs then reappeared, also magnified, as he stepped onto Hooknose's shoulders. Goatee then disappeared above the viewport.

From up top, there was a metallic thud.

The enemy had boarded his submersible.

Swallowing hard, Ashlyn stared at the sonar bank. Positioned next to *Echo Sounder*, there was a device called *Sound Probe*, an underwater ear for gathering subsea sounds such as whales' songs.

Immediately switching on the system, he recoiled as an annoying burst of static shot out of the speaker box. He adjusted the fine tuner. More static...less...nothing...muffled water...then several thuds, maybe footsteps, followed by a dulled thunderclap, and a voice, "Gah-ahhh-ahhhh!"

Ashlyn's jittery eyes darted to the roof as he heard a louder thud, then a clear voice rumbled out of the speaker: "Thanks."

"Don't thank me you son-of-a-ff—*[Thunderclap]*—look what

you did to my fu—*[Thunderclap]*—nose!"

Ashlyn shuddered. Both men were on deck. His eyes followed their movements without the use of *Sound Probe*. They were trying to spin the hatch, their heavy-handed efforts vibrating through the hull. "Open up, motherff—" Ashlyn lowered the volume but he still heard the man stomping, yelling, pounding, threatening to rip him apart if he didn't open up.

The wheel held steadfast.

After ten minutes the men were enervated. Their fury fused into frustration. Then they fell silent.

Time passed.

One of the men said he was so cold he couldn't feel his hands, his toes, or any part of his body. There was a brief stony silence. The other said he was even colder. One of them kicked the conning tower, and Ashlyn heard the "arghhh…fahhhh!"

Ashlyn couldn't help but grin. The man could obviously *feel* his feet. They fell silent again.

Ashlyn doused lights, video cameras, monitors, to save battery. Maybe there was an alternating current generator aboard to restore battery levels but he wasn't sure.

Once again he had to wait. This had been the flow of the day. His mind drifted to Autumn and Ko.

AUTUMN TRIED TO BE PATIENT but every second seemed like twenty. Her skin was sallow, her lips purple, and her teeth wouldn't stop chattering. The horizontally placed sail was a fine shelter against rain, but it transpired to be useless against swamping waves, and Autumn had been swamped, swamped, and swamped again. At one time, *Indigo Empyrean* had almost sunk.

Of course, Ko would never allow it to really sink.

The night now owned the ocean. The dark didn't really bother Autumn, but the waiting, the silence, the uncertainty was challenging. She felt pangs for her brother. Where was he? Was he okay? Was he coming? Or had he been discovered? She had no answers for her time with Ko was chillingly silent. She dreamed of being in the safety of her warm bed in Grandma's house with Bigsey in the back yard. She almost didn't care about escape anymore. She almost didn't care about anything anymore.

A light glowed. So what, after all this time…a light?

She closed her eyes because it was a harsh light. For a moment she drifted off, but she thought about that light. What was it doing there, stupid light? She forced her eyelids open to see if she'd imagined it.

Wait a minute…it was Ko's light! Ko was doing her thing, *luminescing…blooming*. Wasn't it dangerous for her? The men could track her.

Ko caressed Autumn's face, lovingly, but this time Ko's touch astounded Autumn. The touch was temperate, and Autumn immediately felt warm energy cascading into her body. Her seasickness instantly vanished. Her teeth stopped chattering. She was suddenly feeling wonderfully warm, as toasty warm as if she were standing by a roaring campfire. As her shoulders became relaxed, her angst for Ashlyn faded away. Feeling cozy, almost perfect, she took a long, deep, relaxing breath, and she closed her eyes and fell into the most wonderful, dreamy, warm sleep.

A wave soared up over *Indigo Empyrean's* bow, instantly filling the small sailboat with water. For a few moments the vessel stayed afloat, its freeboard level with the ocean's surface as if suspended by magic or perhaps a failure to comprehend its ability to sink.

But then, as if the magic faded, the small sailboat slid down beneath the waves.

Two thousand yards to the west, a brightly pulsing shooting star skimmed the ocean's surface, as Ko vanished into the blackness of the stormy night.

-24-

First Reaction

AT ABOUT THE TIME THAT *Indigo Empyrean* sank eight miles west of Deadman's Bluff, Sheriff Wiggins arrived at the address on Dunbar where the Miller teens had been staying with their grandmother. What he found was a full-fledged hullabaloo with seven, not three, navy folks in the street arguing over rights and orders and something that Ashlyn and Autumn might have done.

While the feisty grandma rightly so hadn't let any of the men into her house, the ruckus had drawn most of the neighbors into the street, and rumors were flying hard like the rain. One rumor in particular chilled the hearts of nearly all—that the kids had accidentally stumbled upon a top-secret government testing facility, and three men in a white Cadillac had abducted Ashlyn and Autumn, presumably to silence them.

Adding pepper to this ruckus, the sheriff looked up to see the arrival of the local TV newsman Dan Shockbottom and his cameraman.

"Is this an abduction, sheriff?" Shockbottom asked, propping the microphone under the sheriff's chin.

While the sheriff had to admit that the low-priority investigation might be something more than a runaway case, he was guarded with the larger implication. "Can't rule that in or out, not just yet. The investigation is ongoing," he replied.

When Shockbottom asked about the navy connection, the sheriff was genuinely nonplused.

A crafty smile began to form on Dan Shockbottoms's face, despite   the "no comments," he later received from the navy personnel.

UNDER STORMY SKIES, WHILE THE police, believing the teens might truly have been abducted, began searching the neighborhood, and while several other reporters arrived at the cul-de-sac, Dan Shockbottom sat in his news minivan, editing together a bizarre, nevertheless real, scoop to be aired that night.

20:40....

Ashlyn must have dozed because he opened his eyes with a start and a feeling that something had bumped. The men up top were yelling, icy cries for help mixed with colorful expletives.

The submersible abruptly skidded right.

Proteus II was afloat!

This was it! Time to leave the cave!

The men?

Ashlyn flipped on the exterior lights, cameras, trimmed the ballast to settle the submersible—for their sake. Why did he care what happened to the men? Would they care about him?

No, but he wasn't about to stoop to their level. He would wait for their Zodiac dinghy, but keep the sub on standby for an immediate getaway.

The forward floodlights blasted a cloudy path filled with sparkling detritus. He couldn't see the cave walls. He needed to see them to safely clear the cave. *Echo Sounder* began to draw something. He cocked his head, trying to understand what the abstract lines, curves and shady areas on the screen represented. Maybe this picture made sense to someone, a trained eye, but not him.

Pressing his face against the front viewport, he cast his eyes upward. Greenish-black water.

A new type of sound whined out of *Sound Probe's* monitor—a low growl. The men up top started jumping up and down, shouting joyously.

Zodiac.

Throwing himself back into the pilot's seat, Ashlyn spun the dial to reduce ballast, again floating the submersible. Flicking all three gears up two notches, he tilted down the navigation joystick and pulled it back for reverse thrust.

"I am the master of you, submersible."

Yes you are, the machine seemed to reply as the pitch of the turbines steadily increased.

The submersible's nose rose up. Through the bottom viewport, Ashlyn saw the entrance bombarded by his floodlights, and the Zodiac racing toward the cave.

BANG!

The collision into the rear wall almost bounced him out of his chair. As the sphere groaned, he quickly neutralized the thrusters. "No problem. I did that on purpose."

Sure you did.

Aft thrusters, port, starboard—he rammed both throttles forward, full power.

Runway time! Go!

The nose tilted back down; the visual of the cave entrance through the portal disappeared.

Go! Go! Full power! Go!

The hull seemed to shiver. Vibrations, scurrying under his feet, rattled the instruments, his chair, the entire sphere. But just when he was about to really panic, the whir of the turbines softened. The sub was at full throttle, max power, but it was suddenly...quiet. He wasn't positive but he thought he felt a driving motion.

BOOMPH!

The thud into the ground bounced him up in his seat, and instantly the pitch of the turbines turned loud—vibration and hum amplified by the ground.

Not enough buoyancy. Get her up. Up! More buoyancy! Ballast trim up!

"Oh Jesus. Now what?"

He was blind. He couldn't see anything through the portals. For a fleeting moment, his common sense, his logical mind, thought about crash prevention, about withdrawing at that instant, switching everything off. But a surge of spine-tingling energy rifled through his body.

Be brave! Go! Go! Go!

The nose surged and shook with a pounding that surely meant one thing—

Waves? Was he out of the cave?

Now he could see frothy bubbles and foam through the viewports. A clump of seaweed whipped by the starboard viewport.

Yes, he was out of the cave.

He felt the sub sliding left, then a harsh jolt pushed the submersible all the way around, making him feel giddy. Was it a halfway turn or a complete 360? Even if the submersible was designed to endure this kind of beating, he definitely wasn't.

Must get under these waves. Right! Air back to the holding tank. Dive. Dive. Get under these waves.

With each pounding wave the digital compass moved in an erratic dance: east, south, north—an agog wind charm, making him unsure of his direction. *Get out of this, Ashlyn.*

The next wave hit portside. North...obviously north! He rammed the joystick hard to port. And then he remembered...

"Sea stack! Where are you?" He pulled back the throttle, straining to see though the viewports. He saw clouds...turbulent clouds...clumps of churning seaweed.

Sonar acoustics whined and screeched:

Wawa wa wa WO WO.

The loud *WOs* meant close. Which way? Starboard. He jerked the joystick right.

Good guess—the chiseled stack loomed by the port viewport. He had missed it by thirty feet.

We're diving. Good.

The depth gauge read 9 meters—29.52 feet. It was still a bumpy ride, but the compass was settling. Direct west. Equalizing the amidships thrusters, Ashlyn positioned the nose of the submersible straight out to sea, full throttle.

Fifty feet....

Sixty feet....

The small bumps he now felt were only as rough as slight air disturbance on an aircraft flight; much better than the surface.

Specks of light drifted by the viewports—millions of specks, like snow falling upward.

Ninety feet....

One hundred....

WaWa....

Keeping an eye on *Echo Sounder,* Ashlyn made out an upward slope or a ridge. He leveled the angle of descent. The submersible's speed began to drop. The ride was now smooth. In fact, it felt like there wasn't any motion.

One-hundred-and-thirty feet.

More tingles ran up his spine, not nerves—thrill. He was pilot-ing the submersible. He was underwater, in control.

Ashlyn Miller, the real master of the submersible.

Going deep…to a new universe.

What would his old classmates say?

22:00….

Blustered by angled rain slicing under his umbrella, Dan Shockbottom stood before a paused ENG—Electronic News Gath-ering—Betacam, waiting for an on-camera cue. An assistant direc-tor's voice in his earpiece cued the countdown:

"Ten seconds, nine…."

Dan's heart raced. He remembered the advice of an old pro-ducer friend: "Be prepared. Make it lean, make it slick, and shock 'em!"

Dan was as prepared as he'd ever been. Slick? Maybe not, but he was about to blow the lid off the runaway teen mystery. As for shocking them, all he needed was enough zing to entice the big me-dia boys. Of late, there'd been a scarcity of sizzling national news, a media lull so to speak. His scoop had a contentious element, with breakout potential—at least he believed so. Would the networks agree? He could only give it his all. No, he would have to shock them!

The Betacam's record light was blinking. On the monitor, Dan saw the superimposed Chyron caption fading up….

'Breaking news' followed by a still photograph of Ashlyn and Autumn with the news anchor saying, "Runaways or abducted?"

The camera shot switched to a graphic of a white Cadillac, dis-solving into an egg-headed alien with huge black eyes, the news an-chor saying: "Or victims of a close encounter?"

Dan's cameraman held out his hand with three fingers, then two, one, and….

Dan was on.

Fighting to keep his umbrella from flying off in the wind, Dan Shockbottom told the local Oregonian community that according to a reliable source, prior to the teens' disappearance, the navy had been investigating Ashlyn and Autumn Miller's possible interaction with an intelligent deep-sea life form known in navy circles as the *Seabed Phantom*.

The viewers were shown a series of prerecorded clips to support this claim: archival footage of the navy's *Seabed Phantom* searches five years ago, shots of navy officers outside the Millers' house videotaped earlier that day, a navy car speeding away from the cul-de-sac, and finally a photograph of Ashlyn and Autumn with some audiotape playing over it.

Ashlyn's voice: "We've been invited somewhere with her...only she doesn't look like that, except her tail...a bit...that's why we need your submersible."

Autumn's voice: "It's true! She promised to show us places no human's ever seen."

Unidentified man's voice: "You talk to her?"

Ashlyn: "I do...telepathically. Autumn can't—"

Autumn: "But she held my hand and we prayed." Pause on the tape, and then. "She's a being, a kind, intelligent being."

AMONG THE MANY VIEWERS WATCHING the broadcast that evening was the jeweler's son Bogdan, whose face turned purple with rage. Bogdan considered himself to be a righteous man living in a progressively sordid and debauched world, where gays marched proudly in parades and liberal abortionists strong-armed the legislature, where sinning was acceptable, blasphemy promoted, and God's Christian values were torn asunder. But God had spoken to Bogdan, instructing him to take a stand; it was time to stop the cancer, the mockery. The commandments were to be obeyed, and sinners needed to feel the wrath of God. And God told Bogdan that it was his—and those of like mind—responsibility to counter-punch, to reeducate those fallen from grace, to debunk the ubiquitous new age propaganda—the claims that alien encounters, channelers, and spirit masters, to name but a few of the heresies, were real.

Being one of God's policemen, Bogdan took his position as chairperson for the local chapter of the nationwide organization C.R.F.O. (nicknamed Cry-for) Christians Rebelling For Order—very seriously.

The preacher man could hardly believe his eyes and ears. Reporter Dan Shockbottom was outside the same house he'd followed the kids to, telling the people of Oregon that according to reliable sources, the navy was investigating the teens' interaction with an intelligent being from the sea—a being sporting a fish tail that could talk...and pray!

The television shot switched from the teens' photograph to

Shockbottom outside the grandmother's house. "It might sound like tomfoolery, some elaborate prank—" Shockbottom paused as a thunderbolt boomed around him.

For Bogdan, it was God's fury. How could a serious newsman, even in jest, claim that an alien from the sea prayed?

The reporter continued, "But there's a series of contributing facts pointing to a very dire situation for these young teens. Last night, a coast guard helicopter intercepted a ship chartered by retired admiral Andrew Lightstone —"

Bogdan turned down the volume to make a call. He was so furious he could have cussed, at least kicked his TV. The kids with the pendant were now involved in some heinous new age plot.

Bogdan made five telephone calls to members of the local C.R.F.O. chapter, announcing a meeting at the boathouse at nine the next morning. Blasphemy was ugly enough when it showed its demonic face elsewhere.

But this was their backyard.

-25-

Ko's World

IT WAS A REMARKABLE PLACE, the undersea. Glistening spheres of small jelly-creatures and luminous specks of darting life glided by the viewports: white dots, blue, green, yellow, roaming life in abundance.

230 feet...220 feet...200....

Ashlyn was returning to the surface, soon to be back in choppy water.

180 feet...170....

"What's the weather like up there, Ko?"

"Sweet and salty and alive with raw energy. You would call it rain. Hurry."

"Here I come."

130 feet...120....

Ko made a slow, wide berth, swimming on her side. She sensed Ashlyn's position, and placed herself close to where he was about to surface.

Ashlyn now felt the current heaving, the rumble of the waves vibrating through *Proteus II's* hull. "Forty feet...arghh, I feel that."

As the submersible soared to the surface and rolled over in the punchy swell, Ko felt Ashlyn's distress. She quickly placed a firm hand on *Proteus II's* nose, stabilizing the craft.

The hatch hissed with a burst of escaping air pressure, and Ashlyn's proud face pushed up through the conning tower. "I am the master of this submer—" His eyes widened as he gasped at the sight— his sister lying limp over Ko's right arm, eyes closed, with her head barely above the swell. Bigsey in his cage was on Ko's back, soaked.

"She was cold...so very, very cold."

"What did you do?" Ashlyn threw himself onto the deck, almost slipping into the ocean as he reached for Autumn.

But as he touched her face and neck, expecting the worst, he found her flesh to be surprisingly warm, a lot warmer than he was at that moment. "She's warm."

After giving her two light smacks on her rosy cheeks, her eyes snapped open. She blinked once, wiped her mouth and sat up. "Oh, there you are. Did I fall asleep?" She yawned, quite happily. "What took you so long?"

Ashlyn glared at her as he shivered in the rain.

Aboard *Proteus II*, Autumn changed out of her drenched clothes while Bigsey ran circles inside his cage. The rabbit did this when he was upset and he was beaucoup upset. Autumn donned a pair of dry pajamas and pulled on two sweaters. Taking Bigsey out of the cage, she cuddled the little guy under her bed comforter.

Ashlyn changed into his one remaining dry outfit, a running suit and a pair of socks. No shoes, no sweater. Everything else was sodden. He sat in the pilot's seat, his comforter wrapped around him.

"Now we go."

"Now we go, Ko."

Autumn became absorbed, as they got under way, pressing her nose against the side portal. Whipping through a kelp field, the sub's floodlights bombarded a massive school of rockfish. Beyond the field, the ride became smooth. She felt she was aboard a plane at night flying through the stars—there was that much twinkling undersea light. Luminescent sea lilies, ethereal jellyfish, rainbow-colored salpae, lantern fish, and tiny stars falling upward made this a realm of fairyland light.

Ashlyn watched the speedometer spinning. There was minimal sensation of motion but the meter proved they were accelerating.

70... 80...85 knots....

No submersible had ever traveled at such velocity before.

Passing through the *thermocline*—the thermal strata separating warmer oxygen-rich surface water from the frigid, oxygen-poor deep-sea depths—the outside became darker. There were fewer bioluminescent creatures, and the larger fish species vanished.

"What's that?" Autumn inquired.

"Squid."

The small cluster of Pacific squid scattered.

Ashlyn kept a keen eye on the information windows, especially the leak detector light. Ko was piloting from the outside, determining direction and speed, but he carefully monitored their progress, prepared to alert Ko at the first sign of a problem. Hopefully, she wouldn't do anything the submersible or her occupants couldn't withstand.

The atmospheric pressure outside continued to rapidly build. At 1510 feet, the pressure had increased to 676.6 PSI—the weight of forty-six atmospheres, easily enough to crush the brain of a human.

But inside the sphere the pressure remained a comfortable:

ONE ATMOSPHERE...NORMAL

Ashlyn's foremost concern was leaks. Even a pinpoint leak could produce a spray of bullet-like force capable of shredding flesh. Fortunately, the leak detector light remained unlit. In fact, there were no trouble-prompts or warnings of any kind.

Once again, he wondered why the sub had sunk.

"It was a gift." Ko suggested, reading his mind.

"No kidding. Who from?"

"The universe. You asked...you received. Simple."

Ashlyn found it interesting that Ko didn't seem to be concerned with how the submersible came to be conveniently lying on the seabed. She was satisfied and thankful. He on the other hand, with his human logical mind, wanted answers. He was conditioned to want to know. Great minds were inquisitive minds, weren't they?

"Ashlyn, can you see it?"

Ashlyn looked through both portals but couldn't see much of anything. It was very black out there.

"Close your eyes. Close your eyes and see it."

Obliging Ko, Ashlyn soon felt a sensation of prickly tingles covering his back. He saw himself soaring through showers of speckled light, unrestrained, going fast, faster yet, like a soaring undersea bird. This is how Ko had to feel in the open ocean, salty spray caressing her skin, riptides and heaving currents being but sunshine and a gentle breeze on her face.

"It's incredible."

"I feel you, Ashlyn. I am happy."

"I'm happy, too."

Briefly, they flew into a cloud of snowy sediment billowing up from the seafloor. Bursting out of the cloud, Ashlyn found himself glued to the forward portal as they approached a steep ridge. And suddenly the sea floor was gone.

As his ears popped, he checked the inside pressure. It was .85 higher than normal, but not enough for due concern.

Their angle of descent was acute.

At four thousand feet the temperature outside had plummeted to a biting one degree above zero. Even fewer species roamed here. It was a black silent cosmos.

The viewports were covered in a dewy condensation. The walls of the sphere, the control surface, information screens, even the tops of the comforters, felt damp. The ride became bumpy, and there was an unsettling noise. It sounded like someone outside was banging on the hull. Autumn's eyes rolled to the right following the noise as it scurried down the hull.

"What's going on, Ko?" Ashlyn asked.

"It's a river. We're crossing it."

Echo Sounder's needle began sketching a picture, readily recognizable as a moonscape of mountains, plains and ridges.

As the bathometer gauge turned to 8400 feet, the submersible's floodlights found the seafloor, and *Echo Sounder's* drawing proved to be an accurate rendition. The benthic zone—sea floor region—was a spectacular plain of rugged slopes, moon rocks and ridges—as if the Arizona desert had been placed here minus the cactus. At this depth almost no vegetation existed.

Ko flew fifteen feet above a grooved ridge, now bombarded by light—her own pulsing brilliance and the submersible's spotlights.

"It's another world."

"I wouldn't like to live here." Autumn remarked.

"But it is beautiful."

Beyond the ridge, Ko hovered over a *chimney city*—as she called it—where dozens of frozen basalt stacks jutted out of the seafloor. None bore signs of thermal activity, however, several thousand years erstwhile the water directly above these stacks shimmered and up from the belly of the earth came boiling geysers of sulfides, minerals and metallic elements. For most creatures of planet earth, this would have been a deadly place, yet scores of mutant creatures, mostly of the mollusk, limpet and crustacean orders, had thrived here, propagating in the sulfur-rich waters.

The *dead* vents gave the area the feeling of a ghost town.

Coursing through the stacks, Ko approached a long dark line in the sea floor—a fissure, chasm or perhaps even a manufactured culvert. Ashlyn estimated it at thirty feet wide.

The speedometer shrank back to an almost motionless two knots.

A sediment cloud enshrouded them.

THUMP....

Unable to glimpse much through the foggy sediment, Ashlyn figured they had touched down at an oblique angle because his pilot's chair was titled. "Ko, what's going on?"

"The machine is large... uneven dimensions...maybe it will fit."

"Fit? Whoaaa. Wait!"

Ko was planning to transport them *into* the chasm.

The submersible's aft tilted up...up, way up. Bigsey's cage slid forward, the luggage, pizza box—everything not attached or locked down—started to slide forward. "Too steep! Ko, too steep!"

"I have to. The only way in."

Ashlyn grabbed the pedestal on his pilot's chair. A swaying, hanging strap caught his attention—his seat belt. He grabbed it. "Put on your seat belt!" He yelled at Autumn.

Autumn already had Bigsey tucked between her legs, her other hand gripping the back of Ashlyn's seat. She absolutely wasn't going to surrender her grip to find a seat belt.

Now vertical, they began their descent into the chasm.

Through the portals, rocky, reddish, grooved walls loomed up on both sides, sheer and massive.

One hundred feet down into the chasm....

Two hundred...the digital numbers on the bathometer kept spinning.

Pressing her face against the viewport as they passed a small cave, Autumn watched an ugly fish swim out to investigate. Spooked, the fish darted back into its hole.

At twelve hundred feet, they came across another cave, a much larger opening, and Ko slowed their descent.

This is obviously where they were headed.

"Yes...here," Ko confirmed, as she started to back the submersible into the aperture. Once again, the pizza box, luggage, odds and ends slid along the floor. A tortuous groan echoed through the

hull.

YAAARR-EEEE-YAGHHH-EEEE!

CRUNK!

Ashlyn gripped the navigation joystick like a handhold, perhaps hoping to affect their course. "Ko, Ko, easy!"

Where the hell was she taking them?

THUMFF!

CRUNK! A big hit! Bouncing up in their chairs, the lights buzzed and crackled. Bigsey squealed. Ashlyn's eyes shot to the leak detector light.

The agonizing wail now scurrying through *Proteus II's* titanium hull was no less than a person's plaintive sobbing, deep and resounding. Expecting to be minced by a killer spray of water at any moment, Autumn's nervous eyes tracked the painful sounds assailing them.

Despite the frigid temperature, Ashlyn wiped a bead of seat from his brow. "Ko! We can't do this!"

"The machine is inflexible."

"Of course it is! It's not designed to take —!"

Abruptly, the starboard side dipped.

The teens hung on tightly as their anchored chairs keeled to the right, and once again all the loose ends slid to new locations.

Ashlyn pushed a swaying microphone out of his face. "Ko, listen to me. This sub's not designed to…it will break. You'll kill us! You have to—"

There was silence.

The lamenting had ceased, and the submersible was level, immobile. They were stopped in a narrow tunnel, only six feet of space on either side of *Proteus II.*

Ashlyn observed Ko's luminescence intensifying, becoming as bright as the time at Deadman's Bluff when she'd grimaced moments before diving out of sight.

"What's happening now? Why's it doing that?" Autumn asked, pointing to the bathometer gauge.

The numbers were spinning.

No the submersible was not stopped, but flying, warp speed.

Straight down.

They were in a chute or shaft of sorts, an elevator to some lower place.

Bigsey was the first to sense an abnormal vibration. The rabbit pressed his nose into Autumn's armpits.

Then Autumn felt her body quivering.

The floor was trembling, making a rumbling sound, like an earthquake. Autumn's face paled. "What is it?" She cried, her eyes widening, expecting the walls to cave in on them any second.

The rumbling had massed itself into a thundering roar, the shaking so severe that Bigsey's cage looked like two cages inching along the floor, as if by alchemy.

Through the bottom viewport, Ashlyn saw sea stars and limpets spiraling downward. "It's an eddy!" He shouted above the din.

"Don't worry!" Ko said at last. *"This is normal."*

"Normal?" The skin on Ashlyn's face was oscillating. He hoped she didn't mean this shaking was the norm of her world. Turning to Autumn, he shrugged: "She says it's normal!"

Unable to hear his words of comfort, Autumn remained terrified until they had descended another twenty-five-hundred feet into the chute, when the swirling and rumbling lost its punch. As peace and tranquility returned to the sphere, she hugged Bigsey with all her heart, while Ashlyn stroked the control surface. *Proteus II* was obviously a fine, sturdy piece of equipment.

They were moving forward again, not fast by Ko's standards, heading along a channel with craggy blackish-green walls.

The bathometer numbers were climbing.

"Ashlyn!" Autumn cried with angst.

Ashlyn's attention was also on the starboard viewport.

It was cracking!

Then he realized—

"It's a waterline! We've surfaced." The viewports began to fog over. Ashlyn realized that they were stopped—truly stopped—the instruments were proof of that. He released his safety belt. "Where are we, Ko? What is this place?"

"You can come out if you want."

There was air out there? Breathable air?

"Hmmmm. I'm not…yes…yes…I think there is."

"That's reassuring. See you topside."

Popping the hatch release, Ashlyn felt a stream of air from the burst of escaping pressure—the sub's air. Prepared to slam the hatch shut if he smelled acid or some other nasty fumes, he gingerly raised his head into a misty, noisy atmosphere—noisy because yards ahead lay a roaring waterfall.

He took a tentative breath.

Air. Cold musty air. Sheets of freezing mist washed over his face. The smell was no worse than a wet afghan, he mused.

Looking around in the dim light, he saw that they were at an intersection of three channels, each some twenty yards wide, converging into the waterfall. The glassy walls of the channels were sheer, disappearing way above him into black infinity.

Ko released the submersible and swam out wide, almost triggering in him heart failure—he hadn't adjusted ballast. "We'll sink" He was about to throw himself below and yank the hatch shut when she calmly retorted: *"It's land...you are sitting on land."*

The submersible was in shallow water, resting on a sandy bank, and quite safe, unless it was quicksand, which apparently it wasn't.

He felt Autumn tugging his leg. "What's going on?"

"She's taking a rest."

Autumn tried to squeeze into the funnel. "Where are we? Can I see?" Ashlyn clambered onto the deck to make room for her. With Bigsey clinging nervously to her forearm, Autumn poked her head into the damp atmosphere, where it took a moment for her eyes to adjust. "Wow, who could imagine a place like this? We're under the sea, Bigsey." She crinkled her nose, "Stinks. But cool."

Ashlyn blew warm air on his hands. From the corner of his eye, he spotted something moving.

"There's something over there. What's that bright thing?"

Autumn followed his gaze. "What?"

Ashlyn pointed to the widest channel. But it was gone, whatever it was. "There was something there. Looked like a flashlight. Hey, Ko? Did you see? Ko?"

It was suddenly dark. Almost pitch.

Ko didn't reply.

Autumn held onto Ashlyn's arm. "Where is she?"

A scary thought dawned on Ashlyn. "I don't know. Get the flashlight."

As Autumn scurried for the flashlight, Ashlyn focused his thoughts on Ko.

Had something awful happened to her?

"Here, take it!" Autumn handed Ashlyn the flashlight. He began sweeping the area with a strong beam of light, shooting down one channel, then the next, probing the waterfall.

No sign of her, no word from her.

Surely, she hadn't abandoned them. It had almost been five minutes since....

"I am here."

Ashlyn saw a light coming from the same direction that he'd seen a spark of illumination moments before the darkness fell. "Ko?"

"I needed to ask permission."

Once again Ko's luminescence re-bathed the cavernous passageway with a misty glow. Ashlyn's thoughts ran hard and fast. Where had she been? Why did she leave without saying a word? Permission?

"We must move on."

"Is there something you'd like to tell me?"

Of course there was something; Ashlyn was aware of at least one mystery or secret ever since their first meeting, but he figured she'd confide in him at the right time. Now seemed like a pretty good time. "Well, where did you go?"

Ko's body was pulsing vibrant shades of green and blue as she rested a hand on the sub's amidships thruster. *"We must move on."*

"Where I come from friends tell—"

"Trust me...please."

Ashlyn didn't understand Ko's reticence but he did trust her.

As soon as he slammed shut the hatch, they were moving again, straight into the fury of the waterfall. Ashlyn slid down into the sphere, grabbing the back of his pilot's chair for balance, as the sub shook violently, dipping down under the weight of the falls. He quickly swung around into his seat, buckling himself in as he stared at wide sheets of water rushing by the portals.

Slowly, the roar of the falls began to lessen. The ride turned quiet and smooth. Fully submerged, they were barreling along a subterranean channel at eighty miles an hour.

East the compass said.

The sub abruptly veered left, then hard right, no deceleration, just a sharp turn around a massive chunk of rock. As Bigsey's cage took the customary skip along the floor, Ashlyn saw that they had entered a field littered with bulbous rock formations, some jutting up from the ground like stalagmites, others protruding from an unseen ceiling. The submersible abruptly nosed down with another burst of acceleration.   Ashlyn gripped the navigation joystick tightly.

"Where are we?" Autumn asked, maintaining a compact hold on the back of Ashlyn's seat. She was beginning to get a kick out of the wacky underwater ride. Ko flew inches above high-ridge ditches, rising over mounds at the last second, rocketing through honeycomb-like structures and around huge rocky globs and nodules at mind-blowing speeds.

Ashlyn shook his head. "Your guess is as good as mine."

Checking the clock on the master display screen, Ashlyn saw they had been traveling in the obstacle course for twenty-five minutes. With the bathometer now reading only 4700 feet—they must have ascended 6000 feet—moving east most of the time. He surmised they had to be somewhere under the mainland, about twenty to thirty miles inland.

Ko abruptly threw her tail fluke into an arching curve.

The speedometer numbers rapidly dropped.

The sub's floodlights bounced into the end of the channel—a dead-end. With effortless arm propulsion and one swish of her tail fluke, Ko set *Proteus II* down onto a sandy bed.

"Now what?" asked Autumn.

Ashlyn checked the view on both sides of *Proteus II*. They definitely had run out of channel. He echoed Autumn's sentiments. "Now what, Ko?"

"Home." Ko replied curtly.

Suddenly, the dead-end wall began to glide aside effortlessly, like a giant stage curtain, and Autumn's lips parted in disbelief, as an immense rush of light from the other side spilled forth, surrounding them. "Oh, my gosh!"

What they saw was dazzling, sparkling, radiant, breath-stealing. From every portal, light dazzled: silvery light, golden light, pearlescent resplendence laced with strands of indigo and emerald green, sapphire blue and ruby red glints; all of it gleaming in sublime motion.

Ko wasn't the only being of her kind.

There must have been fifty or sixty of her kind, like angels dancing in the water; some nearly twenty feet long, pulsing light and color; others like clear gelatin, almost invisible, except for their massive winged bodies, tapestried with delicate filaments of light.

This was Ko's family—the Iquana.

Ko pushed the submersible forward and soared several hundred feet until the conning tower slid out of the water.

They had surfaced.

So had the Iquana.

-26-

A Growing Reaction

WATCHING THE NEWS THAT NIGHT, Boomer and Carter were both flabbergasted…and worried. When Boomer tried to call Ashlyn, he heard the usual prerecorded cellular phone message: "—the customer has left the service zone."

They swung by the marina but couldn't remember the slip number. They searched, to no avail. Returning home, they were tempted to call the police, except Boomer had to think that one through. After all, the jeweler's white Cadillac had been sighted. He decided to wait a day, see what happened.

He and Carter settled down in front of the TV, drank Stoli and talked about the old days.

In the old days, when Boomer worked aboard Jerry Miller's Sea Lab, he had seen many odd subsea sights, but never a piscine alien. Officially, the team had been employed to collect data on the environmental hazards of the sludge channels and document new species. But everyone knew that Jerry was looking for one species only: *Hydromermadis Gigas*—the hypothetical mermaid.

Most of the team thought the boss was insane, but the salaries were decent and the equipment state-of-the-art, so they had endured Jerry's insanity…for a while, until the team turned greedy and contentious.

Boomer hadn't shared the team's opinions. He wasn't a scientist, wasn't chasing a degree or a Nobel Prize, and he wasn't in the game for money or glory. He was simply a diver who loved diving and Jerry had become a friend, although Boomer would have liked to have told Jerry that it was okay to search for the pot of gold, which, after all, was a heck of a lot more interesting than the team's pile of crap. And now after all these years, the notion of Jerry's *hydromermadis* never seemed more plausible. Maybe there really was something. As the old adage says: "Where there's smoke, there's fire." The US navy and retired admiral Andrew Lightstone and the famed animal hunter, Ed Lazerath, whom they'd just seen on TV, all thought *something* existed.

"What if it really does exist?"

The flesh on Boomer's back goose pimpled with the mind-boggling thought: a spiritual fish-like being. It made him seriously think about God for the first time in a long while.

Like 95% of Swedes, religion had been a part of Boomer's upbringing, but the toll from some of life's hard edges, notably two marriages, two divorces, and then caisson disease, had left him with his spiritual luster somewhat dampened.

But if this alien encounter was true—and the evidence was sure hard to dismiss, such as the voices on the audiotape that sent shivers down his spine—then maybe this really was proof—proof beyond any doubter's mind that God really existed. "Can you imagine, Carter, two species totally separate, without any interconnection, living worlds apart, yet both acknowledging God. It would change the way we feel about religion, about life. No wonder it drove Jerry nuts."

"Uh?" Carter blinked.

"If it's true," Boomer added.

"If what's true, God?" Carter blurted in a slur.

"The alien fish that prays."

Carter, with a cube of ice in his mouth, mumbled, "Yeah, it smokes a pipe and watches Beavis and Butthead." He chuckled.

"Seriously, Carter. You say you believe in aliens, yah?"

"Yeah but—"

"Up there…why not down there? It's uncharted. It's huge. Jerry was convinced, and I tell you, my friend, Jerry might have been strange, eccentric, but he wasn't crazy, and he wasn't dumb." Boomer glanced at the TV. "Are you going to tell me the admiral and his sea-hunters use that high-tech floating lab to catch shrimp? Add it all up, what do we have?"

Carter clumsily placed his empty glass on the table. "What do we have?" He hiccupped. "We got, uh bouillabaisse. Fishy stew from fishy poo."

"Bro, come on. Tell me this does nothing to you?"

Carter shook his head, somehow trying to sober himself. "Okay, let me think. Uh yeah…you're right. Something here is very…fishy."

ANDY LIGHTSTONE WAS AMBIVALENT ABOUT the newsbreak. IT was both propitious and unfortunate. The last few days had been solid. Tax man had come through with his promise—delivered Jerry Miller and his den of high-tech toys, including a disassembled ocean-floor workstation, two aging submersibles: *Miranda* and *Encaladus*, as well as hundreds of *A-zone Ingression* maps showing plausible entranceways to subterranean passages and lakes. In addition, they'd now acquired the best lead on the phantom yet: Denton's kids—truly an unexpected boon.

But on the downside, James Swift had allowed the kids and their submersible to slip through his fingers. The investors had all called about the sea alien and the young girl, asking if this was their intended catch? While two of the investors were outraged, another passively appeased, only one thought it was good news.

Andy hadn't expected such strong reactions. Anyway, he decided, one or two fewer investors might not be such a bad idea. It dawned on him that reporters would soon be breathing down his neck.

But mulling over the notion of reporters didn't seem to be a negative…maybe it was even serendipitous.

The publicity wheels were already in motion.

-27-

Iquana

KO'S WORLD, FORTY-FIVE HUNDRED feet below sea level, was a steamy lake inside a soaring cavern bristling with stalactites, stalagmites and sheer glassy columns glowing purple from the bioluminescence generated from millions of limpets, sea slugs and sponges. These critters clung to every surface, creating a pulsing carpet of subdued light. Scattered here and there were rocky islets, some steaming. These were obviously the source of the cavern's slow moving, wispy mists.

Ashlyn and Autumn stood on *Proteus II's* deck, wrapped in their comforters, inhaling frigid air that smelled vinegary.

The Iquana who swam closest was bulkier than Ko by a third, with an angelic multi-colored dorsal now splayed wide to his shoulders. His eyes, green and gold and very vibrant, were settled on Ashlyn.

According to Ko he was an elder, and he was addressing him, although Ashlyn couldn't hear anything.

For Ashlyn's benefit, Ko voiced his words: *"He says, 'Hello Man. Do you hear me?'"*

Ashlyn shook his head slowly, and then bowed, deciding politeness was in order.

The elder reached up and touched the submersible, running his huge webbed hand over the bow. He then nodded, seemingly satisfied, as if the machine pleased or impressed him.

"His name is Ee'uo'ee'ell'ee'oo'ee'i'ti."

"That's a bit much. Do you think he'd mind if I abbreviated it, like I do with you. Say, EO?"

After conversing with Ee'uo'ee'ell'ee'oo'ee'i'ti, Ko turned to Ashlyn, grinning. Apparently, it was a done deal.

EO squinted affectionately, baring his miniscule teeth in smile.

While most of the Iquana kept a distance, a few swam up close, as if they had been given the okay. One stroked *Proteus II's* hull as if the machine was a living animal. Another inspected his reflection in the metal. A smallish female with a peacockish plume, much longer than Ko's, waved goodbye. Perhaps this was the only humanism she was aware of. Delighted with herself, she laughed, shaking her head from side to side.

Watching this female, Autumn couldn't help but giggle, too.

The female covered her mouth coyly, and ducked out of sight.

When one of the males threw his hand into a rigid palm, Ashlyn buckled his knees and extended his tiny palm for the greeting. This seemed to break the ice. Suddenly, webbed hands were reaching up from all corners of the sub. Autumn jumped into the act, shaking hand after hand, receiving flirtatious smiles, and even a couple of very official salutes.

Brusquely, as if they had been given a new order, the clan withdrew. Only EO and Ko remained in the vicinity, swimming back and forth slowly, as if pacing.

Ashlyn's mind was silent of Ko's voice. He figured she was engaged in a serious conversation with EO. Fleetingly, the elder looked over at him. Of course, it was the first time humans had stepped foot in their environment. But were these glances of interest or disapproval?

Autumn snapped Ashlyn out of his thoughts. "Why have they backed away from us?"

"I think they're evaluating us; deciding if we're welcome."

As the Iquana elder dived out of sight, Ashlyn heard Ko's voice, but not necessarily directed at him. *"You should trust me."*

"I should trust you?" Ashlyn sat on the cold deck, his legs dangling over the side. "It's what I've been thinking about you."

Gently pulsing shades of emerald and deep blue, Ko rested her palm on the sub. *"Elders! Huh. What do they know?"*

"So we made a real good impression?" Ashlyn folded his arms. *"They're giving you room to adjust."*

"I guess *it's not yet time?*"

Ko looked directly into Ashlyn's eyes. *"For me, it is time."* She cupped water onto her plume.

While Ko and Ashlyn chatted about the elders concerns over the human presence, Autumn, estranged from their telepathic conversation, soared her eyes to the cavern's ceiling, which was perhaps two or three thousand feet above the lake, but well-lit enough for the naked eye to admire it. The glittering pillars and ice-dripping balconies reminded her of the painted backdrops and theatrical sets straight out of Walt Disney's magical kingdom. But Autumn would later learn that the purple and blue lights that graced every inch of those glittering pillars were living organisms—millions of tiny sparkling creatures illuminating the cave.

Noticing his sister's tourist-like gaze, Ashlyn also took a moment to really observe their surroundings. He estimated the lake at two to three miles wide but longer than he could guess because of its curvature. Most amazing about this place, it was under the mainland. How was it possible that a lake this large existed without it being known? Obviously, that's why the elders were upset. Now someone did know.

Ko playfully pulled his leg. *"Why don't you and Autumn climb upon my back. I promised I would show you a new world, and I will."*

"What about your family? They disapprove."

"I did not say so. They are giving you room to see and think for yourself. Now, would you like to climb upon my back?"

Ashlyn hesitated. Though he wanted to visit the sites of this underworld paradise, there was something bothering him, had been bothering him all along. Ko seemed to harbor a few secrets, one of which was of grave concern to him.

Having listened to Ashlyn concerns, as if he had been directly addressing her, Ko responded: *"I made you a promise, Ashlyn. I will never hurt you. I will never hurt Autumn. You and I share something special, do we not?"*

"That's not the point."

"Did this submersible not materialize?"

"I'm not criticizing that."

"And did you not become its master?"

Ashlyn answered modestly. "Well, I...I don't know about that."

"You are the one who piloted the submersible; you took it from

the cave, not I. You are the master of the machine."

Ashlyn conceded: "I guess."

"Then I have not deceived you...not failed you."

"Well...not like that but—"

"Then come with me, my good friend...and I will explain all."

The teens sat on Ko's upper back, horseback style, between her binary dorsal now butterflied open like two small sails. Her body was hard, slippery, but no different from seats on some amusement park ride.

As Ko catapulted away from the submersible, a holler fell out of Ashlyn's mouth. The G-force acceleration was always a rush.

Ko sped across the lake's taut skin, carving a narrow wake behind her, heading for the towering purple wall on the far side of the cavern. Then she took off on a new path following the curvature of the wall. Speeding along, minute after minute, Ashlyn realized that the lake was much larger than he'd first thought.

Veering around a protruding rock-pool, Ko spoke: *"Would you like to know how this happened?"*

Ashlyn wiped moisture from his eyes. "How what happened?"

"How all this happened. How and why we came to be here?"

"Sure."

Ko led them into a deep cleft in the rock face. Not far ahead, rising sharply up out of the water, stood a large shimmering object, very angular, very tall, very glass-like. As they approached, it became intensely bright, virtually impossible to look at.

Flicking her tail fluke while sweeping her arms back to create reverse thrust, Ko slowed to a harbor pace. As the brightness of Ko's bloom faded, the shimmering object's intense light simultaneously faded. Now Ashlyn could see that he was looking at the largest polished crystal he'd ever seen, maybe seventy-five feet tall, shaped like a pyramid.

Ko ran a hand though her plume as she slowly circled the pyramid. *"A long, long time ago our ancestors used to live on land, as you do now."*

As Ashlyn gasped in surprise, she repeated herself.

"On land, same as you...bipedal—walking upright on two legs. It was a great age of technology and science. We built gargantuan structures, fantastic machines, cities. We even flew to the stars."

Ashlyn had always thought that earth had seen many advanced technological eras. But there appeared to be a very sane argument against that theory: Where was the proof? Not one trace of proof had ever been found.

Ko placed her palm flat against the crystal…perhaps to review or retrieve information, Ashlyn figured.

"It was a divided world. Some of our ancestors valued the arts, the expression of beauty and ethereal knowledge, and we called them "the artists." Most of our kind however were only interested in technology, finance and self-serving power. Ultimately, we were a greedy race, over-harvesting not only technology but also the natural resources of the planet. We were indifferent to the symbiotic needs of a healthy nature, all in the name of progress. The artists warned the scientists of impending disasters, warned that we were consuming too many of our resources, too quickly! And that if we didn't take counteractive measures, the consequences would be catastrophic. But the intellectuals, the scientists, declared the artists radical and dangerous. They attacked and denounced their ideologies and philosophies, claiming them to be fear-based and heretical. Artists were persecuted. Artists became outcasts. And our society became increasingly corrupt and decadent.

"There was one being. His name was Eye, and he was a great scientist. But he was also a prophet. Knowing that the artists' warnings were correct, he foresaw the great flood, and knew that if he and his loved ones were to survive the deluge, they would have to master the water. So he devised a method to biogenetically alter himself and a small group of artists and scientists so they could live underwater, as beings of the sea. Those who ventured with him left behind their inventions, their possessions, and all of the technology of that age, everything…everything except this one crystal. This contains the memory of that age."

Ashlyn was breathing deeply. "This contains that memory…like a computer?"

"Yes. In this crystal is all that…and much more. It is our paradigm for living, our code of honor."

"So you used to be human?"

"No. We were always Iquana."

Ashlyn drew parallels with modern-day society. "We don't exactly have a rift between artists and scientists, but we're divided by class—the haves and have-nots. And we're exploiting and trashing the planet, pushing for greater technology. And right now we have the worst storms on record—*our record*, that is."

"Yes...this seems to be true."

His conversation with Ko was briefly suspended as Autumn pleaded for some explanation. "What kind of tour is this when no one tells you what's going on?"

So as the teens exchanged ideas and notions about environmental wrath, Ko withdrew from the pyramid and slowly swam back to the main lake. Over on the left, a group of her kinfolk appeared to be dancing—at least that's what Autumn suggested.

"I don't think so," Ashlyn replied. "What are they doing, Ko?"

Ko didn't respond right away. Whisking them around a steaming rock pool to the far side of the group, she answered in a roundabout way. *"Do you love music? I love music."*

Ashlyn frowned. "Singing? You mean singing?"

"That, too...but I love music."

"How do you know music? You have no instruments." Ashlyn asked, seizing the contradiction. Her ancestors had forsaken all possessions except for the pyramid crystal, and they still followed that paradigm today—she'd just told him that. So what sort of music was she talking about?

"Music sustains us. I couldn't live without it. None of us could. It's our food." Ko swished her tail fluke, and they began moving in a slow circle. *"Look."*

Following Ko's gaze, Ashlyn saw another group of Iquana swimming below. "You actually hear music?"

"Look."

"I am looking."

"Then look closer."

Ashlyn counted seven beings, swimming gracefully back and forth, pulsing magnificent colors...but they seemed no more special or magnificent than Ko's spectacular coloring— "Whoaaa! Patterns...rhythmic patterns!" The colorful bioluminescent symmetry on the Iquanas' plumes and dorsal fins was moving in rhythmic patterns, flowing from being to being to being.

"Now close your eyes...feel ...feel the vibrations."

Eager to see what would happen next, Ashlyn was happy to oblige. Within seconds, he began to feel the vibrational hum of a large speaker. At first, he thought he was imagining it, his desire playing a trick on him. But as the sound intensified, he found himself listening to music—real music, becoming louder and louder—cymbals, strings, flutes, as if he'd donned a set of great headphones. He was listening to a philharmonic orchestra playing the symphony of the universe. Snapping open his eyes, he could still hear the music, loud and rich in timbre—better than headphones, as if he was inside a theatre, sitting in front row seats.

There was yet more wonder to behold. Ashlyn watched in awe as the rhythmical patterns on the beings began to form the illusion of worldly images—3-D cinema style—to complement the music.

He was watching an underwater volcano spewing flaming red coals amidst showers of spectacular sparks.

"Look at it!" he pointed to the beings.

"What?" Autumn frowned, unable to visualize or hear any of the phenomenal sounds.

As he watched spellbound, Ashlyn now understood so much more about his hosts. It made perfect sense. The artists came to the undersea with their art, but instead of painting on canvas and carving up trees to fashion fine musical instruments, they used their minds and bodies to paint pictures and score symphony, fashioning cerebral images of crashing sea storms, volcanic explosions, fiery hydrothermal vents and life being born. And sometimes, when they felt inspired, they danced to it.

Yes, the six on the surface, just as Autumn had suggested, were dancing.

Flowing with the music, Ashlyn sensed heartbeats, pulses, and strange aural vibrations coming from around the cavern, from other Iquana beings further afar, in the water and above—vibrations from the cavern walls, even from the luminous little critters clinging to those surfaces.

"You are becoming sensitive."

"Sensitive? Is that what it is?" Ashlyn had been feeling changes within him for days, even before Ko had found the submersible. Only he hadn't truly trusted these senses. Being *sensitive* excited him yet it also terrified him. He would never be the same old Ashlyn again. He wondered where would this path ultimately lead? How different would he become? Perhaps a freak to some, the envy of others.

"It is good to be sensitive."

"I hope so."

Not far to his left, Ashlyn spotted a large globe of underwater light, becoming glaringly bright, its surface rays refracting into spectacular multicolored bands and rainbows on the cavern wall.

The group of Iquana that had been dancing near the surface

dove down to this pulsing globe of light.

"What's happening down there?" Autumn asked.

Ashlyn did not answer, for a primordial shiver was snaking down his spine. There was something dark and cruel in that globe of light.

Why would Ko bring them here?

Staring at the globe, transfixed and trembling, Ashlyn's mind flashed back to another time when he'd felt that same sense of horror: when he'd been at the cliff's edge at Deadman's Bluff.

Though he was physically straddled on Ko's back with Autumn by his side in a magnificent subterranean cavern where spectacular shafts of light were sculpting breathtaking rainbows on the cavern walls, the third eye of Ashlyn's mind was now three-hundred feet underwater...and he was witnessing Ko's secret:

This was really a filthy blackness.

"I am sorry, Ashlyn...I didn't know how to tell you."

Sixty members of Ko's family were forming a circle of healing light. Inside this circle, there were sixteen beings, two of them floating on their sides, mostly gray in color, hardly moving, clouds of blood rising from their mouths. One of these was a beautiful female with pleading eyes that tore into Ashlyn's soul. Her skin was peeling away, red-raw and burned off, her angelic dorsal blistered and void of her own natural light. Nearby, a male was convulsing as blood oozed from the corners of his clouded eyes. His chest was covered with black crusting scabs. He reached out to Ashlyn, as if begging to be held, to be hugged. Another female, flexing in pain, found relief from the light of the others now caressing her body. A pulpy, oozing sore on her neck was shrinking, being healed by the magic of light. Wiping away the pink discharge from her mouth, the female moved to the rim of the circle where her own chemosynthetic incandescence once again began to bloom, falling back upon other beings in need.

Tears silently traveled down Ashlyn's cheeks.

"Ashlyn, look away."

Autumn was tugging his arm. "What's the matter? What is it?"

Ashlyn remained hypnotically glued.

"Look away, Ashlyn. Look away."

THE PHONE RANG AT JOURNALIST Dan Shockbottom's house. "Gutter-level tabloid," the voice at the other end bellowed. It was just one more call in a night where Shockbottom had fielded more than thirty calls since going to bed. He could have left the receiver off the hook, but answering was his way of gauging the impact of his alien segment. In a few short hours, he'd been congratulated, laughed at, threatened by angered fundamentalists, and accused of manufacturing the scoop and trying to pull it into the spotlight with pliers and string.

Dan was tired but he felt good. He felt that his scoop was as good as any in this wizened season. Admittedly, it wasn't another presidential scandal or the discovery of a terrorist cell or a glitzy movie star trial but, fortunately, the world was slumbering, from a journalistic perspective. So could an intelligent piscine being and a teenage girl have the potential to collar national news podiums? Surely, it was possible. At the core, children were missing. Perhaps abducted. Shockbottom knew that during lean times like these, the national scoop-vultures hovered, hungry and alert, ready to chase down any yarn at the sound of a buzzer. Why, anything could catch fire. Squirt a little gas, drop a match, watch the inferno.

AN HOUR BEFORE SUNRISE, Eastern Time, Labor Day Saturday, an early morning radio shock jock in New York plucked the Wayside scoop off Reuters, and broadcast it fifteen minutes later. A television network weatherman reeled it in from him, and by 6 A.M. dozens of TV and radio stations across the country had reported the Wayside abduction. The news clincher was Autumn Miller's candy-like voice saying she'd prayed with an alien. Whether true or not—as if the broadcasters cared—it both stirred imaginations and spawned semi-contentious early morning debate.

Dan Shockbottom's manufactured "pliers and string" scoop was catching fire.

POOR BOGDAN BOLESHKO! WHEREVER HE tuned, he heard and saw the same sort of heretical garbage. With each passing minute his anger multiplied like a metastasizing cancer.

Spawned by the Wayside incident, CBS even slipped in an unscheduled prerecorded magazine segment on UFOs. The male anchor said, "—a debate that's gone on ad infinitum, are we alone? Are there other intelligent entities elsewhere in the universe?"

The female added, "They may be even closer than we suspect. Right here on earth, perhaps living underground or under our oceans. That's the claim of UFOlogist Scott Liebermann, author of *Middle*

Earth Really Exists."

Shaking his head in ireful disbelief, Bogdan switched off the TV, and made notes in preparation for his counterattack.

KO'S WORLD WAS NOT QUITE what Ashlyn had hoped for—a magical undersea hideaway where he and Autumn could find refuge. Was the disease afflicting the sea beings contagious like Ebola or AIDS? Was there a carrier? Or was this an infection caused by something in the water? Radioactive waste? Poisonous chemicals? These thoughts ran through Ashlyn's mind as he sat on a rocky ledge next to Autumn, his legs drawing figures of eight in a small rock pool of steamy thermal water.

Ko, in the main lake a few feet away, glided back and forth slowly, her mind as confused as Ashlyn's. Her elders had warned her that contact with humans was unwise, and would likely yield more harm than benefit. Ashlyn's voice interrupted her thoughts: "Is this why you brought us here?"

"I don't know why I brought you here. I know it's not yet time for your kind and ours to live in unity. I was just hoping...hoping to make a friend, hoping...maybe that is all." She glided to the edge of the rock pool, staring into Ashlyn's eyes.

At a loss for meaningful words, Ashlyn sighed.

Ko reached for one of his hands and held it firmly. *"I promised I would never hurt you. After we leave, I will bathe you in my light. You will not suffer from the water."*

So it was the water.

"After we leave here, where are we going?"

Ko lowered her eyes. "Your home."

"And you?"

Her eyes still lowered, Ko attempted to release Ashlyn's hand, but he held onto her. "And you? What will you do?" he asked even though he already knew the answer.

"It is the way it is."

"I don't understand, you can find another cavern where the water is good."

"It is the way."

Ashlyn shook his head. "What way? Whose way?"

Ko fell silent but Ashlyn felt her internal conflict, as if her emotions were his. The bond they shared had been steadily growing. He could feel her emotions, feel her pain, feel her joy. "Whose way?" he asked again.   And then in the same breath: "How many sick?"

Ko rested her forearms, now a silvery blue, on the ledge and looked up into Ashlyn's face. He found it hard to meet her gaze head on. He knew she was dying. He'd known all along, ever since their first meeting at Deadman's Bluff. But the thought had been too painful to digest.

Ko's radiant eyes roamed over Ashlyn's features as she read his thoughts. She wiped a strand of his hair from his eyes, before gazing up at the glittering ceiling. *"Beautiful, isn't it?"*

Ashlyn casually looked about him. "I'm not so sure anymore."

"It is all beautiful. That's the way life is. Like when you soared into the canyon, faster than a sky bird; was that not beautiful?"

Ashlyn nodded, but the pain in his heart prevented him from reminiscing.

"I used to fly to a real chimney city, and bathe in the steaming water. Before… before the machines came."

"I've been feeling your pain. I thought it was me…but it's you."

Ko held Ashlyn's hand, as she looked into his eyes. *"Ashlyn…I am with you. I am with you, always. This is what counts."*

"Always? You mean, like, we're going to hide out at Deadman's Bluff, all of us together?"

"If you cannot see me, if you cannot talk to me, close your eyes and rest your head on your shoulder…and you will find me. I'll have my arm around you." Ko pulled herself half out of the water, and placed her arm around Ashlyn's shoulder. They sat in silence, bathed in thermal steam, just holding each other.

Two members of her family swam by, pulsing brightly. Reading Ashlyn's immediate thoughts, Ko spoke. *"Yes, the light is a healing power, especially when it is magnified by many beings. But we are few. Too many of us are too sick to project light."*

Ashlyn shook his head. "You really don't get it, do you? It's a lie, that's what this place is. These sweeping ceilings and your rock pools and your glassy walls, it's all a lie, a cesspool that's killing you. Why do you stay here?"

Ko took her time before responding. Then she told Ashlyn another story, not from the memory of the crystal pyramid, but from her own recall. There was a time, not so long ago, when the Iquana lived in the open seas, free and unrestrained from any barrier of border, totally unconcerned with their walking cousins on land. But as

Man's technology grew, as Man began to invade the coastlines, building larger and faster vessels, some that could launch deadly projectiles, the Iquana decided to inhabit the subterranean water-ways. They knew that some day Man would make a leap in con-sciousness, and that he'd come to love and respect the planet and all of its life forms…and at that glorious time, Man and Iquana would live side-by-side in harmony. But until then—

"That's beautiful." Ashlyn said. "It makes perfect sense. And I agree. It's not time for you to swim out and flaunt yourselves. But you can't stay here. It's suicide!"

"Dear Ashlyn…don't you see, we cannot risk being seen…and we cannot, and will not, interfere with your evolution." Ko cupped some water over her plume.

"So you are willing to die, because my kind are stuck in the dark ages. How do you think that makes me feel? How do you think most humans would feel about that?" Ashlyn shook his head defi-antly. "I agree it's wrong we're cutting down the forests and pollut-ing the oceans. We're not all that great. We're not all that bad, either. But what you and your elders are doing…that's wrong too. You have a duty to yourselves, to all of the life forms on this planet. You have to survive. There are places, there are places where there's clean water, no pollution. You don't have to die."

"You make death sound so final. It is merely a passage…a jour-ney from one place to another. Spirit does not die."

"That's them talking, your elders. You're different. You want to live."

To a great degree this was true. Ko, the youngest of the Iquana clan, was unique amongst her kindred. She was feisty, inquisitive, daring, and EO had reminded her on numerous occasions that she was overly fascinated by her land cousins and speckled with human-isms.

Even now, Ashlyn could see a child-like human glimmer in her eyes. "Admit it, Ko. You want to live."

Ko acknowledged that she loved living. But the Iquana mind, the mind of her family, wasn't willing to fight for life, to fight for anything, for that matter. She shook her head. *"I think you can un-derstand, Ashlyn, I will never side against my family."*

"Why should I understand something that's wrong? Face it, they're bogged down with their own brand of self-righteousness! Man is so bad and you're oh so good!" Ashlyn knew he was acting with darn right indignation, but he couldn't help himself. "You have to leave here!"

Ko's eyes sparkled. *"Now I know, Ashlyn...now I know why I wanted you to come here. You are my hope."*

"How can I be your hope? You won't allow me to do anything for you."

"You will find your way."

Ko was one-hundred-and-fifty years old. Some of the Iquana were over a thousand, and Ashlyn was a fourteen-year-old kid, a minor with marching orders to Inverness. If he was really her hope, she'd listen to him, and they'd leave, vacate the place at that very moment, find a clean environment. Ko mentioned that Iquana relatives lived two million body lengths away. Doing the math, figuring eighteen feet as their average length, Ashlyn calculated about six thousand miles. "Which way?" he asked excitedly.

"Which way?"

"Which direction? In the direction where the sun sets?"

"Yes...but too far, too long in the open sea...even for a strong Iquana. Too far."

"But what if—"

"Too far...it won't work, Ashlyn."

Ashlyn fell silent for a few moments while he pondered on another idea. "All right...selective aid from humans, people who are only environmentalists and planet lovers?"

Ko shook her head, and once again Ashlyn felt spasms of frustration over her stubbornly held resolve, which he knew was really EO's resolve—no human aid.

Rubbing his weary face, Ashlyn tried to organize his thoughts. How was he her hope? How could he reap a result without performing an action? It was like asking a baseball player to go out and hit a home run without a bat, with his hands and feet hogtied, and with the umpire shouting "out" before he could even take up position on the plate. "I can't score that way...nobody can."

"You will find your way," Ko said sincerely and simply.

Ashlyn rose to his feet. "Where's the source of all this water?"

"Several places. Would you like to see?"

Ko shuttled Ashlyn and Autumn to the far end of the cavern where icy water from far above cascaded over a balcony dripping with dagger-like stalactites before splashing down into the black lake. As Ashlyn touched the glistening wall, frigid water streamed over his knuckles. He looked up.

Maybe the poison's entry was beyond the ceiling. What and who was up there?

Grandma had bragged that Oregon was the cleanest place on earth. No pollution, only fresh air and fresh water.

Perhaps not clean enough.

Ashlyn filled two soda bottles with the contaminated evidence. Maybe the cavern's water could be filtered or neutralized. How, he had no idea. All he knew is that somehow he had to solicit some trusted help and somehow, with or without a blessing, save Ko.

-28-

Labor Day Weekend

IT WAS DAWN ON THE west coast, just before six. Five early-morning joggers flew down the steps of The Five Blossoms Motel, almost knocking over a street protester wearing judgment day boards. "The beast has risen from the sea!" claimed the protester, waving his fist angrily.

The joggers agreed in jest, as they continued toward the beach, laughing.

On this Labor Day Saturday, the air was filled with the aroma of freshly baked bread, sweet cakes, and salt from the ocean. The town was quiet, no traffic at first except a road sweeper, its rotating bristles licking clean the quaint pebbled streets. But a news minivan from Los Angeles startled the joggers when it blasted by them, roaring off in the direction of the coast road. Before the joggers had reached Taylor Avenue, three other newsvans shot by, heading the same direction.

Something was afoot. Plane crash? Couldn't be, the joggers agreed, no fire engines. A shooting? Car crash?

Just then a high-revving Ford sedan screeched around the corner, one of its rowdy occupants yelling something about aliens landing.

The joggers looked to each other with blank stares. None had watched TV that last evening or listened to ABC's morning radio show with Scott Lieberman, the wacky and indomitable UFOlogist, who claimed the US government continually turned a blind eye to abductions, like the case of the "abducted" teens in Oregon. And none of the joggers carried a Walkman radio, so they couldn't know that at that very moment, as they cut across the promenade onto the beach, the local news was reporting that police had found evidence suggesting Autumn and Ashlyn Miller's recent presence inside the cave at Deadman's Bluff.

6:14....

The road alongside the bluff was noisy and congested. A dozen newsvans had parked nose-in on the sandy verge bordering the ridge-top. About a hundred cars had also parked nearby, most illegally.

Sheriff Wiggins ordered the beach cordoned off. Crowds attempted to peer over the cliff, despite the warnings of treacherous winds.

On the narrow beach below, a team of forensics from Eugene combed for evidence, while a coast guard helo buzzed overhead. Another helo skimmed wave-tops a mile out, sweeping the area zone by zone. There were already fifty boats off shore—more than the sheriff had ever seen at one time at Deadman's Bluff.

THE DIGITAL CLOCK ON THE submersible's control surface blinked 6:15. Morning or night, Ashlyn didn't know or really care. He'd lost track of time.

He slumped into his pilot chair aboard *Proteus II* while Autumn fiddled with her seat belt.

"Ashlyn, do not despair. Know that my family feels you. They say you are good energy, a good man. And they feel your sister. Please tell her."

Ashlyn relayed Ko's words to Autumn, whose eyes were puffy from tears. "It's not a good-bye, it's a...'a see you later.'" Ashlyn added, trying to sound upbeat.

"And you, Ashlyn, I am with you, always. Remember...always."

Despondent, miserable, sick to his stomach would, perhaps, describe Ashlyn's real accord, not only for having to say goodbye, but also for the burden he now felt. Ko's life and the lives of her family were now in his custody, their hope riding on his shoulders. The elders said he was a good man. Yet his gut reminded him that he was a runaway, a boy in the eyes of Man's law. Unless he maintained his independence, his mission would undeniably fail. But even if he managed to stay clear of his grandmother and the police, even if he found allies and determined the causative pollutant in the lake, he would still fail unless he could convince Ko and her elders to engage in some sort of action.

He was her hope, yet she had rejected every one of his suggestions. Of course he felt sick to his stomach. Ko's future, and his, didn't seem very promising.

You'll find your way, she'd said numerously.

Yeah, find it into trouble…find it to Inverness.

As he flipped the appropriate switches, the submersible's thrusters began whirring, and cool oxygen flowed into the sphere. The hatch locked with a burst of hissing air pressure. The on-board computer beeped.

Ko asked if he was ready.

No, he wasn't ready to encounter the human world again, but he replied the affirmative.

Proteus II began the long journey home.

THE HUNT SHIP *ARGONAUT* WAS once again on the prowl twelve miles offshore.

Admiral Lightstone had ordered his newly appointed animal acquisition specialist Ed Lazerath to dismiss the three weeks prep time promised, and board his ship immediately. Ed's protest had been feeble, at best.

So, here he was, Labor Day Saturday, pacing the upper deck in a foul mood. He'd signed on to catch a rare fish, to be the brains of the hunt. Now this fish was being touted a spiritual animal and he was no longer the brains, but a servile patsy searching for a submersible and two teenagers.

Heading to the bow on the lower-level deck, ignoring everyone he passed, Ed leaned over the railing, and as he sucked in salty air, he thought about his girlfriend Wanda. They had had plans for this day—and they didn't include his being aboard Andy Lightstone's stinking ship. Wanda had just flown in from New York, and she was now back at the hotel, alone, and he wasn't there to see how adorable she must look in the skimpy teddy he'd purchased for her at Victoria's Secret.

Angrily rubbing his face, Ed looked up and down the ship. Here he was, Labor Day Saturday, heading out to sea. Adding insult to injury, in every direction he looked, there were boats, hundreds and hundreds of boats. How the hell was his sonar man going to spot a tiny submersible in this holiday minestrone?

Andy's orders.

Ed spat in disgust. He hadn't surrendered his life to Andy Lightstone...had he? He reminded himself, there was money here, big money. "Dammit, Wanda! I'm sorry!"

Ed thought about leaning over the rails and shouting at the top of his lungs to vent some of his bottled up anger.

Perhaps he should have...but he didn't.

BOGDAN BOLESHKO ARRIVED AT THE fishery early to work on the finalities of his sermon. The local chapter of C.R.F.O. had forty members. Bogdan's plan was to stand before the entire throng at ten, get them all angry and fired up so that they'd run off and spread whatever rumors he fed them. But first, he needed to sit down with his inner trusted core, his dirty half-dozen who kept their glorious credits hidden from the rest of the chapter. Those credits included the bombing of two gay bars and a women's clinic.

Sitting on a worn leather swivel chair in the tiny mezzanine office upstairs, Bogdan sipped on a Donut King coffee, before posing the question to his attentive clan. "Well boys, how do we quash this vile infirmity?"

Bud James, a heavyset man with a round red face, spoke first: "Fish it out the water and stick it on the barbecue." He laughed.

Nodding with a cynical smile, Bogdan answered, "I guess you know how to catch it?"

Face turned to face in the room, but no one uttered a word.

Bogdan casually plopped the remainder of a cherry donut into his mouth. "But you're on the right track, Bud. Metaphorically." He swallowed the donut and then got down to brass tacks. "In my humble opinion, the best way to debunk this crap is to defocus it, with a well planned counterattack. We *defocus* it by causing folks to think...of something else, like a perpetrator." Bogdan manufactured a pause to build anticipation. "Oracle Publishing, the largest new age publishing house, right here in Oregon. That's our perp. They're behind this."

Bogdan's brothers nodded in agreement.

Bogdan leaned forward. "Free publicity, that's how Oracle benefits. Hype for a new age book! And this, my brothers, is a malicious attack on good Christian values!"

"Over a stinkin' book," remarked Bill.

"Penance to pay," grunted Arnold Hechtcliffe, a man whose bark always fell in line with his brothers.

Bogdan continued: "Three-pronged attack: We discredit the kids. Arnie, you handle their background. Pete, Bill, and me will go after the publisher. We'll plant sketches of this fish-being and a few pages of a book proposal in their office—then we'll leak it to the press."

"That still leaves the navy," Mark Duncan said. At fifty, Mark was the eldest and meanest of the squad. It had been said that during the Gulf War he'd killed a man with his bare hands.

Bogdan tabled his coffee. "We have friends in high places. They'll take care of that end. As for Admiral Lightstone, he's fixing to net this thing to make him rich. He thinks it's some kind of luminescent Loch Ness monster. Well, maybe he knows something we don't."

The squad appeared to be stunned by Bogdan's admission.

Bogdan grinned. "It's another avenue. And it works for us. Maybe there is something…a big, unclassified fish, maybe a rare seal or cetacean. See what I mean about defocus? Any way we can."

"We could spread that—rumor of the day. It's only a dolphin."

"Wouldn't have it any other way, Mark, your job; back it up. Get your friend, your printing buddy, to hustle together some oceanic study. Use any of the reports flying around, CNN, whatever. Doctor 'em up. This story's spreading like wildfire. The media's here; let's use them.

Ten minutes later, Bogdan's pep talk to the full congregation, the regular fundamentalist Christians who knew nothing about the secret agenda, was quite different.

He stood on a crate, Bible in hand and read aloud: "And I stood upon the sand of the sea, and saw a beast rise up out of the sea, having seven heads and ten horns, and upon his ten horns ten crowns, and upon his heads the name of blasphemy." Bogdan looked up. "My friends, we cannot sit and be silent. The streets of heaven aren't lined with cowards. In the name of our Lord Jesus Christ we must fight the blasphemer! We must pluck out these lies and discard them as we do chicken feathers."

"Let's pluck them feathers," someone in the throng added.

"As I speak, there are many souls falling under Satan's spell. They are watching TV and sobbing, crying foolishly, falling to their knees over these wicked lies. We must fight...not just for our own souls but for theirs, too."

"Amen," in unison.

"Spread the word...and let's kick some devil butt."

"Amen."

As Ko HURTLED THE SUBMERSIBLE onward through the clear aquatic night, Ashlyn sat in his pilot's chair, silently and anxiously watching tiny pinpoints of light zipping by the viewports. They were at 2050 feet, only minutes from the surface when his anxiety suddenly turned into a violent burning in his midriff. As he doubled over, clutching his side, *Proteus II* lost its momentum and began nosing downward.

"What's happening?" Autumn shouted.

Hardly able to breathe, Ashlyn fumbled with the controls. Autumn started screaming. "Oh my God! Oh my God! She's dead! She's dead!"

Ko was floating in a fetal position, encapsulated in a dim glow, not pulsing, her mouth open, eyes frozen in what appeared to be her last pose.

The submersible was now moving on its own power, gradually leaving her behind.

With a voracious gasp, Ashlyn sucked in a breath and flew his hand to the joystick, yanking the submersible slowly about. His stomach pain was rapidly leaving him.

But he felt strangely different.

He reached for his shoulder, to where Ko's arm was just moments before, as it had been since the cavern, as it was meant to be for always. "Ko! Please no...."

She was straight ahead, still curled in a fetal position, gray and inanimate—

No, not inanimate...a dim light pulsed inside her chest, a weak light, but nevertheless expanding and retracting—a heartbeat getting stronger again.

"Ashlyn?"

Ashlyn felt Ko's presence returning to his shoulder, as if the flesh of her arm genuinely lay on him, gentle and comforting. "I'm coming, Ko."

"Ashlyn?" Delicate strands of luminous amber and emerald began to lighten her skin.

"I'm here, coming up behind you." Ashlyn pulled back the

throttle, slowing the submersible. He had already decided to escort Ko back home.

"Yes...home...I must return home."

"I'll escort you!"

"No," Ko replied softly.

"I'm not listening to you, Ko."

"Ashlyn, you will listen for your desire is noble but misguided. Be strong for both of us. Continue. Be my hope."

Ko was beginning to gleam, her base color turning violet. *"See, I have my strength."* Resting her open palm against the bottom viewport, her eyes fell on Autumn.

Acting on Ashlyn's request, Autumn placed her palm flat against the side portal while Ko placed her palm on the opposite side of the acrylic. Hand against hand, it was a tender hug separated by three inches of clear hard plastic. As Ko had promised, Autumn felt a sensation of prickly heat permeating through her hand, flowing up through her arm and into her body, no less than a sunlamp tingling her flesh, curing any possible contamination from the cavern.

Then it was Ashlyn's turn to feel the light of Ko's healing power. Though he detested leaving her, he conceded. This was her realm, and what use would he really be, anyway?

Ko forewarned him that at times she'd be silent to conserve energy. Her free-spirited antics, soaring at the speed of a cannonball, pushing a heavy submersible, had worn heavily on her. She needed to recharge. Yet silent or not, she would be with him...always.

Ashlyn canted his head.

"Yes there...always. Be strong. And remember, you are the master of the machine"

"I love you, Ko." Autumn said, holding Bigsey in her arms, pressing her face against the viewport.

Ko's mouth warmed into a wide smile.

Ashlyn conveyed Ko's return message. "She says she feels you and loves you, too. And she wants you to sing and laugh because it is good for you. And...and this is not a farewell."

"I know," Autumn replied, wiping away the tears on her cheeks.

Turning back to Ko, Ashlyn didn't need to voice anything for his heart spoke volumes. He held his head up high, because that's what Ko wanted.

As Ko released *Proteus II's* skids, allowing the submersible to pull away on its own power, Ashlyn kept his eyes on her, indelibly planting into his memory cells that image.

Ko stayed in that same spot for several moments, like a loved one watching a train depart from the station. Then, as the gap broadened, even though she was at a mere one-quarter bloom, she cupped her hands and retroflexed—creating a curve with her body so that she could accelerate—and she began making smooth driving sweeps.

Ashlyn still watched her until she became a mere amber dot, and then vanished from his viewport.

He increased throttle and tilted the submersible's nose up, wondering if he'd ever see her again.

There wasn't any sensation of motion, but the gauge confirmed the acceleration. It was peaceful, silent…empty without Ko…empty knowing they were returning to Wayside.

With her nose still pressed against the starboard viewport. Autumn watched the blackness outside hinting a snippet of blue. Larger fish started to appear—deep-sea species speckled with twinkling lights.

It wasn't long before the aquatic sky was a deep indigo blue—the undersea dawn known as the twilight zone.

Ashlyn maintained a vigilant eye on the scopes, the sonar in particular which was bristling with blips. "Must be good weather."

"Where will we dock?" Autumn asked.

Ashlyn had given the docking subject quite a bit of thought. The submersible's battery meter indicated four hours of remaining power. Estimating their position at forty miles offshore, at fourteen knots, by his calculation they'd just make the coast. But there was no room for error. Most coastal areas would be too dangerous to attempt a landing: Rocks, waves, vicious currents. They would likely run out of juice if they cruised the shoreline, looking for a landing site. He had to pick a spot ahead of time and stick to that choice. The safest place he could think was: "The marina."

Autumn leaned forward. "The marina? That's really keeping a low profile!" She exclaimed. "You are kidding?"

"Marina's the safest place. Wherever we go, we're gonna be seen."

"How about Deadman's Bluff?" Autumn suggested, believing that to be a solid, practical idea.

Ashlyn adjusted the sonar magnification. "I don't think I can distinguish it. See all these blips here in neat lines—that's the marina, I'm pretty sure. Moving north, this looks like the headland, so this might be Deadman's Bluff, but maybe this is or this. I've been thinking it through. We don't know the tides and the marina is about the only place I can pinpoint and navigate to with any decent kind of accuracy."

"What about cops?"

Ashlyn sighed. "As long as we don't break the speed limit, we're just a boat."

"Keeping a really low profile."

"Got any better ideas...that might not kill us?"

She didn't.

At a depth of three hundred feet, spangling showers of blue and green cascaded down from the surface. Ashlyn switched sonar to maximum magnification. The coastline vanished from the graphical display. The new grid had a circumference of three miles. He counted twenty-one green specks, the nearest at a thousand yards. "Wish we had a periscope. Who knows what these are. Ships? Whales? Waves?" He rubbed his chin thoughtfully. "Okay, this is how we do it. When we surface, I'll open the hatch. You sit here in the hot seat. Don't touch unless I say, 'dive!' See this, push it forward like this, and push this joystick like this, and press it down a bit...that'll make it tilt down."

Ashlyn vacated his seat. "Oh, and when I say 'pump' press this. You have to do that! It's the emergency pump in case we're sacked by a wave, so we don't sink. Whenever we open the hatch in the open sea, we turn it on, as a precaution. Now sit in the seat."

Autumn looked perplexed. "Why can't you stay here? You're making me nervous."

"Just do it. You'll probably only be pressing the one."

"Which one?"

"Pump. We're almost there. You can do it." He smiled.

The submersible dipped. Through the viewports they could see the rifling surface sparkling with streams of azure light.

50 feet...30...20....

"Get ready." Ashlyn climbed into the conning tower. He held on as the submersible surged forward and dipped down. No doubt about it, a surface swell. "Hit it! Pump!" He shouted.

Ashlyn pulled the hatch pressure release, spun the wheel and pushed. Ears popping, he drove his head through the hole, and was greeted by real air—fresh, windy sea air. The sky was a powder blue.

Greedily filling his lungs, he saw only a few boats in his immediate vicinity but the horizon was speckled with hundreds of sails and dot-sized motor yachts. Land was obviously beyond them. He held on tightly, as the submersible rolled down a glassy blue canyon, then slowly rose. He held back the feeling of nausea.

"Okay?" Autumn hollered.

"Don't touch anything!"

"What? Do it?" she hollered again.

"No!" Ashlyn scrambled back down into the sphere. "I'll take it." He slipped into the pilot's chair and juiced the thrusters. At full speed, the swells were manageable. Canting his head to the side, he took an anxious breath.

Yes, Ko was still with him.

ED LAZERATH WASN'T A SONAR expert. To his layman's eyes, the *contact* on the scope looked insignificant, no different from any others on the scope.

Yet the sonar man was so sublimely confidant, he said he'd bet a week's salary on it. "That there's a small submarine, just surfaced."

WARM SALTY WIND AND SEA spray tousled Autumn's hair as she stood up in the conning tower. But for an uncomfortable knot in her gut, she could have slept right there with the sea elements caressing her face, yet that knot constantly reminded her of her grandma and of being shuttled off to Inverness. Ashlyn's brazen plan of sailing straight to the marina seemed to seal that fate, even though, she had to admit, it was probably the wisest choice for a mooring site. In the span of a few days her brother had grown up beyond his years. She could see the changes in him. Ashlyn, older by only eighteen months, an outsider at school, the one considered the most unlikely to succeed, was Ko's hope...and right now, he was her hope, too.

Autumn rubbed her tired eyes. The flotilla of sailboats and cruisers were closer now. In the distance she could barely discern a hazy coastline. To her right, a large boat was approaching.

Ashlyn was studying the same boat on scope when he heard a ring, a familiar sound, although he couldn't place it as a part of the submersible's mechanics.

Phone.

Where did he put the cell?

Autumn kept her eyes on the large boat...no, more than a boat, a ship, getting closer and closer.

She yelled down into the sphere. "Ashlyn! Ashlyn! A ship's coming!"

Finding the phone tucked at the bottom of his backpack, Ashlyn stabbed the talk button. "Hello?"

The caller's voice was drowned out by Autumn's yelling as she scrambled down the metal rungs. "There's a ship coming, right for us!"

Ashlyn turned back to the scope. "It's twelve hundred yards!"

"No! It's gonna ram us!" Autumn cried.

"Hello, can you hear me?" asked the voice on the phone.

"Who is this?" Ashlyn asked impatiently.

The reply, enshrouded in static, did not enlighten Ashlyn. He flew past Autumn, up into the conning tower where he saw a ship all right, about the length of a football field, eight hundred yards off. Closing. Surely, it had seen them!

"Ashlyn, can you hear me?" The voice on the phone demanded.

"Boomer?" Ashlyn replied.

"Thank God. Are you okay?"

"No! We've got a ship bearing down on us. I've gotta go!"

"A ship?"

"I can't talk, Boomer."

Ashlyn was about to drop back down into the sphere when a voice droned out of the ship's loudspeaker. "Ashlyn, Autumn, wave if you're alright!"

Ashlyn halted in his tracks, and slowly turned around.

How did anyone know they were on a submersible?

"What's happening?" Boomer cried down the phone.

Ashlyn scrutinized the ship. No coast guard flag. The name *Argonaut Explorer* was painted on the ship's side. "I guess it's not going to ram us, after all."

Autumn called out. "Ashlyn! What's going on?"

"Hold on, Autumn!"

"Is it coast guard?" Asked Boomer.

"I don't think so…"

"Ashlyn and Autumn," the ship's loudspeaker droned. "—My name is Ed Lazerath. We are the oceanographic explorer Argonaut. We would like to bring you aboard. We have an A-frame for your submersible."

"Talk to me, Ashlyn. Is it coast guard?" Boomer demanded.

"No. It's some exploring ship, Argonaut."

"Don't go with them!" Boomer yelled.

"What?"

"Don't go with them!"

"They're getting close." Ashlyn replied nervously.

"They are animal hunters, extraction specialists!"

Ashlyn paled.

Boomer continued: "Everyone's looking for you. You're on the news. Because of the alien...Autumn prayed with it. Yah, it's the headlines. It's everywhere."

Ashlyn's body tensed. "News? Headlines?" How was it possible?

"Where are you?" Asked Boomer.

Ashlyn was speechless.

"Ashlyn? Where are you?"

"We're...we're at sea, two, two and a half hours from the harbor. I can't believe it...people know!"

"Did you say submersible?"

"Yeah."

"You have a submersible?"

"Uh-huh."

"Amazing...amazing. And good. Dive. Use sonar. I'll meet you at the harbor."

"Boomer, wait! Don't tell anyone we're coming!"

"I won't...oh, Ashlyn, what slip?"

"F-112."

ARGONAUT WAS SLOWING, BUT STILL slicing the waves at eighteen knots as she closed to within two hundred yards of *Proteus II*. Four divers with undersea jet packs were on her deck, waiting for the right moment to drop over the ship's side.

"Steady as she goes," announced the first mate. But his expression hardened as he watched Ashlyn slam shut the hatch on the submersible.

"They're going!" Ed Lazerath roared at the diving captain as he watched aghast. "Go! Go! In the water!"

But the diving captain, a skinny figure they called Popeye because of his bulging tattooed triceps, shook his head. He quickly assessed the ship's speed, wind, swell, and he didn't budge.

"Jump, man! They're going! Now!" Ed screamed at the top of his lungs. In frustration he watched *Proteus II* dip down below the waves in spumes of blue bubbles. "Go! Go!"

Popeye shook his head. "Too fast!" He and his three divers weren't going over the side at fifteen knots.

Argonaut's sonar technician reported the submersible descending to one-hundred-and-fifty-five meters, before leveling, he estimated at fifteen knots. "Little underwater bullet, that thing."

Ed Lazerath kicked the railing and cussed. "This is crap! This is bull!" He wasn't a submersible catcher; he was a marine extraction specialist, a professional. "Now what?"

The skipper proposed two options. "Track it in, let the ground team pick 'em up. Or forge ahead; let the divers get into position. Your call, Ed."

-29-

The Wharf

"WE'RE ASKING FOR IT, YOU know that," Carter whined as he trailed Boomer into the back alley behind the Wayfarer store. Throwing open the garage doors, Boomer jumped into his rusting carcass of a car that had once been the pride of British motoring, Carter reluctantly following. "This is stupid. I mean how stupid is this?" Carter sighed as he slammed the Jaguar's door shut. As much as he was willing to maintain a degree of open-mindedness, he feared Boomer had really flipped his lid this time.

Boomer gunned the old car's accelerator, reversing at a stupid speed into the main street, while Carter fell mute.

Both men were lost in thought.

What really disturbed Boomer was that Admiral Lightstone had located the kids when the police, media, and everyone else hadn't been able to. Argonaut would obviously track Ashlyn's submersible on sonar. Would Lightstone also try to intercept?

Carter's advice for all intents and purposes was logical, rational, clear-headed counsel: "Call the police, the coast guard, let them handle the situation."

But Boomer resisted logic. Logical minds tended to explain the unexplainable, they found ways to neutralize magic and make light of true wonder. And Boomer couldn't stop thinking about the wonder of Ashlyn piloting a submersible. Piloting it, dammit, coming back from God knows where. He absolutely had to speak to Ashlyn before the cops and the press could contaminate any of the account of where the kids had been.

Boomer swung out wide to pass a Volkswagen before roaring through the intersection at Collins and Third, oblivious to Carter's look of despair.

His mind flashed back to twelve years ago, to the months he'd spent with Jerry Miller aboard Sea Lab. In the beginning, the energy had been good, the morale upbeat, the hunger for discovery—any new discovery—intoxicating. But the search was long and hard, and gradually the crew turned ugly and disgruntled, placing unreasonable demands on Jerry. Most everyone branded Jerry a fool, a nutcase, a loser. Boomer had watched the man's inner spark dying before his eyes. All those logical minds that could never consider the possibility that something magical had happened extinguished it.

To this day, Boomer felt remorse for staying in the shadow, for never telling Jerry that it was okay to believe.

A car horn snapped Boomer out of his reverie. He suddenly realized that Carter was blabbering. He turned to his friend. "What?"

"I said if friends can't be jail buddies, what good are we? So how do you plan on dealing with the admiral? I heard he eats diver intestines for breakfast."

Boomer nodded thoughtfully. He was fully aware that Lightstone was a dangerous man.

WITH THE CONCENTRATION OF A brain surgeon, Ashlyn navigated the submersible through a field of swaying stems resembling squid tentacles—huge bottled-green and black leafy kelp.

They were three miles from the coast, whether at Wayside or someplace miles away, Ashlyn wasn't sure. Though sonar was brimming with *blips*, his attention had never strayed from the one *blip* he knew to be his nemesis—*Argonaut.* "Maybe they're as close to shore as they dare go. Could be our chance!"

Autumn frowned. "What?"

"I bet they've run out of water!" Ashlyn trimmed ballast, pulled back the navigation joystick one notch, slightly elevating the sub's nose. Then he jumped out of his pilot's chair. "Same drill as before."

"What are you doing?"

"We're surfacing."

"Boomer said no."

"We might have an advantage, and I'm not going to waste it.

See that—that's our battery. We're running out of juice!"

Autumn's eyes scrutinized the controls nervously. "Are you sure?"

"You'll be okay." Ashlyn ushered her into the hot seat. "I know what I'm doing; Boomer's not here, I am."

Ashlyn charged up the metal staircase. "Get ready."

The moment he felt the submersible rolling in a surface wave, he yelled: "Hit it! Pump!" And he yanked the hatch pressure release.

Poking his head out into the brightness of day, Ashlyn immediately saw *Argonaut* anchored. Her crewmen were lowering a submersible and two Zodiac dinghies over the ship's side. With Olympian speed, Ashlyn jumped back down into the sphere. "Full throttle!" He shouted with a crafty smile and a wink of confidence. "You can do it, thrusters all the way forward!"

Ashlyn's confidence helped quell Autumn's anxiety. "Aye-aye, captain." She pushed the thrusters forward.

"I was right. The ship's anchored. It's us versus their dinghies…oh, and their submersible."

Autumn's grin sank. Dinghies? Submersible?

Ashlyn's brow hardened. "Dog meat! Stay the course!" Ashlyn slipped a finger through an O-ring on the floor. A square metal plate came up in his hand. He peered down into the sub's hold—eighteen inches deep, two feet long, containing lifejackets, freeze-dried foods, a five gallon bottle of water, and a box of SOS flares. "Cooked dog meat."

Autumn turned around. "What are you doing?"

"They screw with us, they can eat these!" Holding one of the emergency flares, he read the instructions. "Hold at arm's length away from face. Never point at objects, animals, or people. Aim high and pull string here." Tucking the flare box under his arm, he scooted up the conning tower.

The Zodiacs where on the way, strafing foggy trails of white water. Ashlyn counted three men aboard each craft. Side-by-side, they covered the half-mile in less than thirty seconds. Ashlyn took a deep breath to calm his butterflies.

The dinghies screamed into a tight crescent curve, then split up to flank *Proteus II.*

Ashlyn now had four flares tucked into his waistband, one under each arm. Autumn was holding the other six, ready to pass them up if needed.

Breathe easy. Here they come.

The approaching Zodiacs buzzed him on both sides, engines roaring, shooting back sheets of steamy spray that slapped hard into Ashlyn's face. He hardly flinched, knowing the flashy maneuvers were intimidation tactics. The boats swung about in tight arcs. Ashlyn steadied himself in the wake, feeling Autumn steering the submersible out of the turbulence. "Good girl," he mumbled under his breath.

He watched the enemy carefully as they reduced speed, approaching his stern. Of the six divers, four were in wet suits. One shouted, "We want to help you. We're going to throw you a line. Cut your throttle."

Pretending not to hear, Ashlyn awkwardly waved, while pressing the concealed flare tighter into the fold of his armpit. The knots in his gut tightened. "Breathe deep. Stay calm," he told himself. "I'm in control."

The Zodiacs drew level, ten yards on either side. One of the divers flicked four fingers across his neck. "Kill your engines!"

Ashlyn nodded and made the same four-finger flick. The diver acknowledged with a thumbs up. On that cue, Ashlyn ducked down in the conning tower, and in the same fluid motion, transferred a flare into his palm. "Now!" he shouted at Autumn.

While Autumn jumped out of the pilot's seat with the other six flares, Ashlyn rocketed up through the hatch, aiming and pulling the string. As a red smoky glob flew out of the flare's tube, he heard panicked shouts from the dinghy but he was so focused on firing the second flare, then the third, that he didn't even notice the results.

What the divers on the Zodiacs saw was a scowl-faced commando shooting a miniature bazooka, for which they were virtually defenseless. They gasped, yelled, and ducked as the projectiles fell upon them one after another.

Ashlyn's motion was smooth, constant. He fired a flare, whirled port side to the other dinghy, fired a flare, whirled, fired. He glimpsed a yellow flame flickering out of the first dinghy, then a shower of sparks, a bang.

He hurled another pitch, another strike over the plate.

More sparks, a bigger bang.

He uncoiled flares eight and nine. As they soared toward the targets, purplish-red smoke was billowing. The divers were scrambling, trying to evict the fiery charcoals.

Ashlyn aimed another flare. But the men were jumping overboard. He turned to the second dingy. But they'd already jumped. He pulled the last string anyway.

PAUL MOSSENBERGER AND HIS FRIEND Kirk watched the flare battle from the deck of their Tartan 10-meter sloop. Each had quaffed a dozen beers and smoked some primo Hawaiian bud. With glassy eyes, an occasional stoic head nod, Paul uttered only two words, and only when the submersible flinging the smoky bombs disappeared in a froth of bubbles below the waves. "Cool, dude."

Kirk simply nodded, and said nothing.

Meanwhile, *Argonaut's* chase submersible *Gracy* accelerated to her maximum speed—six knots. She was outclassed by *Proteus II*. The fourteen-knot little bullet pulled away, swiftly distancing herself from the enemy.

AT CANVELLE'S BOATYARD ON THE wharf, Boomer and Carter were scrutinizing a seventy-five foot iron-hulled fireboat bearing six high-pressure water pumps. Dick Canvelle, Boomer's good buddy, claimed *Firebelle* could do sixteen knots, but any more than eight, she would probably sink.

Boomer shook his head, grimacing. High-powered water jets would have been great. His attention sidetracked to Dick's *Sea Ray Sundancer*—a sharp forty-three footer with twin Caterpillar 357 engines.

Dick Canvelle shook his head adamantly no. "Firebelle is all I got...and don't give me that 'come on Dick, you owe me.'"

Boomer's eyes ping-ponged, back and forth, from *Firebelle* to *Sundancer*. "You said it, I didn't." Boomer began checking the mounting brackets on *Firebelle's* water hydrants. "Carter, toolkit in my trunk."

"I know what you're thinking and the answer is no way!" Dick bellyached. "Not on my baby!"

"And Carter..." Boomer yelled. "...furniture pad, bring it, too. We'll mount the pump on it." Boomer then turned to Dick. "On her transom."

As Boomer and Carter began removing the water hydrant from *Firebelle*, Dick paced the yard, stuttering a protest that fell on cloth ears.

Struggling with a stripped bolt, Boomer said, "Dick, you're

sounding a lot like Etta, your ex."

"You mean like a wind-up doll with a stuck battery, morning till night, nag nag nag."

"You said it," Boomer guffawed.

"Yeah, lucky for me she took her ass to one of them alligator parks in Florida, and never came back. Seriously, Boomer, this boat is my pride and joy."

"Hey, I dent it or smash it, I own it."

"What?"

"Joking…not a scratch. You won't even miss us…we'll be gone and back in a flash. "

Pulling his baseball cap down over the bridge of his nose, Dick whined, "No over-revving. The engines need to breathe, to be taken to their pinnacle gently, like passionate lovers!"

"Got it. We'll glide."

"Not a scratch, you hear—"

"Not a pimple."

NEWLYWEDS JOHN AND JENNY KEESLING were amongst the boating crowd off Wayside that Saturday morning, flooring their Sea Doo water bikes along the velvety crests several miles off shore. Deciding to take a breather, Jenny pulled back the throttle on her Sea Doo, allowing the bike to drift along with the tempo of the ocean, when a large dark *something* passed right under her.

"Move!" her husband yelled, thinking a shark was about to attack.

Throttling her Sea Doo, Jenny was about to peel the hell out of there when the fin broke to the surface, only it wasn't a fin. It was a submersible's conning tower gently slicing up through the waves.

Watching in awe, Jenny heard a steaming burst of air pressure as the submersible's hatch opened and up came a pretty young girl, her long blonde hair flying in the wind.

Jenny Keesling could hardly believe her eyes. She was gazing at the face from the morning news broadcast.

Who says honeymooners don't watch TV?

Jenny tried to recall exactly what she had seen on TV—*We need to borrow your submersible.*

"Don't tell me they rent those things?" Jenny's husband said as he slid his Sea Doo about, banking it toward the submersible.

"It's the girl from the news."

John Keesling frowned.

"The Wayside abduction!" Jenny gently throttled her Sea Doo to keep pace with the submersible. "Hello, nice day," she called out, knowing only too well it was a lame greeting. The girl on the sub-mersible—prettier in real life—smiled at her warmly, but said noth-ing. Jenny then said, "Looks like a fun boat…need any help?"

Continuing to ignore her, the girl on the submersible briefly ducked down out of sight.

The newlyweds had a quick conversation about the morning news, and when the girl reappeared, John positioned his bike even closer to the submersible. "Hey, kid, what's up?"

Ashlyn had already instructed Autumn to ignore the cou-ple—ignore as in 'don't answer them'—and keep her eyes fixed on the flags of the harbor approach. But ignoring them didn't feel quite right to Autumn, so she turned to the couple and said, "We were go-ing to scuba, but you know, why scuba when you can go real deep?"

"Man, that's a fine piece of engineering," John quipped. "Say, you're not those missing kids, are you?"

Autumn brushed her hair from her eyes. "How can I be miss-ing? I'm right here."

"I don't recall your name," Jenny interjected. "On TV they said you prayed with an alien. Was he green?" Well, it seemed funny to Jenny when the newswoman said it, but when Autumn's demeanor visibly tensed, Jenny quickly wiped the stupid grin off her face. Though a statuesque six feet, she suddenly felt all of two-foot-two. "I didn't mean to offend you. You okay?"

Autumn turned away.

"Hey, look I'd pray with an alien too…I mean, I would if I could."

Autumn slowly nodded. She felt compelled to respond, to say something meaningful, despite Ashlyn's admonition. And what spilled out of her mouth was a laconically poignant message for mankind, a message that would later be repeated time and time over.

"We're fine. But they're sick. And it's our fault. We've poi-soned the ocean and they're all dying…and they are beautiful." Autumn wiped her eyes.

"YOU TOLD HER WHAT?" Ashlyn exploded. "We agreed, Autumn! Whatever anyone says, asks, implies, we say nothing!"

"I'm sorry. But they knew already. All I did was set the record straight! Anyway, they seem kinda nice."

"How the hell do you know what they are?" Ashlyn barked.

"Then you go up there!" Autumn barked back, which is exactly what Ashlyn did.

Topside Ashlyn quickly discovered that the Keeslings were not only nice, they were also accommodating. *Proteus II's* batteries were riding on fumes, and the harbor was still a way off, so Ashlyn supplied the rope, and the Keeslings supplied the tow.

Once on the move, Autumn parked herself in the conning tower, her hair blowing in the breeze, while Ashlyn tied himself to the deck to escape the rising temperature below. The sun-baked deck had turned the inside of *Proteus II* into a Swedish sauna.

It wasn't long before the submersible was a major focus of attention—boaters honked, shouted, waved, and sailed alongside in convoy.

Ashlyn shuddered. Where was all this attention leading?

Approaching the breakwater, north side of the marina, a metallic scream pierced the air.

From his periphery, Ashlyn saw several jet skis leaping over the breakwater's rocky wall. Airborne, at full rev, the jet skis looked like shrieking birds of prey.

Then they landed with a roar!

Momentarily frozen, like the proverbial deer in the headlights, Ashlyn's mind at last jammed into gear when he saw lassoing ropes flying toward him. "Down!" He screamed at Autumn. He quickly tallied a total of six jet skis driven by frogmen in black wet suits. "Down inside!"

Jenny was the first casualty. Tripped up, she hit a wave hard. Ashlyn watched her Sea Doo tumbling away from her.

One of the frogmen slammed a set of magnetic suction cups onto *Proteus II's* deck. More circles of rope flew over Ashlyn's head, one of them ensnaring the conning tower. Ashlyn threw himself into the hole, groaning as he careened into a metal rung. Reaching for the hatch above him, he glimpsed John Keesling entangled in rope, struggling to stay aboard his bike. Divers were already on *Proteus II's* deck.

"Move!" he yelled at Autumn a few steps below him.

She dropped down into the sphere. Ashlyn pulled the hatch and it clanged down shut, but he couldn't spin the wheel! A frogman was struggling to open it!

The frogman was strong.

Too strong! Ashlyn stepped off the rung, using all his body weight.

Still not enough muscle.

He was being lifted up...up...back into daylight. Horrifyingly, he found himself staring at two ugly frogmen who were smiling at him. Now Ashlyn recognized them: Evil Goatee and Hooknose, bandaged and ready for revenge.

Ashlyn's future—maybe even his life—hung in the balance of that long stare, which seemed to linger forever in slow motion. But when a loud *hissing something* whizzed overhead, Evil Goatee's grin quickly drained from his face. Before Goatee could even say "not again!" he was flying off the deck, zapped by a rocketing blast of pressurized water.

Déjà vu!

As his stunned partner Hooknose looked up, he glimpsed a white streak of water, like a laser beam, hissing toward him. Then he was punched in the midriff, and the air was knocked out of him. He found himself flying.

Carter at the helm of the race boat *Sundancer* zeroed in on the next Jet Ski villain, while Boomer on fire hydrant duty squeezed the trigger, discharging another powerful water blast. Boomer's aim was good, the powerful stream of water landed on the frogman's chest, immediately ejecting him from his machine.

Carter spun the boat, shooting across his own foamy wake, causing sheets of backwash to fall on the last two Jet Skiers like hard rain. Boomer's sights quickly picked off another frogman, while the last perp gunned the throttle of his machine, trying to outrun justice. Boomer found his mark in the Kawasaki's exhaust pipe. The Jet Ski flipped into the air, its engine coughing and spluttering, its frogman helplessly tumbling away from it.

Carter spun *Sundancer* around almost on a dime, and drew alongside *Proteus II*.

The cavalry had arrived, the enemy was down, and boy, was Ashlyn grateful. Jenny and John Keesling were shaken but not physically hurt. As newlyweds hoping for a long and healthy life, no one could really blame them for making a swift departure.

Boomer threw Ashlyn a new towline...and once again *Proteus II* was in motion, surfing around the breakwater, ignoring the 5 mph buoy, and barreling down the channel into Boatyard Alley.

When Dick Canvelle saw the submersible entering his boat yard, he felt like bowel fluxing. The kids from the media storm were in his boatyard! Boomer leapt off *Sundancer* and pulled the submersible into the dock. A small crowd was already gathering.

"You didn't tell me," Dick moaned plaintively.

Boomer threw the line over the bollard. "You didn't ask." Following Boomer's lead, the teens, laden with luggage, bottles of contaminated water, and Bigsey, jumped off *Proteus II,* and ran to Boomer's Jag.

Meanwhile Dick Canvelle paced, his arms flying in bewilderment. "Wait. What do I do? What do I tell them?"

"The truth," Boomer shouted out of the Jag's window.

"What about *that*?" Dick gaped at the submersible.

"We'll come back for it." Boomer yelled. Then he jammed his foot down on the accelerator and sped out of the yard.

THOUGH THE DAY WAS A scorcher, a peg under a hundred degrees, the ride in Boomer's car started off chillingly silent.

Boomer was thinking about his purpose in life…and *Proteus II.* At first glimpse, he'd recognized her lineage. The original *Proteus* wasn't as long or wide, she had propellers instead of thrusters, but overall the submersibles were twins. *Number II* had been under construction when Jerry died, and scrapped soon after, he'd believed. Now Boomer was even more convinced that the male voice on the audiotape was that of a ghost. What a turnaround! What a day of amazing events.

Ashlyn was lost in his own thoughts. He was thankful to Boomer and Carter, but should he trust them? It was all happening too fast. The Iquana's plight had been broadcast, people were looking for them, and some, it seemed, wanted his skin. The best plan of action, he decided, was to lie low while he made new plans. He locked eyes with Boomer in the rear view mirror, and broke the silence. "Where are we going?"

"We can drive for a while."

"And then?"

Boomer twisted in his seat. "Your options are limited. Cops need to speak to you, and so does your grandmother."

Ashlyn adamantly shook his head. "We can't. No cops. No Grandma."

"Ashlyn, I am sorry. But you must surrender yourselves. You

saw the commotion back there."

Ashlyn slowly nodded. "I understand…you can't help us. Just drop us off. We might as well get out here." Ashlyn's hardened look confirmed his intent to remain aloof, underground, a fugitive, so be it.

Boomer grimaced. "There are too many people…everyone's looking for you. Carter and I, we're already in a lot of trouble."

Ashlyn reached for the door handle. "It's not a problem. We'll manage on our own."

Boomer braked, but didn't completely stop the car. "I want to help you—"

"Oh, yeah. You want to help? You have no idea…you have no idea, if we surrender—" Ashlyn stopped. He really didn't want to bail out of the car at that moment. Surely, there was a way to soften Boomer's resolve. Deciding on a different approach, he tentatively released the door handle. "You want to help us? I need to know what you guys know."

"Same as everyone, from the news, the audiotape…maybe a bit more."

Boomer turned into a side street and stopped the car. "Look, if you're wondering if I believe you…if I believe in…you know, I have an open mind. Where you've been, what you've been up to, whether you tell me or not, it's up to you. Me and Carter, we're with you, we support you, whatever you decide, as long as you haven't broken any laws. That doesn't mean I don't want to know. But understand this, Ashlyn, some people are going to push…they're going to demand answers. Some people, not us."

"What audiotape?" Ashlyn asked.

"Audiotape, you and Autumn and er the man with the submersible. It's all over the news."

"He taped us?" Ashlyn was stunned. "Why did he do that?"

Boomer looked into Ashlyn's eyes. "You tell me."

Ashlyn gently touched his shoulder, almost tenderly, Boomer thought. Ashlyn then faced Autumn, shrugging, looking for guidance.

Autumn also shrugged. Her instincts affirmed that Boomer and Carter were gentle souls, but she didn't want to verbally endorse them. She answered: "Up to you. Remember what Ko said—*You'll find your way.*"

Ashlyn exhaled a weighty sigh. Maybe he was going to find his way, but at that moment, he was truly lost. Turning to Boomer, he said, "I guess I should thank you for saving our asses."

Boomer winked. "You'd have done the same for me. Would you like to start from the beginning?"

Biting his lip, Ashlyn pensively nodded. "A few weeks ago, Autumn and I were on the beach at Deadman's Bluff—"

While Ashlyn recounted the events of the past few weeks, with Autumn dotting his i's and crossing his t's, Boomer headed to the Sheraton. He suspected the cops would be at his storefront after the wharf. By going to the Sheraton, he'd have time to hear Ashlyn's story...before being arrested.

Ashlyn's account was lengthy, despite being a censored version. Boomer sat spellbound listening to the cavern of death, how amidst so much pain there was peace, beauty, joy, even music and dancing.

Finally, sitting in the hotel parking lot, the story was told.

The car turned quiet.

While Ashlyn studied Boomer and Carter for their reactions, the men's minds fought for direction. Was Ashlyn telling the truth?

Boomer's skin was tingling with goose bumps. Carter felt moisture in his eyes. The men seemed to make their decision at the same time.

Boomer held up the two bottles of cavern water, while he slowly gathered his thoughts. "It makes me want to weep out loud. What have we done?"

"What we've done is not that important right now. What's important is how we proceed from here." Ashlyn reached for the water bottles. "These two bottles, for example."

"Running won't work. You'll spend more time running than being productive. If I were you, I would dig in. Yah. That doesn't mean you have to talk...you can deny everything, if you want. We can analyze the water privately; we can hire chemists. With the money from the pendant, you can do a lot. But think, Ashlyn, the discovery is no longer a secret. People are talking. Ask me what I would do? I would use it to your advantage. Stand up on a platform, and speak loud. Use your position and your notoriety to force environmental changes; make noise and get folks all riled up with emotion. It's what your father used to do."

Ashlyn rubbed his aching temples. "Ko would say that's noble but misguided."

"And you, yah, is that what you think?"

Ashlyn lowered his eyes. If only he could do as he wished, if only Ko would endorse such a plan, if only— he ran his fingers through his hair. "It's not that easy. I need to think about it."

Boomer smiled. "Of course." He hoped with all his heart that Ashlyn would make the smart decision. Together, they would become warriors for justice. The notion made him feel alive and invigorated. Fate had a strange way of balancing the scales. If not for his caisson disease, he'd still be diving, probably in some far off place like Grenada or Florida, instead of being burrowed into a quiet life on the Oregon coast, and now into an association with Ashlyn and Autumn, Jerry's kids. His role was already identified: mentor, supporter, surrogate uncle.

"So, now what? You going to turn us over to the police?" Ashlyn asked.

Boomer furrowed his brow. He was never going to turn them over to the police. He'd only suggested they surrender themselves. But regardless of whatever Ashlyn's decision was, they needed protection. The explosive news had already caused a ruckus and it was nothing compared to the full story. As their trusted confidante, he simply couldn't drop them off at the cops or the grandmother, not until they had a lawyer, a great lawyer. And as it so happens, he knew the perfect one. "Change of plan." Boomer replied. "We need some extra time."

Carter lowered his glasses, his face showing overt signs of angst. "Hey, buddy, I'm with you but—"

"Relax, my friend. I know what I'm doing. We need some time…and a lawyer."

Ashlyn stirred. "That's a good idea. Do you know one?"

"The best. In Portland," Boomer answered. "First, let's get a room, okay."

Boomer asked them to wait in the car while he scurried into the Sheraton. A few minutes later he was back, holding a room key.

They snuck into the hotel through a side entrance, up to a room on the top floor. The air conditioner was humming full pelt. It was a welcome contrast from the stuffy car. Boomer called his lawyer pal in Portland, but was told by an officious secretary that he was at a luncheon, and wouldn't return until after two. After replacing the receiver, Boomer heard a stomach growl—Carter's.

"Me, too. I could eat a horse if I wasn't so tired." Autumn sighed, slumping down onto one of the beds.

Boomer called room service, and ordered the Chinese special, while Carter flipped TV channels. "Holy smoke!" he exclaimed. "It's us!"

The news broadcast was at least as hot as the broiling weather. There were shots of the submersible at the wharf, investigators swarming, eyewitnesses with different versions of the submersible battle, and a female reporter saying, "…were seen on this submersible, engaged in a fierce water-hydrant battle with a number of frogmen on Jet Skis. Witnesses say two Caucasian males on a speedboat joined the foray and whisked the teens here to Fisherman's Wharf. As of this hour, police and federal investigators are still combing the area, looking for the two men and the teens. And as for this multi-million dollar submersible, how the teens managed to operate it, and where've they been for the last two days remains a mystery, but these questions have to be on the minds of investigators, as this tale twists and turns and gets more extraordinary by the moment."

"Rock-and-roll!" remarked Carter facetiously, his eyes rolling in despair. "You guys are famous, we're infamous, and we're all in for it!"

Ashlyn exhaled a guttural sigh, "I'm sorry."

Carter quickly downed a beer from the mini-bar "Makes me wish I was a dog, Jennifer Aniston's. What do you say, Boomer, run for the hills? Yeah, you're right, a little spice to the life. How about an autograph, Ashlyn? Maybe I can sell it in the slammer."

After chummily snarling, Boomer switched to channel 8 where another story about the kids was breaking. Ditto with channels 7, 13, even CNN, their anchor saying with a smug grin, "And in Oregon, Close Encounters of the Piscine Kind."

Some of the channels were featuring the story as breaking news, others like NBC from New York used it as a light closer. One of the stations ran Autumn's message, relayed through newlywed Julie Keesling. "'They're sick. It's our fault. We've poisoned the ocean. Unless we stop, they'll all die. And they're beautiful.'"

The reporter reiterated, "And *they* are beautiful! Meaning more than one?"

The shot switched back to the news anchor: "Although police continue to investigate this as an abduction, there's a growing consensus that this is a very elaborate environmental ploy or, as some are claiming, an ingenious publicity stunt."

There was a knock on the door. Four hearts momentarily froze but resumed beating when the voice outside said: "Room Service."

The food's aroma was sweet and spicy. "Yup, add a little spice to life," Carter mumbled as he poured soy sauce over his paper-wrapped chicken.

As they were eagerly loading up their plates, a TV fiction began to grow. *Action Headlines* was reporting that the teens were members of a new age cult, and that their father, the late Jerry Miller, was a quasi-environmentalist and initiator of Oregon's legendary Seabed Phantom searches.

Switching back to channel 4, evangelist Billy Bob, donned in a red velvet robe, was being interviewed. He appeared livid. "When it looks like a dog, when it fouls the sidewalk like a dog, when it stinks like a dog, believe me, it's a dog! This isn't breaking news! It's a dog! Where do these kids come from? I'll tell you where…unhinged parents! We're not talking wishy-washy liberal here—*the kids can figure it out themselves*—we're talking loco! Father, a certifiable schizophrenic! Mother intimate with Marshall Applegate. Remember him, the leader of the new age wackos who vacated their 'containers' to rendezvous with a spaceship?"

Ashlyn felt his blood boiling. "How can they say that?" How can they report such far-fetched, out-and-out lies?"

"They do whatever they want, print whatever, edit however, slant it however. Who's gonna stop them?" Carter replied.

His appetite lost, Ashlyn pushed aside his plate. Was it worth adding to the madness by responding? What benefit would it be to get up on a platform to speak only to be mocked?

Knowing he needed answers, and fast, Ashlyn lay on the bed. He closed his eyes, breathed deep, letting the TV commotion and the voices in the room blend away, as Ko had taught him.

But in that created silence, he became aware that something was wrong…*very wrong*.

Ko was no longer touching his shoulder.

His heart thrumming, he shook his head, as if denial could produce a different reality. His hands and neck felt cold and clammy.

How could it be? She'd said, *"I am with you always."*

"Speak to me, Ko. Anything." He touched his other shoulder, hoping, wishing, praying, but he felt absolutely nothing…nothing but a cold, vast emptiness.

She had promised…she'd said for always.

Wasn't always forever?

-30-

Funeral

IN STREAMING SPANGLES OF LIGHT and color, the entire Iquana family flew along the outer channels of the subterranean system, heading for the open sea. The Iquana rarely ventured out en masse, but today was one of those rare occasions.

Today was a funeral.

Two of their members had passed on through the portal, and the Iquana were risking a seven hundred mile round trip to the fire springs, so that the bodies could be vaporized in the shimmering-hot jets. From water they were born...to water they would return.

WHILE THE IQUANA SOARED OUT of the seabed chasm into the open sea, four submersibles including Denton Clark's *Miranda* and *Encaladus*, now operated by Andy Lightstone's extraction squad, were diving down to the benthic realm to explore several A-zone ingression points—according to Denton's maps.

The submersible *Miranda* was a thousand feet above the seafloor, descending at one hundred and fifty feet per minute, when the sub's electronics panels began to malfunction. The navigator first realized something was awry when the sonar turned intensely bright. Then the overheads dimmed and the battery meter dropped. The pilot's diagnosis of a power drain was confirmed when the thrusters died. But when he flipped the reserve switch, instead of a power boost, the engines continued to expire.

Then there was an arcing buzz from within the control panel

and everything went black.

Every system had shut down.

The pilot flipped on a pocket penlight. It was a bright beam for a small device, eerily falling onto his navigator's face, which was grim, his mustache twitching. Then the bright little penlight beam died, its energy sucked into some sort of weird energy vacuum.

"What the hell—?"

"Got a match?"

"No."

In that pitch, in that silent darkness, in those terrifying moments of uncertainty, came the cracked voice of the navigator. "What's that?"

It was light...but not the submersible's. Viewed through the portals, it looked like the aurora borealis—the northern sky phenomenon where dazzling streamers and arches of light fall from the sky. It was an awesome sight. As they watched in awe, the lights became huge, bright, brighter...as if the sun had fragmented and was—

The submersible was vibrating.

"Oh Jesus! They're going to hit us!"

As the vibrating swiftly intensified, the seats on the submersible shuddered and the instruments rattled into a deafening clamor. Shafts of laser-like light sliced in through the portals. Now the charging fragments appeared as a singular brilliance, the headlights of a roaring train, and it was almost on top of them!

As the navigator crossed his heart, praying for mercy, the submersible was picked up like a piece of scrap paper in a gusty wind, whirled, turned upside-down and thrust aside.

The navigator felt himself heaving, sour bile pushing up through his throat. For the sake of the pilot, he held it back.

The pilot coughed, and found a breath. "I think it's over." The spinning was subsiding, *Miranda* slowly settling. Her buoyancy tanks automatically turned the submersible the right side up.

The brilliance outside was diminishing with every passing second.

And then it was black again....

Quiet as death.

The penlight switched on first. Within seconds all the systems were reengaging.

The navigator licked his parched lips. "What the hell was it?"

Even though the pilot knew exactly what it was, he was slow to respond. He blew a soft whistle of relief. "Well, good luck if they're trying to catch that, good luck to them. Once is enough for me."

The navigator nodded in agreement. "Right...I saw nothing. Sweet damn nothing!"

The radio squawked to life: "Miranda, do you copy? This is base."

"This is Miranda, we copy loud and clear, base."

"You see anything down there?"

"Like what? Clarify that, base."

"There were contacts. Right by you! You must have seen them!"

"Negative, base. We had a power out down here."

THE IQUANA JOURNEY TO THE fire springs was a swift endeavor. En route, the underwater universe found a way to provide the Iquana with supplemental energy. They realized some of this energy was courtesy of Man. They accepted it thankfully and moved on.

The crews on the submersibles *Encaladus, Mimas* and *Gracy* also saw nothing...absolutely nothing. Like the *Miranda* crew, they had endured electrical disturbances and sonar failure.

On the ocean's surface, *Argonaut's* sonar had malfunctioned, the sonar technician concluding three possible causes: either there had been an electrical anomaly, sabotage, or eighty Seabed Phantoms had emerged from the seabed and escaped the ship's target-lock.

Seven hours later the anomaly repeated itself. Despite the haywire sonar, *Argonaut's* technician was able to record small amounts of data: *contacts'* speed, depth and overall direction. Unable to precisely determine the *vanishing point* but by using simple extrapolation, the technician offered Captain James Swift a best guess—the beginning of the Olympus ridge.

Forty-three miles west.

Within three miles of the ridge, there just happened to be several chasms and sink holes marked on Denton Clark's A-zone ingression maps.

-31-

News Conference

ASHLYN STOOD ON THE HOTEL balcony overlooking the glimmering ocean, a late afternoon breeze tugging at his tee. Every bone, muscle, and tendon in his body ached, but none so much as his heart. Ko was gone. What difference did it now make if he went public? What difference did anything make? The TV was mocking them—cynical, hateful minds eager to prove that Man was the only spiritual entity, and that he and Autumn were either liars or demented freaks of a new age clan. New age? He didn't even know what new age was. And even if he was new age, so what? Would that alter the truth? What did those people know about truth? What did they know about love…and friendship?

He felt a hand on his shoulder and for a split second—

It was Autumn, her eyes red from crying. "I think…I think you must speak."

Ashlyn felt a burden of immeasurable weight.

His mind flashed back to the subterranean cavern when he'd noticed EO's cold stare. Would Ko really want him to side against the Iquana elder? Back in the cavern, he'd argued with Ko, telling her that the elders were wrong.

But on that balcony, watching the golden orb on the horizon, he no longer felt quite so adamant about right and wrong. What would really happen if he spoke up? Would the pollution be curbed? Or would he merely be pouring fuel onto the fire, enticing undesirables to participate in a heinous search, and others to attack with verbal venom?

There again, if he did nothing, Ko's family would certainly perish.

You will find your way, Ashlyn.

Turning to Autumn, he whispered, "I truly don't know. We'd be going against the elders and it's not my place to—" He felt a tingle on his shoulder. Perhaps imagined, but no, there it was again…tiny pins of electricity.

As he ran his hand to his shoulder, Autumn's expression spiraled into a glimmer of hope.

"I'm not sure," he rasped. "It's faint, but I think…."

Did it mean that Ko was alive, barely hanging on, waiting for him to save her?

Autumn clasped her hands, as if in prayer. "Ashlyn, please, please speak up!"

ON HIS THIRD PHONE CALL, Boomer finally connected with his friend, attorney Marvin Rappaport. Seven years ago, Boomer had saved Marvin's life in a boating accident, so Marvin always tried to field Boomer's calls however busy he was—and at thirty-six, fast becoming noticed as a brilliant environmental lobbyist, Marvin was nearly always busy.

"Boomer, my friend! Alice says you called a couple of times. What's up? I see you got some action over there your neck of the woods."

"That's why I'm calling, Marvin."

"Miller's kids, your old diving buddy, no?"

"I'm impressed you remember. Anyway, this is about the kids."

"You know them?"

"You could say…I'm with them right now."

Sitting behind an oblong glass table in his thirty-seventh floor plush office suite, Marvin immediately picked up the receiver, cutting off the speakerphone. Leaning forward, the smile disappeared from his suntanned face. "What's going on, Boomer?"

"What's going on? Uh, kind of a long story. I'm one of the fellas in the white Cadillac." Boomer paused, momentarily lost in the scope of the saga. "The kids are with me. They're fine, but …"

"Boomer, you didn't detain them, did you?"

Boomer frowned. "Detain them? You mean hold them against their will? Of course not."

"They're free to go?"

Boomer was almost offended. "Of course. Any time they want. Marvin, we need some help here."

"Okay…first we've got to call the police."

"Not so fast. Hear me out."

Boomer then rumbled off the kids' story: Ko, the submersible, the subterranean cavern, the eighty-member family of Iquana, and so on. Marvin was a good listener and didn't interrupt, even when the details seemed implausible, at the least extremely unlikely. Boomer finished with a plea: "These beings have been chased, hunted, poisoned, and now media whipped. Ashlyn needs to make a statement. We need to set the record straight and…and maybe we can do something…something really positive. We need you."

Marvin cleared his throat as he attempted to assemble his thoughts coherently before responding. Known nationally as a strong voice for the planet, Marvin was a believer in the sacredness of nature and the ecosystems, but he had never endorsed spiritualism, not the religious kind. Praying piscine aliens? He rubbed the stubble on his chin. It didn't have a ring of truth. Prayer was a concept born out of fear and the human need for protection, its genesis dating back to caveman times. His ideology was, however, another matter. On the way to the office, he'd heard a rumor about some new age book ploy. Marvin understood Boomer's passion. He also considered himself a passionate man. But he didn't want to end up with egg on his face, or, for that matter, for Boomer to end up with egg on his face, either. On the flip side, the kids had been somewhere in the submersible.

He thought about the book ploy. Thin, he concluded. There was obviously something to the Seabed Phantom, otherwise the navy and Andy Lightstone wouldn't be involved.

"Well?" Boomer interrupted his thoughts. "You're not going to say anything?"

"No, no. I was thinking. You say they have a water sample?"

"Yah. Two bottles," Boomer replied.

"We could do tests."

"Exactly!"

"Detailed analysis… will cost some bucks."

"I almost forgot. They've got a pendant, got it from one of the beings. It's a valuable medal of honor that sank in a shipwreck in 1605."

"I see," Marvin mumbled, not fully comprehending.

"As far as maritime records go, it's still there, lying on the ocean floor."

Marvin picked up his pen and started jotting down some notes. "Uh-huh, okay," he mumbled.

"Undiscovered. And we have it appraised. Twenty million dollars."

Marvin almost chocked on his own saliva. "Appraised twenty what?"

"Let the cynics get out of that one," Boomer added.

Marvin scribbled on his pad:

Twenty mill. Undiscovered treasure.
How?

He found himself grinning, knowing that Boomer's hook had grabbed hold of his ankles, or was it his brain? Not that he was sold, but he was definitely fascinated. "Alright, let's start with where are you?"

"Sheraton, suite 807. We're staying here until you clear the way."

Marvin looked at his watch. "I'll take the helo. I can be there in two hours."

Boomer then asked, "Can we get some sort of restraining order on Andy Lightstone? I don't want him trying any of his antics again."

Marvin jotted another note. "I'll work on that, too."

WITHIN TWENTY MINUTES, MARVIN WAS out of his office, driving through busy downtown Portland.

On the way to the helo-pad and throughout the flight, he was on the phone to the mayor, to his press agent, the kids' grandma and numerous times to Boomer. Mayor Hawkins was sympathetic, but said that if the kids were telling the truth—he reserved his opinion—if they'd spent even one minute in a subterranean cavern with an unidentified species, especially one that appeared to be sick, he would have to call in County Health Services and probably the CDC—Center For Disease Control, which would mean tests on the kids and possibly quarantine for all those in contact with them.

Marvin relayed this to Boomer and the kids, much to their chagrin. Marvin assured Ashlyn that he could still release statements through a third party, such as himself, which was probably for the best, anyway.

THROUGH THE HOTEL ROOM'S WINDOWS, the sun was setting in a blaze of red and orange flares. Autumn chewed on her nails while Ashlyn, the last to eat, picked on tepid paper-wrapped chicken and fried rice. Waiting for Marvin's next instruction was like waiting for the executioner's axe. For a brief spell, they talked about Jerry Miller in preparation for expected questions about the submersible. Ko might have discovered it on the seabed, but it was fully primed and in perfect working order, and it didn't take a neurosurgeon to fathom that it had been remoted. Boomer felt sure he knew by whom. His concern was that many individuals would recognize *Proteus*. Soon, if not already, the submersible would be linked with the kids' father, which would only further endorse the notion of an environmental ploy.

Ashlyn was confused. Why did his father deny them the submersible, then immediately remote it to the seabed? If he wanted them to have it, why not simply give it to them in the first place?

"He was never a simple man," Boomer replied.

The craziest inconsistency of all was why did he audiotape their conversation? "He's doing everything backwards," Ashlyn suggested.

Carter snickered. "Backwards…maybe a dead man thing…sorry guys."

Stretching his back, Boomer stood up and paced. "Jerry's a smart guy. He doesn't do things backwards. If you ask me, these are the actions of someone being scrutinized, someone being watched, even in trouble. That also might explain the tape. He's thinking ahead."

Carter looked up. "Andy Lightstone?"

Ashlyn flashed back to Denton's driveway. "I remember a man in a car at the end of his driveway, sitting there, doing nothing. We thought he was a traveling salesman."

Boomer rubbed his face. "Poor Jerry. His whole life he's chased shadows and now they're chasing him. Maybe Marvin can help there, too."

Ashlyn pushed aside his plate. The thought of his father trying to aid them and being hounded by Lightstone didn't sit well. Ashlyn gently reached for his shoulder. Was it Ko's touch he could feel? It was infinitesimally faint, perhaps nothing more than his yearning desire to feel her life force. Selfishly, he wished for a pain in his stomach—her pain. Then at least he'd know without a doubt that she was alive—they'd be sharing energy both positive and negative, and the link would be strong. If only....

OUTSIDE THE HOTEL, SIX LOCAL police units pulled up, quiet, no lights flashing. The officers piled out of their squad cars and spread out along the sidewalk, in no particular hurry. A sergeant conferred with his superiors over the radio. A crowd gathered.

A youth inquired, "Hey, someone wasted?"

Saying nothing, the cop moved the youth along.

THE PHONE RANG. IT WAS Marvin, letting Boomer know that he was on the way, but he'd just been informed that CDC had entered the picture and would be taking the 'contaminated subjects' into seclusion as soon as a recovery team was in place, probably around nine.

Boomer asked Marvin, "Are you allowed to see us?"

"No, but I'll be there, downstairs. No one's allowed in, no one's allowed out." Marvin assured Boomer that he'd make the CDC expedite the examination.

The token good news didn't pad Ashlyn's growing frustration.

Carter jumped up in his seat. "Hey, check this out! It's the hotel!"

The television shot was revealing the exterior of the hotel. Police had strung yellow tape to cordon off a swelling crowd including a few protestors with gospel billboards. There were shots of the surrounding mayhem—police cars from local, state, and federal agencies, news minivans, a county health services car, and a van from the National Oceanic and Atmospheric Administration.

Carter turned up the volume.

The attractive female reporter had a permanent smile, even as she spoke. "The Center For Disease Control is expected here any moment now, apparently to take Ashlyn and Autumn Miller and two male Caucasians into quarantine." Pushing her audio piece closer to her ear, the reporter continued. "The earlier report that Ashlyn and Autumn Miller have been exposed to a virus is still unconfirmed, and most of what we're receiving is sketchy. There are many rumors of alien contact and a cavern beneath the seabed. While we've heard it, we have no way of knowing if any of this is true. What we do know is that this hotel is condoned off, no one is allowed in or out, so authorities are obviously taking the possibility of contamination of some sort very seriously."

The phone in the room rang. It was Dan Shockbottom, the reporter with a volley of questions. Boomer told him, "No comment at this time," and hung up.

A few minutes later, the phone rang again—a prank call. Then it rang again…and again…and again.

Finally, Boomer asked the concierge to screen the calls.

At seven, Marvin arrived at the hotel, although, as expected, he was denied access. Speaking to Boomer from the parking lot, he offered a suggestion. "I don't think a detailed press statement would be wise or appropriate at this juncture. We don't want this to backfire. If the water sample doesn't contain any contaminants, we'll look like charlatans. And we better not rule out a viral disease like AIDS or mad cow, mad fish?"

Boomer cupped his hand over the mouthpiece while he relayed Marvin's concerns to Ashlyn.

"A disease? Well, anything's possible, I guess," Ashlyn conceded.

Keeping Marvin on hold, Boomer continued: "He wants to address the press with a concise statement from you. You'll make a full statement after we've analyzed the water. Okay?"

Ashlyn slowly nodded his head.

NIGHT HAD ALREADY FALLEN WHEN Marvin stood in the hotel parking lot before a thick crowd, Betacam record lights blinking in his face, and camera flashes popping like antiaircraft fire.

Upstairs, they watched it on TV.

Marvin was a good-looking man, wavy blond hair, blue eyes, suntanned from running, the athletic type even though he was dressed in an elegant gray silk suit. "My name is Marvin Rappaport. I'm an attorney, representing Ashlyn and Autumn Miller. As you know, my clients are being quarantined, so they can't address you here. I will read a short statement from Ashlyn." He removed the paper from his inside breast pocket. "This is to ease the wild rumors and innuendo. Firstly, we have no affiliation with any cults of any sort whatsoever, nor did our mother. You've heard that we traveled in a submersible to a subterranean cavern. This is true. A sea being named Ko, a loving member of a species unlike any ever documented, escorted us there. In the cavern my sister and I met some eighty members of Ko's family. They are intelligent…extremely intelligent, in a way that rivals our own intelligence." Marvin paused because there was some laughter and some boos, slightly unsettling but he remained straight-faced. "I look forward to speaking with you, the press, directly, as soon as I am discharged from quarantine. Thank you."

Amidst an explosion of overlapping questions, and popping flashbulbs, Marvin folded the paper, and started to move off.

"Did they say where this cavern is?"

"No comment."

"Any photographs?"

"No comment."

"Are they claiming these beings are sick? Are Ashlyn and Autumn sick, besides mental?"

Marvin shook his head. He backed away, the volleying questions and camera flashes still popping in his face.

-32-

Quarantine

"HOLY TOLEDO!" EXCLAIMED CARTER AS they stormed through the door—five men and one woman in orange decon spacesuits with air tanks, soft hoods, sealed visors, protruding gas masks. Four of them carried king-sized hatboxes, red biohazard stickers plastered all over them, the other two spacesuits shuffled in with aluminum tanks of phenolic disinfectant and rolls of blue plastic wrap.

The door slammed shut. The hatboxes opened. Out came similar suits, but blue. They were told to strip and get into the blue suits. Autumn was escorted to the bathroom by the one female of the team.

"No one said anything about a rabbit...damn, Johnson, there's a frickin' rabbit in here!" The orange suit was speaking into an intercom on his shoulder.

"You better not hurt him!" Ashlyn cautioned with a warning finger.

Orange man nodded. "A pet...okay...copy." To Ashlyn, "Don't worry. We might look like demons, but we're really just a bunch of Halloween goblins. We'll look after him. Gonna have his own little compartment. All right, everything into these boxes. We've got more, if we need 'em."

One of the orange suits talked about the media zoo downstairs, and amidst this very serious procedure, managed a few jokes.

Once dressed in the blue chemo-immunity suits, covered head-to-foot, the quarantine subjects were sprayed with phenolic disinfectant, and their clothes and possessions were dropped into hermetically sealed bags, and tagged. The hotel's linens and towels were also bagged. Bigsey was placed inside a special air-filtered cage.

They were escorted quickly along the empty corridor to the fire stairs. The room they'd just left was already being thoroughly disinfected. No one would be allowed back in there for five days.

On the hotel's roof, a CDC Bell Ranger helicopter was waiting. No press, no crowds. But, as the helo took off, Ashlyn glimpsed the media hoopla below. Pressing his nose to the window, he thought about his life, how different it had become. The problem was: He hardly felt in control; hardly felt that this was his way. He remembered something his mom had said: 'A sign of character is having the courage to make a tough decision, but a greater test of character is to admit it when you're wrong.'

Was he wrong to talk?

The flight took a little over an hour. They landed in Benton, a hundred miles north, forty miles east near Oregon State University. They boarded a van for a short ride along highway 99. It was midnight when they turned off the highway onto an unlit road that looked like an entrance to a farm. The driver said it was a private clinic. They stopped outside a hideaway two-story cinder block and glass building.

Ashlyn noted some sixteen cars in the parking lot. He couldn't see a name anywhere on the building or even on the glass doors. They were told to disembark and stand by the van for a quick inspection of their suits—a precaution before any of the nurses or orderlies could come out.

Standing next to the van, Ashlyn heard a strange drumming sound coming through the speaker in his facemask. He smiled, realizing it was amplified crickets. He stood with his arms out wide while the driver inspected his suit, which was obviously intact because the nurses and orderlies, in regular green scrubs, suddenly strutted out to welcome them.

The lobby was small, with stark white walls, white tiles, spotless. They were led up two steps, through an electrically beeped door into a long corridor with many doors. Their accommodations were four separate rooms, side-by-side. Except for a double layer of clear plastic sheeting with zippered entry points that ran floor-to-ceiling and wall-to-wall, they were regular hospital type rooms—mounted TV above metal cot, small table, two chairs, magazine rack, phone, private bathroom, closet for clothes—although in their case they had none except the cumbersome biohazard suits.

Autumn took one look at her room and shuddered. "It's like death in here. I'd like to share with my brother. Where's Bigsey? What did you do with my rabbit?"

The nurse politely informed Autumn that her rabbit Bigsey was being taken care of, however sharing a room wasn't permitted. Autumn reached behind the hood of her biohazard suit, threatening to release it, although she didn't have a clue how. As an afterthought, she grabbed a section of the room's plastic sheeting, quite prepared to engage in some heavy-duty vandalism.

"That's not necessary," announced a voice.

Autumn's eyes focused beyond the nurse to the doorway where a man in a short doctor's coat was browsing over a chart on a clipboard. He was perhaps sixty, although well preserved with kind but challenging eyes, an avuncular smile, and, quite surprisingly, his facemask was dangling around his neck. "If you want to share with your brother, I see no reason why not, unless your brother complains. Nurse."

"Yes…er, of course, Doctor Norton," the nurse answered submissively.

Ashlyn didn't complain, and they wheeled in another bed, and then delivered Bigsey. Two orange suits helped the teens out of their biohazard suits, handed them pajamas, gowns, a plate of cookies, and a choice of soda, water, or milk.

Night one of quarantine.

Climbing into bed, Autumn whined, "Who do they think they are? Ordering us around like we're in some third world prison!" She pulled Bigsey's cage closer, and stroked the little guy through the bars. "Lucky rabbit, you have been places no other rabbit has." Rolling on her side, she pulled the covers up to her chin. "Bigsey's lucky…I guess we are, too."

"What's that?" Ashlyn asked as he climbed into bed.

"We're not on the way to Inverness."

Ashlyn fluffed up his pillow. "I would have never guessed."

"Goodnight, Mom, I love you," she muttered without even realizing.

Within a few minutes she was snoring.

No wonder she was snoring. It had been three days since they had last slept in a bed. Ashlyn was also exhausted, yet he resisted sleep. Having decided that the minuscule energy force he felt on his

shoulder was absolutely Ko and not his imagination, he was determined to connect with her.

But how?

Connecting required his mind to be free and clear of clutter. All
well and good, but at that moment, thoughts of the last few days
were storming around his head. His mind could easily be compared
to the bustle of New York's Fifth Avenue, when it needed to be as
tranquil as a deserted country lane.

He tried to focus on nothing but space, breathing deep, breathing hard. And gradually—very gradually—the mind clutter began to
fade. Maybe an hour passed, maybe two, when at last he began to
feel warm and light-bodied, and the gentle noises in the room that
he'd become accustomed to—Autumn's breathing, the hum of the air
conditioner, and the distant song of nighttime crickets—began to
melt away. The new resonances he felt and heard were the energies
of the inanimate, the high-pitched whirring of the walls and the lab
equipment way down the corridor, the mellow reverberations from
furniture in various rooms all over the clinic. He'd experienced the
symphony of the inanimate before, in the cavern with Ko.

And he began to sense the pulsing energies of the animate—the
clinic's staff members sleeping in their rooms, the birds and animals
in the forest nearby.

"Ko...Ko, where are you?"

Pinpoints of light falling upward cut into the blackness of his
sealed eyelids. In that instant, he knew he'd vacated his physical
body. The symphony of the clinic abruptly vanished, and the pinpoints of light turned into a clear image of rifling water.

He was whizzing faster than Ko had ever piloted him in the
submersible, plunging down into the depths of the ocean, to the seafloor...below the seafloor, flying through sand and rock as if they
were air.

In a flash, he was upon the great rock sealing the Iquana cavern—and he flew right through it.

His desire to connect with Ko was strong.

The Iquana brethren were in ceremony, hand locked in hand,
moving in a slow circle near the cavern floor.

They were pulsing coronas of light onto the one in need.

That *one* was Ko.

Though her family bathed her in sweeps of golden, loving energy, Ko was curled on her side, scarcely moving. When she did

move, it was mostly a reflexive writhe. Her once glorious pulses were slow and labored. A puffy black discharge swam out of her pursed mouth.

"Ko!" Ashlyn shouted, unable to contain his decorum. "Ko, it's me!"

An elder, sensing Ashlyn's presence, turned about, scowling, as he broke clear from the circle, and moved menacingly toward Ashlyn. The elder then flicked his arm in a universal gesture: *Get out of here! Go!*

Just then Ko's eyes flickered open, searching for—and finding—Ashlyn. Despite the obvious pain she felt, her mouth grew wide in tender smile, and a hint of color returned to her eyes that had fallen gray. She reached out with her arm.

Oh, how Ashlyn wanted to take hold of her hand and squeeze it. Yet an impenetrable gulf, only yards to his disembodied self, but in material dimensions as wide as the world, separated them.

Ko's eyes shifted, as if searching for someone else. Following her gaze, Ashlyn found EO. To his surprise, the elder's forlorn face abruptly brightened. Then EO moved away from the healing circle, and attempted to approach Ashlyn. But that same impenetrable gulf separating Ashlyn from Ko kept EO at bay.

EO beckoned with a hand, *"Come...come."*

Ashlyn wanted to leap forward, wanted so much to oblige, still the distance to EO remained an impossible yardage.

"Come," EO beckoned again.

"How?" Ashlyn asked. "What should I do? I want to help."

Something clanked.

From EO's perplexed look, either he didn't understand or that clanking sound confused him. "EO!" Ashlyn shouted. "EO, can you hear me?"

Something clanked again—and a brittle voice echoed through the water. Ashlyn spied an orange blur moving around the cavern—only he suddenly realized he wasn't in the cavern anymore.

A woman dressed in a plastic orange suit lay down a breakfast tray of cereal, breads, and juice. "Morning. Sleep alright?" she asked.

Ashlyn gathered his senses. Where was he? Autumn was sitting up in a hospital bed. Bigsey was in a cage on the floor next to her bed.

Quarantine.

"I'm in quarantine."

"Yes. Doctor Norton will be here in ten minutes. You might want to wash up."

Ashlyn nodded. He tried to remember his dream. Had he spoken to Ko? Or was it EO? Did EO say "come?"

You'll find your way—is that what it meant?

He thought about the dream/vision as he washed up. He'd have to reappropriate the submersible, which didn't seem very plausible. But even if he could somehow get his hands on a submersible, how would he ever pilot it through the chasm and the eddy, and the vertical sinkhole?

You'll find your way.

Maybe EO would guide him.

He sat at the small table eating breakfast. Autumn, in a chatty mood, tried to command his attention, but his mind was still away at the cavern, thinking about Ko and EO.

After breakfast three doctors in spacesuits knocked on the door, and entered without waiting for an invitation.

Doctor William Norton and Doctor Nancy Tripp were from CDC. The third doctor was hired by Marvin, Doctor Arthur London, Clinical Professor of Medicine, University of Southern California. Hard to tell what he looked like in the decon spacesuit. Anyway, he was basically a spectator in the proceedings.

The examination began with blood and saliva samples. Then the medics scraped a little skin, shone a light into their eyes, ears, took their ear temperature, checked pulses, and examined them for strange marks.

In fifteen minutes it was over. They could expect the same every day of quarantine.

Once again, they were alone.

Autumn lifted Bigsey out of the cage, and placed him on her lap. Then she turned to Ashlyn. "So, are you going to tell me about EO?"

Ashlyn stopped chewing the biscuit he'd just picked up from the breakfast tray.

"In your sleep. You were doing it again."

Ashlyn slowly nodded. "What did I say?"

"EO. You said EO...kinda loud."

Absentmindedly squeezing the table napkin, Ashlyn sighed. "There's nothing to tell, Autumn...it was just a...dream, a foggy dream." He sat down on the edge of his bed, wondering: Had it been a journey…or a dream?

He casually touched his shoulder.

Ko was there, but oh, so faint.

ASHLYN SPENT THE MORNING ON the phone to Boomer and Carter who were only next door but separated by lock and key. He also spoke with Marvin who had plenty of words of advice. "I'm still hoping to fly up there but maybe not for a day or two. There's a bunch of federal agencies, all wanting to interview you, so I'm juggling. And I've still got to handle some business here in Portland. In a way, it might be best if I don't show up until we get the results of the water tests."

"The water tests?"

"Do I detect a slight anxiety there, Ashlyn?"

"About the water test? No. I was just—"

"Makes me a little anxious, too. Anyway, about these interviews, if anyone shows up unexpectedly, even if they flash a fancy badge and tell you this is serious business, you tell them you're waiting for me, okay?"

"Got it!" Ashlyn replied.

"Good. Okay, last but not least, you really do need to call your grandmother. I visited her today. She signed some medical authorization documents, and she told me more than once, told me she's worried sick for you, and really misses you."

"Yer-right, she misses us. That's why she's been trying to send us to Inverness!"

"Well…she's expecting your call. I think it would be a good idea."

After hanging up with Marvin, Ashlyn contemplated that 'good idea.' He stared at the phone, wishing he didn't have to, while knowing that he really didn't have a choice.

He took a deep breath, and dialed.

The conversation certainly surprised him. His grandmother laughed and then wept and then laughed again. She seemed genuinely concerned, proclaiming her love for him. She said Lucy was baking a raspberry and apple upside-down cake—his favorite—for their welcome home, and she couldn't wait to see them.

When Ashlyn hung up the receiver, he felt like he'd stepped into a parallel world. Was this *his* grandmother? What had happened to her? Incredibly, Inverness wasn't even mentioned.

MARVIN RAPPAPORT WALKED ALONG WAYSIDE'S Taylor Avenue, feeling as anxious about the water tests as his young client Ashlyn Miller pretended not to be. What if the tests were negative? One glance at the newsstand exacerbated his butterflies.

MAN WIPES OUT GOD-PRAYING SPECIES
DISREGARD FOR PLANET WREAKS HAVOC

Another headline:

MISSING KIDS GO TO SHANGRI-LA
HIDING OUT WITH SPIRITUAL FISH

Admittedly, these were tabloid headlines, but plenty of front-page coverage appeared in the regular press. Proof-positive that gutter-level journalism was alive and kicking furiously.

Marvin involuntarily shuddered. Part of him wished Boomer had never called. Only yesterday, he was on the fast track to success. Well liked, well respected—even by his adversaries—he'd not encountered a popularity setback since school days. But since his appearance on television, he'd received some alarming feedback, some from his supposed friends and supporters. Had he jumped aboard the right environmental platform?

Across the street, a passerby pointed at him. "Hey, you're the kids' scummy lawyer!"

Marvin quickly skirted down 2nd Street, almost wishing he could make himself invisible.

IN HIS STERILE QUARANTINE ROOM, Boomer munched on a hamburger and soggy fries while flipping TV channels. He was amazed at the TV coverage. *Sea Beings* had swallowed up the airwaves. One irate woman on *The Jenny Show* shrieked, "It's an attack on Judeo-Christian doctrine! These kids are liars!"

Another woman behind her stood up. "How do you know what they are? Who says humans are the only spiritual species?"

"God! The Bible!" belted a man from somewhere.

"I think humans and sea beings praying together is divine beauty, the coming of a new age," the same woman added.

A dozen spectators in the audience shrieked: "Blasphemy."

Jenny's guest was a scowling pastor who lashed out, "Where

does it say God created fish in His image?"

CARTER WATCHED A LESS CONTENTIOUS talk show. The male host was announcing the results of a phone survey. "Nineteen percent, almost one in five, say the circumstantial evidence, the submersible, quarantine, indicate the teens' truthfulness. However, the vast majority, seventy-nine percent, folks, feel the Miller teens are either smoking some pretty weird stuff, which we at the studio would like to try, or it's a hoax. By the way, those final two remaining percent, they're hanging out in the subterranean cavern eating sushi. See you tomorrow, folks."

Carter shook his head, turned off the TV and picked up a paperback.

ASHLYN REFUSED TO WATCH THE news or any of the talk shows. He and Autumn watched a movie followed by an old *Brady Bunch* episode, then sometime during another rerun of the show *Friends* Autumn fell asleep.

Ashlyn lay on his pillow with his hand resting on his left shoulder. "What do you want me to do, Ko?"

He could hear the TV from next door, but not a sound evoked itself from his inner self.

"EO...EO...can you hear me?"

THE MAN WHO HAD LAUNCHED the media storm, journalist Dan Shockbottom, sipped a demitasse in the studio newsroom. Some of the fifteen monitors in front of him were showing news clips from around the globe. The escalation of his scoop was beyond his wildest expectations. CNN had broadcast it internationally. He'd watched a Frenchman cackling, a British Cockney saying "Only in America!" Even a Vatican official in biretta and canonicals found airtime—"No comment."

Shockbottom was in the studio to edit another major twist to the Wayside scoop, having learned that the submersible *Proteus II* was a trademarked design of the late Jerry Miller, the teens' father. Admittedly, the debunkers would love it. But if he didn't broadcast this, some other journalist would.

One of the monitors suddenly caught his attention. He peered over the rim of his coffee cup. "What's on monitor five? Volume."

The studio engineer slid the audio fader up several notches.

A CBS reporter stood outside Oracle Publishing House, saying, "—manufactured to hype their upcoming book *Sea Beings*. In response, Oracle's chief executive officer, Sunny Yu, issued this statement. "This is a baseless, malicious attack on our company. We are not publishing a book called *Sea Beings* or any book even remotely like it. We have no opinion one way or another on the veracity of the Miller teens' statements. What we do know is that early this morning someone broke into our offices and planted this manuscript in an attempt to malign—"

"What the hell—?" Shockbottom exclaimed.

BACK IN HIS OFFICE IN Portland, Marvin also watched the swelling news coverage. Several commentaries were downright vicious, remonstrative attacks against the Miller teens and anyone believing in them. Two prominent TV evangelists even went as far as calling them "Devil's disciples!"

Marvin cringed. Was his reputation, even his career, now hanging on the results of the water tests?

His wife Nancy consoled him over the phone. She believed in Ashlyn and Autumn and assured him she wasn't the only one.

The governor of Oregon, however, wasn't one of those believers. He and several other politicians had called to express abject disappointment. Earlier that day an old lady spat at Marvin as he disembarked from the elevator. The owner of the club where he played racquetball had refused to renew his membership, and even the IRS had called, the agent informing him that *Proteus II* had been seized.

After hanging up the receiver, Marvin realized he'd bitten the eraser off his pencil. Who else wanted his neck? He scribbled a note by the name Jeweler Boleshko. Yes, he mumbled to himself. The pendant was strong evidence that could at least puncture the right-wing attack.

Was this the direction he really wanted to go?

He pressed his intercom and told Alice to hold his calls.

Then he rocked back and forth in his recliner, rationalizing, reasoning. In a courtroom, he figured he'd have a decent circumstantial case, although much hinged on the outcome of the water test. He also acknowledged that he potentially had a great platform to lobby from. But was it too volatile to be productive? The thought of recusing himself entered his mind. If there were a conflict of interest he'd recuse himself immediately. Was there? No...just a conflict of belief.

Praying piscine aliens.

Of course it had folks outraged. The prayer thing was what most unsettled him, too, although for a different reason. Marvin had never endorsed religion. He called himself a deist, believing that a supreme intelligence had engineered the molds for life, and then left the bare creation alone to unfold, without a desire or even an ability to inter-act thereafter. This made sense to him. But....

"Prayer...prayer," he mused aloud. "Why, oh why...it'd be a snap without prayer." Then another thought occurred to him. "That's what's giving us this audience."

-33-

Bugs

IN THE ICY BLACKNESS OF the abyss, the roving workstation *Mimas*—a mini sub with a galley and night cabin for sustained dives—descended toward the seafloor, the weight of six hundred and eighty atmospheres, or ten thousand pounds per square inch, pressing up against the craft's eight-inch thick titanium skin.

Knowing that the vessel's stress limit was supposedly nine hundred atmospheres was of little comfort to Ed Lazerath. If there were imperfections in the metal's composition hitherto not detected, the craft could implode at any moment. And from what he understood, they'd never fully tested the thing.

They were approaching a line in the seafloor.

Buck Whitman, the loquacious pilot at *Mimas'* controls, rolled his bushy handlebar mustache. "It's a chasm, alright, pretty narrow, looks to be about fifteen feet wide. About to touch down. Stand by." With one hand still rolling his mustache, the other manipulating the control joystick, Buck maneuvered *Mimas* to a safe touchdown on the seabed next to the lip of the chasm.

Masking his cowardly anxiety, Ed Lazerath breathed a concealed sigh of relief. They were on the ground, couldn't go any deeper and thank God they hadn't imploded. During the three-hour descent, Buck Whitman hadn't stopped talking, a diatribe about different species of eels and crabs and mollusks, and how this one was named, and what this one's excretions could cure. He assumed Ed, a zoological man, was just as enthralled. Wrong. Ed couldn't care two hoots. He was beginning to despise the whole show. He despised Andy's orders, which he was supposed to jump to with sublime obedience. He despised the cramped, damp quarters of *Mimas*. And piscine aliens had too quickly become a volatile subject. He wasn't experiencing the usual chills and thrills of a hunt. Besides, if they were as intelligent as the youngsters insisted—and from what he'd so far observed on sonar, he believed they were—his entire bait-bag of tricks was useless.

Buck flipped some switches, pulled a lever, and from somewhere underneath Ed's feet there was a *clank.* Buck said, "Alrighty-o fellas, Scuttle Bug on the way."

Trying to appear upbeat and involved, Ed rejoined, "Now for some action."

Through the forward portal, he watched *Scuttle Bug,* one of their three AUVs—Autonomous Undersea Vehicles—scuttling away. The squat, jet-powered suboceanic robot quickly covered the short distance to the chasm, its powerful xenon gas headlight illuminating a beam of milky detritus. The video bounced around as the robot started the climb down, its multiple pincers and suction cups clawing against clay and rock.

With one hand still rolling his mustache, the other on camera and direction controls, Buck nodded appreciatively. "There she goes. Down vertical. Clever girl. Adjusting stabilizer...murky, murky, come on, come on, come on girl, let's find us one of them ingy things."

Ingy things to Buck were *A-zone ingressions*—possible passageways to navigable terrain beyond the seabed. "Murky, murky...yeah, that's better, whoa, hey, look...look...see that?"

Ed squinted. The video was extremely muddy and bouncing around.

"See it there...coming up, ten feet...five...."

Now Ed saw it. The robot was approaching a flat shelf. The image suddenly turned very dark.

Buck made some quick control adjustments. "Good girl. That's it. All right, all right, horizontal again." The video became quite clear. The robot appeared to be traveling along a level path of red craggy rock.

"It's a tunnel?" Ed asked, suddenly feeling rather excited.

Buck shook his head. "Nah...a ledge on the main wall. Dead end!" Buck was about to reverse the robot when something caught his eye. Ed saw it, too. In the chalky red wall, on the top left edge of the video monitor, they were looking at a dark circular patch.

Scuttle Bug began to advance toward this patch. The ground now appeared to angle down. The walls on either side of the robot were receding. The robot was moving forward, quickly now.

"I'll be! Ingy!"

THE INSTANT *SCUTTLE BUG* PLACED the first of its eight metal limbs inside the subterranean passageway, the collective Iquana consciousness sensed the intrusion. Occasionally, a stray sea ray or other deep-sea fish would inadvertently wander into one of the channels and would invariably perish unless they rescued it, which they usually did. But this intrusion, they sensed, wasn't a stray fish.

ED AND BUCK WATCHED THE images with mounting anticipation. *Scuttle Bug* was inside a suboceanic pathway, a five hundred foot wide canal beneath the sea, sending back invaluable data. The little robot had almost reached its maximum distance, almost a mile from *Mimas*, when the video images began to rotate.

Ed found it difficult to look at the screen—the images were making him giddy. "Can you steady that thing before I puke?"

Even though Buck tried to adjust sync, the image continued to rotate, faster and faster, clockwise. Buck twirled and twirled his mustache the opposite direction. "Sync is fine. There's no reason—"

BEEP!

"Whoaaa!"

The picture had vanished, along with the flow of data.

"Let me guess, that's not supposed to happen?" Ed rubbed his eyes.

For a change, Buck was quiet. He flipped some switches. He reset the computer. He still said nothing. When the system booted back up, he shook his head, slowly turning about in total bewilderment. "Poor girl. She's gone."

"Gone? You mean a…technical gone?"

"Gone. Vanished. Scuttle Bug's nowhere. She was only a mile away. We should be able to read her emergency beacon." Buck stroked his handlebars contemplatively. "The admiral ain't gonna like this."

"She can't be gone. Maybe something fell on her and broke the beacon," Ed suggested.

"Yeah. Maybe we should send out Ladybird...see if we can retrieve her."

Ladybird was a very expensive AUV.

Ed shrugged. "I don't know. You're the expert, I mean down here you're the expert."

Yes, Buck was the expert.

So *Ladybird* descended into the chasm, sending back a stream of data and sharp video. The AUV scuttled along the ledge, into the same passageway where *Scuttle Bug* had ventured. The unit had traveled a thousand yards when the images Buck and Ed were watching began to spin.

BEEP!

"Oops!"

The screen was black.

WIRELESS COMMUNICATION DEVICES SUCH AS cellular phones and radios work well on land, work well in the air, even in the sky thousands of miles above earth, but these communication devices become impotent in the deep-sea. In the deep-sea wireless signals, whether from radiophones, cellular or satellite, end up bouncing into an impenetrable steel-like wall—the communication vacuum of the abyss.

The answer to deep-sea communication is cable.

An hour after the robots vanished inside the subterranean channel, a communication bell dropped by *Argonaut* landed near *Mimas,* enabling a cable wired communication link to the surface.

Andy Lightstone's furious voice slammed out of the speaker. "You lost WHAT?"

Trying to maintain a level of composure, Ed explained how they had discovered a subterranean route that maybe led someplace.

"Someplace? What the hell is someplace? Las Vegas? Downtown LA?" Andy screamed.

Ed backed away from the speaker, rubbing his ear. "Well it probably—"

"Probably!" Andy hollered as loud as he could. "Listen here, you mentally defective muttonheads! I hired the best, and what do I have? A hole in my pocket and a sack of excuses! You haven't got a goddamn clue if you've found King Tut's ass or a pigeonhole to China! Is that about it?"

Ed tightened his fists angrily, yet he somehow managed to restrain himself. "The AUVs are in there, inside the ingy, I mean, entry point. I'm sure of it. We can get these creatures, Andy. But they're smart. They got some kind of biological sonar, echolocation. The moment they sense us, bam, they're gone! Here's what I suggest...we lay titanium wire netting, tension-sprung, mechanical, triggered by motion to snap shut in the blink of an eye. We lay it strategically and split. When they don't see us, don't sense us, sooner or later, they'll come out and BAM—two hundred square feet of the strongest netting ever made will slam down on them like lightning! Gotcha!"

If Ed could have seen Andy at that moment, he would have watched his eyes lighting up. "Trapped piscines."

"In the bag!" Ed said, but he thought, fat chance.

"How long is this going to take?"

"Get me topside, a few days, we'll be in business."

-34-

Moral Obligation

MARVIN MARCHED BREEZILY ALONG San Luis Street to the heliport. It's amazing how a single day can so change a person. He was no longer concerned with the governor's opinion, no longer worried about the protesters still camping outside the Wayside Sheraton, or of any potential downside to his law practice—because in the last twenty-four hours, he'd met with Boleshko, seen the pendant, made copies of the MARAD papers, visited the toxicology lab, and rendezvoused with his publicist. And now he had come to a resounding conclusion: He had a great circumstantial case. Who cares if the creatures were spiritual? Quite honestly, it really didn't make a difference whether Ashlyn was telepathically communicating with them or not. It was the powerful, environmental message that Ashlyn could bring to the world that mattered here.

"NICE DAY FOR A MOON walk," was Boomer's jovial greeting as he met up with Ashlyn and Autumn in the corridor. Ashlyn returned the smile. They were together again, back in the blue biohazard suits, striding up a flight of stairs to another stark corridor.

They were ushered into a hermetically sealed room with a long metal table on which lay four plastic business folders, lined up by four foldable chairs. There was nothing else in the room except for a plate glass observation window, behind which Marvin sat patiently at a desk.

An orange suit helped Ashlyn out of his hood and unclipped his airflow pack while other orange suits aided his companions.

Marvin grinned. "We're looking good. The report is on your table." He adjusted his microphone level.

Ashlyn picked up his copy.

HARVARD LABORATORY
MILLER, ASHLYN, WATER SAMPLES
QUALITATIVE ANALYSIS

The first page was technical; the second outlined elements and toxicity percentages; the third was a detailed description of corrosive and biohazard agents; the last page was a summary.

"Let me paraphrase." Marvin cleared his throat. "Extremely low salinity, still considered seawater. Above normal levels of iron, lead, arsenic, possible carbon tetrachloride or benzene, all potentially deadly. But the bottom of page two is our skull and crossbones: praseodymium, the sample shows a very heavy concentration, lanthanum and thallium, even worse. No known biology can sustain itself in this kind of water."

Ashlyn didn't move despite the revelation—the water *was* polluted.

Marvin continued. "In the summary, they've redlined a common denominator. Might indicate a single source, one culprit dumping toxic waste. Top of the list, specialized glass industry—colored glass manufacturer, ceramics, photoelectric factory, infrared detector makers—down the list, furniture maker, a toy factory, automotive plant, boat maker, so on."

Ashlyn studied the paper, silently.

"Is it possible to track the source?" Boomer asked.

Marvin frowned, "We have a plus in that the cavern is under the mainland."

Ashlyn looked up from the paper. "How do you know that?"

"Toxicity levels. The open sea disperses chemicals, except when they're in tin drums, then there'd be traces of metal oxidation. Mind you, there are plenty of leaky tin drums lying on the ocean floor. Anyway, that's the plus. But it's not a big plus. Pinpointing it—" Marvin shook his head. "Even if we had the cavern's exact coordinates, water traveling paths are deceiving. You know how the leaky roof is: tar's cracked at the front of the house, the puddle on the floor is all the way at the back. The culprit could be directly above their cavern, or thirty or forty miles away in any direction. Our suspect list is enormous."

Marvin watched the faces through the glass slump in dejection. "Understand I'm telling you this just so you realize...we could spend a fortune and still not find the culprit or culprits. But even if we do, and we stop him, there's still a problem. The water will probably get worse before it gets better. It's not a swimming pool. You can't shock it with chlorine. You do, you'll kill everything in a few hours. Time is what will cure it. One, two, three years, even longer. But there is an upside...."

Ashlyn was shaking his head. "We should have never made the statement. I don't want any of this reaching the press."

Marvin loosened his tie. "Let's not be rash. If we go public, we'll be making a powerful environmental statement. We get an artist or an animator to show what's happening down there. We bring the tragedy into people's homes, and we make them think! We make them think so maybe the next time they're about to flush the paint thinner down the toilet, they'll think again."

"That's an upside? I don't trust the media. They'll warp and distort the truth. We're already liars and freaks! And the scumbag hunters, do we really want to feed their fantasies? All we're doing is making it worse. Face it, Mr. Rappaport, they're going to die. You've just proved that fact. At least let them have their dignity." Ashlyn bowed his head.

Marvin leaned forward. "With all due respect, Ashlyn, I think you're missing something. I know there's been some bad press, but you've got a lot of support, too."

If there was support, Ashlyn didn't know about it. Most everyone was calling them liars, new age freaks. If they kept quiet, the interest in sea beings would eventually die down. He shook his head.

"You want to help these piscines, right?" Marvin asked.

Boomer jumped in. "How about moving them?"

Inconspicuously, Ashlyn touched his shoulder, perhaps hoping for an answer from Ko. He shook his head. "We'd only be delaying the inevitable. Sooner or later we're going to pollute the rest of the world."

Anxiously tapping his foot, Marvin said, "You're right, unless we educate the public. There are people who genuinely care about mother earth who know if we don't respect her, she'll make the land

and sea inhospitable. But they're a minority. The rest, they might think they know, but they really don't—at least they're not reminded of the consequences." Marvin paused while he gathered his thoughts. "Not far from where I live there's this mountain lookout. It's misty and green and lush; first glimpse you'd have to say, 'What a paradise.' But if you look over the edge all you see is beer bottles, cigarette butts, cans, diapers—refuse. How many mountainsides do you think look like that? How many cities can you visit where there aren't cars and trucks spewing filthy smoke? How many people do you think dump engine oil? How many toss six-pack holders into the ocean? Do they know that young fish get stuck in them, that the plastic cuts into their flesh? How many spit out chewing gum even though it can seal a bird's digestive tract? I could go on and on, Ashlyn. We need to educate. We need to remind. This is airtime. We have a moral obligation."

Ashlyn nodded understandingly. Marvin's argument was thoughtful and under normal circumstances— "I realize, there's much to consider. I need to sleep on it."

Obviously disappointed, Marvin slowly nodded. "All right. I'll call my press guy. We won't release the test results. But before we tackle the next issue, let me give you something else to digest: the polluter might think he's dumping harmlessly, maybe onto a chunk of wasteland, or shooting it down an old mine shaft. We go public, he might just realize it's him, and if he's got half a conscience, who knows, he might just stop." Marvin could tell from the look on Ashlyn's face, he'd scored.

Autumn whispered something to Ashlyn. Because of the sensitivity of the speaker set-up, Marvin could hear, "Perhaps they can heal themselves if the poison stops."

Marvin nodded, no doubt trying to influence Ashlyn's decision.

But that's what lawyers do, don't they?

Ashlyn remained uncertain, his gut seemingly telling him to refrain from making a decision, while his brain was convinced that Marvin was right. Somehow he found himself siding with his brain. "If I say yes, I'll only do so as long as I can review all materials, all ideas, before anything else is released to the public."

Marvin smiled broadly. "Of course. It's the right decision, Ashlyn." He took a deep breath and segued the conversation. "Okay, next on the agenda. We have interviews scheduled for tomorrow." He read from notes on his legal pad. "The U.S. Department of Fish and Wildlife, the Department of the Environment, National Oceanic and Atmospheric Administration, and CIA—Central Intelligence Agency."

"CIA? What do they want?" Boomer, Ashlyn, Carter, and Autumn voiced the same question simultaneously.

"My guess is they're interested in Ashlyn's unusual ability. Don't worry. They're just a bunch of pencil pushers." Marvin glanced at his notes. "Okay, we start at ten. Any time you need a break, we'll stop. And of course we stop for lunch. I'll be here, this side of the glass. Don't answer anything in a hurry. These people are pushy, but think about what you're going to say before answering. If you're not sure, tell them you're not sure. Your inner thoughts belong to you, Ashlyn. You don't have to share them if you don't want. You're not criminals, and you're not charged with anything. You don't have to jeopardize what you believe in. Would you be willing to take a lie detector test?"

Both Ashlyn and Autumn said yes without hesitation.

Marvin liked that.

ASHLYN HAD CHOSEN BRAIN OVER heart, but as he sat on the edge of his bed in his quarantine quarters watching the evening news, he already knew he'd picked the wrong part of his anatomy.

The experts quickly attacked the validity of the water samples, suggesting the water had been doctored or sampled from a dank pond in somebody's back yard. And even though the pendant appeared to be valuable treasure from an undiscovered sea wreck, a bearded expert on channel 4 discounted it as a wild assertion without validation. The evening news devoted more time to city councilman Paul Schamm's protest on the expenditure of taxpayers' money on quarantine. "One hundred thousand dollars! It's obscene!" the councilman ranted with clenched fist on the steps of city hall.

Not surprisingly, the news broadcast angered Autumn, but Ashlyn watched with a numbness of mind, strangely and passively detached from the verbal lashing.

Sea beings were the focus of the late night *Danny Hall Show,* featuring a panel of experts, including an oceanographer and a UFOlogist.

In the audience, a sour-faced woman in a tweed jacket stood up, Danny Hall's mike under her chin. "With all the high-tech gear they got, satellites, submarines, sonar, I mean, come on, we know what's down there—if these beings exist, how come there's no proof? Real proof! Give me something real, body parts, photographs. Maybe I'll believe."

Half the audience cheered, clapped and shouted. "She wants something real," Danny mediated. "If these things really exist, surely we should have some hard-core proof."

The oceanographer, a woman in her sixties, with a breezy, confident smile, spoke passionately. "Yes it's true, space satellites and echo sounders have been able to map most of the ocean floor, but mapping from a satellite versus physically getting down there and exploring, well it's sort of like standing outside a cinema and imagining the film inside. Yes, you might draw several reasonable conclusions from the title and the publicity, but the real image—the laughs, the tears, the thrills—those you'll never know. The fact is the preponderance of the undersea, ninety-eight percent, has never been seen by human eyes, let alone explored. So to say spiritually aware creatures from the deep couldn't exist because there's no physical proof... I'm sorry, it's just one more example of human arrogance."

"Give me something, a bone, anything, that's all I'm saying. What's wrong with that?" rebuked the sour face in the tweed.

Danny responded. "Visual proof. Why so important? We have Ashlyn and Autumn's word, we have the submersible, and now a twenty million dollar pendant from a yet-to-be-discovered shipwreck. In a courtroom, a good circumstantial case, isn't it?"

A wiry man in spectacles stuck his arm into the air. "All those that believe, meet me outside, I got some magic sand to sell."

The audience laughed and applauded.

"They're kids! I got kids. Kids lie! Kids and lying, it's like Tom and Jerry, cereal and milk, bees and honey. Give 'em a polygraph, then we'll talk." He sat down.

"What about the submersible?" Danny reiterated. "Does it prove anything?"

The UFOlogist Scott Liebermann nodded. "I think it certainly does. But the skeptics and cynics who live for the status quo are going to manufacture excuses. The bottom line is no new lines are drawn, despite—and I think this is a shame—despite the importance of the message: We're poisoning our oceans!"

Again, half the audience cheered, half booed.

Danny held up a hand up for decorum. "We're back to I agree with the message, not the messenger. When we come back from this commercial message…."

As the theme music played, the picture cut to a commercial.

Ashlyn turned off the TV.

A few months ago, being called a liar would have angered him. Now he felt nothing except guilt. He'd exposed the Iquana to the human world, against their desire.

Surely, this wasn't his way.

Even if the polluter was watching the broadcasts, did he believe it? Did he feel any culpability? Any remorse? Would he stop? Not if he shared the views of the pedantic TV experts.

A GUST OF BRUTAL HEAT rocked Ashlyn, almost knocking him to the ground. A fraction of a second later, he heard the blast from the explosion, then screams!

Was the clinic on fire?

As hot dense smoke billowed, he ran. Confused, barely able to see through the smoke, he fled down a wooden deck, flames lapping at his feet, more flames falling from above. Everywhere people were yelling and screaming, knowing they were about to die!

Something was *wrong*.

Why are my hands dripping with blood? I'm not in the clinic! I'm in the wrong place! This has to be a dream!

Then he remembered attempting to visit Ko at the subterranean cavern. How did he end up aboard a sixteenth century caravel, slashed, stabbed, and fighting for his life?

Unlike the swashbuckling movies he'd seen, this foray was brutally vicious and graphically gory. His shirt was red from blood and black from being scorched.

I'm in the wrong place!

Just then a monster of a man came charging out of the smoke, his grotesquely scarred face grinning with glee as his blood-dripping cutlass rose into the air. Not knowing whether to run or fight, Ashlyn froze.

That fleeting moment of indecision would later haunt him.

The only time Ashlyn ventured below the waves that night was when he was thrown overboard, blood gushing from a slash across his neck.

He awoke with a splitting headache, exhausted from his night of battle, which seemed to have replayed itself over and over.

He was not exactly vexed with dream analysis.

He'd been indecisive in the face of an enemy.

Run or fight?

It had been the dilemma in the dream, as in real life.

"Give it a chance," Boomer urged as they strutted back along the corridor, late for their interview with the first government agency.

As they entered the hermetically sealed interview room, two suits next to Marvin in the observation booth began scribbling notes, perhaps describing the appearance or demeanor of the subjects, Ashlyn thought.

Although lengthy, Ashlyn found the incessant questioning to be painless—it broke up the monotony of confinement. He answered truthfully, in detail when he could, and with a level of imprecision when the subject was sensitive, such as the whereabouts of the Iquana cavern and the identity of the male voice on the much-publicized audiotape.

When it came to the CIA's turn, the agents pushed hard. Fortunately, Marvin was there to curtail the harassment. He and Autumn were asked to take polygraph tests. Both teens gladly accepted the challenge. They were hooked up right away.

Finally, the last snotty-nosed suit left the room.

Marvin smiled. "Good job, all of you. Don't take their crap to heart. There's more open-mindedness on the street than they'd let you believe."

"Is that an admonition?" Ashlyn queried.

"No, just a nod of encouragement."

"What about the creeps that are poisoning them? What about them?" Autumn asked.

"Give it time. We're working on it. Well, you guys are probably starving." Gathering his papers, Marvin stood up and bid them farewell.

Back in the quarantine room, Ashlyn and Autumn ate a supper of rubber chicken, soggy mixed vegetables and potatoes au gratin. Afterward, Ashlyn sketched while Autumn watched TV.

MEANWHILE, SITTING ON AN OIL drum at the back of Pete's fishery, Bogdan Boleshko admired a flaming red sunset, while speaking clearly into a flip-top encryption cell phone. "Send new instructions. Oracle ploy not succeeding…Wayside is unseasonably crowded. We are here for you. End message."

Bogdan pressed the send button. His voice, now memory recorded on a digital chip, was automatically scrambled into code, and then transmitted via satellite to C.R.F.O. headquarters in Washington DC.

Several minutes later a green light on his phone blinked as the return encrypted message was descrambled. He heard a synthetic playback: "*CONTINUE NORMAL DISRUPTION...WE ARE WORKING ON A NEW COUNTEROFFENSIVE...BE PATIENT, BROTHER.*"

After hitting the phone's erase button, Bogdan straddled his cycle and set off for the beach. Passing by the newsstand at Taylor Avenue, his face hardened.

The *Western World* headline read:

MILLER TEENS PASS POLYGRAPH

QUARANTINE DAY FOUR WAS QUIET. No outside visitors, more tests, exercise in the gym, supper, TV. Ashlyn watched a young preacher standing before a crowd on the beach, his arms waving flamboyantly, portending the coming of the antichrist. Ashlyn noted he was a powerful speaker, however he failed to recognize him.

"Mark my word, this is an alien, but not one of God's kind!" Bogdan Boleshko raised his voice, oratorically: "Think...who has the power to get a fifty million dollar submersible for children? Think! Who has the power to undermine your Christian faith? Who has the power to cause such chaos and disruption, such worldwide lack of belief and respect? What we are witnessing today was foretold in the scripture. They say that the alien is sick. Feel sorry for it, they say...pray for it to heal...

"That's what the demon wants!"

Opening his Bible, Bogdan quoted from Revelation: "'And I saw one of his hands as it were wounded to death, and his deadly wound was healed; and all the world wondered after the beast; and they worshipped the dragon which gave power onto the beast.'"

Ashlyn sat dumbfounded, wondering why were the TV stations allowing this blatant bias.

As the evening progressed, it deteriorated.

Whether fanned by the positive polygraphs or the lack of current news spectacle, the missing Wayside teens saga that had turned into a tabloid tale of deep-sea phantoms and navy conspiracies was beginning to turn into a media war. From *Larry King Live* to *The To-*

night Show to every magazine show in between, the existence of sea beings was debated fiercely. Guest warred against guest, expert battled expert, scoffing, accusing, and ridiculing each other.

The hues from the television reflected on Ashlyn's forehead, but he was no longer absorbing the madness, the hate, the anger—he was a world away....

He was looking at Ko.

She was floating on her side, inanimate, devoid of any light, a miserable gray from head to fluke.

"No!!!" Ashlyn shouted.

Abruptly, he felt a rush of energy as her kinfolk stormed through his vision, like one autonomous unit—as if an emergency siren had been triggered. Patient flat-lining.

They surrounded Ko.

They lifted her and caressed her, bathing her in brilliance, and they cried to her and cried for her.

The treatment was so uniquely different from a hospital ER yet in some ways so identical.

Ashlyn urged them on; every ounce of his being urged them on, his love, his token of light adding to the cumulate.

Perhaps Ko heard him, because just when he was about to surrender his hope, she sparked a pulse—meager, but an embryo of life force.

In that very instant, Ashlyn felt her on his shoulder—a faint, almost imperceptible twinge of electricity.

From Autumn's perspective, as Ashlyn watched television, tears trickled down his face. She assumed the show's hateful content had caused the emotion. How could she have known that something remarkable was now happening to Ashlyn?

Ashlyn wiped his tears. Crying was selfish. Crying wasn't going to save Ko. He was her hope. It was clear to him now. Clear, as if a switch had been flipped.

He saw *his way*.

The elders had said no, but that was before. This time they would agree because this was *his way*. They would have to agree. He ousted the notion of rejection, and the notion of failure.

There was much to plan, much to prepare, but it was already coming to him, coming to him quickly, and clearly—*his way*.

While the vilifying, vitriolic blabber continued to pour out of the television, the hues from the screen playing on his forehead,

Ashlyn found himself in a different ether. The pistons of his mind were accelerating, as they'd never done before. Clarity was sparking itself, new ideas forging into his mind. And by the time Autumn hit the television's off switch, plunging the room into darkness, Ashlyn the loner, Ashlyn the master of the submersible, Ashlyn the man of heart, had built a solid but complex plan for the greatest rescue in the history of the world....

Only the world could never know.

PART THREE

EO

-35-

Discharge

AT ELEVEN IN THE MORNING warm bright sunshine soaked the clinic's parking lot, and glints and sparkles danced off scores of camera lenses and tripods.

It was the sixth day of quarantine.

Discharge.

Four burly bodyguards arranged by Marvin met Ashlyn and company in the lobby, then escorted them out into the sunshine, where there was a surge of bodies and a roar of questions. "Ashlyn, if these *beings* are as intelligent as you say, and have lived on this planet longer than humans, why are they now only making themselves known?"

Ashlyn walked on silently, his head bowed.

"Ashlyn, are they going to give you other pieces of sunken treasure?"

"Did you take any photographs?"

As the beefy bodyguards fought to keep the throng back, microphones on fish poles still found their way into Ashlyn's face. "Ashlyn, Ashlyn, did you ever read the Bible?"

"Ashlyn, isn't it true you belong to a new age cult and your mother had a book deal with Oracle Publishing?"

Ashlyn glared back. "Did you make that one up all yourself or did you borrow it from the little boys locker room?" It was the only question he answered.

"You're a demon!" rebounded the last reporter.

They climbed into Marvin's Mercedes.

Ashlyn wasn't talkative during the drive to the coast. He appeared morose and detached. In another world, Boomer thought.

In truth, Ashlyn was deeply focused, cognizant of every word spoken in the car and many words and thoughts outside of the car, but he decided that now wasn't the time to share his thoughts…or reveal his plan.

Boomer, in the front passenger seat, grinned at Marvin. "Pendant, polygraphs, submersible—the evidence is mounting. So, now what do you have to say, my secular-minded friend?"

"What do I have to say? Well yes, it's a good case. I agree I'm not as much a skeptic."

Autumn leaned forward. "You're still a skeptic? Why are you helping us?"

Marvin laughed. "Boomer's paying me."

"Seriously," Autumn insisted.

"Seriously…seriously, I'm probably going to dig myself a watery grave here. Okay…I believe you were at the cavern. I believe you discovered a new species. I even believe Ashlyn has an unusual connection with them."

Carter interrupted, "Them? Pray tell what *them* is?"

Marvin turned up the air conditioner. "I'm getting to that. Umm… yes they're smart…I can pretty much accept—"

"That they're really dolphins? Oh dude. Whammy!"

"I know, I know…we lawyers should be at the bottom of the ocean; better us than the radioactive waste. The point is, what if Ashlyn didn't exactly understand."

"Understand what?" Boomer queried.

For a moment, Marvin locked eyes with Ashlyn in the rear view mirror. "All of us comprehend things we're familiar with; we process information by sight, smell, touch, taste, sound. If you eat something foreign in texture and taste, something that doesn't remind you of anything at all, how do describe what it tastes like? How do you give me a clear unequivocal understanding?"

Carter quickly responded. "I'd still know I was eating something, I'd know if it was chewy or on the sweet side or savory or…."

"Even if it had no taste—forget it. How about this: You're a seeker searching for enlightenment. One day on the good path you come across a white-faced alien in a flowing white robe, kneeling in what you think is a pose of worship. Now, what you don't know is this ET is actually an atheist and he's come to our planet for one reason: chocolate! And he's kneeling because it's his way of picking up cocoa vibes."

Carter snorted, "The Hershey alien. This is a good one."

Marvin adjusted his sun visor. "So this Hershey alien, this very unspiritual ET, who doesn't speak any of our earth languages, says to you 'Ram scabata baswi dew fatish god.' Now because you're on the spiritual path, you naturally assume—"

"—But Ko didn't say 'rum scaba whatever God,'" Autumn insisted. "And we weren't on any path."

Boomer chuckled. "Marvin, Marvin, Marvin. You know what I think? I think you're confused. Yah, all your life you say, 'there's nothing; this is all random.' And now along comes another species praying to The Almighty! One leaves room for doubt. But two, oh boy!   You've been dogging God so long you don't know what to think. Hey, you still want to fly all the way to the moon to prove we're a round planet? Let me save you the airfare. Round."

Marvin burst into a loud guffaw. "I love it. Practicing evangelism or psychiatry in that storefront?"

"A Swedish thing. I'll bill you later."

Ashlyn abruptly looked up, unfolded his arms and offered his first words since they'd left the clinic. "Guys, I've been thinking."

Sudden quiet.

"I've been thinking about the pendant. How soon can we sell it?"

Turning to face Ashlyn, Boomer answered, "Welcome back. Well, we've amassed plenty of publicity. No reason why we can't get on with an auction…a week, two."

"Make it quick." Ashlyn grinned.

"Are you up for a press conference, later?" Marvin asked.

"No," Ashlyn replied coldly.

"Well, we really shouldn't stall too long."

"No more press conferences. No more interviews."

"But I thought—"

"I've changed my mind. I'm finished with the press!" Ashlyn offered no further explanation. His chilly attitude silenced the ride.

Autumn observed him gently moving his head from side to side. She knew he was reading vibes and energies, seeing with his heart and practicing the art of sensitivity. Watching him, she felt slightly envious of his newfound abilities.

Eyes closed, Ashlyn breathed deep, exhaled slowly. A couple of times he quivered. After some thirty minutes, his eyes flickered open. "You are good energy, Marvin."

Marvin glanced in his rearview mirror. "Oh, thank you." He assumed Ashlyn's comment was a term of endearment.

"I'll tell you tomorrow. I'll tell you all tomorrow. But right now I want to talk about my dad before we get to my grandma's."

THE MEDIA FRENZY AT GRANDMA'S mirrored the electricity outside the clinic. Crowds and newsvans and large uplink antennas choked the sidewalks from Spruce Lane all the way down to the coast road. Helos girded the skies, cars honked, a few teenagers screamed, "I love you, Ashlyn; I love you, Autumn," while a few others yelled: "Take us with you!" and some even shouted "Blasphemers!" "Sinners!"

To Ashlyn, the entire scene seemed diffused, as if the clamor was being channeled into a sealed vacuum—perhaps another trick he had learned from Ko.

After his grandma released Ashlyn from a hug, and whispered in his ear, "You shouldn't have done it, you know that?" they all sat down in the lounge. Lucy served up lemon tea and raspberry upside-down cake with fresh whipped cream, meringue and fresh berries, while Marvin carried the conversation, per Ashlyn's request.

Marvin made a steeple with his hands. "It's important for you to understand because of your grandchildren, Mrs. Phillips." He cleared his throat. "Ashlyn and his father are drawn to each other. They both experienced something unique and special. I'm not excusing what Jerry did. What I'm saying is Jerry and Ashlyn have a connection beyond lineage…and Ashlyn doesn't want you to break that connection…or for you to try to break it. Do you understand?"

Grandma's blank stare suggested she didn't really understand much of any of this. Marvin paused, knowing that he needed to be firm without appearing bullish. "You see, Mrs. Phillips, given these very unusual circumstances, Inverness probably isn't an appropriate measure for Ashlyn and Autumn."

Grandma frowned. "Inverness? I thought you kids wanted…."

Autumn swallowed a large mouthful of raspberries and meringue. "Anyway, Grandma, when we sell the pendant, you'll never have to use this place as a bed-and-breakfast again. We'll be rich.

You too, Lucy."

Grandma was trembling. "Of course, if you don't want to go—"

"We don't," Ashlyn interjected adamantly.

Grandma pulled and squeezed her fingers until her fidgety hands found comfort on the rims of her wheelchair. "You poor children, having to go through this. They better send him to prison; that's all I can say. What is this pendant again?"

Ashlyn couldn't help but smile warmly at his grandmother. She was totally flummoxed.

ALONE IN THE BEDROOM, ASHLYN sat on the edge of his bed, flipped open his sketchpad, and using a charcoal stick, began sketching with energetic up and down strokes. He drew two side-by-side tubes, which looked like flat-topped boats with deep V-hulls. Drawing fore and aft two-story bridges connecting the hulls, the image began to resemble an enormous catamaran. Ashlyn sketched three sails, a net platform below the freeboard running hull to hull. He jotted the length: one hundred and fifty feet; beam: eighty feet; area between decks: fifty. Galley quarters: fifty by eighty. His calculation of the two levels was eight thousand square feet. He sketched armed guards on deck, doctors on deck, Iquana swimming between the hulls.

Ashlyn took a moment to scrutinize his drawing, then made some minor adjustments, before placing the charcoal on the night table.

He then lay down with his arms crossing his chest, closed his eyes, and began a new sketch—this one in his mind. With painstaking concentration, he began to see EO's luminous face.

"No!" Came grandma's angry voice from downstairs, momentarily throwing him. There seemed to be an argument downstairs. Trying to ignore it, he again focused on EO.

Practicing the art of "sensitivity," he was soon feeling the euphonious energies of the room...and the noises downstairs melted away.

An owl hooted.

Ashlyn was suddenly aware that he was listening to a chorus of crickets. It was some time after eight. Dark outside. He sighed, knowing that he'd been on the bed at least two hours. He'd been out of his body, traveling among the stars in some far off nebula, unable to redirect himself to the ocean and to the subterranean cavern. He was upset but not dispirited. Not much more than a month ago the idea of venturing out of his living body and traveling millions of miles at the speed of a thought would have seemed as ludicrous as a talking horse. Yet here he was, Mr. Ed himself, no less.

He knew that his poor navigation was the result of being an untutored student. He would have to improve his skill, even without Ko's nurturing voice guiding him. He was resolved to become a master of this new science. He'd try again later and even if he didn't succeed he'd try again and again and again.

-36-

Good Energy

ASHLYN AWOKE SLIGHTLY BEFORE DAWN after a long night searching for EO. Although tired, he rose from his bed. He found comfort feeling Ko on his shoulder. Her pulse was weak but no worse than before.

Quietly shuffling downstairs, he made himself hot tea and toast. He sat at the breakfast table, slowly sipping the beverage, thinking about EO and the plan. What plan? If he couldn't reach EO—

Don't think that way, Ashlyn. Know that you will reach EO and you will.

Perhaps he was trying too hard. He flipped on Lucy's portable TV, low volume. One of the morning shows was: "Politics, Religion, and Sea Beings." The assembled collage laid claim that politicians were terrified of sea beings. When asked about the subject, even in the context of myth, they recoiled as if the cameras and microphones were contaminated with Ebola.

"Mr. President, what are your feelings on sea beings? Are you a believer?"

The president flashed his pearly teeth. "The underlying issue here is pollution, and the polluting of our oceans is unconscionable. So once again, I urge congress to pass my clean planet bill that provides much stiffer penalties for—"

Ashlyn switched off.

Through the window, the sky was awash with the pinks and magentas of dawn. He found himself thinking about logistics, which made him edgy. He'd promised to tell the gang today. But he still didn't have EO's blessing. He could stall but—

I have to do this, he told himself. *For Ko.*

BECAUSE OF THE MEDIA CARNIVAL and the assemblage of onlookers, the sheriff's deputies had now barricaded the entrance to the cul-de-sac. Boomer, Carter and Marvin arrived at ten, and almost weren't allowed into the street.

Grandma wasn't feeling well, so they strolled to the back yard. Boomer walked with his arms around both kids. Ashlyn had the sketchpad tucked under his arm. It was a hot morning, and Marvin quickly took off his jacket and removed his tie. They sat by the newt pond.

Ashlyn picked up a pebble and rolled it around his fingers. "You are good energy, Marvin, for a disbeliever...I mean, you have a good heart." It was his way of getting down to business.

"Well, thank you. Does this mean we're going ahead with the press conference?"

"No. No more press." Ashlyn paused before he continued. "I've decided to put together a team, people like you, people that are good energy."

"A team?" remarked Boomer.

Ashlyn dropped the pebble into the pond, and opened his sketchpad. His drawing, now bearing infinitely more detail of the giant rescue catamaran, revealed a ship sailing alongside the catamaran. "There's a safe place...west, far west. In their weakened condition, it's not a viable option. Too dangerous a swim. That's why we need this catamaran. They can swim alongside or in between the hulls and they can rest on this net."

"I thought they weren't leaving their beloved cavern, whatever, whatever." It was Carter.

Slowly nodding, Ashlyn did not answer immediately. He was thinking about his plan, the time it was going to take to organize. Time Ko didn't have. If he waited until he reached EO, waited for the blessing, an extra day, two days, a week, Ko might very well not be around to—

He touched his shoulder. "They've changed their minds," he blurted, staring at his somewhat guilty-looking reflection oscillating in the newt pond.

Was it a lie?

Was he becoming what so many experts were claiming? A charlatan?

You'll find your way.

No, it wasn't a lie.

It was his way! But what about EO? He'd seen EO urging him. Surely, that wasn't a dream. No, he couldn't believe that. EO hadn't yet agreed to his plan but he would...he would soon. He had to!

Marvin dabbed his forehead. "Wow, Ashlyn. This is...this is one hell of a pretty ambitious idea. Are you sure—?"

Ashlyn interrupted. "The support ship will carry supplies and extra personnel. We'll have a defense unit aboard the cat, medical team, veterinarians. This is all hush-hush. No press, no announcements. Everybody we employ is sworn to secrecy."

Still scrutinizing Ashlyn's sketch, Marvin whistled. "It'll take months to put something like this together, let alone the cost."

Ashlyn turned over the page. Inside an oval ring, he'd sketched the numeral '9'. He then said, "I'd have sketched a '2' but I didn't want to be too unrealistic. In numerology nine is the number of completion. I believe we can pull this together in nine days."

Boomer, studying the craft's written dimensions, pulled his hair back into a ponytail. "Twin Wind," he said deadpan. "In Cabo...if she's still there. Yah...two Tradewind schooner hulls...an American was building her. But it's been...I guess about three years."

"Nine days!" Marvin brushed a bee out of his face. As always the logical advocate, he found it hard to believe that Boomer was actually considering this meshuga idea. "What about money...logistics, coordination? And I'm sorry to say it again, nine days...."

For the moment ignoring Marvin, Ashlyn's eyes were on Boomer. "How big is she?"

"She's big. One-thirty, maybe one-fifty," Boomer replied.

Ashlyn's eyes brightened. "I was thinking one-fifty to two."

Carter grinned. "Hey, rock-and-roll; we're really going to do this."

Marvin interjected, "Cost, time...I hate to be the dampener...."

Picking up another pebble, Ashlyn answered, "Trust." Then turning back to Boomer, he asked: "How quickly can we sell the pendant?"

"Sotheby's one week from Wednesday. They've asked for a pre-sale examination no later than five tomorrow. I've arranged an armored car pickup tonight."

Feeling the sun's heat on his back, Marvin pulled open another shirt button. "You're prepare to spend all your money—"

"My share, too. Whatever it takes." Boomer said.

Carter waved another persistent bee away from his face. "Mine as well, dude."

Ashlyn beamed. "Thanks."

Pouting his lips, Marvin was about to say something, but changed his mind. The flow was set, and there was no reason to swim upstream. He did, however, voice one legitimate concern. "Keeping this secret in the shadow of the auction, the press sticking to us like leeches...."

"We can do it." Ashlyn rebutted with total certainty.

"Boy, Nancy's going to love this," Marvin retorted.

"Who's Nancy?" Ashlyn inquired.

"My wife. Your biggest fan." As Marvin wiped away a bead of perspiration on his forehead, he felt a spark of inner warmth that he couldn't quite explain. He figured that Ashlyn's enthusiasm was contagious. Strangely, he felt like rubbing his hands together like an excited schoolboy.

Ashlyn smiled. With all Marvin's reservations and admonitions, the man really did have a good energy.

MARVIN FIGURED THE NINE-DAY plan was probably impossible to cement, yet on the flight back to Portland, thinking about various doctor friends he'd solicit, he found his neck and back goose pimpling, and concluded that if he was this energized others would be too.

Picking up the helo's phone, he called his publicity agent to cancel all of Ashlyn's appearances, Oprah, Larry King, Barbara, et al.

When the agent asked why, Marvin simply answered, "Ashlyn feels there's already been enough publicity."

AT BOOMER'S WAYFARERS STOREFRONT, BOOMER and Carter made a myriad calls to boat builders, marine brokers and charter companies. Boomer also spoke with Boleshko, reminding him about the pendant's pickup.

Boleshko clicked the back of his throat. "The sooner, the better; once it's out of here, I'll breathe a little easier."

Of course he'll breathe easier, Boomer thought. Marvin had harangued Boleshko over the security of the pendant; he'd wanted it locked up in a bank vault, but Boleshko insisted that it was just as secure in his upstairs jewelry safe. That was before the reporters started snooping and Boleshko began receiving some nasty phone calls. Marvin arranged to keep two security guards on hand, but that didn't assuage Boleshko's nervous tension.

And the inquisitive crowd outside the jewelry store didn't make any of them breathe easier.

ON DAY TWO ON ASHLYN'S countdown clock, several minutes before three in the afternoon, a Dodge Ram van pulled up at the curb in front of Boleshko's store. A man in a white tee and faded denims jumped out of the van and took off across the street.

Inside the store, Petro Boleshko was cleaning a watch while Bogdan was soldering a safety catch on a gold chain. The two security guards sat by the locked front door, idly watching the passerby. "That's odd," remarked the taller security guard as he observed the van driver running away.

Just then the phone rang.

Picking up the receiver, Boleshko heard a husky voice in the earpiece. "Look outside! You'll see a gray van."

Sure enough, through the window, Petro Boleshko saw a parked gray van. "It's a bomb," said the husky voice. "If you wanna live, get out now!"

The phone went click.

As Boleshko stood stock still, the color draining out of his face, Bogdan looked up. "What? What's wrong, pop?"

"Bomb threat. He said if you wanna live get out…."

Dropping the gold chain, Bogdan grabbed his father's arm while he shouted at the security guards: "Open the door!"

"No!" Petro protested, trying to resist his son's firm grip. "The pendant upstairs…it's a heist! Let go of me! It's the pendant!" He attempted to move toward the stairwell.

"Don't be a fool, pop!" Bogdan swung his father about, pushing him toward the door, the security guards now aiding him.

Foaming at the mouth as they ran him into the street, Petro screamed, "Let go of me! Let go! It's a heist!"

Ignoring his father's protest, Bogdan yelled at passing tourists. "There's a bomb! There's a bomb! Take cover!"

One of the security guards fired his revolver into the air. "Everybody clear the area!"

Now that people were fleeing, Bogdan ran with his father across the street and pulled him down behind a parked Durango truck. They were a hundred feet from the jewelry store. Peering over the Durango's fender, Bogdan observed the brave security guards stopping traffic, ushering pedestrians away from the gray van.

Two minutes passed, and nothing had happened. "I told you, it's a robbery!" Springing to his feet, Boleshko slipped out of his son's grip.

Bogdan gasped in horror as his father raced into the street. "Pop! Pop! No!"

The jeweler had covered half the distance back to his store, when there was a silent bright white flash, and the ground beneath his feet bucked up like an angry sea wave. In that moment, an unfathomable roar bit into Petro Boleshko's eardrums, and he was lifted off his feet.

The force of the explosion also slammed into Bogdan, throwing him backward. Showers of glass from nearly all the storefronts rained down on the street. Bogdan saw his father thudding into a parked car as the jewelry store collapsed inside a billowing cloud, followed by the bakery next door.

Bogdan had asked the bomb maker to construct something fancy, but he'd never expected this. Though his ears were ringing, muffling the horror of so many screaming voices, the agony of the shocked and injured played before Bogdan's eyes like a slow-motion mime. He was stunned. The van—the evidence—was gone, vaporized.

Bogdan staggered to his feet, pretending to be in shock, which wasn't difficult. Dulled sirens were already whining in the distance. A small boy was wondering in a daze, blood running down his tee from a slash in his neck. Bogdan ran to his father lying in the road, unconscious. He knelt down next to him…and wept like a baby.

THE EVENING NEWS REPORTED TWENTY-SIX injured by flying glass. Bogdan's father, one of the more seriously injured, was suffering from internal bleeding, multiple face and body lacerations, three broken ribs, broken right arm, and a dislocated ankle.

Amazingly, no one was killed.

The safe from Boleshko's Jewelry store had been found in the rubble, lying open...empty.

IN THE TWILIGHT HOUR, BOGDAN and three of his brothers from CRIFO boarded *TeaKup,* a small fishing trawler. Eight miles from shore, Bogdan muttered a prayer as he held the pendant in his open palm, agleam in the early evening sunlight. Then Bogdan closed his eyes and let the pendant drop over *TeaKup's* side.

The jewels glistened as the twilight struck them, and then with a gentle plop the pendant hit the water and disappeared below the waves.

VIEWERS WATCHING TV THAT night saw evangelist Billy Bob on *Larry King Live* calling the bombing incident another part of the ugly ploy. "Isn't it convenient?" the evangelist snarled, "On the very eve this apocryphal pendant is supposed to go to Sotheby's for evaluation, it's gone. Coincidence I think not! And where's the infamous press conference they're promising? What? Not having one? You know why? Because they can't stand up to the scrutiny. Yes, saints, we zapped the devil! Zapped him! Praise the Lord! Hallelujah!"

ASHLYN AND AUTUMN WERE AT Boomer's at the time of the bombing. They heard the blast and the subsequent sirens, but it wasn't until around six when a neighbor relayed the news to Boomer that Ashlyn looked up from an inventory list he was compiling and nodded understandingly. The news didn't pierce his heart; it didn't surrender his shoulders to a slump. He seemed neither perturbed nor discontent. He didn't even stand up.

Sitting next to him on the sofa, Autumn lowered her head onto his shoulder. "The pendant's gone. What do we do now?"

"I'm ready," Ashlyn replied calmly.

"Ready?" Boomer asked, concerned with Ashlyn's reaction.

"The pendant's gone," Carter reiterated.

Ashlyn's eyes refused to hold focus on anyone or anything. "I know."

"Our plan. Everything's gone!" Autumn said.

"No, not gone." Ashlyn answered quietly. He wasn't upset or shocked because at some level he'd known beforehand, even expected this. The pendant had been a problematic cog in a wheel of spectacle. There were already claims that it was linked to his father. The IRS was snooping. Sotheby's would have been a circus. He'd known these things for some time, but resisted the notion of dismissing the pendant, and searching for another solution. Now, it had dismissed him. "Almost spooky," he said as an afterthought.

Boomer pulled up a chair next to the sofa. "Spooky…yah, spooky." He sighed, burying his face in his hands.

"I know you guys think I'm a little weird. But I'm asking you to trust me. Now we really begin." Ashlyn stood up and faced his cohorts. "What does Nancy do?"

Boomer blinked. "Nancy? Nancy who?"

"Marvin's wife. Nancy. Her name keeps coming to me."

Boomer frowned. "I don't know. I think she's a homemaker. Why?"

"The pendant's gone but it's a blessing. We were making too much spectacle."

"Too much spectacle?" Out of respect for Ashlyn, Boomer refrained from laughing.

Carter added. "No money, no funny."

Ashlyn picked his sketchpad up off the counter, opening it to the rescue drawing. "I admit we've lost a few days. But this is still on! We continue. We have to raise money…quietly, person to person. We can do it!"

Toying with a pen, Boomer seemed to be shaking his head. "Ashlyn, son. I've never doubted you. But this…I'm sorry, we're at the end of the road. "

Ashlyn shook his head. "We can do it!"

DAY FOUR OF ASHLYN'S COUNTDOWN clock saw crowds continuing to flock to the tiny seaside town of Wayside, where piscine alien shirts, caps, tees and flags sold like hot cakes and wily-eyed local fisherman spun fanciful yarns of piscine alien encounters and conned many a visitor into a tour of a favorite hideout.

Out of Wayside, however, the TV experts had done a nifty job of debunking Ashlyn and his sea beings. Believers were scorned and ridiculed, and according to Marvin's press agent, the Miller kids were now bad news.

When nine-year-old Bobby Ray Wilson Jr. returned home from school with a bruised eye and a missing front tooth, he proudly held his head up and told his father that some kids were throwing rat poisoning into the storm drain to speed up the death of the Iquana. "But you told me to stick up for what I believe in, Dad, didn't you? So I did."

Bobby Ray Sr. hugged his son for sticking up for the Iquana.

Bobby's Ray's story didn't find its way into the newspapers or the evening news that night, nor did thousands of other similar stories like it across the nation.

But the voice of belief was alive and well.

Many individuals who believed spiritually aware beings were living below our oceans were scared to admit their feelings—scared to admit that the Bible, particularly the story of Genesis, seemed to be either flawed or misunderstood. What these individuals voiced in public and what they held to be true in their hearts weren't always synonymous. Some of these silent believers were public officials scared of losing position or ranking by voicing their contrary opinions; some were clergymen, high profile figures, even statesmen, not daring to admit in public their real feelings. But behind closed doors, family members, loved ones, trusted friends and confidantes talked of the Iquana beings and the terrible predicament we the human race had manufactured for them.

One of these believers was Nancy Rappaport, Marvin's lovely wife. A terrific homemaker with two young boys, she also happened to be the president of the local Starving Children's Foundation…and for the last few days Ashlyn's financial wonder woman. When Marvin had conveyed Ashlyn's hopeless desire to raise money for his rescue effort, Nancy's eyes had sparkled. While Marvin insisted that it couldn't be done, reminding his wife that the Miller kids were now bad news, she'd turned and said, "When was the last time you were in the supermarket?"

"Uh?"

"Grocery store?"

"What are you getting at?"

"People believe Ashlyn. You think I wouldn't donate two or three thousand dollars to his fund? You think Giles Graham wouldn't?" Giles Graham, hardly a liberal, was one of their best friends.

Grabbing the portable phone, she placed herself comfortably on the sofa, and began calling friends and acquaintances, one after the other.

Sipping a brandy, Marvin had watched her in awe, noticing how deft yet passionate she was. She winked at him as she jotted down another pledge. With five calls she had secured ten thousand dollars and appropriated ten new names. Ten thousand was a paltry sum within the scope of Ashlyn's rescue, not a patch on the thirty million they'd expected from the sale of the pendant, but in those few minutes, watching his wife, Marvin had glimpsed the operation coming to fruition after all. He saw the ease with which Nancy imparted the need to save these sea beings from the perils of their poisoned habitat. He too had raised money and he knew some mighty deep pockets.

Once again, Nancy was on the phone. "We need to build a rescue vessel. We need doctors, medical supplies, security…of course…of course. All confidential." She held up five fingers, followed by another five.

The dollars were mounting.

Marvin blew his wife another kiss.

-37-

Gates

THE DIRECTOR OF THE CIA, Larry Gates, was sitting alone at his desk in his office, tensing in anger as he read a statement from Pastor Brown of the Christ Consciousness Church of Manhattan.

> *If such creatures exist and they worship God this is both wonderful news and at the same time a travesty in that we, their neighbors, might very well be responsible for their demise.*

It was one of a handful of statements coming from liberal churches. The director rolled the paper into a ball and tossed it into the trash.

Gates had been cautiously optimistic that the piscine interest would fizzle but that now seemed unlikely. Just yesterday, a fifteen-year-old boy had stoned a fisherman on the banks of Crater Lake after witnessing a news report where demonstrators supporting Ashlyn Miller were intimidating hunters and fisherman, and spray-painting 'murderers' on their cars. The fisherman had survived the attack, but the incident had spawned even more contention. The American Sport Fishing League denounced the media for inciting hate and retaliation against law-abiding fishermen. Now the Fishing Club, the American Anglers Association, even the United States Gaming Commission were warring against Greenpeace, SPCA, Earthtrust, Global Cetacean Coalition and dozens of other environmental organizations. Sadly, this only kept these piscine things in the limelight.

Organizations like CRIFO, which Gates secretly endorsed, were doing their best as a counter-voice to debunk the whole notion of spiritual piscines, but almost one in four Americans now believed the creatures existed. Gates felt confident that, if anything, they were probably something like a new species of dolphin. Intelligent, no doubt, but the idea of them being spiritual was demeaning. It was also dangerous. What Gates feared most was that it could get much worse. God forbid if one of these things would ever show itself, or be captured—a piscine on television! There'd be hell to pay. In that regard, the thought of Andy Lightstone's hunting expedition to capture them sent shivers down his spine.

Gates picked up the phone and called his very close friend Admiral Benny Wilkes. The admiral was a man not unlike himself, a firm believer in the literal interpretation of the Bible, America, apple pie, Christian prayer in schools, and that Jews, Blacks and Muslims ought to know their places.

"I see your old pal Andy Lightstone's back in the press," the director said with a cynical after-laugh.

"Can you believe this crap?" the admiral scoffed.

"Yeah, it's a crazy yarn."

"Damn media, treacherous whores, giving it all this air time."

"Can you imagine what would happen if one of these creatures ever showed itself, Benny? Good God, there'd be no way to controvert what the kid says."

"The fish blinks, he tells us it's praying, and we're all no better than a beetle!"

"Be a dark day, wouldn't it, Benny? Say, what do you think? Maybe we ought to help Andy Lightstone track these things down. You know, before someone else does, before it really gets out of hand. EFPRO would give him quite an edge, wouldn't it?"

EFPRO was an acronym for Energy Field Production Recognition, a nascent reconnaissance system.

"EFPRO...we can't...I mean, how do you mean? Unofficially?" asked the admiral.

"No, no, of course not. Completely above board. He's got that oceanographic ship. Surely we can subcontract. Official beta-test site."

"Dangerous. Lightstone's not an easy man to steer."

"Agreed. So we don't let him steer. Your men can still operate, even in a subcontracting situation, can't they?"

"Well...I guess, if we write the contract that way," the admiral replied.

"Then we will. You'll operate and if you don't like what you see, well, your hands will be on the trigger."

Admiral Wilke's pulse hastened. It was a rogue plan. Something that could explode in his face, but it could also perhaps be one of the defining moments of his life—an opportunity to preserve the ideals of tens of millions of like-minded Americans. There'd be no direct navy involvement, but he'd be in control. If he wanted to, with the flip of a switch, he could— "Deep-sea fry." He chuckled. "You're a sly dog, Larry, you know that."

"Gotta be, haven't we, Benny?"

-38-

Enlisted

SITTING IN A SMALL OFFICE overlooking the naval yard at Port Oxford, Andy Lightstone chewed the end of his unlit Davidoff cigar, while reading every word on the document just handed to him. Andy didn't trust the stocky man with the toupee on the other side of the desk, Admiral Benjamin Wilkes, but Andy was smart enough to keep his thoughts in check. "You got yourself a deal."

Andy was agreeing to a one-month contract to test the subsea version of the latest reconnaissance technology called EFPRO—a spying system that detected and tracked a target's own energy field.

Besides actually seeing the benefit, Andy knew that if he declined, the navy would be one step behind in the hunt. It was better to be joined at the hip, in mutual disrespect, so to speak.

He signed the nondisclosure, opening the gate for navy engineers to board *Argonaut*. Admiral Wilkes signed the non-competition agreement giving Andy Lightstone exclusive license to market and exploit any new species made during the union and for an additional five years thereafter.

Wrapping up the meeting, Admiral Wilkes made a remark Andy found amusing: "You've a sharp mind, Andy, good acumen. What's better, the freak show or an arcane society of deep-sea salvage workers?"

The remark conjured up an interesting image: chained and

shackled piscine slaves combing undiscovered shipwrecks for treasure. Even for Andy, it was a rather heinous thought. No, he didn't trust Admiral Wilkes but he knew how to play the game. He re-lit his cigar and puffed smoke into the admiral's face. "Great idea!"

-39-

Committee

WITH HIS CELL PHONE CRADLED to his ear and a nervous knot in his gut, Ashlyn watched the birds on the pear tree through his bedroom window. Boomer was on the line, yapping away but Ashlyn's mind was speeding along on a different track, although not as speedily as time itself. Time raced faster than he liked to admit. Another few days were in the books. He didn't know how many people had jumped aboard his rescue team—it seemed like an army. Money was flooding in, over two million pledged. The plan's foundations were being laid: An appropriations committee had been formed; twenty-eight medical doctors and fifteen veterinarians had offered their services, and an overload of design engineers had volunteered to design the rescue vessel.

But at that moment the plan was simply his desire.

In terms of reality, it was a meaningless pipedream with no factual basis because there was no rendezvous appointment with the Iquana. No deal. Of course, Ashlyn hadn't mentioned this core fact to anyone. And he had no intention of mentioning it. Especially to the folks Boomer and Marvin had arranged for him to meet that night.

Even though the plan was engineered to be all hush-hush, per Ashlyn's request, talk of the rescue operation had spread like the winter flu. And that gave Ashlyn an additional dose of anxiety.

"Ashlyn, are you still there?" Boomer asked.

"Yes, sorry. I was just… never mind."

"Fundraising is conducted in a very social way. What I'm saying is we can raise a ton of money tonight. By the way, do you have a suit?"

"A suit?"

"Don't worry. We'll figure something. I'll be there at six sharp."

When Boomer arrived at the cul-de-sac, a small gathering of piqued tourists remained on the sidewalk. Gone were the newsvans and eyesore generators. Boomer waved at the two sheriffs who were stationed outside the house to prevent trouble, especially in the light of several threatening phone calls.

Opening the front door, Autumn whistled flirtatiously because Boomer was wearing a tuxedo. "Ooh, baby."

Boomer laughed, vainly adjusting his bow tie.

Ashlyn, feeling even more unsettled about this evening, trotted down the stairs. "How many people do you have coming?"

Boomer shrugged. "A few. Don't worry, all you have to do is smile, eat dinner, and we'll collect the checks. Nice suit. Nice."

Upon arriving at the Sheraton, Ashlyn and Autumn were recognized by some tourists. But Boomer quickly ushered them into the hotel lobby where Marvin's wife greeted them with open arms. Ashlyn instantly liked Nancy. Tall and slim, with long, wavy brunette hair, she generated a warm presence.

After releasing Ashlyn from a hug, Nancy took Autumn by the hand and led her through the lobby to a very expensive boutique, where three servile assistants placed Autumn into a stunning silver and black gown. Picture-perfect in eight minutes, she looked seventeen, not twelve.

Back together with Ashlyn and Boomer in the lobby, the group marched along the fancy corridor to the west wing.

The sign read: 'EMPIRE ROOM.' Ashlyn thought it seemed a bit too quiet. Boomer winked at him, and then opened the ballroom's double doors.

Ashlyn froze.

This wasn't exactly a small gathering, as Boomer had indicated, but a sweeping ballroom packed to capacity.

As Ashlyn gulped in wide-eyed shock, thunderous applause and cheers shattered the quiet. Spotlights danced around the floor. A four-man band played: "For They are Jolly Good Fellows."

Ashlyn glared at Boomer, "Just a few, huh?"

The explosion of cheers and applause grew even louder as the guests stood up from their tables—distinguished-looking men in suits, ladies in fine sequined gowns, teenagers, adults, seniors. Flash-bulbs rained. Wolf-whistles and yelps deafened, and an amplified voice burst through the mayhem: "Ladies and gentlemen, your hosts for the evening, Ashlyn and Autumn Miller."

Ashlyn's legs jellied as he felt Boomer's hand on his back coaxing him forward. Nothing was more nerve-racking, not his near-death experience with the mother sea, the whirlpools, eddies, the submersible's collision with the jagged chasm twelve thousand feet under the sea, nothing was more terrifying than standing on the stage, unprepared, with a foggy mind, while a hundred and fifty "supposedly" important guests shouted at the top of their lungs: "Ashlyn! Ashlyn! Ashlyn!"

Boomer held up Ashlyn's hand, the referee at a boxing bout. After a final burst of hoorays, the cheers slowly fizzled. Boomer whispered. "You don't have to make a speech. Just thank them for coming. They're paying ten thousand dollars...each one."

"Wow!" Ashlyn said aloud. As light laughter washed across the room, he felt heat rising to his cheeks, which must have turned tell-tale pink.

Then the room fell chillingly silent.

Ashlyn found himself listening to the heartbeats of almost every person he looked at, as if he'd nestled his head against each of their chests or bosoms. He locked eyes with a man who looked remarkably like the famous film director Steven Spielberg. "You are good energy," he said softly, before turning to the next person. "And you are good energy." Focusing on the next table, he said: "I feel your energy. Thank you."

After each acknowledgment, there were sprinkles of applause, some light laughter. If someone had been asked, "What do you think?" no doubt the reply would have probably been: "Cute, a little Hollywoodish."

The audience would soon change their minds.

Ashlyn paused, his attention shifting to one particular table all the way at the back of the room.

There were two men in the company of two beautiful women, smiling, laughing and applauding. There was nothing suspicious about their behavior. The four had paid for their tickets, spoken cordially to the other couples at the table, and had done nothing to arouse suspicion. The first man, salt-and-pepper hair, washed-out blue eyes, a strong chin, was about forty, fairly handsome, wearing a red and green tie. The other man, with a receding hairline, a long straight nose and thick horn-rimmed eyeglasses, was older.

Ashlyn cleared his throat. "Excuse me, sir...you at the back, you with the red and green tie...and the man in the glasses, what are you doing here?"

The man with the red and green tie pointed to his chest. Me?

"Yes, you!"

The man wiped his nervous palms on his pants. How on earth did this new age boy know of him? "What am I doing here?" he said.

"Yes." Ashlyn replied.

"I'm like everybody else," the man retorted through a forced smile.

"No sir. You are not. With everyone here I sense a warmth. I can feel their kindness...but you...is there someone here you hate?"

Murmurs and whispers filtered across the room. The man stood up slowly, his fallacious smile hardening into a glower representing the eyes of his inner sentiment. "I paid ten thousand dollars for this. What do you say to that, boy?"

Ashlyn momentarily froze. Perhaps he was mistaken. He sensed his already flushed face turning an even brighter hue.

Two heavyset security guards approached Red Tie's table. Red Tie looked livid. His friend rested a hand on his sleeve, trying to calm him, but Red Tie shook off the hand. "You people think this here is alright? This charade! Trendy, right? Ten thousand a pop? Help your needy alien? Well, I'm telling you, you are being fooled!" His voice rose into an oratorical shriek! "You are witnessing the beast at work! The beast!" He pointed to Ashlyn! "Him! See how he knows I'm his enemy? He ain't human! Can't you see that? He ain't human!"

Two more security guards entered the ballroom. But Red Tie and his partner backed up toward the exit door before the guards could reach them. They went peacefully, without force, their lady friends lowering their heads, silently following.

As the murmuring in the ballroom attenuated, a breathless silence settled upon the room. Ashlyn cleared his throat. "Wow! I've been called a lot of things in my life but 'beast,' that guy sure was creepy!"

The room burst into laughter and dense applause. The crowd had experienced something remarkable, and now the energy in the ballroom was electric. Mustering the courage to address his guests, Ashlyn held up a hand for silence. He spoke with a wavering voice. "Thank you. Thank you." They kept on cheering. "Thank you. Thank you...thank you for coming." As the cheers died down, Ashlyn said, "I'm not really a speaker but I just want to let you all know that you really are good energy." The crowd was about to applaud again but Ashlyn held up his hand. "You know, when Ko told me 'You've got good energy,' I think I thanked her like, you know, I really didn't have a clue. I figured, hey, that's her way of saying what's up? Have a nice day."

There was some laughter and a small round of applause.

"But I think you all know, there's more to it than that. Much more. Thank you very, very much."

Once again, the guests were on their feet, shouting, whistling, applauding. One man backstage, out of Ashlyn's line of sight, clapped his large hands louder than anyone.

His name was Denton Clark.

A FEW HOURS BEFORE DAWN, Ashlyn climbed into a bed at the hotel. So much had happened in the last few days, yet so much was uncertain. His plan was on a fast-moving escalator, but in a way he felt like a criminal, a fraud. Whether the rescue vessels were at the ready or not, there would be no rescue unless EO committed to the plan.

Emotionally drained, he closed his eyes. "EO, please give me your blessing. Please, EO, please...."

As the now familiar tones and resonances filtered into his mind, Ashlyn knew that he'd soon be traveling.

DENTON CLARK ALSO SLEPT AT the Sheraton, a room booked by Marvin. Anxious thoughts also pervaded Denton's mind that night. Where was life taking him? Andy Lightstone and his men had literally transited from his house the previous morning after he had woken to the sounds of hammers and electric drills. Four Atlantic Moving Company trucks parked outside his estate were being loaded up. They stole his Queen Anne furniture, his aquariums, mermaid sculptures, paintings, all of his equipment, even the closed circuit monitors. Finally, Andy's crew ripped up the floors and demolished the walls to make sure nothing else was hidden. By five, his house was bare, much of it demolished except for the heavy gear in the basement, which they'd dismantled, ready for pickup the next day. They were kind enough to leave Denton his bed. Not that he cared ever to sleep in it again.

After they left, despite their admonitions, he fled. He felt no remorse. The stale old house had harbored nothing but sour memories.

Lying in the bed at the Sheraton, Denton tried to rid himself of the thoughts of the old house. It was time to get on with a new chapter in his life.

But was he worthy of being reborn?

COME...EO BECKONED.

The elder's bioluminescence was subdued, his delicate strands of multicolored light blending into the void in a way that reminded Ashlyn of scorched, oscillating blacktop.

Come, he again beckoned, not verbally but with a wave of his arm.

As Ashlyn moved closer, he saw sadness yet compassion and understanding in EO's eyes. There was no inner-voice dialogue akin to his association with Ko but ideas and feelings began forging their way into his mind. Perhaps these were only fragments of EO's thoughts nevertheless there was a telepathic nexus.

EO conveyed an image of Ko, floating, gray and lifeless. A wispy vapor resembling her form rose up out of her body.

Ashlyn interpreted this as her released spirit. Even in sleep, he immediately ran his hand to his shoulder. He breathed a sigh of relief. Ko was still there, somehow holding on.

He then communicated his own counter-image: Ko on an island beach under the sun, playing, laughing, as healthy and luminous as she had ever been. "She must hang on; she promised me," he telepathically voiced, not knowing if EO could hear him.

Appearing to understand, EO reached for Ashlyn's hand. As Ashlyn felt the warmth of the elder's compassion, fresh images found their way into his mind: A procession of Iquana beings were carrying Ko's body to a benthic chimney city, like he had witnessed through the submersible's portal. But the water above these hydrothermal vents was shimmering, which meant the chimneys were thermally active.

The subtext Ashlyn gleaned was that Ko was to be liquefied in the chimney. Suddenly the image vanished, replaced by what appeared to be a time-advanced continuation: Ko's disembodied spirit was dancing through the starry empyrean. Once again, she was alive and vigorous. This scene then surrendered to a yet another vision—and Ashlyn found himself witnessing the birthing of a life form: Ko's spirit was about to merge with the flesh of a newborn—a baby human being.

Ashlyn understood the normalcy of these images. But he continued to reject every notion of Ko's death. "I understand, but these are only potential outcomes. Ko is still alive. I can feel her. And I now tell you this: It is not yet time. Do you understand me? It is not yet time for Ko to go. Not now. Not for a long time."

As EO probed deep into Ashlyn's eyes, reading him, feeling him, Ashlyn felt that his entreaty had been received, and was now being weighed.

After many moments—perhaps ten seconds or ten minutes—EO slowly bowed his head.

Ashlyn crossed his heart and breathed a sigh of relief. "Thank you." He then telepathed a new image:

In his mind, he opened his sketchpad revealing the rescue catamaran and support ship. He pointed to the shelter areas, doctors, aides, security personnel. Turning the page, he showed EO sketches representing a journey across the sea. "We can do this. You can live. Ko can live. But EO... only if you want this...only if you agree. But please, I urge you, I urge you with all my heart and all my love, please agree. Let me be your friend."

EO canted his head, perhaps concentrating on Ashlyn's message. Then Ashlyn felt what he perceived as a reply. One word—

Trust.

"Yes...trust!" Ashlyn nodded.

EO then telepathically conveyed to Ashlyn a repeat image: Ko's funeral at the hydrothermal vent.

"No! It is not her time! She will hold on! I am begging you...don't stop the healing light! Please!"

EO opened his palms in surrender, and Ashlyn sensed these words:

"It is too late, Ashlyn."

"No! It is not too late!" Ashlyn immediately conjured up another of his own images: An image of the bedroom at the hotel, where at that moment he was sleeping with Ko's face nestled against his neck, resting there, barely pulsing, but holding on, keeping him safe, as she had promised. "I am her hope."

EO stared at Ashlyn for a length of time that seemed an eternity. And then the elder extended his arm toward Ashlyn.

"Hope." Ashlyn actually heard EO's voice.

"Yes. Hope."

WHEN ASHLYN GROANED AWAKE, THE early morning rays were streaming through the curtains. Sitting up, his head felt muzzy, as if he were hung over. Overworked and under-rested, he figured. He tried to remember the finer details of the encounter with EO. He remembered talking about hope, but couldn't recall whether he'd received the blessing for the rescue. He chastised himself for not being blunt, asking in plain language something as simple and succinct as: "If I arrange the rescue vessels will you join us?"

Standing up, his legs felt weak and hollow. He stumbled into the bathroom and threw cold water on his face. He needed to pull himself together because today was a huge day.

THE RESCUE COMMITTEE HELD THE meeting in suite 601 at the Sheraton, which instantly became known as the war room.

On the large round table there was a covered platter of scrambled eggs, toast, coffee, croissants and juice. But Ashlyn wasn't hungry. He was still feeling lightheaded.

Marvin brought the meeting to order. Even though he was a quasi-believer, and they all knew it, the table voted him the chairperson. Good old paradoxical Marvin, a doubter of sorts, was a master organizer. He immediately announced that five million dollars had been collected, due to two very large donations, and money was starting to come in from overseas.

The twelve people at the table applauded.

Marvin continued: "Alright, first, so that we all understand exactly what and when the mission is, we're escorting approximately eighty Iquana sea creatures—"

"Beings," Ashlyn corrected him.

"Beings. I meant beings, sorry. We're escorting eighty Iquana sea beings across the Pacific to—" He paused glancing at Ashlyn, "—an as of yet an undisclosed location." He opened Ashlyn's sketchpad. "Our rescue vessel will be a super-wide catamaran, the area between hulls must be wide enough to use as a harbor for the beings. This will accommodate our principal rescue team. The support ship is for the rest of the team and additional supplies. Before we get into vessel selection, for those who don't know, preplanning time is extremely short, almost nonexistent due to obvious reasons. Date of departure is tentatively set for next Wednesday, exactly one week from tonight, subject to change, maybe sooner, so don't make any plans." Despite a few stunned murmurs, he telegraphed a warm smile to Ashlyn, and took a sip of orange juice. "All right, brass tacks item one: vessels." He turned to Boomer. "You've got something in mind, right?"

Boomer lay down his plate of eggs. "Nine different prospects, all super-sized catamarans. Twin Wind still seems best. I spoke to her owner; apparently she's in bad shape, but we can take care of that. I'm flying out this afternoon."

"In bad shape?" Ashlyn queried.

"Spit and polish; we'll fix it up." Boomer assured him.

With a trembling hand, Ashlyn poured himself some juice. "Do you think we should get it?"

"You're the boss."

"Okay. Let's do it."

"I already did," Boomer replied with a wink.

Rip Tedderston, an ex-CIA man, appointed security chief of the rescue, cleared his throat. "If we can afford it, we should get them all. Decoys. That goes for most of what we're doing. Decoy bases, boat yards."

"As long as it doesn't delay us," Ashlyn said, rubbing his temple.

"We won't let it," Rip replied.

Everybody was in agreement. The instruction would be passed down to the sub-purchasing committee. "By the way," the ex-CIA man added, "we should use code names. They might sound hokey but believe me they serve a very valid purpose."

"I have a name." Autumn said quickly. "Noah."

"Your name or the project's?" asked Rip.

The project's," Ashlyn answered for her. "I like it, Autumn."

"Sounds good to me," Rip agreed.

There were no objections. The project name became *Operation Noah*.

Marvin reintroduced his friend Doctor Arthur London, in charge of the medical side of *Noah*. The doctor wanted to know if he could get a head start, even a single examination in order to put together his medical team.

"You mean a prior rendezvous? No, not possible," Ashlyn told him.

Marvin interjected. "Expect blood infections, cancer, immune deficiency, liver, kidney, heart failures, and so on. Be prepared for any and all."

Next, Captain Michael Bixton was introduced. A merchant seaman, he was to be in charge of ancillary vessel, the crew and the route. His first choice was a tub called *Sister Mary*. She was 260 feet long, 2,900 tons. Originally built in the sixties as a floating marine laboratory, the Red Cross took possession of her in 1999 with the intent of turning her into a hospital ship. After sitting in dry dock for three years, a group of investors acquired her and they were now close to completing the conversion. What made her attractive was that she was at Edmonds, just north of Seattle on the Puget Sound, which was close. And she could be rented or purchased.

"How much?" several voices asked simultaneously.

"Fourteen million purchase or rent seventy-five thousand a week plus insurance plus crew."

Marvin liked it. "Book her as a rent now," he said.

"By the way," the captain added, "there's a couple of huge storm fronts coming in Sunday or Monday. One of them looks real nasty. Sooner is not a good idea."

"Got it," Marvin replied. "Let's say tentatively Wednesday, storms permitting."

When the meeting adjourned for lunch, Marvin took Autumn and Ashlyn aside. He first asked Ashlyn if he was feeling okay. Apparently, Ashlyn looked sallow.

"Didn't sleep much, too much nervous tension," Ashlyn replied.

Patting him on the back, Marvin came to the point. "Your father is in a room down the hall. He's been pretty beat up, emotionally. Long story. But one might say you guys hold the key to his future."

Ashlyn frowned. "How do you mean?"

"He's going to prison...unless I can prove these beings really exist."

"They do exist," Autumn interjected.

"Well, if I prove that to the court, if I prove that they caused him to literally lose his mind, I think I could get him off, as long as he pays back the taxes with penalties and interest."

Ashlyn shook his head. "Proved to a court, you mean go public? Everything we're doing here is cloaked in secrecy because that's the only way it can be. We can never go public. Surely, you understand that. There must be another way."

"We don't have to go public, no press, no jury, all in judge's chambers. Would you be willing to put a retired judge on our team?"

"I'd agree to that, sure, no problem," Ashlyn quickly replied.

"Good. I'll take care of it. Room 612. Go easy on him. He's just about bitten off his nails."

Ashlyn grimaced. "He's nervous?"

Marvin smiled. "No, hungry."

DENTON WAS SOBER—ALREADY ON the wagon three days; it didn't mean he processed his thoughts with greater clarity. In fact, at this moment his mind was awash with shame and self-repulsion. "Shall we sit?" were his first awkward words.

Autumn and Ashlyn sat on the sofa. Denton pulled up an armchair. He cleared his throat and ran a hand through his freshly styled haircut. He was at a loss for words. Could he even dare think of them as his kids?

Ashlyn's thoughts were virtually as troubled as his father's. He wanted to apologize for his behavior and to acknowledge him as a decent man after all, the way his mom had always described, but bringing up Mom probably wasn't an appropriate idea. The room maintained an eerie silence until Ashlyn managed a smile and remarked, "Nice room," almost wincing at his ineptitude.

Denton shifted in his chair. "I'm glad Proteus worked out. I had a hunch you'd figure it."

"She was awesome. Really awesome. I'm sorry we lost her."

Denton brushed the remark aside.

"Maybe we can get it back," Ashlyn added.

Denton shrugged his shoulders. "Yeah."

More hollow silence followed. The air-conditioning blew a frigid stream onto Denton's face, but he still loosened his necktie and fanned himself. "Would you like a drink? Coke? 7up?"

"Not for me," Autumn said. Ashlyn also shook his head no.

Denton took a deep breath and began: "You turned out to be swell kids, in spite of...in spite of the hardship I caused." His head slouched downward, shoulders burdened with an unbearable weight. "Things happen in strange rhythms and discontinuities...I think you've discovered that. Maybe this is the way it was meant to...."

"I know," Ashlyn said softly.

Denton appeared surprised. He looked up.

"You followed a path, Dad. You thought it was the right thing to do. You made a choice. Right or wrong, you made a choice and you stuck to it. That's the way it goes. It's what I've been doing, too."

A sparkle of moisture found its way to Denton's eyes. Being called Dad didn't escape him. "Yeah, it's the way it goes." He swallowed hard, trying to mentally suppress the flow of emotion he was feeling. The last thing he wanted was pity.

"What are you going to do?" Autumn asked. The question's underlying implication being, are you going to stick around?

"I think I've done all the hiding and running one can do in a lifetime. Wouldn't you say?" He mustered a grin.

"We don't want you to go to jail," Autumn said.

Denton shrugged, using his arms in an expressive manner, but they seemed to open wide. At least they did to Autumn. She took it as a cue for a hug, which is exactly what she gave him. Ashlyn realized that's what he wanted, too.

Denton hadn't intended to show his emotion, but the tears trickled down his cheeks, anyway.

LUNCH WAS IN THE WAR room. Denton, now a part of the rescue team, sat between his kids. Chicken Caribbean fajitas were served.

As Ashlyn began to eat he felt hot—as if the sun was scorching down on him. The conversation at the table was lively—Autumn laughing at one of Carter's jokes, Marvin and Boomer chatting about old dives—but the voices, the clutter of cups, plates and cutlery was fading away, disappearing into a vacuum.

Without even realizing, Ashlyn dropped his orange juice clangorously, spilling most over himself and Denton, and drawing the attention of everyone at the table.

Ashlyn stared straight ahead, at no one person or thing in particular. His mouth was cast slightly ajar. His eyes were glassy.

As Dr. London jumped to his feet, Denton held out a restraining hand, for Ashlyn was inhaling deep long breaths. His father watched him with a mixture of joy and sadness. For the first time in twelve years Denton felt the presence of a sea being, albeit a vicarious connection through his son.

Ashlyn was back at the Iquana cavern, his vision as clear as reality, his senses as dimensional as if he'd physically returned to the subsea. EO was hovering at Ko's side, accompanied by the entire Iquana family. They were all pulsing light onto Ko.

EO beckoned with his hand.

Come… come….

"Yes…I understand," Ashlyn replied.

A collage of images burned into Ashlyn's mind, no less than a homemade movie: The life of Ko.

He glimpsed her swimming like a speeding bullet near the surface, and playing ball with a dolphin; he saw her watching humans at a beach party; he saw her cradling Denton Clark twelve years ago after his near-death episode in the sea.

Ashlyn was momentarily confused. Was this a testimonial?

EO broke away from the healing circle. With one swish of his tail fluke, he seemed as close to Ashlyn as Marvin was on the other side of the conference table.

Again there was intense concentration etched into EO's features, and another home movie played into Ashlyn's mind.

Ashlyn saw himself standing with wide-open arms atop a pitch-black mountain, poised as if he were the king of the hill, only his hands were as luminous as the Iquana, his body pulsing intense light, which fell onto the black mountain. A bioluminescent webbed hand approached him. It was Ko's hand.

The vision reminded Ashlyn of that moment in the cave at Deadman's Bluff when Autumn and Ko first touched hands, where one webbed hand, one human hand came together in union. Except that in this vision his hand was pulsing with as much light as Ko's.

He suddenly understood.

To EO, he was light.

No, this wasn't a testimonial. EO had decided that he and Ko were lights shining through the darkness—pilot lights that would show the way and unite the families: human and Iquana, sea being, earth being.

It was the elder's blessing.

EO crossed his heart as Ashlyn had done last night as a universal measure or symbol of understanding: *"Thank you."*

As if her prayers had been answered, Ko's eyes gently flickered open. At first, she seemed to be without focus or cognition, slowly emerging from a deep, painless sleep, but as she moved into a state of awareness, she began to feel the savage, unrelenting pain tearing through her body. Her eyes turned upward in shock. She jerked in spasm.

Oh, how Ashlyn wished she hadn't been woken. Her gray, anguished eyes then fell upon him, and gradually her suffering blended into tranquility, as if he were her morphine.

"Ashlyn."

"I'm so sorry. You were sleeping."

"You did it...you found your way."

"Yes, I guess I'm sort of using my heart."

"I knew you would. I knew it.... Now I can go home."

"Wait for me, Ko. Don't go anywhere. You're going to get well again. I've got a plan. You wait and see; you'll be doing the wolf whistle dance, soon."

Ko sighed a peaceful sigh, then closed her eyes.

Ashlyn wiped away the single tear from his cheek, witnessed by the eleven around the conference table. Slowly discharging the breath he was unconsciously holding, he released himself from the astral state. He was back in the war room, every eye upon him, as spellbound as he'd just been.

"What are we waiting for?" He said. "We have work to do!"

-40-

Preparation

Friday 10 A.M. Noah-minus 5 days

A SCRAWNY BAREFOOTED BOY WITH an iguana lizard dangling over his shoulders handed Boomer an ice-cold beer. Pocketing the two American dollars, the boy then turned to look back at the frantic construction going on near the water's edge. The boy had seen much boating construction in his eleven years, but none like this.

On a makeshift jetty on the pristine Baja beach, an army of carpenters and welders were hammering, sawing, gluing, sanding and sealing, all oblivious to the broiling Cabo heat. And why wouldn't they be building with such pace and determination? After all, the big Swede overseeing the completion of *Twin Wind* was paying top dollar.

Bruce Maggin, the man who'd owned *Twin Wind* until the day before yesterday, never thought he'd see the catamaran sail, but Boomer's one hundred Mexican boat builders were working around the clock to complete the construction of the one-hundred-and-sixty-three-foot-long double-beam boat. Bruce stuck around as the foreman, part of the seventy-five thousand dollar purchase price.

Already the catamaran's two eighteen-foot-wide hulls were secured, connected by aluminum arches called crossarms. Sixty-five feet separated each hull, which meant that once afloat, the area in the middle of the catamaran would resemble an Olympic-sized pool. Above the forward arch, the construction crews were erecting the first mast, while carpenters were finishing up the bridge and main galley. Builders on the stern arch were housing additional berths. The craft was designed to sleep more than thirty people in reasonable comfort. In addition to the two sky-scraping masts designed to fly six thousand square feet of sail into the fiercest of sea breezes, Boomer had purchased four refurbished Caterpillar 1250 HP engines and two 6,000-gallon fuel tanks. The Californian engineer he'd hired to mount them said she'd slice through the waves like nothing else that size.

Boomer polished off the ice-cold beer before calling Ashlyn on his cell phone. "The cat looks great…ahead of schedule."

OMINOUS RAIN CLOUDS LOOMED OVER the city of San Francisco. The drab sky had cloaked the bay area for two days. Like Boomer, Carter chugged a beer as he sat on a paint-splotched barstool, watching oil tankers and barges drift by. He was at Pat's Boat Yard, one of many damp and dreary establishments along the front, a place where the salty sea air was tainted with the commercial aromas of gas, paint, acetate and smoke. Behind Carter, six strong Irishmen were turning *Wendell,* a seventy-eight-foot catamaran, into a seaworthy vessel.

Wendell was the first decoy vessel.

"EVEN IF YOU'RE NOT, ASSUME you're being followed," is the advice security man Rip Tedderston bestowed upon *Team Noah.*

Following this advice, Denton left the Sheraton and stepped into a waiting taxi. He went nine short blocks, jumped out of the taxi, ran across the street into another taxi. In Old Town he repeated the ploy. The third taxi drove him up the coast to North Bend where he rented a Chrysler Sebring from Hertz. He then took a two hundred mile drive south to Eureka, Northern California, where, at the marina, he located the eighteen-year-old catamaran *Picaresque,* a forty-eight-footer with an 85 horsepower diesel engine. She had good sails, two helm stations, wind instruments, VHF, wind vane. She was in a slip, clean and pampered. Her owners were an elderly couple, who took Denton for a short spin. They were asking $88,000. He offered $75,000 cash on the spot. The deal was made.

Picaresque became decoy vessel number two.

MEANWHILE, DECOY VESSEL NUMBER THREE, *Penny Lane,* lying in a slip in Astoria, almost on the Washington state border, was being prepped for her voyage. Her captain and first mate, Mr. and Mrs. Henry Seggerman, friends of Marvin, said they'd be delighted to make an additional contribution. The Seggermans set sail for Way-side.

Saturday 5 P.M. Noah-minus 4 days

AFTER STEPPING OFF THE PLANE, Rip Tedderston took a bus to Way-side, then an eight-mile jog through Old Town, continuously zigzagging from one side of the street to the other. Darting in and out of several back alleys, he scissor-jumped a small wall, walked into the Wayside Public Library, and loafed out through the rear door into another alley.

For the punctilious security chief of *Operation Noah*, the gait was a breeze. Rip also got a kick out of giving his *shadows* a ripe old workout. His pursuers were disadvantaged by being overweight, out of shape, and for wearing dark suits and heavy shoes. By contrast, Rip was wearing a featherweight jogging suit, running shoes, and a twenty-pound backpack—peanuts for him, even in the muggy heat. As cars were not allowed access through Old Town, Rip was doubly advantaged. Looking over his shoulder, he watched his pursuers falling back, one of them limping, another ambling along with his suit jacket slung over his shoulder, while the last one waved his arms in disgust.

When Rip knocked on the door of the war room—suite 601—he wasn't even huffing. With a calm and collected tone, barely a bead of perspiration on his forehead, he told the teens and Denton, who'd just returned from Eureka, that it was time to pack up the gear. He checked his watch. "We're leaving in one hour." He slid the back-pack off his shoulder.

"What happened?" Denton asked.

"An inconvenience, that's all." From his backpack Rip produced two jogging suits, a tape measure and a digital still camera. "We've got some eyes on us I'd like to lose. Kids, do you mind, I need you to wear these."

Downing a bottle of water, Rip sat on the sofa while he waited for the teens to get ready...and he thought about the last few days.

Rip Tedderston had been in the information business for twenty-five years, first as a government agent, then into the commercial spy world where he taught major American companies the art of keeping trade secrets secret. After becoming *Noah's* security chief three days ago, his first order of business had been a trip to Los Angeles where he had rounded up a dozen topnotch mercenaries including his favorite point man, Ace Jenkins—nicknamed "the Lion."

Then he went fishing.

Now that Boleshko's store had been bombed, it was clear that certain individuals—perhaps organizations—were capable of engaging in lethal practices to further the demise of Ashlyn Miller and his followers. To secure the safety of *Operation Noah*, Rip decided to harvest information on potential enemies, which included individuals, radical groups, even the United States government.

Shortly after arriving in Los Angeles, he made a series of phone calls to some old chums still in the game, hoping to pick up a lead, anything that might point him in the direction of an enemy. He quickly learned that Ashlyn Miller's name was on the navy's troublemaker's list, but was unable to glean further information in that regard.

He hooked up with a thirty-eight-year-old CIA cryptologist named Isaac Mandell, the son of a friend. They ate dinner at The Black Angus in Burbank, a suburb of Los Angeles. During the meal, Rip asked a few questions about Ashlyn Miller and piscine beings. Both men knew beforehand this was a fishing trip, where to a degree a discrete tidbit was okay, but Rip was surprised by the overt nervousness that fanned through the younger man. "Isaac, I'm not asking for weapon codes."

"There was a brief…I didn't get to see it."

Rip pushed aside his coffee cup. "I love my country, Isaac. I'm a proud American. I'm also a human being, a Christian, and I know you're a good Jew. I'm concerned we as a nation don't always make the best decisions. Put it this way—we don't always see the interest of all humanity and our planet. Piscines not weapon codes. If you get my drift, I'll continue. If not, no hard feelings."

The younger man's eyes remained glued to the tablecloth. "Gates sent out a memo. We've been warned."

Larry Gates, Director of the CIA had put them on notice.

"Sorry I asked," Rip replied facetiously.

"Look, I'll keep my eyes open. I can't promise anything."

Rip hadn't expected to hear from Isaac again. He spent the next day interviewing retired marines, navy SEALs, and purchasing state-of-the-art military equipment. By nightfall he'd hired twelve men. Returning from dinner, he was surprised to find Isaac waiting for him outside the hotel. They drove along Olive Avenue, Isaac slurping a double-chocolate malt. "I was a total schmuck last night. You saved my dad's life. Here…but don't ask me where I got it." He tossed an A-4 envelope onto Rip's lap.

Inside the envelope there were five sheets. The first was a Top Secret directive from CIA.

To: General David Pandexter
                 USAF Duke Laboratory, Texas.
From: The Central Intelligence Agency,
                 Langley, VA

Re: TRAIN:

This exploration exercise is classified TOP SECRET. The exploration has been allocated the codeword "KRAKEN." All train contractor personnel assigned to KRAKEN are to have a current TOP SECRET clearance approved by HQ prior to tomorrow's briefing. TRAIN is to be tested in the suboceanic Bathypelagic Zone. You are directed to rig for suboceanic maximum length. Date of departure TBA but probably 5/6 days.

It was signed, dated, with some other abstract code numbers, which didn't mean much to Rip.

Rip noticed Isaac grinning. The next document was:

To: Kraken Command Center
                 4th Floor, The Pentagon.

From: The U.S. Naval Post
                 Port Oxford, Oregon.

Re: BATHYPELAGIC EXPLORATION.

Argonaut has located suspect ingression. Traps have been set. No activity so far.

Rip shuddered. If he could remember correctly, Kraken was a legendary Scandinavian sea monster. Here it appeared to be the codename designated to piscine beings. *Argonaut* was the name of Andy Lightstone's ship.

Traps had been set.

The third, forth, fifth documents were equally informative. They related to the Sphinx Reconnaissance Satellites and EFPRO—Energy Field Production Recognition, a fledgling recon system, which was targeting key individuals of *Operation Noah*. Thus far, the EFPRO targeting had failed.

Rip knew why.

The EFPRO technicians first needed to capture a *biosignature*—unique imprint of the subject's mass, bulk and generated energy field. Failing to obtain a close-up snapshot of the target's *biosignature,* Kraken Command would resort to standard surveillance practices.

"So, someone's been following you?"

Autumn's question snapped Rip back to the present. "They tried. Just an inconvenience."

When the teens were dressed in the jogging suits, Rip snapped several digital photos, jotted down their height and weight measurements, then relayed the information to Ace Jenkins, his point man, on an encryption cell phone.

Rip couldn't be sure whether EFPRO operators had nailed the biosignatures, also known as "stamping the subjects" but he had to assume they had. Once stamped with a device not unlike a camera, held by an operator close to the subject, the exact location of *Team Noah's* representatives could be pinpointed at any given time thereafter. *Team Noah* would in essence be broadcasting a global positioning signal. But Rip knew the EFPRO surveillance system had an Achilles' heel, and he had every intention of aggravating that heel.

It was dusk when Ashlyn, Autumn, Denton and Rip hopped into a waiting taxi outside the hotel. The driver took them just five blocks to Wharf Way—single lane traffic, impossible to U-turn. Out of the taxi, they dashed across the street into a waiting sedan where they embarked on another short ride three blocks back the way they had just come. Back on foot again, they ran helter-skelter across traffic to the bike path, through the pedestrian zone into Brooks Ave, where they threw themselves into a waiting five-ton truck.

Three minutes later they were dropped off at a warehouse on First Street. The ducked under the partially elevated warehouse freight door, which clanged down shut as soon as they were inside the building.

A blast of steamy heat greeted them—heat as hot as a Swedish sauna, and loud rock music filled their ears.

Thirty people were waiting for them, including two sets of look-alike doubles who were the same build and height, dressed in identical running suits. Ashlyn found himself staring at his twin—well, not quite a twin on closer inspection, but good enough. No one spoke, per Rip's instructions.

Ashlyn recalled Rip talking about the EFPRO Achilles' heel.

If the subject's energy field were to abruptly metamorphosis, say by an instantaneous temperature loss, the lock on the subject was usually lost.

Ashlyn figured it was probably a hundred degrees in the warehouse. He was already feeling flushed when Rip ushered him forward, placing him next to one of many electric bar heaters. He took a quick inventory of the hardware in the warehouse: four trucks, four cars lined up by the main exit doors, three children's paddling pools filled with ice and water, a dozen fan and bar heaters running full pelt, and a set of disc jockey speakers blasting the music. Faces were flushed, armpits running, the air odorous.

Autumn, standing as close to a bar heater as she could bear, twitched her nose. Stinky bad.

"Four minutes, twenty," somebody whispered.

Ashlyn knew that in four minutes and twenty seconds, still wearing his clothes, he'd be taking an icy plunge.

The four minutes and twenty seconds seemed like an eternity but a sudden change in music signaled the marker.

Feeling as if she'd faint any moment now, Autumn felt a coaxing hand shepherding her to one of the freezing pools. She knew what to do but Rip still prompted her. "Go! Completely under, quick!"

Autumn gasped as icy water bit into her thighs and buttocks. Her impulse was to jump right back out, but several hands were guiding her down. As cubes of ice touched her waist, she suppressed a scream, held her nose, and slid under.

Instantaneous temperature loss.

Ashlyn dipped down into his pool. Even though he was primed for it, the shock sucked the breath out of his lungs. Rip nonchalantly slid under the water of his pool, while Denton was spared. His mission was to be paired off with the first set of decoy kids—the bait.

With rippling black muscles glistening with sweat, Rip's number one man, ex-navy seal Ace Jenkins, signaled for the B-team to get into the water.

The B-team comprised of three extra bodies per pool, just a little added confusion for the EFPRO operators.

A new song played. The three-minute marker.

"Time!" Ace shouted over the blasting rock-and-roll.

The C-team, known as the pool escorts, helped Autumn, Ashlyn and Rip out of the pools.

Autumn could hardly feel her legs but someone was pushing her, making her use those frozen limbs. Virtually numb from head to toe, not even feeling cold anymore, she ran toward three large refrigerators with doors wide open. Breathing holes had been drilled on all sides.

A hand on her back guided her into the first refrigerator. The door slammed shut, and a small battery-light taped to the door lit up. Already, she could feel that they were moving her. The wheels under her juddered, then clanged on metal. She knew that they were running her up the ramp onto one of the 5-ton trucks.

Autumn suddenly felt cold and her teeth began to chatter.

Lapsed time: pool plus thirty seconds.

The truck rumbled to life. They were on the move.

"You guys okay?" a female voice called out. Her name was Wendy Smith, head of the D-team, interior truck escort.

"Freezing!" Autumn cried.

"Good. Keep talking. That way we know you're okay. If you can take your clothes off, go right ahead, alright."

Autumn felt comfort knowing that the D-team truck escorts were waiting with warm blankets, flasks of hot soup, coffee, and dry clothes. One of them was a doctor. She had a defibrillator on standby…in case.

"Okay, you guys, not long now…about a mile."

Thirty seconds later, a buzzer sounded. The D-team yanked the refrigerators doors open. Bone-chilled is how Ashlyn would have described himself as a toasty-warm blanket was thrown around him. He and Autumn looked a little blue in the face, their teeth wouldn't stop chattering, but all in all, they were none the worse for the experience. Ashlyn sipped delicious, steamy cocoa and hugged his blankets.

Conchita, a pretty brunette girl, gave Autumn a circulation massage, arms, back, legs, toes. The color soon returned to her face.

Wendy said, "Here, slip these on." She tossed the group black jogging suits and sneakers, which they donned over their damp undergarments.

Ashlyn waited expectantly for part two of the getaway—the switch-point.

Rip had explained that even though the EFPRO operators would lose them during the sudden temperature loss—if they had been *stamped* in the first place—old-fashioned surveillance still remained a threat. Rip hoped that when Denton and the bait kids, the doubles of Ashlyn and Autumn, left the warehouse in a Crown Royal, enemy agents would follow. But Rip couldn't rule out the possibility that they also were being tailed.

Rip opened a 3x3 metal panel in the truck floor. Ashlyn leaned forward and saw speeding blacktop, while Rip's driver spoke to someone on a cell phone. "Pork chop, five seconds."

Rip dropped his blanket. "Get ready. This is it!"

They were approaching an intersection.

Just then, a rickety old pickup truck—*pork chop*—backed up across their path and stalled.

The 5-ton screeched to a halt.

It seemed to be one of those annoying road mishaps—car stalls blocking the path of the right-of-way traffic. Only the 5-ton was now in perfect position, stopped right above a manhole cover.

Rip's driver honked his horn and yelled out his window: "Move that damn piece of scrap metal or I'll ram it!"

On the blacktop, under the 5-ton, the manhole cover slid out of its hole, and one of Rick's mercenaries poked his head up from the underground sewer.

"Go!" Rip whispered aloud. Ashlyn dropped down through the hole. A pair of strong hands wrapped around his ankles. "Gotcha," whispered the gruff voice below. Ashlyn had been told to stay quiet and follow the mercenaries. That's exactly what he did, except there wasn't much following. These guys—five of them in military greens, blackened faces—were built like brick houses. The moment they grabbed his ankles, they were in control of his body. Down he sank into a dark and putrid sewer tunnel. With lightning speed, and almost complete silence, the mercenaries attached a pulley-ring to his waist with a rope looped through it. Then Ashlyn found himself being placed on a flat wooden plank with wheels. Another strong set of hands helped him keep balance.

"Sit!" the mercenary ordered.

Autumn was lowered next, then Rip. The manhole was closed. The five mercenaries flicked on miners' lights strapped to their foreheads.

Autumn squeezed her nostrils hoping to block out the stench, but the sewer's odor was so thick, she could taste it. Above her, she heard the drone of the truck in motion. One of the mercenaries whispered into a communicator: "Tally ho." And they began moving, sloshing through foul water. The cart's wheels rode about a foot above the sewer floor. Rumps got soaked, again.

"Low roof! Duck," warned a mercenary.

They all ducked.

Other than those words of admonition, there was silence during the ride. After three minutes at a steady clip, they heard sea gulls, then waves crashing, and fresh air began to return to their nostrils. Then the carts flew out of the tunnel onto the beach, and they came to an abrupt halt.

"Walk with me!" said the new escort, a young woman in a bikini holding half a dozen towels and an igloo cooler. The trio ripped off their malodorous jogging suits, and left them behind on the beach. The escort tossed Autumn a tube of sunscreen, handed Ashlyn the cooler, and Rip three sandy towels.

They walked along the beach, up six steps to the parking lot. The young woman, Jenna, opened the back door of a Toyota van, and they piled in.

Just another family having had a wonderful day at the beach.

They drove for twenty minutes, arriving in Porterville, a small town ten miles inland. Rip had rented the house for a month, even though they'd use it for only one or two days. It was a quaint little place with four bedrooms, fully furnished with pink and blue accents, very summery. There were fresh clothes and refreshments waiting for them.

Rip swilled a beer from the fridge. "If the eyes are gone, we'll move you to the palace tomorrow."

Palace was codeword for the farmhouse—the place where N-day would be launched.

Ashlyn couldn't help but think Rip was a whiz at his job.

DENTON DROPPED THE DECOY CAR off at Main Street, where a waiting taxi took him and the decoy kids straight to Grandma's house. Earlier, Ashlyn had managed to get word of the ploy to Lucy and his grandma. He'd told them to open the door and let the look-alikes into the house.

Lucy did as she'd been asked. Once inside the house, the girl decoy—Sally was her real name—held out the promised five thousand dollars, which was more than fair for one night's bed-and-breakfast. They were crispy new notes bound by a rubber band. The boy, Brad, opened a palmtop digital video player and played for Grandma a message from Ashlyn stating that he and Autumn were fine, to make supper as normal and watch TV as normal. Sally and Brad were to use their room as if they were really Ashlyn and Autumn.

Lucy and Grandma understood the deal. "If anyone calls, just take a number. Say we've retired for the night," Sally reiterated

The plan was for Denton to pick up the decoys kids in the morning and then whisk them in very roundabout way to a new, large house, brimming with activity, codenamed *Lighthouse*. The detouring and backtracking maneuvers were designed to give credibility to the ploy. If any prying eyes were watching, hopefully they would assume that *Lighthouse* was *Operation Noah's* headquarters.

-41-

The President

THE PRESIDENT OF THE UNITED STATES opened the Top Secret pouch that had just been handed to him. It was a communication from Director Gates of the Central Intelligence Agency.

RE: SEABED PHANTOMS AKA SEA BEINGS

Mr. President, I believe you are aware of the navy's undersea exploration around the purported entranceway to the Miller children's much publicized sea being lair. While the preliminary survey has not rendered conclusive proof of these creatures' existence, it is the opinion of this office, based on interviews with the Miller children, eyewitnesses and the review of the available scientific data, that the existence of a hitherto unknown deep-sea species is not extreme. The Millers have created a romantic illusion that these creatures are God-aware beings as intelligent as humans. This claim is not only preposterous, it has the potential to disease the minds of tens of thousands of Americans. While this office is willing to concede that these children might have discovered an intelligent group of mammals or fish, we flatly reject any notion of them being spiritual beings akin to Man. Such beliefs taken seriously could only emerge from individuals rejecting the God of our Bible, individuals adhering to heathendom. Yet a growing percentage of Americans with such beliefs are known to support a clandestine operation to relocate these creatures. Despite the secrecy, this endeavor will undeniably turn into a public circus. Even now, without proof of existence, opinions on sea beings are polarizing our nation. If the American public and the family of nations were to witness images of these creatures, there would be dire consequences. Bear in mind, 70% of our population are Christians, the Christian doctrine being the quilt of our stable democracy. To flaunt these animals as God-praying fish and Man's equal, in all likelihood would collapse the worldwide church and potentially make anarchists out of millions.

Accordingly, this office respectfully suggests the general public be spared the anguish and turmoil of discovery, if necessary by our own intervention in the relocation.

I understand intervention may seem harsh, but I submit that in the extremely unlikely scenario that the Millers have uncanny knowledge of the creatures' demise, relocation would only defer the inevitable. By allowing a public display, we would simply be announcing our environmental wrongdoing and, in the bargain, destroying that which is sacred to us, our own spiritual beliefs.

Therefore, my recommendation seems to be the only equitable and human course of action. For your further evaluation, I have enclosed a transcript of the interview with the Millers. You will see that the boy, the more vocal of the two, is indeed delusional.

The president leafed through the transcript.

Q.   How do you know the creatures are intelligent?
A.   How do I know you're intelligent? Scrap that, you're right I don't know you're intelligent.
Q.   Is it true you speak with them in your mind?
A.   Yes.
Q.   Do you speak with other people or entities in your mind?
A.   Mmm, let me see. Santa Claus, Batman, Easter Bunny.
Q.   Is that a joke?
A.   [Boy's attorney] Facetious question. Asked and answered.
Q.   So, this type of communication is a first for you?
A.   It is.
Q.   I see. Did they, the Iquana, make communicating sounds?
A.   Communicating sounds? No, not really…well in the beginning, before I learned, before I started becom-

ing sensitive, I used to hear static and whispers, spacey sounds.

Q. Are you hearing those spacey sounds now?

A. No.

Q. Did they do or display any sort of actions you thought remarkably intelligent?

A. Of course; [long pause] what's the point of this? You don't believe anything.

Q. What were you taught?

A. I told you. To read vibrations...feel different energies...see with my heart.

Q. You can see with your heart?

A. [Long pause] I'm working on it.

Q. Did you see anything with your eyes that suggested they were intelligent? Dexterity? Tools? Weapons?

A. I told you, that's not important to them.

Q. The Iquana don't build anything?

A. By and large, yes.

Q. Yet, they hide themselves in a shelter?

A. I didn't say that they hide. It's unwise to live in the open sea.

Q. Because of Man?

A. Your type, maybe.

Q. What's their shelter like? Could you remember how to get back there?

A. Of course not. Ocean all looks the same.

Q. What about the shelter—?

A. You don't care anything about the pollution do you?

Q. You don't remember it?

A. I do. It was beautiful. Dark, but magical.

Q. In what way?

A. The walls glowed...hazy mists drifting aimlessly. I kept thinking I'd find pirate's treasure. Well, I guess I did, didn't I?

Q. I see. But they didn't build this shelter?

A. Correct.

Q. If they're so smart, why don't they come out of hiding and instruct us on the ways of *smart*?

A. We're not ready...not yet.

Q. Not ready...meaning backwards...I see.

After reviewing the material, the president folded the papers and pondered. He had always suspected that complex life existed elsewhere in the universe. But within the workings of industry, economics, foreign affairs, and every day politics, otherworldly phenomenon and the supernatural were low totem pole affairs. Intelligent life on earth other than Man? Where would that leave the religions, the story of the Creation? He thought about his fragile presidency. CIA Director Gates had been around much longer than he. His advice must have been weighed. There again, Gates was a fundamentalist. Maybe containment was the answer, not eradication—a government evacuation of the species, placed into safe keeping under lock and key. Maybe they could hand them over to the Pope, let *him* deal with them.

The president reluctantly drafted a directive. Afterward, he laid his pen on the blotter, pinched the bridge of his nose, and mumbled, "God help me."

DIRECTOR LARRY GATES OF THE CIA didn't believe he'd obtain the president's scribble on an elimination order, but in his book there had been a limited risk asking. The president's directive was to contain the piscines inside marine tanks and, pending on their evaluation by top scientists, have them transported to a safe, secret location.

There were conditions. No containment unless it was entirely safe to humans. Plan to be aborted if any of the piscines escaped. Under no circumstances was the United States to engage in a chase with the creatures or the independent team planning to rescue them, and under no circumstances was there to be any attempt to eliminate or harm the creatures.

But the president's directive was ample ammunition. It was a green light. Not that Gates needed anything from the White House to send a special task force to the ocean bed. But now he had a scapegoat. If there was ever a leak, if the press ever discovered that the United States had eliminated the piscine *whatever* he could point the finger and say, "Yes the plan went awry but the number one man gave the order."

-42-

Obstruction

IN CABO SAN LUCAS, SEPTEMBER 18TH, under a seared fiery orange sky, Boomer smashed a bottle of champagne against *Twin Wind's* port bow.

The Mexican boatmen cheered, waved their hats.

Twin Wind sat audaciously wide on the launch ramp, a gleaming white with royal blue side sashes and color-matching sails. A sailing aficionado watching the launch laughed: "That elephant's gonna be dead in the water."

"Betcha fifty she'll fly," countered the man next to him—who happened to be the boat's design engineer—even though he knew that *Twin Wind* was hardly a purist's vision of a super-sized multi-hull. Typically, a super-sized catamaran (also known as a multihull) would be built for racing. Long and featherweight with narrow hulls for slicing water, the craft would have daggerboards instead of keels, and it definitely wouldn't have engines.

Almost everything about *Twin Wind* was a contradiction. She was heavy, wide, keeled, and she did have engines.

Boomer waved his arm at the fishing trawler hovering off shore. With a guttural cough, the trawler's diesels ejected a gaseous cloud, and the trawler slowly chugged away from the beach. As the ropes stretching back to *Twin Wind* went taut, Boomer signaled more throttle. The trawler barked another smelly cloud, and *Twin Wind* groaned like a big old bear.

But the boat didn't budge.

Boomer dusted his baseball cap on his knee. "What did we do, nail it to the ramp?"

"Joo no spit for luck, Senor Boomer," cried one of the boatmen.

"Champagne not good enough, huh?" Grinning, Boomer performed the ceremonial spittle on the hull.

Now the boatmen really cheered, tossing their hats into the air.

And the boat slid straight down the ramp into the turquoise water.

When Boomer fired up the four Caterpillar engines, they made deep, healthy guttural sounds. When he throttled, they roared!

Moving away from the beach, *Twin Wind's* bows dipped down and rose up effortlessly, planing through the azure water like her design engineer had always known. Boomer soon discovered that running full sails free as a bird or bare-poled under the rumbling power of her four Caterpillar engines, *Twin Wind* performed like her namesake—she was a double blast of wind.

Under a silvery Cabo San Lucas moon, Boomer set sail for Oregon.

Noah's Ark was on her way.

"LINGUINI, CLAM SAUCE, AND A nice dry Bordeaux."

"T-bone steak, baked potato, sour cream, butter, chives, ummmm," came Ed Lazerath's reply.

For a minute, neither of the two men in the claustrophobic capsule spoke, they just listened to the monotonous whir of the generator.

"I hate this place. I hate it with a passion," Ed mumbled to himself. His nose was pressed up against the glass portal of the seabed habitat *Mimas*.

It was black out there, eerie and silent—the black nothingness of the abyss. By contrast, everything inside the habitat *Mimas* was white and stark—a pearly white coffin. Ed had been holed up in the miserable place for...he didn't know how long. Forever.

Through the portal, he stared at the fan-eject nets, the devices he'd devised to ensnare the piscines, lying untouched. Beyond the nets twelve huge iron cages, large enough for a T-rex or two, had been dumped into the sediment, anchored and tethered by the navy. They looked like the frames of small buildings, as if they'd once been a part of a town before being swallowed up by the ocean...and now forgotten.

"What day is today?"

Captain Buck Whitman smacked his lips. "Thursday, I think. Strawberry cream pie, fresh custard and cream, with a thin crust, two helpings."

Ed was tired of the food game. Maybe it was two days ago or three that he'd suggested they move to another ingression. Or was it just hours ago? He chuckled under his breath, finding humor in the tragedy of having a mushed brain—zapped of cohesive thought by the deep sea. Oh yes, now he remembered. It was when sonar tracked what appeared to be a *phantom* twelve miles south. But Andy's orders were to remain in position because *Argonaut's* new spy equipment had detected something close to their current position.

So, here they were, waiting…waiting…caged in their white coffin, waiting and—

"What is that?" Buck nudged Ed's elbow. He pointed to a moving object forty-fives degrees east.

Pressing his nose further into the portal, Ed now saw it—a bulbous titanium pod thing, being lowered by steel ropes to the seabed. "What the hell is that?"

Buck shrugged his shoulders. "Don't look like an AUV."

Andy Lightstone had informed them that the navy would be supplying a new, stronger type of AUV. But this *thing* had to be twice the size of *Mimas*.

As Ed watched, he noticed several another objects being lowered, long, skinny things with suction cups and claws. He counted six separate objects that made him think of metal centipedes or snakes.

"I don't have a good feeling about this, Buck," he said.

SNAPPING OPEN HIS EYES, ASHLYN jumped out of the dream, landing on his feet next to the bed. Unable to see anything, he blinked. Then he remembered—the curtains were drawn. That's why it was black in the room. He could still see into his dream—a slithering metal snake with probing lights, coming for him, preparing to strike.

Ashlyn quickly flipped on the bedroom light, and the snake vanished. But it was not gone from his thoughts—the beat of his heart was proof of that. In the dream he'd been aboard a Zodiac dinghy in the dead of night; there was a storm, huge waves, rapid-fire lightning flaring like warfare. In the discord of the dream, the boat flipped upside down and he found himself staring at the metal snake, a very long metal snake with spotlights ripping into his soul, forcing him awake.

Shuddering with the thought, Ashlyn turned the doorknob, and tiptoed out of the bedroom. Quickly downstairs, he grabbed the encryption cell phone Rip left for emergencies. He pushed the first three digits, and paused, noticing the silence…it was very silent. Looking out of the window, he saw stars…no rain…no lightning. What could Rip do? He'd simply confirm that he was dreaming.

Was it a dream…or was it a vision?

Noah's sea captain Michael Bixton had talked about the upcoming storm. The forecasters projected a Monday night arrival, saying that it would be one of the worst storms in a decade.

Sitting on the last step in the hallway, Ashlyn closed his eyes. What was the metal snake?

You must feel.

Twenty minutes passed.

Ashlyn massaged the back of his neck as he felt the chill of the early morning settling into his bones. He was tired, and would have welcomed the bed covers upstairs. But he stayed on the stairs, waiting for an insight.

Feel.

Perhaps another fifteen minutes passed before he opened his eyes. Although he hadn't concluded what the metal snake was, he was convinced of two things: The metal snake was real, and N-day couldn't be launched as scheduled.

How can we move up *Noah* day? How? During the storm? Then he told himself, we just have to do it. We have to because time won't defeat the metal snake—only bait can.

"Huh," he said aloud as the idea just dropped in.

-43-

Chocolate pie

Saturday 6 A.M.

TWIN WIND, NOW KNOWN AS *Noah's Ark,* pitched into a gentle ocean swell sixty miles southwest of Las Escabos, northern Baja, her billowing sails propelling the multihull along at nineteen knots. Both the sky and sea were a cerulean blue, winds temperate, and seven hundred and fifty miles were now behind Captain Boomer Larson. He calculated that they'd easily make the rendezvous hour, without rushing. He didn't want to arrive early and be seen loitering.

He had just finished taking a cold shower when his first mate Caesar Arreaga yelled, "Senor Boomer, fax, more storm!"

Toweling off, Boomer loped up the steps to the bridge and took the fax in hand. Studying the report, he ran his finger over a line of storm cells now shadowing the entire west coast. The weather prognosis had gone from grim to grave in a heartbeat. The deep blue sky would soon be replaced by gray thunderheads and the ocean would turn angry. Skewing his head to the heavens, Boomer didn't even have to give Caesar the order to fire up the big Caterpillar engines.

"Engines going to sing in five minutes, senor Boomer boss man. Good for joo?"

"Yah. Good for me, Caesar.

The phone rang.

Flipping open his new flip-top, Boomer heard Marvin's voice, talking in code. "Soldier, Poor Man." The code translation: *Boomer, Marvin.* "There's a new bakery order: forty-eight crème puffs and a chocolate pie!" Code translation: *Noah's a go, forty-eight hours ahead of schedule!*

Forty-eight crème puffs meant they'd be slam-dunk in the middle of the storm.

Boomer whistled. "You are joking, Poor Man?"

"Big order, urgent, must be filled."

"That's some order. Okay, we're battening down the shelves, lighting up the oven!"

"Good luck. See you later, Soldier."

As the eight-man crew reefed the sails, the catamaran's big engines wound up into a roar.

Noah's Ark surged forward.

Boomer tucked his fatigued eyes back into the weather fax. Sustained winds were expected to reach seventy miles an hour, a grain under hurricane force. Ashlyn's plan was only to conduct the exodus during the worst storm of the decade, maybe the century.

IT WAS A BLEAK DAWN as the decoy catamaran *Wendell* captained by Carter Benwall sailed north of San Francisco with its captain still in bed. The choppy seas and immense wind drone had kept Carter miserably awake all night and he was trying to get his first shut-eye in almost three days when he realized that his phone was ringing. "Yeah," he groaned into the flip-top.

"Tinker, Poor Man," Marvin sang.

"I'm sleeping."

"Well wake up; there's a new bakery order...."

Saturday noon, Noah T-minus 36 hours

A MISTY RAIN WASHED OVER the decks of *Operation Noah's* support ship *Sister Mary* as her crew readied the ship for departure.

Captain Michael Bixton, who had also received an early morning call from Marvin, signaled the linesman on the gangplank to release lines.

As the ropes came off the bollards, *Sister Mary,* laden with twenty-four million dollars of medical supplies, a team of physicians including Doctor Arthur London, three hematologists, two oncologists, a serologist, three radiotherapists, a mammographer, an immunotherapist, five veterinarians, twelve nurses and orderlies, nine well-paid soldiers of fortune, and a sixteen-man crew, pulled away from berth 1409.

The ship headed north along the harbor channel, slowly making way toward the Strait of Juan de Fuca.

-44-

Metal snake

ED LAZERATH COULD NO LONGER contain his anger. With his nose pressed against *Mimas'* portal, he watched more apparatus arriving on the sea floor. Another submersible, *NIR IV* was the fourth navy sub. The area surrounding the chasm was taking on the appearance of a battle camp. It was obvious that the navy had taken charge, obvious that they weren't about to share their proceeds—in fact, obvious that any proceeds were targeted for elimination.

The huge metal snake, now assembled as a weapon of war, was Ed's last straw. He'd already given Andy Lightstone a mouthful. But Andy was just as furious, protesting that they had all been duped.

Hours earlier Andy had been informed of the navy's unrelated Top-Secret experiments in the vicinity of the subsea beta-test site. It was an infraction of the agreement. But what was he to do?

Andy screamed back at Ed, instructing him to keep the navy out of the hole—as if Ed needed to be told. Of course he wasn't going to let the navy into their *ingy*. He and Buck had discovered it, safe-guarded it all these days. It was theirs!

Buck Whitman noticed the veins in Ed's temples visibly darkening. Poor Ed had recently lost his girlfriend over this gig. He'd spent day after agonizing day on the seabed with nothing but freeze-dried food. They had endured weeks of Andy's verbal abuse, and as troubled as Ed was with worldwide opinions on sea beings, he wasn't ready to surrender his $250,000 stake in the operation.

"Oh-hoh, it's moving," Buck cried.

Through the portal, they watched the snake-thing arch its back and slither forward.

DESIGNED AND BUILT AT THE Geoscience Institute of Technology in Houston, the snake-thing was supposed to be a harmless remote-controlled probe capable of descending deep into earthquake faults. But the CIA had appropriated it one week ago—supposedly for evaluation.

Only six men knew it had been modified: Director Gates, Admiral Wilkes, one programmer and three construction engineers, all members of CRIFO.

Now called TRAIN—Titanium Rope Automated Inversion Nodule—it was a robotic, synthetic larvae brimming with sensors, focusing lights, cameras, claws, drills, high pressure suction cups and cyanide and mustard gas pellets.

Three hundred feet long, designed to withstand the rigors of intense heat and cold, *TRAIN* slithered toward the chasm.

TO ED LAZERATH, THE SNAKE was a thief attempting to steal his dream. The only device on board *Mimas* barely sufficient as a weapon was the AUV—*Creepy Crawly*—designed for maintenance and repair, not exploration, and definitely not combat. Ed's eyes settled on *Creepy Crawley's* remote joystick.

When Buck saw what Ed was planning, he tensed. "Don't do it, Ed!"

Too late—Ed had already stabbed the AUV's release button.

The three hundred pound squat unit with eight arms sank to the seabed, kicking up a small cloud of sediment.

As the unit approached the navy's circular habitat, from where *TRAIN* received its remote instructions, *Mimas'* radio squawked, and a voice rumbled out of the speaker. "Mimas, US navy Lieutenant Commander Ellis. Why did you launch your AUV? Over."

Snatching the mike, Ed snarled back, "Why did we launch? This is our site! We have an exclusive navy contract! Why did you launch? Over and out!"

Through the portal, Ed watched *Creepy Crawly* approaching the navy's habitat.

"Reverse your AUV!" warned the lieutenant commander.

"Sorry. Runaway unit out of control," Ed shot back with a smug grin.

"I'm warning you!"

Out of the speaker box, Ed and Buck heard a metallic *CLA-KLUNG!*

From inside the navy's habitat, the lieutenant commander heard the same metallic sounds vibrating under his feet. The AUV *Creepy Crawly* had attached itself.

"Get that thing off us!"

"Jammed. Sorry," Ed replied with a wink to Buck who gave Ed a nervous nod. Ed could now hear through his headphones dull voices and the hum of equipment from inside the navy station.

"Mimas, I repeat, we are the United States navy. Withdraw your AUV or we'll take the necessary steps to preserve the integrity of our operation. Do you understand? Over."

"We understand. Now you understand this—get that *thing* away from the hole or we'll blow our AUV! We are United States citizens trying to protect sea beings!"

"Are you threatening us, mister?"

Ed realized he might have overstepped his bounds. There weren't any explosives aboard *Creepy Crawly* but by representing it, he'd given the navy a viable reason to open fire. But would they fire upon American citizens? Self-defense, they'd claim. Ed knew they'd probably get away with it, too. But he convinced himself to keep the bluff going. "I'm holding this button, the moment I let go...BOOM! Checkmate!"

There was no further verbal response from Commander Ellis but through the portal Ed watched two navy submersibles lifting off from the seabed.

One of the submersibles slowly approached the navy's habitat while the other headed their way. Buck Whitman was now sweating bullets. "Ed, back down! For God's sake, for my mother's sake, back down!"

Ed's forehead was also glistening but he put a finger across his lips. Navy sound probes could be listening. He pushed the mike button. "Get back, you sons of bitches or I'll do it! I swear! Five seconds...four...three! I'm doing it!" he shouted.

"Okay! Okay! We're pulling back! Don't do anything!"

The submersibles sank back to the seafloor.

Brow dripping wasn't confined to *Mimas*. Aboard the navy's habitat, aptly named *Station,* Lieutenant Commander Richard Ellis toweled dried his armpits. He turned to his chief petty officer. "Those guys are crazy."

"Where is it?" Ed Lazerath bawled.

During the standoff the snake had slipped unnoticed into the chasm. Ed stabbed the mike button: "Reverse it! Reverse it or we're all gonna die!"

"Reverse?" Commander Ellis sounded surprised.

"The snake in the chasm! I swear I'm letting this button go—"

"Wait...wait, sorry! Our mistake. Didn't even realize."

On board the navy's *Station,* Commander Ellis gave the appropriate order.

TRAIN's operator acknowledged: "All systems reverse, Commander."

Watching the metal hardware reemerging, Ed took a long sigh of relief. He winked at Buck. "We came, we saw, we conquered!"

"You're nuts, Ed, you know that, certifiable."

Ed grinned, swooning in vainglory.

His smugness would have abruptly vanished if he had realized that only two hundred feet of *TRAIN* had reemerged through the chasm.

But how could he have known that?

TRAIN's OPERATOR HAD TRICKED THE eyes observing the nodule, including his commander and the marines sitting right next to him who'd watched him pulling the lever clearly marked "reverse."

A one-hundred-foot-long section of the nodule was now slithering into Iquana territory.

The rogue operator maintained a straight face. Admiral Wilkes would be proud of him. If the marines next to him didn't know the mission had been changed from seek-and-capture to seek-and-destroy, how could the civilian crew on *Mimas?*

-45-

Countdown

Noah Day, 4 P.M. T-minus 8 hours

THE SKY WAS GRAY WITH misty rain washing down onto sweeping acres of verdant farmland as the Jeep chugged along a dirt road flanked by chain-link. Rip stopped next to a herd of cows while a farmer opened a wooden gate, allowing them access into the field. Rip then drove another hundred yards, approaching three buildings, before skidding to a stop.

It had rained hard several times that day, so when Ashlyn and Autumn stepped out of the Jeep their boots squelched into thick mud.

They had arrived at Calloway Ranch, codenamed *The Palace*—nine hundred and fifty acres of farmland near Blythe, northeast of Wayside on the Calilee River.

Of the three buildings, two were grain silos, the other an empty hangar large enough to accommodate a Boeing 747.

Rip tossed Ashlyn a military issue backpack. "Foul weather gear inside and Dramamine, if you need it." He tossed Autumn her backpack.

They walked across the mire toward the first silo. When Rip opened the door Autumn grimaced—blood made her feel queasy, and in this silo there was plenty of pungent blood.

Under humming fluorescents, a group of men and women in overalls and goggles were ripping up hulking whale carcasses and chunks of purple meat, while others were pouring rocket fuel into tanks woven from beef rawhide. The floor was strewn with large marine skeletons and fairy lights, beef rawhides and plastic explosives and streaming with blood, blubber, and computer chips. At a glance, the nexus intertwining these incongruous elements would seem macabre, more than likely illegal, but in fact there was a very sane, practical explanation.

They were decoys—the bait decoy Iquana beings envisioned by Ashlyn to sidetrack their enemies.

Named IBRs—Iquana Bait Rockets—the self-detonating torpedoes were being camouflaged within carcasses and carrion, bundled up with resilient Chinese seaweed, rope, and strings of flashing fairy lights. Seventy-five of the eight-foot-long decoys had thus far been assembled. They were configured to travel even faster than the Iquana. If these devices didn't totally fool Andy Lightstone or anyone else hunting the Iquana, the hope was that they would cause enough confusion, so that in conjunction with the storm and decoy boats, the real Iquana would be able to swim to *Noah's Ark.*

After Ashlyn voiced his approval, Rip patted him on the back.

Walking back into the misty rain, a 10-ton truck was rumbling up the farm's long dirt road. Even before it pulled to a stop, both cab doors swung open and sixteen men, including Rip's point man, Ace Jenkins, dropped to the ground.

The men unloaded M6A2 assault rifles, CAR-15 assault rifles, Stoner M63A1 light machine guns, AN/PVS-9A night vision goggles, AN/PAQ-4 laser aiming lights, AN-TAS-6 thermal acquisition sights, four twin Mercury 400 outboard Zodiacs, Colfax encryption phones—CIA issue, HP palmtop computers, scanners, and a whole bunch more.

"Move it, men! Pass it, pass it!"

Rip led the way to the next hangar. "Going like clock work."

Ashlyn smiled, but his gut told him that he'd missed something.

7 P.M. Noah T-minus 5 hours

IT WAS RAINING BUT NOT heavily when Denton arrived at a house on Knowles Road—decoy house number three.

When the front door opened, Sally and Brad greeted him warmly with a hug. They were wearing yellow plastic coats, hoods lowered on purpose, faces exposed but partially shielded from the street by Denton's body. From close up they looked very natural, very much like the real deal, so to any spying eyes further away they must have definitely looked like Ashlyn and Autumn.

Denton bundled the kids' gear into the trunk of his car, and delivered his line for the edification of any microphones in their vicinity—and there were several. "Autumn, did you take the Dramamine?"

"Of course. I'm not stupid." She replied, sounding remarkably like the real Autumn.

BY FIVE IN THE AFTERNOON, thirty to forty mile an hour gusts were throwing themselves at the coast. Except for the foolhardy, the beaches were deserted. Wayside's stores and sidewalk cafes closed early, many of them boarded up. The hotels, however, were jampacked. At the Sheraton, there was standing room only at the Sloop Bar where the conversations were either about the storm or sea beings. The buzzword was that something was going down this very night.

The radio was reporting that the heaviest storm would hit at ten. But as Denton drove into the marina, gusty winds were already whipping across the channel like salty breath from an invisible dragon. Sixty-foot masts drew loops in the slate-gray sky. Mooring ropes stretched tight and cried from the torture. Hundreds of plastic wind vanes spun and metal cleats and shackles clinked and clanked in a wild marina symphony.

Denton and the bait kids were greeted at the dock by two of Rip's men, who helped them speedily board the decoy vessel *Picaresque*. Six real doctors boarded right behind them, enhancing the salability of the ploy. The catamaran was the only boat at the marina about to set sail that night.

Fletcher, the captain, gave the engine some juice, and as the 85-horsepower engine ejected a burst of smelly smoke, the decoy catamaran chugged away from the dock.

7:50 P.M. Noah T-minus 4 hours, ten minutes

AS THE CLOCK COUNTED DOWN, Ashlyn felt horribly anxious. He stood on the banks of the Calilee River, buffeted by wind and moderate rain, watching Rip's mercenaries load the IBR decoys onto a fifty-six-foot fishing trawler named *Unselfish*. The captain of the trawler tugged on his baseball cap, which was his way of saying, "All's clear."

Unselfish throttled up and pulled away from the small jetty. Ashlyn watched the trawler until it approached a bend in the river and disappeared inside a patch of fog. His departure was still two hours away.

He touched his shoulder, moved it around a bit. Sometimes it was hard to tell if Ko was still there. Her touch was so light…so very, very light. "I'm coming, Ko. Hang on."

Shaking his wet hair, he pulled up his hood, flicked on the Maglight and headed back to the main silo.

Autumn greeted him with a plate of sandwiches. "You didn't eat."

"No thanks."

"Go on. I made them especially."

"I'm not hungry."

"You know what they say about sailing on an empty stomach."

He pushed the plate away as he spotted Rip on the silo's far side where the temporary command post had been set up. He headed off in that direction.

Autumn tagged along, munching a sandwich.

Ace Jenkins was at the 40-inch LCD screen, an electronic stylus in his hand, charting the operation's progress.

In essence, the plan was to cause so much confusion and mayhem with the IBR bait rockets and with numerous speeding vessels, right in the middle of the largest North Pacific storm in over a decade, maybe the century, that when the real Iquana made a beeline for *Noah's Ark*, neither the government nor Andy Lightstone would know who or what to chase.

Rip tapped Ashlyn on the back. "Your baby, Ashlyn, your genius. We might have reeled in the elements but it's your... what's wrong?"

Ashlyn was trembling.

"What is it?"

"There's a machine…in their subway, closing."

-46-

Attack

AT FULL THROTTLE, MERCURY ENGINES screaming, *Noah's* four Zodiac dinghies, *Olpha, Bolpha, Dolpha,* and *Golpha* flew down the Calilee River, throwing back stinging contrails of white water. Schedule off, plan in jeopardy, the helmsmen drove like hell.

Autumn and Ashlyn were in Zodiac *Olpha* along with Ace and two paramilitary boys, their heads poking out of unzipped sections in the tarp cover. They were wearing foul weather gear, strapped in with quick release belts and safety ropes.

The two paramilitary boys, helmsman and navigator, wore night-vision goggles. They drove without lights, leaping wave tops at more than a mile a minute. Autumn and Ashlyn couldn't see a thing…but they felt it all right. Their boat screamed around bends, canting hard left, then hard right like a stunt car on two wheels. The buffeting wasn't that bad, Autumn thought. Little jockey thumps. But she knew this was novice steeplechaser's domain. The real stuff was coming up.

A sheath of vertical lightning split the heavens. For a brief spell, they could see rain falling in sheets. Moments later they felt it.

The storm of a hundred years had arrived!

THE IQUANA EXODUS DIDN'T REQUIRE the gathering of supplies, the packing up of old possessions and the closure of preexisting business. It required nothing but two elements: willingness and trust.

The Iquana had never placed themselves in the trust of another species before. Yet to EO this felt right, even though in two breaths human beings were both benevolent and malevolent. This paradox was never more pronounced than at that very moment as the dangerous mechanical device moved deeper into their subway system.

Yet EO felt the trust of Ashlyn in his heart. So the Iquana beings gazed upon their cavernous abode for the last time. The other sea animals in the cavern, their longtime companions in this symbiosis, seemed to understand the magnitude of the moment for they made unusual sounds and their biochemical light wasn't as luminous as usual.

The Iquana thanked these denizens for their friendship; they thanked the steaming pools for the joy they had shared, and they thanked the rocky walls for housing them. There was no sadness in the farewell, no remorse, only feelings of love and hope.

Only two of the Iquana beings were unable to support themselves: Gal'ee'ial'eeli'ee and her younger sister, the one being whom Ashlyn knew lovingly as Ko.

EO took Ko's limp body into his leviathan arms, and holding her firmly in his grasp, dove to the cavern floor, the entire family following closely. They were no less than one massive descending spaceship, their gleaming bioluminescence bathing the basalt walls for the very last time.

In union the beings retroflexed to a virtual stop at the boulder sealing the entranceway.

It was a mean rock, no less than thirty-five-hundred tons, one hundred-and-thirty feet wide. During Ashlyn and Autumn's visit, the rock had glided aside as if controlled by a mechanical pulley. Yet, the only mechanics used by the Iquana were the mechanics of the mind.

As the massive rock moved aside, the ground shook and rumbled. Water ripples ran across the surface of the cavern.

And on the other side of the rampart, where moments before there had been stillness and blackness, brilliant light streamed forth.

THE ONE-HUNDRED-FOOT-LONG section of *TRAIN* instantly picked up the signals: electromagnetism, radiation, motion, multiple biological forms. The data automatically routed back to the navy's *Station,* although nothing registered on the pilot's computer screen. The clever programmer had performed such a skillful deception, had done everything so very right…or so he thought.

The alarm suddenly bleated.

The programmer had forgotten to disconnect the audio alarm.

The alarm howled. It shrieked. It took the programmer and everyone else by heart-leaping surprise!

Aboard *Mimas,* the unearthly silence had existed for so long, Ed had almost fallen asleep. But now a howling siren and panicked voices screamed out of his headphones.

"What's that alarm?"

"CO, don't touch that!"

"What's this flashing icon?"

"I told you not to touch!"

"It's the nodule's signal. Radiation, electromagnetism…where's it coming from?"

"It's too late. It'll all be over!"

"Multiple biology…you idiot!"

"You had to touch that, didn't you?"

"What the hell did you do? I ordered you—"

"—you're not in charge. I am!"

"Pull it back! Pull it back! Mimas, we're pulling it back!"

"No!"

"Kill that damn siren!"

"Idiot—"

"Too late!"

"Kill it!"

The siren died.

"Oh my God. They've heard everything."

Ed Lazerath's face turned crimson as the veins in his temples darkened. It looked like fluids were pumping into his eyes, making them bulge, making them huge, Buck Whitman thought.

It was all the years of bottled up anger, all the years of controlled behavior, animosities shoved into the basement yet still there, brewing, simmering, waiting to surface during a moment of turmoil. Andy Lightstone had been the fuse. Yes sir. No sir. Three bags full, sir.

"Those bastards!" He shrieked, grabbing the AUV's manipulator controls.

Buck watched in hapless horror, a spectator watching a macabre pantomime. Ed had started up the AUV's drill and was drilling into the navy's *Station.*

This was no longer a game of bluff.

Buck found his voice. "Ed, no!" he screamed but his words seemed to be shallow, without gusto, drifting off nowhere. He watched his own hands reaching for the controls, pushing Ed's hands away.

Had his brain at last kicked in?

If so, why was everything in slow motion? He saw Ed's clenched fist floating toward him, not flying like a speeding hammer, but floating—yet he was still too slow to veer away from the punch. And even when he felt the blow, it didn't really hurt that much. His knees buckled and he felt his eyes taking a swim. He'd heard that crunching sound before. It had earned him a nickname during his youth: China chin. Four times hit, four times broken.

This broken chin was to be his last.

His ears ringing, Buck Whitman lay on the floor, blood and spittle running over his knuckles as he held his jaw. And as he looked up and saw Ed at the controls, he felt a very strange sensation.

How odd, he thought. Ed was standing in front of him, yet he could have sworn he'd been smacked in the head again.

Then Buck saw a light, a dazzling white light—and the ringing in his ears stopped.

Buck Whitman knew he was dead.

THE CREW INSIDE THE NAVY'S *Station* observed the lash of death. Where *Mimas* had been anchored only seconds ago, there was now only a ball of underwater fire. The torpedo from *NIR IV* was a direct hit. The crew observed the visible concentric shock wave a fraction of a second later, just before they felt it—the force of a seven-pointer on the Richter scale. Equipment racks crashed to the floor. Lights buzzed. Lips quivered. It was over in fifteen seconds.

But that's when *Station's* crew realized....

It wasn't over!

Creepy Crawly's drill bit was still producing a sibilant whine. It was still drilling into the skin of the habitat.

"We didn't stop it! It's still drilling into us!" cried a marine.

The Lieutenant Commander threw off his headphones to make sure. "Radio, alert NIR Senior! We have to evacuate! Escape hatch, leave everything, move it!"

As the submersible *NIR IV* approached *Station's* docking port for the rescue, the captain of the submersible *White Panther* piloted his submersible to *Station's* aft, hoping to pry off the AUV.

Monitoring the rescue submersible's approach on the Heads Up Display next to the escape hatch, Commander Ellis spoke into the intercom. "Steady…three meters…you're almost here."

"The current's strong…it's pushing me," replied *NIR IV's* commander, a man named Redding Hathburn.

"You're doing fine. Hold it there…one meter, closing…a little more. Good! Touchdown!"

"We acknowledge, touchdown." Hathburn almost giggled with relief. "Let's get you people over here quickly."

A hundred feet around *Station's* port side, the manipulators on *White Panther* clamped onto the AUV *Creepy Crawly.*

"Gotcha!" The pilot snarled. He was about to pry the AUV off *Station's* side when, shockingly, the habitat jumped up like an animal in shock, and the pilot heard the voice of an old woman…screaming.

The old woman screaming was the sound of air being squeezed out of his own submersible—the last sound he would ever hear.

THE CREWS ABOARD THE OTHER TWO SUBMERSIBLES *NIR II* and *Thrasher VI* watched the horrifying implosions.

It began with undulating ripples on *Station's* skin. The habitat then jumped up like an animated monster, snapping, snarling, its titanium body folding in on itself, and birthing razor-sharp shards that instantly became scimitars of death lashing into the two submersibles sharing its boundaries. *NIR IV* no longer looked like a submersible but an extension of the crazy metal monster eating it. An iron dagger cleaved off *White Panther's* conning tower as if it were soft butter. *White Panther* collapsed like a crushed egg, its steal and titanium hull bleeding into the carcasses of the other two hulls.

The vessels may have been forged from the strongest metals known to Man but to the six onlookers aboard *NIR II* and *Thrasher VI* they looked like scraps of paper crumbling into a singular mass.

The implosion of all three vessels took less than five seconds.

No longer galvanized, the amorphous mass of metal drifted down to the seabed where a haze of sediment quickly washed over it.

A cold, eerie stillness, typical of the benthic zone, returned to the area. A chain of ethereal, gelatinous salps glided over the unrecognizable metal heap. To the salps, this heap was no more or less significant than the shapes that previously existed. Either way, intruders had encroached upon their environment.

THE LOSS OF *STATION* WAS an insignificant factor to the section of *TRAIN* advancing into the Iquana's territory. The nodule was programmed to act autonomously. Slithering forward, its echo sounder built images of what lay ahead. The on-board computer processed the information. Targets were closing in. Fast water was approaching. The safety mechanisms on the firing tubes automatically disengaged.

EO SENSED THE DANGER, SENSED the impending disaster. As non-warring beings of love and harmony, he simply held Ko tighter in his arms, waiting for the moment....

    TRAIN'S flashing red numbers counted off the seconds....

    Five...four...three...two...one....

    WHOOSH.... WHOOSH.... WHOOSH....

    Twelve torpedoes containing the poisonous gases flew out of the tubes, screaming down the channel at two hundred miles an hour.

    No living organism could survive the explosion set to take place in a few seconds—any living biological form within a six-thousand-yard radius was about to perish.

10:05 P.M. *USS Whitehorn,* Pacific Ocean, 40 miles west of Wayside

ADMIRAL WILKES LEARNED OF THE seabed debacle moments after a distress buoy from *NIR II* was fired to the surface. Wilkes held first class seaman David Jackson, the cryptologist who decoded the SOS, to sworn secrecy.

    After Jackson saluted and closed the door, Wilkes slumped down at his desk. He had no way of knowing if *TRAIN* was intact or if it had finished the job. He decided to move forward with plan B on assumption that the subsea mission had failed. According to Director Gates of the CIA, the Millers had boarded a catamaran named *Picaresque*

    Wilkes paced his ship's quarters as he formulated his next move. Protocol required that he call the Chief of Naval Operations to report the loss of life and property at the seabed chasm. Of course, he'd only tell the CNO a fraction of the truth. Wilkes rehearsed his revised subterfuge. *The creatures did it...a herd charged out of the chasm! Bulls, no intelligence, wild bulls fleeing the lair! Hard to imagine on purpose, but we ought to go on alert...just in case. Seeing as this is such a sensitive issue, I'd rather not burden my men....*

Wilkes chuckled aloud, surmising that once on full alert his backup plan wouldn't be too difficult to engage.

There was one weak link—the six special task force survivors on the seabed. The best way to deal with them, he decided, was to keep them on the seabed, waiting for a pickup that would never materialize. They'd probably try to surface—two miniature submersibles in a killer storm. Even if they got their hatches open, they'd be swamped and they'd sink. A shame, but men die in action. There was a seventh witness, however—the cryptologist. He would also have to take care of seaman Jackson. Another shame, but alas a sacrifice of war.

THE ELDER WAS A BEING of peace and love. But as the twelve gas-filled rockets hurtled toward him, without thinking or debating a defense strategy, EO allowed a wave of water to surge away from the family. Perhaps this wave was a mere reflex, a flinch coming from these peaceful, passive beings, an action that could be compared to a group of monks ducking away from flying stones, as opposed to a conscious decision to participate in battle.

But it would be hard to dispute the ferociousness of that wave, or even to simply call it a wave, for it was traveling at five hundred miles an hour! It was a speeding wall of water—a tsunami!

As *TRAIN's* deadly rockets exploded into that speeding wall of water, the gas was repelled at the speed of sound.

In a nanosecond, the tsunami was atop of *TRAIN,* uprooting the machine as if it were a loose weed in a hurricane, snapping off its antennas like twigs, imploding its lights, buckling and warping its suction cups and linkages. The long, skinny machine careened backward, breaking into multiple pieces, rebounding into the canal's side walls, snapping into car-sized sections, smaller chunks, meaningless discarded metal fragments, all whizzing backward.

"UP! STARBOARD SIDE!" YELLED *OLPHA'S* helmsman. The Zodiac dinghy soared up...up beyond the pinnacle of the towering wave...airborne. The boat's engine buzzed like a chainsaw on metal as the propeller stabbed at rarefied water. Then they came back down again, hard.

"Like a mad bull!" the helmsman shouted.

Indeed, the ocean was an inflamed bull, hell bent on punishing anyone riding her surface—heaving, spitting and bucking *Olpha* from all directions. "Down!" shouted the helmsman as another mountainous wave rose to their right. The sea dipped way down, dropping the tiny dinghy with her, before bucking up and throwing the boat back into the air.

Ashlyn shrieked—a shriek of glee. Not because of the thrill of the ride. "The snake's gone! They got it!" Ashlyn had to repeat himself three times to be heard above the roar of the ocean. The helmsman suddenly realized that both kids seemed to be yelling with excitement. Gluttons for punishment, he figured.

"What?" Ace shouted. "Gone? They told you that?"

"I saw it!" Ashlyn yelled.

Ace, hardly a believer of mystical things, grinned. If Ashlyn was psychic, then perhaps his big toe was psychic too. But what did he care? He was a mercenary. Get paid…don't worry.

The navigator poked his head up from the dinghy's tarp. "Ark can't go faster, storm's wrapped 'em up! They don't even know if they can make point X on schedule!" he shouted.

Ace put his mouth to the navigator's ear. "Tell Rip Ashlyn says subsea danger is reduced!"

The navigator looked mystified.

Ace shouted, "We're reverting to X-hour, right, Ashlyn?"

Ashlyn nodded his head. "Same old schedule!"

"Boat's up! Big one!" yelled the helmsman.

Autumn grabbed the handholds fitted to the tube as they sidled acutely up a twenty-foot roller, then careened down its backside. As a wad of slimy seaweed smacked her in the face, she shrieked.

"Bigger one!" the helmsman shouted. He feathered the engine as they skied thirty feet up the roller, then gunned the throttle to escape a closing canyon, which exploded behind them. A firehouse of sea spray broadsided the boat.

"These waves are bigger than my apartment building!" The navigator yowled, adjusting his night-vision goggles.

Ashlyn and Autumn couldn't see the size of the waves. They weren't wearing night-vision goggles, and could barely see each other's faces, let alone much out of the boat.

"How big's your apartment building?" Autumn inquired.

"Here we go! Up! Hang on!" cried the helmsman.

"Big!" yelled the navigator.

Up they shot, rollercoaster up ...

Way, way up.

Then down.

Warp speed.

Fire hose spray.

Lightning stabbed the sky, ripping it open in several places. As the navigator shielded his goggles from the enormously magnified light, Ashlyn and Autumn saw the seething mountains. Far from being terrified, Ashlyn thought about Ko, how she so loved to fly through these monstrous waves.

Ace tapped him on the shoulder. "If we spill, yank your safeties! We can't sink, but we can overturn!" Ace turned to Autumn, and repeated the advice.

"Got it!" Autumn shouted back.

"Don't worry. It probably won't happen!"

"I'm fine. I have faith. How 'bout you?" she yelled back.

It was too dark for Autumn to see, but he winked at her. He liked this spunky little girl who'd refused to stay back.

The navigator threw himself back under the tarp. He stuck a nineteen-inch radome antenna up through a gap in the plastic and studied the compact green screen. The patterns looked the same as before, irrefutably way too many *blips* on radar. Storms do that. Radar returns go haywire in confused seas. But the bolder *blips* seemed to be immobile—ships not going anywhere. Loitering. Waiting.

WHEN CHIEF OF NAVAL OPERATIONS Gary Brown, ended his phone conversation with Admiral Wilkes, the seabed debacle was twenty minutes old.

Brown, in his pajamas, paced his living room, his eyes intermittently falling upon the red phone—the direct line to the president. It wasn't the first time a political bombshell had been tossed in his lap. But this was probably the most sinister. He could have refused Admiral Wilkes' suggestion of going on a Pacific Northwest alert. But what choice did he really have? If he'd denied the alert and something happened to an American ship— well, he really couldn't deny it.

Admiral Wilkes promised not to engage without consent. But, of course, that was a hollow guarantee. If Admiral Wilkes' ships were attacked, he would act autonomously, and he'd have every right to defend himself under the Rules of Engagement. By the same token, Brown had now given the admiral the license to eliminate the piscines, if they really existed, which it now seemed they did.

Brown felt his armpits turning moist. He looked at the red phone again. The baton of responsibility would be passed if he called the president. By the same token, the baton would almost certainly blow up in the president's face. Dammit, these were fish, unarmed. How could they have destroyed the subsea station? A shudder ran up Brown's spine. He realized he knew very little about Admiral Wilkes. Surely Director Gates couldn't have, wouldn't have, blueprinted such a ploy to eliminate the piscines? But that had been the director's suggestion to the president in the first place.

Brown reflexively snapped his eyes back to the red phone. Then he took a calming breath. "I'm panicking."

THE NAVY'S NORTHWEST PAC MANEUVERING zone covers a forty-mile radius, seven thousand nautical square miles. With seven ships in maneuvers that stormy September night, there was an aggregate of nine thousand seamen, all of whom were aware that they were patrolling an area associated with sea beings. If they had been asked, at least sixty-five percent would have said they were doubters. Admiral Wilkes had no intention of changing that balance of belief. That was the beauty of his plan. The world would never know what really happened. Conjecture would go on for a while, but pretty soon even that would fizzle, and the entire episode would be forgotten.

As swirling winds screamed through the crows' nests and rolling liquid hills rose into heaving mountains, foreshadowing perhaps the greatest north Pacific storm of the century, emergency klaxons rang across the ships' decks.

The men were hustled into briefing rooms.

"Men, we've been ordered on alert," announced *USS Whitehorn's* Commander Davis, per his instructions from Admiral Wilkes. "It's a small ship transporting terrorists. Recon indicates possible use of Zodiacs. Keep your eyes peeled, your wits about you. That's it. That's all. Dismissed."

There was a knock on Admiral Wilkes' door. The admiral stopped pacing, picked his hat off the coat hook, and placed himself behind his desk. "Come in."

Chief Petty Officer Clement Doogins entered. Doogins was a systems design engineer, a devout Christian with aspirations of becoming a television evangelist. He came highly recommended and was transferred to *USS Whitehorn* only that morning. He stood at attention. "Sir, you wanted to see me."

"At ease, son. Sit yourself down." Wilkes casually and aimlessly fed his hat around his fingers. "So Director Gates is your godfather."

"Yes, sir."

"I hear you're a whiz at electronics."

"Yes sir."

Smiling, the admiral stood up, dropped his hat on the coat hook, and returned to his desk. "Son, hypothetically, if I needed to make this ship look like it was being attacked, from under the sea...."

"Torpedoes?"

Wilkes clasped his hands and leaned forward, patiently waiting for the young man to continue.

"Easy. Record the APG radar, animate it; key it back into the system."

Wilkes looked right into Doogin's eyes and smiled. "And you could do that?"

"With my eyes closed, sir."

Operation Noah, T-minus 45 minutes

PICARESQUE WAS RUNNING BARE POLES, her eighty-five horses plowing the catamaran forward at single digit knots. In between plunging canyons, the captain on the enclosed bridge, could barely discern the running lights of the decoy ship *Tipendra* now just a mile away.

"It's too rough," he mumbled as he slid open the bridge door. He then shouted at Denton who had just stepped out of the galley onto the narrow deck below. "It's too rough! Too risky! Get back!"

Denton dismissed the notion with a wave of his arm. He and Sally and Brad and two volunteers were making their way astern, clinging to rigging, railing and each other as they pressed into the wind, ignoring the stinging spindrift that lashed into their faces.

Denton grabbed the ties securing the tarp on the twenty-one-foot turbocharged Novurania tender—a small jet-propelled, rubber-tubed boat mounted on *Picaresque's* transom, which was to be their transport to *Tipendra*.

"Too risky!" The captain shouted again.

"It's just a mile! We can do it!" Denton shouted back.

The ride was going to be wild and risky, but for the plan to work, they needed to sell themselves as the real deal, not a decoy. *Team Noah* was relying on them. As Denton unraveled the second tie, the untethered tarp flew up in a gust and disappeared over the boat's side. "Grab that line, Brad! But don't let it go until my signal!"

Brad nodded.

"You guys and Sally strap yourselves in!"

"I can get the other line!" Sally yelled back.

"Sit in the boat...sit down! Strap in! This is going to be hairy!" Denton jumped into the tender and keyed the starter. "Brad, now!"

Brad released the safety line.

"In! In! In!" Denton yelled. Brad lay a foot on the boat's side and gave one last shove before jumping aboard.

Denton juiced the Novurania's throttle, and, with a whirring blast of jet air, the small jet boat leapt off the transom...but, shockingly, instead of landing on the ocean's surface, a fierce gust carried them upward into the air.

Denton gulped as a heaving liquid mountain rose up to pluck them out of the air, and finish them off. There was no escaping the eye of this monster—a sixty-foot tall curling wave!

As they braced for impact, Denton floored the jets. "Heads down! Hold breath!" he screamed at the last moment, not knowing whether this was his last moment alive!

They sliced into the wave just below its peak. Denton could only imagine what it must have looked like—the tiny tender abruptly vanishing under the oppression of the monstrous wave.

But he was still alive and so were the engines...revving to the max.

No one dared move, not even to release his or her safety belt. The Novurania wasn't a submersible, but even completely underwater the boat's twinjets kept spewing foam.

And just when Denton thought he couldn't hold his breath any longer, they exploded to the surface, flying at full speed.

Gasping for a breath, Denton yanked back the throttle, feathering across another peak before once again gunning the throttle to outrun a closing canyon.

Brad and Sally cheered. What a blast!

The lights on *Tipendra* were dead ahead now, very close.

Another few minutes, they'd be out of their wet clothes, sipping a mug of nice hot cocoa.

USS Whitehorn 23:20

THERE WERE TEN OPERATORS IN the radar room when CPO Clement Doogins slipped nonchalantly behind one of the master equipment racks, but none paid him any attention. He was a top-notch engineer, acting on captain's orders, supposedly to fix a glitch.

It took CPO Doogins just three minutes to plant a mini digital video recorder and create a wireless patch to all the ship's radar screens.

Glitch fixed.

Back in Admiral Wilkes' quarters, Doogins handed the admiral a small remote control pad. "Press the button, it will chroma-key the animated sequence of an APG radar screen during a torpedo attack. Press again, gone."

"You'll dispose of the recorder in the morning?"

"Over the side…like it never existed."

The admiral stared at the tiny remote control pad in his palm, and his thin lips turned upward in smile. "You'll go far."

-47-

Noah

Decoy catamaran *Wendell*...the first decoy IBR launch

CARTER WATCHED THE SECOND HAND ON HIS WATERPROOF watch approach the ten-minutes-to-midnight marker. Five IBR decoys taken on board after the rendezvous with the trawler *Unselfish* were strapped to *Wendell's* deck, ready to be cut loose.

As the seas heaved, Carter's knees buckled. He hung on to the gunwale, keeping his eyes on the second hand on his wristwatch, his heart racing.

Twenty seconds...fifteen....

The first mate, like a statue, was poised over the decoys, his razor-sharp switchblade at the ready.

"Cut the ropes!" Carter shouted.

Two seconds...one....

BOOOOOOF! Over Wendell's side went the first IBR.

BOOOOOOSH! Went the second, third, forth, and fifth.

Swiftly tumbling below the clamor of blistering waves and shrieking winds, the decoy devices plunged into the silent darkness of the subsea. At eighteen hundred feet, almost three minutes later, fiery jets leapt out of the IBRs—this first ignition was just a two-second positioning burst. Then, as the IBRs turned north by northwest, the rockets fully ignited.

"CONTACTS AT FOUR-TWO NORTH, one-two-four west bearing zero-two-two at sixteen hundred feet," blared the brittle voice out of the public address system aboard the *USS Whitehorn.* "Five contacts at fourteen hundred feet, now bearing zero-two-three. Speed: one-six-five knots."

On the bridge, Admiral Wilkes studied the four-by-four-foot screen. He was confused. The *contacts* were moving in the wrong direction. If they were piscines why weren't they heading toward *Tipendra,* the ship Director Gates assured him was the rescue vessel? "Identify?" Admiral Wilkes barked.

"Negative ID...likely organic, depth: eight hundred feet, bearing zero-two-three. Speed: one-eight-five knots."

"Heading where? Who's in the path?"

The chart showed nothing directly in the *contacts'* path. The closest vessel was the *USS Matthews,* fifteen miles further north, eight miles east of the *contacts.*

"Contacts now at four hundred feet...three hundred feet. Speed: two-two-five knots."

"Organic?"

"Yessir. Contacts approaching the surface...bearing...ugh.... Uh...they're gone."

"What's that, sonar?"

"Gone, sir. Contacts vanished."

Admiral Wilkes stood stock-still, his brain momentarily numbed. What had happened? He felt the tiny remote pad in his palm. Had the piscines escaped into the stormy night right under his nose? Had he been tricked? His head was spinning. "How can they be gone?" He asked. "Helm, take us northwest to those last coordinates."

A S THE *USS WHITEHORN* ALTERED course, the crew aboard the trawler *Unselfish,* fifteen miles north, were preparing to discharge the balance of their on-deck cargo.

Noah's zero hour had arrived.

The captain waved his arm. "Cut them loose!"

BOOOOOF— BOOOOOOSH— BOOOOOOOOF—

Seventy IBRs were dropped over the trawler's side, down into the frigid subaquatic realm. Three minutes later, seventeen hundred feet below the ocean surface, the rocket boosters ignited, and all seventy of the devices cannonballed back toward the surface, to coordinate point "Y."

USS WHITEHORN'S PUBLIC ADDRESS SYSTEM squawked: "Control, so-nar, multiple contacts alpha to omega at forty-two, one-eight north, one-twenty-four, forty-three west, at fifteen hundred feet, bearing three-one-three degrees. Speed is one-six-zero knots."

Up on the bridge, as the electronic chart ran a trajectory, Admiral Wilkes could barely contain himself. The trajectory intersected with the Millers rescue vessel *Tipendra*.

"Sir, Tipendra's picked up speed. Bearing zero-eight-five."

"Change course! Zero-eight-five! Bring us up to full speed!" The admiral's heart pounded. His palm concealing the tiny remote pad was moist, his mouth tart and dry. He placed his shaking thumb lightly over the activation button knowing that the creatures were making a beeline for the rescue vessel. He was the man, the one who could put an end to the ridiculous saga. Any minute now.... Any minute...as soon as the *contacts* reached the rescue vessel, he'd press the button. At that instant, his ship's sonar would see bogey torpedoes in the water. He'd give the order for countermeasures, a second order to engage. In a flash, it would be over. The charred remnants of *Tipendra* would sink to the seafloor. His official report would describe how multiple sonar contacts were identified as terrorists' underwater sleds returning to their ship. It was too dark, too stormy to really see anything. Contrary enlisted men's reports or officers' reports would be dealt with as necessary.

Wilkes smiled to himself. He could even end up a hero.

"Contacts bearing three-one-five degrees at two-zero-zero knots."

LIGHTNING FLARED THE SKY AS *Tipendra* plowed down a steep roller.

Denton, Sally and Brad, wearing life vests, with safety ropes around their waists, clung to the ship's railings. There was no need to be on deck. It was warm and dry below, comparatively safe, but they wanted to see the detonations of the IBR decoys—the plan in action, especially now that several navy ships were converging. Denton knew the hunters had taken the bait. And he was leading them astray.

But never in a million years could he have imagined the heinous plot unfolding on the US navy warship now bearing down on them, that very soon the cross-hairs of the ships' guns would be lined up over *Tipendra*.

"There!" Denton yelled. "See them!"

Below the bombardment of pell-mell rain and confused sea

spray, a stream of undersea shooting stars twinkled and pulsed. Briefly vanishing in the glare of lightning—heaven's light being the conductor's cue—the detonations began. Red and blue flames lashed out of wave tops and eruptions of fiery sparks rained upwards in a spectacular fireworks display.

USS Whitehorn's sonar man called the events over the intercom. "Fifteen, eighteen gone, twenty. They're going fast."

On the bridge, Admiral Wilkes glared at the electronic chart. The *contacts* fell away five, ten *blips* at a time, until every single *blip* except *Tipendra's* was gone. Wilkes' throat was tight. "Sonar room, did they reach the ship?" he inquired, more than an element of desperation in his voice. His thumb remained poised over the remote pad's activation button.

"No, sir. Contacts failed to reach Tipendra."

"It's not possible," he said sotto voice. "Vanished...aquastealth?"

"What's that, sir?" queried Lieutenant Commander Briggs standing by his side. The admiral didn't reply. But Briggs noticed that the admiral looked white, like he'd seen a ghost.

The phone rang.

The first officer of the watch picked up the receiver. "Bridge. Yes sir." The caller on the other end of the phone was the commander of the entire Pacific fleet, Admiral Moses. "Yes, sir," replied the first officer. He immediately turned to Admiral Wilkes. "Admiral Wilkes, sir, Pacific Command, Admiral Moses. He says it's urgent."

Admiral Wilkes looked down at his clutched hand containing the small remote-pad. It was now or never. He closed his eyes....

And pressed the button.

"Conn, this is sonar! We have a torpedo in the water!" belted the voice out of the intercom. "We have two, now three. Three torpedoes! Bearing two-two-five degrees, twelve thousand yards!"

Klaxons pierced the air.

"Helm, left full rudder!" barked the commander.

The helmsman swung the ship's wheel.

"Sir," cried the first officer, trying to pass the phone to the admiral. "It's Admiral Moses, sir."

An automated voice sang out of the public-address-system. "Countermeasures in two seconds..."

The first officer overlapped: "Sir, Admiral Moses...!"

"Hang up, sailor! Can't you see this is an emergency?"

"Sir, we've been ordered to stand down, sir." The first officer was trembling.

"Countermeasures away," resounded the automated voice.

"Gunner, control…fire!" shouted the admiral.

"Sir! He wants the call on the public address!"

Silence.

There was no earsplitting roar from the ship's 40mm cannon, despite the admiral's order.

"Gunner, fire!" The admiral shouted again.

The cannon remained silent.

Commander Davis seemed to snap out of a trance. "Oh Lord!" He found his own hand slamming down on the telecomm. "Admiral Moses, sir. You're on the speaker."

A familiar voice resounded out of the PA.

"Officers and seamen of North Pacific maneuvers, I order you to stand down immediately! I repeat, I, Admiral Moses, hereby order you to stand down! Do not engage in any self-defense action until further notice! Captains and commanders proceed to verify. Rear Admiral Wilkes, surrender yourself to the Master of Arms. Commander Davis surrender yourself to the Master of Arms. Is Lieutenant Commander Briggs there?"

"Yes, sir. Here, sir!"

"Commander. Thanks for your call. Take over."

"Yes, sir. Thank you, sir. Detonate countermeasures!"

The gunners in the local control cabinet heaved sighs of relief. The gunners in the shell room heaved sighs of relief. The gunners in the handling room heaved sighs of relief. None of them, not one of the seventy men in the gunning crew, were willing to open fire on *Tipendra*. No one takes terrorism lightly, yet no one in the gunning crew believed they were under attack by terrorists. Astoundingly, out of the seventy gunners, fifty of them, almost two thirds, believed in sea beings, and they had no intention of destroying them.

The countermeasures exploded harmlessly, the pounding booms sounding like another barrage of thunder, the sparks from the discharged ordnance not so unlike the exploding IBRs.

"Control to sonar room, status?"

We have multiple contacts, alpha to omega at three-zero-zero-zero, bearing zero-zero-five degrees.

"Speed?"

"One zero-zero knots.

"Any ID?

"ID light is green, sir…organic, definitely organic, sir."

If those are dolphins, I'm a monkey's ass," remarked CO Briggs.

"HUGE…HANG ON!" SCREAMED THE helmsman as he watched the wave through his night-vision goggles. Lightning once again ripped open the sky, and in that moment, Ashlyn saw a towering black wall closing in.

Flying up the incline, the helmsman banked hard port, and suddenly they were airborne, drifting sideways. Autumn ran a hand to her safety line.

Safe!

They came down hard, boat side up. Horizontal white water whipped into Ashlyn's face, forcing his head back, as it had done numerous times over the last twenty minutes. The skin under his eyes was now chaffed and feeling sore from slashing winds gusting at seventy miles an hour and forty-foot waves exploding one after the other under a sky of machine-gun lightning.

"We've lost Bolpha," yelled the navigator. *Bolpha* was Rip's Zodiac. "Radio's down, cell's silent!"

"Do we abort?" yelled the helmsman. His confidence in sea beings, shallow beforehand, was now non-existent. He would have liked nothing more than to beeline for base camp. It was fifteen past midnight. Ten minutes past schedule.

Ace Jenkins turned to Ashlyn for an answer.

"They'll be here!" Ashlyn shouted at the top of his lungs.

"Dammit! Where are they?" the mercenary shouted back.

"Up! Big!" screamed the helmsman as he feathered the dinghy up another peak, then gunned the throttle to escape two careening walls. As a fire hose of spray hit them broadside, two new black mountains rose up on either side.

"Uh oh! Huge!"

"Gun it! Gun it, dammit! Gun it!"

"Hold on!"

The helmsman banked. Up they went. Up. Up. He pulled back the throttle. But the mountain continued to grow, and they were still going up…steep…vertical…too steep!

Ace shouted, "Release safeties!"

Autumn screamed, just as the dinghy pitchpoled.

They were falling down into the canyon…only this time upside down!

As soon as Autumn pulled her safety, flipping open the buckle on her waist, she tumbled out of the boat, hitting the ocean's surface almost immediately. Cold salty water as raspy as sandpaper blasted up her nostrils, stinging the back of her throat. In the pitch black she could feel bubbles and hissy foam snapping at her eardrums. She kicked her way to the surface, coughing and blowing the water out of her nose.

It was pitch but for a green phosphor glow coming from her life jacket, automatically activated when she'd flipped her safety. She knew to stay calm but that was all well and good in calmer seas. She felt herself riding up…up and up. She knew it must be one of those huge ones. Just then a bolt of lightning illuminated the monstrous wave. But before she could utter a sound, the wave crashed down on her, and she was once again underwater, being forced down, deep down. As her secondary safety pulled taut, she began kicking wildly for the surface, her lungs burning. Her head bounced into the Zodiac's fiberglass hull. Down she went again, swallowing a mouthful of fiery seawater. Then she felt a hand on her back, swiftly pushing her to the surface. She coughed and retched, gasping for air.

The helmsman also coughed. "Are you alright?" he shouted.

"Where's…where's Ashlyn?" she cried.

Ashlyn shouted from somewhere in the blackness. "Autumn, where are you?"

"Ashlyn, where are you? I can't see—" she stopped. There was light under the water—a mass of light. White light, green light, blue, red—it was all around her!

"Oh my God!" She heard the astounded voice of the navigator! "Oh my God!"

THOUGH THE SEAS WERE SEETHING, the skies swirling, the winds biting irreverently into eardrums, *Noah's* four Zodiac dinghies, *Olpha, Dolpha, Bolpha* and *Golpha* were once again upright, skimming wave-tops at speeds close to a hundred miles an hour.

The helmsmen were no longer concerned with feathering mountainous peaks and escaping colliding canyons, for they were no longer in control of every pitch, rise, and fall—the Iquana pilots under the boats were—and the Zodiacs were flying as if they were one with nature, where any and all ocean maneuvers seemed possible.

"LIGHTS!" CRIED THE LOOKOUT ABOARD *Sister Mary*. The medical ship was forty miles distant from *Noah's Ark* when speeding lights appeared off her port deck. The boatswain sounded the alarm:

Bong. Bong. Bong. Whirrup. Whirrup. Whirrup.

Staff and crew, not already topside, scrambled to the deck in time to see *Noah's* Zodiacs riding atop something that resembled an undersea spaceship pulsing with brilliance and color.

But as the *spaceship* neared, the faces on deck arrested into stunned, speechless gazes.

Someone cried, "Angels!"

Aboard *Olpha,* Ashlyn didn't convey a thought or image that would have suggested that EO slow the pace—at least not consciously—but the Zodiacs slowed anyway. Obviously, the Iquana mind knew how important this moment was to the humans aboard *Sister Mary's* deck now waving and yelling and begging them to pull alongside.

Ashlyn touched his shoulder. "EO, please don't stop! Hurry!" He consciously conveyed an image to EO—the Zodiacs racing ahead to *Noah's Ark*. He touched his shoulder again. Perhaps he was just too frozen and aching from fatigue to feel her. "Hold on Ko…we're almost there."

-48-

Unity

BOOMER NEVER DOUBTED THE EXISTENCE of the beings but the sight still sapped him of breath. They looked like angels in the water.

The Iquana beings bathed the catamaran in mesmerizing shafts of light as they rose from the wave-tops, their ethereal wing-like dorsal fins pulsing vibrant strands of color.

The stunned Mexican crew crossed themselves and sank to their knees.

As soon as Boomer cut the *Ark's* engines, the Iquana beings swam between the hulls, and the catamaran leveled. Even though the waves were still the size of apartment buildings, *Noah's Ark* assumed a steady cadence, rising effortlessly to meet the roving pinnacles.

Rip's paramilitary boys, showing unwavering professionalism, immediately assumed guard positions.

Immediately after being hoisted aboard, Ashlyn set about finding Ko, passing dozens of smiling Iquana faces as he searched. He spotted her gently rising to the surface in EO's secure arms.

There was no joy in EO's face, for Ko's body was completely void of light. Shockingly, she looked everlastingly peaceful.

Autumn cupped a hand over her mouth, not daring to scream.

Ashlyn jumped into the water, approaching with deliberate caution. He wanted so much to hug and kiss Ko, without hurting her. Limp across EO's arms, she looked like a princess killed by the wicked witch.

Tentatively, Ashlyn caressed her face. He nestled an ear to her bosom, somehow hoping to find a pulse. "Ko...it's me...it's me...please wake up."

A hushed stillness settled over *Noah's* decks. Even the area between the decks—the pool—turned quiet. Ashlyn felt a hand on his back. "Ashlyn." It was Boomer's voice, but Ashlyn brushed the hand away.

"Ko, it's me. I'm here...we're on a catamaran...made especially for you. There are people here, humans. We're here for you, Ko. Please wake up."

"Ashlyn."

"She promised...."

"I know."

"No, you don't! We have a bond." Ashlyn gently kissed Ko's face. Most of the salty rivulets running down his cheeks were not from the stormy sky, nor from the raging Pacific.

Boomer witnessed EO's twin dorsal seemingly shuddering.

"Ashlyn."

Hearing a voice in his mind, Ashlyn raised his head, hoping beyond hope to see a glimmer of light in Ko.

"Ashlyn...it is I." The elder supporting KO with one arm placed a hand upon his chest in confirmation. *"I can hear you."*

EO ran his hand affectionately through Ashlyn's hair. *"You are aware...I see that now. I see why my daughter...she understood, she knew you were special."*

EO's words spoken past tense cut to the core of Ashlyn's being. "She's still alive. I can feel her. See, right here." Ashlyn grabbed EO's hand and placed it on his shoulder. "It's faint...but I feel her. See!"

EO smiled. *"It is her spirit."*

"No! That's not what we agreed!" Ashlyn dropped his head back onto Ko's chest. "Wake up, Ko!" He shook her. "Wake up! It's me! Wake up!"

Ashlyn felt a number of hands pulling at him, lifting him up out of the water. He no longer even cared to resist. As warm blankets were wrapped around his shoulders, he heard EO's voice again.

"There is nothing greater than love, Ashlyn."

EO then scooped Ko into his arms and carried her down to the net bedding where he pulsed light and love onto her. In EO's mind, if Ashlyn felt Ko's presence, perhaps she truly was holding on.

ASHLYN AND AUTUMN STAYED ON deck throughout the night, praying for Ko, willing her to live. Boomer brought up more blankets and hot soup. He tried unsuccessfully to get the teens below to a cabin. Eventually, he surrendered his paternal efforts and also spent the night on deck.

Sailing west throughout the night, *Noah's Ark* at last outpaced the storm, and as the gray of dawn singed the horizon, the medical ship *Sister Mary* drew alongside.

Several sea beings swam out of the pool area to greet the new arrivals. One of those new arrivals was Carter who had boarded *Sister Mary* during the night. As two Iquana beings kicked their tail flukes, elevating themselves slightly out of the water, Carter's face collapsed into a stony image matching the looks of the catamaran crew the night before. "Jesus Christ!" Like most who said he believed, a part of him must have doubted.

Seemingly understanding his thoughts, one of the beings slowly nodded, seemingly saying, "It's alright, we forgive you."

Marvin—the enigmatic skeptic of *Team Noah*— trembled as a sea being gazed into his eyes. How arrogant he'd been. His heart bled with shame.

Ashlyn paced the deck impatiently as the medics and supplies began trickling aboard *Noah's Ark*. The crew was maintaining a healthy respect for the tall seas, and the process moving supplies from boat to boat was painstakingly slow.

At last the primary doctors were ferried aboard *Noah's Ark,* and upon Ashlyn's request, the elder EO surfaced with Ko. With sublime trust, he placed her on the deck.

To some of the human eyes, watching the Iquana gathering on the surface while Ko's listless gray body lay before the doctors had the appearance of a tribal offering.

Doctor Arthur London stepped forward, followed by his team of physicians including Doctor Sally Reahman, the senior veterinarian. Except for some whispers from doctor to doctor, there was silence on deck.

As a radiographic scanner was placed on Ko's body, Ashlyn, who was standing right behind the medics, nervously swayed his head back and forth, willing Ko to live.

Doctor London nodded his head, and whispered to another doctor, "She's got a pulse." At that moment, Ashlyn's hopes spiraled.

Ko was alive.

Louder whispers, and a few small exchanges filtered across the decks. But silence quickly returned as the examination continued.

The noninvasive procedure lasted twenty minutes, during which time the examiners submerged Ko three times and continuously hydrated her with a fine water spray.

As the team withdrew, silently, Dr. London closed his medic's bag and stood up. Taking Ashlyn aside, he spoke quietly. "This was a long shot from the start, you know that, Ashlyn."

"She can heal; she's not like us!"

"I don't think it would be right to try anything. Seventy-five percent of her body tissue is already dead or dying. Her internal organs are in a state of focal necrosis. Honestly, if she were human, she'd be gone."

Ashlyn wasn't surprised by the doctor's comments. "She's alive; even her own kind are shocked...she's alive, and we have to do something."

Placing his bag on the floor, the doctor faced Ashlyn. "I don't want you to take this with false hope, if she regains consciousness, we'll give her the appropriate palliative care: painkillers, sedatives. Spiritually, I'm sure she's more prepared than—" He pulled off his stethoscope. "Look, Ashlyn, I'm sorry; I know it's painful...maybe there are others we can save." Picking up his bag, the doctor patted Ashlyn on the back, and ambled off down the deck, leaving Ashlyn alone to his thoughts and grief.

"She's not going to die, maybe one day, but not now." Ashlyn called after him, wiping his moist eyes.

EXAMINATIONS OF IQUANA BEINGS CONTINUED throughout the morning, so it was a late lunch when the *Noah* committee convened in the port galley. After the group had eaten potato soup and freshly baked French bread, Ashlyn stood up: "I have a few words to share with you. You know you all have my gratitude; I can't say enough about that. You have sacrificed time and money, and I am forever grateful. But I need something more from you."

Ashlyn paused to gather his thoughts. As the galley turned pin-drop quiet, he continued. "The word 'love' might conjure up a few definitions, mostly describing affection and devotion. But love is not just a word, it is an actual, physical energy that can be focused and used for healing. I have seen it, and so has Autumn! It's how the

Iquana heal themselves! Actually, you've seen it, too. You've seen them holding hands. What they're doing is creating streams of love energy to project into whoever needs healing. The only reason it's not working with Ko is she's too sick, been sick too long, and there's not enough of them. But there's us! If we all focus our love, if in our minds we shower Ko with *our love* at the same time as the Iquana, then maybe we'll tip the scale."

Boomer stood up. "You mean, like, we meditate together?"

Ashlyn smiled. "Sort of…."

Everyone in the galley began to nod in agreement. There was a tremendous feeling of love, yet sadness, knowing that the beautiful angel-like beings were suffering.

As news of Ashlyn's plan spread around the two ships, even the paid mercenaries and boatmen spoke up, pledging their hands and hearts to aide the Iquana.

It was a brisk mid-afternoon upon the high seas when seventy human beings lined *Noah's Ark's* port deck.

EO laid Ko flat on the deck near the water's edge so he could hold her hand. She was inanimate, the bulk of her body a transparent gray except for some pinkish scabbing along her right side.

Lowering himself into the water, Ashlyn took the hand of a sea cousin.

Other humans followed his lead.

From one end of *Noah's Ark* to the other, palms slipped into palm, human being, Iquana being.

Save for a wispy breeze in the sails and the gentle caress of seawater lapping the hulls, a noticeable stillness settled over *Noah's Ark*.

Boomer was expecting a lengthy meditation of sorts, so he was stunned when the cold webbed hand he was holding quickly turned warm, and he instantly felt the power of love. At the same time, Autumn felt a powerful heat swelling up inside her…so did Carter, a heat filtering through his body that tingled every ounce of his flesh.

Light rays as intense as warm spotlights pulsed out of the Iquana beings, flooding *Noah's* decks and bathing Ko in a capsule of light.

Some of the humans prayed with their eyes closed, tears streaming down their cheeks, while others watched spellbound, glued to Ko's form in the center of the healing circle.

The hearts of all become the heart of One.

Not in a church, mosque, or synagogue had the humans experienced anything such as this.

Yet the minutes ticked by....

Ko remained motionless, unaffected.

As sun-dappled shadows fell across the decks, many of the Iquana broke away from the circle and slipped back underwater.

The temperature dipped.

EO scooped Ko into his arms, and, turning to Ashlyn, bowed his head reverently before slipping under the water.

Ashlyn remained transfixed, his hand on his shoulder where Ko's touch was meant to be. He swallowed the lump in his throat. Why had they failed? What a cruel trick. Why had he been teased, led to believe that she'd always be there? What lesson or message was to be found in this?

He saw that tears were also streaming down Autumn's cheeks.

As he climbed out of the water, he felt someone tapping his shoulder. Turning, he saw Marvin, white-faced and watery-eyed. "I was wrong, arrogant, smug...and so clever. Never in my life, Ashlyn, never have I ever felt anything like this."

Ashlyn wasn't angry with Marvin; he just didn't have the ammunition to respond. Ignoring him, he drifted along the deck, his eyes on the vast seascape, which looked purple, almost velvety. "Why couldn't Ko see this?" He leaned against the railing. "I was so sure it would work. It was my way. She said I had to find my way. What else could I have done?"

Marvin took a deep breath, inhaling the ocean air. "Look at this...Noah's Ark, Sister Mary...the beings. I never thought it could be done. You did find your way, Ashlyn."

"We took too long."

"You've done something wonderful here."

Ashlyn shook his head. The truth was he'd devised *Noah's Ark* for Ko. Perhaps he had even been motivated by selfishness. The whole idea was to rescue Ko because that's what was important. That the others came along was gravy, not the main course. He tried to muster a smile but his heavy heart made for heavy lips.

"That energy, I've never felt anything like it. And that was just seventy of us. Can you imagine what would happen with thousands? Or millions, even the world?" Marvin caught Ashlyn frowning. "That's right, the world. Imagine people in Africa and India, Russia, all over the world, all focused on the same outcome, all of them at the same time? Strangers in the street shouting Ko's name, people stopping whatever they're doing to send Ko their love, holding hands, crying together…one outcome."

Ashlyn accepted a towel from a passing boatman. "But people don't want to believe."

"We go public! We make it the most public, interactive event ever! We start off by getting a chopper out here with a TV crew. They can land on Sister Mary."

"What about the rescue? Their safety?"

"We'll orchestrate. We can control the reporters, legally. We'll only invite those who agree to our stipulations. Our whereabouts, our destination need never be revealed. The world will only know what we show them. And if after all's said and done, the Iquana still want to return to seclusion, fine. I'm a lawyer, I'll have the media sign their lives away."

Ashlyn dropped the towel around his shoulders, thinking, imagining….

But Marvin already knew the answer, for it was emblazoned inextinguishably in Ashlyn's eyes.

While Marvin scurried to his quarters to type faxes on his palmtop, Ashlyn noticed that Rip and Ace and two of the mercenaries were moving in a hurry to the cockpit. Something seemed to be bothering them.

ENTERING THE COCKPIT, RIP AND Ace found Boomer scrutinizing the radar. "This isn't good. Eighteen miles…closing," Boomer said.

Leaning over Boomer's shoulder, Rip saw the *blip* causing the alarm. "Can you tell what it is…how big?"

Boomer rubbed his fatigued eyes. "A whole damn ocean, here to Australia, and it's running for our wake. She's big…bigger than us, and her pedal's to the metal."

Rip squeezed his lips while pondering. "No way to outrun it?"

Boomer shook his head.

The wind had dropped, and they couldn't fire up the engines with their Iquana guests hovering around the propellers.

"We're beyond the two hundred mile limit, aren't we?" Ripped unclipped the walkie-talkie from his waist belt.

Boomer acknowledged with a pensive, "Uh huh."

"So, it couldn't be coast guard?"

"Argonaut?" Boomer suggested as his best guess.

Nodding in agreement, Rip beeped his walkie-talkie. "All team, code one, copy!"

Then he and Ace fled the cockpit.

As the Zodiac teams prepped for launch, loading weapons, strapping on ammo belts, Marvin raced along the deck, having just been briefed by Boomer. "Don't start a war yet!" he yelled breathlessly. "Don't engage, I think I can call in a favor!"

Rip signaled Ace: *Go!* Then to Marvin, "Do whatever you can! But as of right now, we're on full alert!"

"Boat's down!" Ace shouted. The Zodiac dinghies dropped over *Noah's Ark's* side, splashing down onto the ocean's surface, followed immediately by the mercenaries.

Rip repeated, "Do whatever you can! You've got fifteen minutes!"

Marvin spun on his heels, and beelined to his cabin quarters, where he flipped on his satellite phone.

Marvin had twice met the president—symposiums on clean air—and held decent conversations with him, although he would hardly call the president a friend, or even an acquaintance, but it was worth a call. After playing automated telephone for ten minutes, a live but pompous male secretary picked up the phone, and then immediately transferred him—despite Marvin's protests—to another recording: *"Leave a message at the beep!"*

Marvin left a rapid-fire message: "Mr. President, Marvin Rappaport, lead council for Clean Air Action Committee. Mr. President, I'm on a vessel called Noah's Ark. CIA knows of it. I'm with seventy members of a species the world has come to call 'sea beings.' I'm sure you've followed the story and know the why's and who's. I've called the press and they're on the way. But we have a problem. A hostile ship— a hunting party—is currently closing in on us. We are armed and if we have to defend ourselves—"

There was a click, then a voice. "Hold on, sir, the president will be right with you."

The president had already been briefed on the seabed chasm incident and Admiral Wilkes' ploy. The crew of the two surviving submersibles had been rescued and Director Gates of the CIA arrested for collusion. The names Ed Lazerath, James Swift, and Andy Lightstone were not foreign to the president even before Marvin began.

"Mr. President, what is the position of the United States?"

"Marvin, you and I are both on the side of decency and human compassion. This discovery, besides mind boggling, is extremely humbling. If there's anything I, as your president, can do, provided it is within reason, I'd be more than willing to oblige."

CAPTAIN JAMES SWIFT WAS AT the helm of *Argonaut*, which was now only seven miles astern of *Noah's Ark*. Swift didn't really have a plan. But he was going to catch a piscine or two by whatever means. Perhaps he'd open fire, create some confusion, drop his nets. Perhaps he was as desperate as Ed Lazerath had been. In a way, this was for Ed.

It was also Captain Swift's last straw. His entire life savings had been emptied into the operation. How could he let it sail away from him?

An earsplitting jet shrieked above.

Raising his eyes into the early evening, James Swift saw three F-16 fighter jets bearing *US Navy* markings screaming out of the partially overcast sky. The jets dipped wings as they buzzed his ship, the roar from their engines painful to the ear.

The ship's radio squawked, "Argonaut, this is the United States navy, Boston flight leader, please advise…what is your destination? Over."

James glared at the squawk box with contempt. What was the navy up to now?

The first mate turned to him, shrugging.

"Argonaut, this is the United States navy, Boston flight leader. Do you copy?"

James flipped the talk button angrily. "Roger, Boston flight leader. Captain James Swift here. We're heading west. Do you have a problem?"

"Yes, Captain. You're running into a restricted path. Why don't you turn zero-one-five degrees?"

"Flight leader, we're traveling southwest. We're in international waters. What's up?"

"Then why don't you run direct south half a day; that'll do just fine by us."

"No can do, Navy. We're in a hurry. Sticking to this course, over and out."

By now the jets had screamed into tight crescents over the

blazing sunset. "Let me relay that to base, Argonaut. Over."

With a deafening roar, the fighter jets flew back over the ship, buzzing her a hundred feet above the crows' nest, allowing the ship's crew to feel the furnace-blasting drafts. In seconds, the fighters were silent specks in the distance.

RIP HAD HELD THE ZODIACS back as long as he dared, waiting for Marvin's called-in favor, but as the final flares of the sun sank into the horizon, and *Argonaut* closed to within eye distance of *Noah's Ark* and *Sister Mary*, he radioed his point man.

Moments later, *Noah's* flying Zodiacs, bombarding misty trails, approached the bandit ship. "Argonaut!" Ace shouted out of a bullhorn. "Andy Lightstone. We know who you are! Keep away from our ships! We are heavily armed!"

Suddenly, machine gun fire erupted from *Argonaut's* deck—a warning blast! The lambasting bullets cut a lethal path a few yards to Ace's right. *Olpha's* helmsman gunned the engine, *bearing off* as they skimmed past *Argonaut* at forty miles an hour. "Sumbitch!" yowled the helmsman.

Olpha's radio squawked. "Olpha, this is base. Disengage. Airborne retaliation inbound."

At that moment, the F-16s plunged out of the sky, screaming into a barrel-rolling attack stance. A bursting flurry of fiery lights flickered from their wingtips...

Rat-tat-tat-tat-tat...rat-tat-tat-tat-tat.

The strafing bullets licked wave-tops fifty yards ahead of *Argonaut's* bow.

These were also warning shots.

The ship's radio squawked. "Argonaut, United States Navy, Boston flight leader. You fire one more pebble, I'll drop a sparrow, the kind that don't sing pretty songs. Capeesh?"

"What's your rag, Navy? We're a Brazilian ship in international waters. We've got hostile Zodiacs buzzing us. What do you expect? By the way, we're transmitting this, you know, in case you guys try something funny. After all, we're a Brazilian ship and these are international waters. Over."

"Nice mouthful, Captain. How about repeating it for the president?"

James Swift brushed off the flight leader's remark as something glib.

Meanwhile, sitting in the cockpit of his F-16, the not-so-glib flight leader stuck a cigar in his mouth, flipped a switch, and let the president's voice warble out of channel sixteen.

"Captain James Swift, men of the merchant ship Argonaut. I think you know who this is," came the president's slightly twanged Southern drawl.

James Swift's eyes abruptly dilated.

"Captain Swift? Can you hear me?"

"Ah...yes sir, Mr. President."

"Good. First, can I ask you if you have a problem altering course?"

"Uh, well, sir, Mr. President. To be frank, we're an oceano-graphic expedition and I was hoping to witness—"

"To the point, Captain. I know who you are. I know who Andy Lightstone is. I know what happened to your partner, Ed Lazerath. I was sorry to hear that. Understand this, the United States cannot and will not stand by and allow you to procure for your own enterprise and commercialization even one of the creatures known as the Iquana. Quite frankly, such a thought is repugnant to me."

"It wasn't intended to be—"

The president continued, ignoring the interruption. "There are concerned people all over the world monitoring the events unfolding on the ships directly ahead of you, humanitarians, lawmakers, decent human beings. Understand this in plain, unequivocal language, Cap-tain Swift, I will see to it that those ships reach their destination, if need be with the protection of the United States. Now, I ask again: Do you have a problem altering course?"

"Mr. President. It wasn't going to be...we have a vested inter-est, we would care for them, put them in TV shows and—"

"Do you have a problem?"

James exhaled a heavy, "No sir."

"So you'll be altering course?"

"You're not exactly giving us much of a choice, are you?"

"No."

The president heard nothing more from Captain James Swift other than a spent sigh.

"Thank you, Captain Swift."

BY EIGHT THAT NIGHT, PACIFIC time, the TV stations and news orga-nizations Marvin had contacted had signed and returned the faxes.

The press visit was scheduled for the morning.

In the interim, the reporters were allowed to telephonically interview individuals aboard the rescue ships, including Dr. London, Boomer, Carter, even several of the Mexican boatmen. Autumn and Ashlyn refused to be interviewed, as they were holding a vigil for Ko.

'BREAKING NEWS' FLASHED ACROSS TV screens in the Los Angeles area. A popular entertainment magazine show on Channel 7 was just beginning when the audio and video vanished, replaced by a silent caption: *Channel 7 Special Report.*

After a few moments, viewers saw news anchor, Mitch Lajohn, hastily clipping a microphone to his lapel. On a screen angled slightly behind the anchor appeared a photograph taken aboard *Noah's Ark*, with a superimposed caption reading: *Sea Beings.*

"Good evening, Mitch Lajohn in the newsroom with this breaking news. Folks, we've talked about them, we've speculated, argued...this just in: Sea Beings—Iquanas—are real! This breaking news is coming in fast and furious. What we can tell you is that early this morning a rescue operation to relocate the piscines from a polluted subterranean cavern did take place, supported in part by the United States navy. As of this moment, two ships, a three-thousand-ton medical ship and a vessel known as Noah's Ark are en-route to an undisclosed location. On board, seventy-seven Iquana sea beings ranging in size from twelve to twenty feet. They are described as luminous, angelic, bright-eyed, and extremely intelligent...intelligent in the way never before seen in a species outside of the human race.

"Folks, this is a huge day. Fifteen minutes from now we are told the navy will be issuing a statement." He paused while someone off camera gave him an instruction and handed him a sheet of paper. He smiled and nodded. "This just in...the president will be addressing the country at eight-forty-five Pacific time, a little over half an hour from now. We're going to stay on the air to bring you these events as they happen. And we will have audio for you directly from the rescue vessels.

"Tomorrow morning, channel 7 will air live pictures from aboard Noah's Ark—the vessel being used to transport the Iquanas to an undisclosed location."

Elsewhere across the globe, similar broadcasts were occurring, or would soon take place.

BEFORE TALKING TO THE PRESS, the president, acting not so unlike many journalists at that moment, decided to gather information directly from the rescue vessels.

Noah's doctors informed the president that in their professional opinions, Ashlyn was absolutely telepathically communicating with the Iquana. Through Ashlyn, the Iquana communicated and responded to the doctors, opening their dorsal fin, holding their arms up, head back. In addition, through Ashlyn's telepathy, the Iquana asked procedural questions, which appeared to be affirmed by their body language, hand signs and facial movements. One doctor even noted that they were polite, excusing themselves prior to diving underwater to air recharge.

The president also spoke with Ace and Rip, who talked about the rescue with the Zodiacs—how the Iquana arrived at the prearranged time and location.

After more than an hour of questioning, and after reviewing some emailed video and stills of the Iquana, the president was satisfied. He conferred with his wife, who hugged him. He then scribbled a speech, which he placed in front of his chief of staff, who immediately experienced heart palpitations. The poor man, only in his early thirties, strongly advised the president to stay clear of religion, spirituality or human-like intelligence.

AT 8:45 PST, WITHOUT EVEN glancing at his script, the president of the United States faced the American public and told them that since the inception of the space program, almost six decades past, Americans have sought to find proof of life, especially intelligent life, elsewhere in the universe. "Today we've discovered it," he said, "we've discovered intelligent life besides Man right here on our own planet."

The president then informed the public about the rescue, that the United States had been, in a limited way, involved, and would continue to help with the rescue effort. He informed the country that the Iquana were a spiritual species in that they understood themselves to be a part of a Greater All—an 'all' that encompassed all matter in the universe—a definition that most would call 'God.'

This was political suicide, according to the analysts, later.

"This is not the time to say, 'I told you so.' This is not the time to say, 'My religion is better than yours or that I'm doing the right thing and you're doing the wrong.' What's important is that we share a common belief in a Higher Power. It's important to recognize that all species living on our planet have the right to clean air and clean water and unpolluted vegetation. This is not a day we should doubt our spiritual beliefs because perhaps we now think there's been a mistake in the written word. This is a day we should strengthen our spiritual beliefs because we know we're not alone in our spiritual journeys.

"It's my hope that our two uniquely distinct species can learn from one another...to better our lives...to enrich our lives.

"As I speak to you, many of the Iquana beings are dying from a disease that also effects us: cancer. Many of you have heard of Ko, the youngest Iquana—the adventurous sea being who formed a friendship with Autumn and Ashlyn Miller. Tonight, aboard the rescue vessel Noah's Ark, Ko lies in a coma, riddled with this disease. Our doctors say her condition is beyond help. But perhaps there is a way we can help. Tomorrow, at five P.M Pacific time, eight o'clock here in Washington, the first lady and I will be out in the rose garden. We will be joining hands in a prayer for Ko. We invite each and every one of you, wherever you are at that time, to join us. What we're hoping for...is a miracle."

The chief of staff threw his arms up in the air, "I don't believe it!"

The president took a sip of water. "We have less than one day to spread the news, one day to rally. Tomorrow night, I'm going to ask for a miracle. I'd like my voice to be one of millions asking for this miracle. Can you imagine if a hundred million, or five hundred million, or a billion—a billion humans went out into their back yards, stood on their balconies gazing up at the heavens, or ventured out into the streets, held hands with their fellow man and, for that moment, pictured Ko well? Can you imagine that sort of energy? The unity of the human mind—that's a powerful thought. I dare you to make it happen."

The chief of staff turned white—all the graft, the hair pulling, for what? The leader of the free world was hanging his entire presidency, six years' blood, sweat and tears, on a miracle! "A miracle you tell them! We're gonna have a miracle! Well, that's exactly what we need now! A damn miracle!" He whined as they marched back to the west wing.

"You catch on fast!" remarked the president with a grin, unruffled by the younger man's insolence. He turned to the vice president, perhaps for a nod of encouragement.

The vice president adjusted his necktie as he strode to keep up with his boss. "Hey, the kid's a little upset. You know, you didn't have to go quite that far."

The president loped on ahead. "Oh, but I did."

HAS THE PRESIDENT GONE FRUIT loops and wind chimes? This was the tag line for the hastily assembled quintet of dueling TV politicos. The show's sentiment reflected the media reaction throughout the late night. Sunup it wasn't vastly different. There was vibe on the early morning talk shows, a strong electrical current in regards to the Iquana, but there were biting words for the president:

"Dangerously unbalanced."

"Loco."

"Out to lunch."

And worse than that....

AT DAWN, AFTER THREE HOURS of sleep, Ashlyn surfaced, showered, and ate a light breakfast in the master galley. Looking up, he noticed many individuals staring at him. A boatman bowed his head reverently. Feeling uncomfortable, Ashlyn stood up. "You don't have to do that. I'm just a man."

A man indeed.

Shortly after nine, under a silky blue sky, two long-range Bell jetcopters, chartered by a pool of media reporters, hovered above *Noah's Ark*. The boatmen watched the visitors' mouths drop open in awe as they sighted the beings.

Flashbulbs showered the decks...and mouths stayed open in disbelief.

The media crews worked swiftly. Up went the camera dollies, tripods, diffusion silks; a transmission dish was mounted, the feed immediately up-linked to the satellite, downlinked across the nation...across the globe.

Five...four...three...two...one....

Television viewers worldwide saw the family of Iquana; they watched the luminous beings deploying their arms and hands expressively, seemingly interrelating handsomely with the humans, especially with Ashlyn Miller who explained beforehand what each sea being was about to accomplish, such as open his or her mouth for a doctor's examination, raise her arms, splash water over his plume.

And because of the low-key manner in which they performed the actions, they didn't appear to be parlor tricks for the pleasure or enlightenment of a theater crowd.

But were these animals really as smart as humans?

So many viewers still weren't convinced. Though the luminous creatures looked spectacular, especially when their dorsal fins separated giving them an ethereal appearance, the magnitude of their intelligence was muted by their inability to verbally communicate.

Some newscasters were even remarking that they were not so unlike apes, monkeys and dolphins...until something happened.

There was a yelp on deck as one of the Mexican boatmen tugging a halyard line slipped and gashed his right leg, severely. The wound could have been stitched up by any of the doctors aboard *Noah's Ark* but EO quickly beckoned with his arm....

Come forward, human.

Ashlyn grinned, knowing exactly what the Iquana elder was up to.

And EO understood the merits of the boxy-shaped mechanical devices with red blinking lights, designed to capture their likeness.

At the deck's edge, one of the beings gently offered a hand to the injured boatmen. The man limped forward, and upon request, tentatively conceded his palm.

As the family of beings gathered, pulsing kaleidoscopes of dazzling light onto the boatman—a glorious sight even in the brightness of daylight—the cameras jockeyed for a close-up of the boatman's leg, which was slashed to the bone and bleeding profusely.

The mood on deck quickly became meditative. Iridescent light rays cascaded over *Noah's* decks, so intense that at times some of the beings vanished in the glare.

Two minutes passed...and as the harshness of the healing light softened, some of the Iquana beings submerged themselves. The spell was broken, replaced by loud gasps of awe. Where minutes before the boatman's leg had been slashed to the bone, blooded and raw, the long gash was now gone, closed as if surgically sealed by laser; the only remnant of the wound was a red line and some surrounding pink puffiness.

Real or trick?

The eyewitnesses on deck were deeply moved, some teary-eyed.

"Magical, mystical," voiced one journalist.

Another wrote: "For the first time in my life, I am speechless—regrettable for a writer, although I feel vindication knowing that I am not alone."

Another whispered into a digital tape recorder. "Standing alongside many of my peers on the windswept decks of Noah's Ark, we watched a brutally injured boatman's leg healed in moments with nothing but a glowing white light emanating from these beings. While this could arguably be called a tour de force of illusion and staging, I believe what we witnessed was spontaneous and magical, and this unforgettable experience has heightened my understanding of being human, while at the same time usurping any desire I might have had to make light of what *must* be described as a miracle—"

THE WORLD HAD SEEN THE Iquana—now was the time to decide.

As the president's miracle hour approached, people from all avenues of life struggled with their ideologies and their consciences. Were these creatures really as intelligent as Man? Were they really spiritual beings?

Iquana beings were on the minds of Christians, Jews, Hindus, on the minds of religious people, atheists, agnostics, businessmen, laymen, housewives, children. For some, especially those who had believed in the sea beings since day one, the choice was easy. Few could deny there was something in the air, a sort of magnetic, spine tingling energy. Petro Boleshko felt it from his hospital bed. Perhaps his son Bogdan, sitting behind cell bars in the local jail awaiting arraignment even felt it, although he would never admit it.

The president's advisers looked to their leader wondering if he could have possibly been right and they wrong.

In American offices, factories, shops, restaurants, airports, people were asking questions such as: "Are you going to…you know, tonight?"

Crowds gathered in parks and open spaces ready to hold hands and pray. Crowds gathered in theatres, halls, and in churches where the resident ministers readily accepted their sea cousins.

Of course, there were those who tried to downplay and ridicule the miracle hour. Confused by the public's fervor, some men of the cloth simply sealed their church doors.

Overseas, there was an equally festive excitement—New Year's Eve in replay!

In London, Paris, Rome, Moscow, people were staying up into the early hours of the morning to join symbolic hands with the

Iquana.

In Tiananmen Square, Beijing, a swarm of bodies as large as the '89 protests held hands and sang.

The Place du Concord in Paris was packed.

London's Trafalgar Square was mobbed.

Children gathered with their parents in their homes, children gathered with their teachers in their schools.

Organs played, bells tolled.

And amidst a fusillade of camera flashes and blinking Beta-cams, the president of the United States, walking hand in hand with the first lady, stepped onto the White House's Rose Garden, followed by the entire executive branch.

On the lawn a twenty-six-foot diamond-vision screen was showing live pictures from *Noah's Ark*.

TV and radio stations were broadcasting nonstop coverage from around the globe.

Moments before eight, the streets of Washington DC slowed to a stop. This was repeated in cities spanning the globe. Drivers wandered away from their cars to gaze up at the stars. Strangers held hands. Car horns stabbed the early night air.

The twin masts on *Noah's Ark* creaked. The sails luffed gently. In the amber dappled hues and shadows of late afternoon, cameras rolled, while reporters whispered their narratives into microphones.

EO rose to the surface carrying Ko. The Iquana beings locked hands in ceremony. Humans locked hands. The healing circle was born, and a gleaming bioluminescence rapidly built into a blinding light.

The humans aboard the catamaran felt heat rising in their bodies, almost a burning, as if the sun had shifted off the horizon and had placed itself aboard *Noah's Ark*.

Despite the harshness of light, Ashlyn kept his eyes open. He saw a silhouetted image in the center of the circle: EO and Ko, she limp and lifeless in the elder's arms.

While the deck remained awash in streaming rays of light, the luminescence directly around EO and Ko softened into an amber glow.

Ashlyn found her name parched atop his lips, and had the strongest urge to say it. So he did, almost a whisper: "Ko."

Hearing him, Autumn spoke it a hint louder: "Ko."

With his eyes closed, and sparks of energy tingling every ounce of his flesh, Boomer whispered Ko's name.

The person next to Boomer was crying.

From person to person, Ko's name blew like a soft breeze across *Noah's* decks.

On the lawn of the White House, the president uttered the name of the youngest Iquana: "Ko."

Watching the television pictures, tears streamed down the face of a housewife in Boise, Idaho. She cried aloud, "Ko."

A five-year-old from Fargo, North Dakota gazed up at the sky, and squeezed her mom's hand: "Please God, don't let Ko die."

In Tiananmen Square they held hands and shouted Ko's name. In Trafalgar Square they sang her name. City streets across the globe fell quiet as cars and buses and conversations stopped, then became clamorous with the unanimous voice….

KO!!!!

Like invisible lasers, tens of millions of imperceptible streams of light riffled up into the sky, away from hamlets, towns, and cities worldwide. But as the energy of that focused thought reached a pinnacle, something magical happened, something never before witnessed in the history of the world.

Every human felt that something, and millions witnessed it with their eyes.

The symbiotic wave of hope and love was no longer *invisible*. A *lightbow*—a truly observable golden-colored bow of light appeared in the sky, soaring westward.

The power of unity was at work. What a wondrous sight to behold.

Epilogue

Somewhere in the South Pacific

AT LAST, ASHLYN AND AUTUMN WERE ENJOYING a real vacation: swimming, sunbathing, playing water polo with wacky sea beings…oh, and trying to move deck chairs with the power of the mind. *Noah's Ark* had become a lively swimming pool with music and laughter.

Carter turned out to be a talented chef du cuisine, only with a ghastly culinary practice of snagging flying fish straight out of the air, *BAM*, into the sizzling pan.

"One more and you're shark bait!" Autumn admonished him.

Today was a great day. Denton arrived by helo, after Marvin had pulled some fancy legal nylon, rescuing Denton from the clutches of the IRS. As long as Denton made good on the old IRS debt, the government would drop fraud and tax evasion charges—which didn't seem too tall an order. After all, Denton's newfound friends just so happened to know the whereabouts of every major undiscovered shipwreck on the planet.

Marvin performed another special task—persuading Grandma to relinquish her sole custody of Ashlyn and Autumn in favor of joint custody with Denton. For now, until the Iquana decided exactly where they wanted to live, the teens would be schooled by private tuition aboard *Noah's Ark*.

Boomer turned Uncle Boomer, Carter Uncle Carter—AKA the flying fish man.

As for the doctors, their jobs concluded in that awesome planet-changing moment.

Not only was Ko cured—all the beings were.

"Look!" Ashlyn yelled with utter disbelief as a deck chair slid across the breadth of the deck, moving as if by remote control "I moved that chair! I did it! I did it with my mind!"

"You found your way!" Ko laughed with effervescent glee as she leaped out of the water, intending to slap Ashlyn's hand with a water-drenching high-five.

Only she misjudged the distance to his hand, landed with a thud, and slid right off the deck.

Oh, what fun to be a klutz.

Acknowledgments

Into the Abyss is entirely fiction. Born out of a vivid dream I had when I was fourteen, Ashlyn (myself in the dream) discovered the portal to the other world lying at the bottom of a public swimming pool—but only he could find this portal, and only he could remedy the disasters befalling the denizens of this new world. Over the years, before I took pen to paper, the dream/tale received many embellishments, such as the departure of the swimming pool in favor of a journey to the deep sea, as it became my young daughter's favorite bedtime fable. Then at age forty-two, I decided to take dream-thought, daughter-story, to the drafting board, as a novel aimed at children of all ages—especially big ones like myself. The decade it took to reach print is another story, but as I look back on this long journey, it's amazing how many people I have encountered, many of whom probably don't even realize that they've helped to shape this novel. In the developmental stage, there was Justin Carroll, who I haven't spoken to in ages, and Matt, Alina, Irene, my daughter Michelle and her buddies in Hawaii—thanks, guys for your encouragement. Gratitude also goes to my sister Debbie for sending me in a better direction. I would also like to thank Cathy at the dealership for poring over the manuscript, John and Ruth Thompson for the editorial wisdom, John Lovick for an outstanding job catching tons of mistakes, and a big thanks to my good friend Hraj for helping me find some very important time when I needed to get cracking. As I wrap up this page, thinking about the next novel, there is one more name to mention: She is a beacon of light, my biggest fan, and the one responsible for opening my eyes—a huge thanks to my wife Svetlana.

And I thank you for reading,

David Marsh